Illegal Avatars

A GameLit/LitRPG Novel of Time Travel and Alternate Realities

MK Eidson
Emila H Thicke

Eposic

DEDICATION

This book is dedicated to Batman and Robin, if
Batman's name were Tom.

The distinction between the past, present, and future is only a stubbornly persistent illusion.

Albert Einstein

CONTENTS

FOREWORD

Welcome to book three of a five-book series. This volume continues the stories of the characters set forth in the first two volumes, and a familiarity with the events of both books is assumed herein. Moreover, this book ends with more loose ends than an unraveling sweater. In other words, this is not a standalone novel. That is all.

CHAPTER ONE

Charli: Jealousies

Mithabel glares at me.

I step back onto the brick sidewalk, involuntarily cringing. Why should I let her intimidate me? "Dylan doesn't care that I killed her, Mithabel. Why do you?" Is she jealous that I earned the million XP instead of her? She had more than ample opportunity to earn the bounty for killing the Longest Survivor. I waited until the *literal* last second, and since no PC had done it by then, I acted. It would have been a million XP wasted if someone hadn't won it. Mithabel should be glad someone in her party earned it instead of XStorm or Quantized.

"Leave her be, Mithabel." Attired in the same skintight brown suede Armor she's been wearing since I met her, poised with the confidence of a Goddess beneath the shiny, hanging metal sign of the Mystical Magical Shoppe, the Polynesian Priestess of Light imposes a hand between the Bikini-clad Elf Tank and my cowering self. She pushes air, mimicking the action of pushing Mithabel back. *"I told you to claim the bounty yourself,* but you're too damned stubborn. Please let it go."

The Tank stomps a bare foot on the warm asphalt surface of Main Street. Earlier, she wore Platform Slippers matching her black leather Bikini, but upon returning to Khertaan after the update, the Elf quickly shed her footwear. While the environment in Khertaan doesn't always behave as an Earthling would expect, the road does emanate heat under the constant glare of the sun. It doesn't faze Mithabel. The Tank has a level two Natural Armor trait and the Anjai subclass which work together to protect her against minor damaging effects.

Without her Slippers on, Mithabel stands at eye level with the Polynesian Priestess. "I didn't want you to die, Dylan, *period*. But I'll deal with it because you want me to."

The Tank turns her gaze back to me. "What I want to know, Charli, is how long you were invisibly traveling with us, not saying a peep to let us know you were okay. Were you with us in the Grass Bladed Field?"

She knows I have the Hide skill, which allows me to hide in plain sight... when it works. I don't register in an affected person's view, whether they're using First Person POV or Third Person POV. It's not that I become invisible. One person might notice me while another doesn't, due to the first person having better observational skills. If I were to travel alongside Mithabel for a while without her noticing me, that would mean my Hide skill is more powerful than her Detect Anomaly skill.

Is that what she thinks? Oh, gee. Is she jealous?

My brown pigtails sway beneath the wide brim of my hat as I shake my head. "The System wouldn't let me come back to you right away. When I did respawn in Maron, it was *after* you entered the city but *before* the fighting broke out over Dylan.

"At first I stayed hidden—just to see if I could... and for how long. A couple times I thought you'd noticed me, but I remained real still and focused, to see if I could stay hidden. I promise you I wasn't scheming to claim the bounty. I was only testing my ability."

Dressed in Leather Armor similar to Dylan's but of a different brown hue, Amarynth clears her throat, hefting her Crossbow. "We know that, honey." The Viking Archer throws Mithabel a look of disapproval. "Have you forgotten she has the Complex Personality trait? We don't know what all that trait entails, but it might explain some of her behavior, and we shouldn't hold it against her. Can we get on with the real business at hand now?"

"Oh, I see." Mithabel doesn't step away. "Because we don't understand what her Complex Personality trait does, she gets to use it as an excuse for every bad thing she does. Do I have that right?"

"Mithabel, *please*." Dylan takes the Tank by the arm and tugs.

A measured clopping approaches, as might be expected from a mounted City Guardsman. "Why are you lot always congregating in front of entrances? Stand aside." Ruby, a female Centaur with long, curly red locks, pushes between me and Mithabel, her Leather Armor rough against my bare arms. Benefiting from the extra height afforded her by hooves and equine legs, Ruby towers over us all, about three-quarters again my five-foot frame.

Forced a step back, Mithabel locks her icy stare on the rude intruder's backside. "There's plenty of room for you to go around us, Centaur. It's not like we're right in front of the doorway."

"You are for someone my size." Ruby beckons for others in her party to follow while she pushes the swinging door open with a hoof.

On the Centaur's back rides a pale Goth woman dressed in snug black Leather Armor. The ends of her straight black hair sway along her jawline. Wearing a grimace as her most prominent facial feature, Penelope doesn't spare a look for any of us as she and Ruby enter the Mystical Magical Shoppe.

Dylan holds up an empty hand, which suddenly holds a Shuriken. "Good day to you, too." She doesn't throw the missile. Two seconds later the weapon disappears from her grasp. The City Guard issued a notice that PC parties weren't to fight each other again while in the city limits, unless otherwise directed by a System announcement. Not that Dylan would be the one to start something.

A man of Asian persuasion falls in step behind the Centaur. His brown Leather Armor, while no more bulky than the armor worn by other PCs around him, looks more rugged than sleek. His wavy cherry blond hair strikes him across the back of his shoulders. Greatly dwarfed by the Centaur, the man stands about my height and wields a Staff nearly as long as Ruby is tall. Bradford, party XStorm's Fire Wizard, doesn't attempt to hide his contempt of us. He pauses to assess Dylan head to toe, clucking his tongue.

Mithabel tenses. I'm waiting to see her Axe appear in hand and cleave the back of his skull, but she stays her hand.

Like Penelope, Bradford says nothing. He follows his fellow XStorm party mates into the shop.

Funny thing is, I have his original Staff, currently stashed in my inventory. I took it and his sister's Cudgel after they fell victim to the Poison Ivy Snakes in the Black Poison Forest. I can't suppress a snicker, but it's quiet enough he doesn't react.

Next comes Bradford's twin sister, Yuni, Priestess of Athlea, the Goddess of War. She's dressed in a flaming red Leather Armor outfit, including Platform Boots. Cutouts in her outfit expose blemish-free flesh on either side of her belly. Her height, weight, complexion, and hair color are a close match to her brother's. She's not carrying a Cudgel—if she replaced the one I took from her, the new one is stashed to inventory.

Like her brother, Yuni stops in front of Dylan. But unlike her brother, she doesn't cluck her tongue. She meets the taller woman's gaze. "No hard feelings?"

The Polynesian Priestess beams like the sun. "Of course not. It's a competition. I'm sure our players could be friends on Earth. In fact, I want you to have this." A Cudgel appears in Dylan's grasp—the one I took from Yuni and gave to Dylan. She hands it to the XStorm Priestess.

Yuni gasps. "Are you sure?"

"I'm sure."

So much for me risking my life to retrieve that Cudgel from beneath a swarm of poisonous serpents so Dylan could have a weapon. But I'm an NPC. Unless the System instructs me otherwise, it's not for me to interfere in the business of PCs.

The Asian Priestess takes the offered weapon with a smile. "My player's name is Aimi. A-I-M-I. She's disappointed not to be in charge of me. How does your player feel about it?"

The Polynesian Priestess chuckles. "Debra is content to let me do as I wish, especially since I'm winning." She shrugs. "Maybe when this competition is over, Aimi and Debra can meet. Debra could use more friends."

"I'm sure Aimi would like that." Yuni offers another smile and then hurries after her brother.

Mithabel's eyes bore a hole through the back of Yuni's receding head. Is the Tank jealous? She bites her lip. "Earth has been invaded by inter-dimensional monsters. Megan Wright's house was burned down by a fireball-throwing Orc Wizard, and then he chased her on a Motorcycle, trying to burn her. He destroyed her car and put a knife in her leg. Giant spiders tall as two-story houses attacked an ambulance she was in, grabbing living, struggling passengers from their vehicles. That's what our players have to face when this competition is over. When we finish our Khertaan training, *there won't be time for socializing on Earth.* There's scarcely time to make friends *during* this competition. We need to concentrate on reaching level 30. Otherwise, there might not be an Earth."

I don't know if she's jealous or scared, or both. It's difficult for me to empathize with PCs and their ties to Earth. My earliest memories are of Morrow, Kylie, and Slithy—PCs whose players woke me and imparted to me some knowledge of their home planet, but they didn't instill in me a sense of duty to Earth.

Still, it's in my best interests for these PCs to train as hard and fast as they can, *all of them*, if that's how they'll protect their planet from its invaders. All their bickering and jealousy is counterproductive. If they fail to repel the invaders—if Earth falls—Khertaan will fall just as easily.

Maybe I can empathize with PCs after all.

"Hello, Dylan." The suave masculine voice belongs to the XStorm leader, ChrisCross. I sense a particular dislike for him from my fellow party members. Their stances and jaws tense, like they're all wolves—and he's from a rival pack. There's no possibility of cooperation between them. With Ruby, I get the sense she'd be accepted into MAD if she wanted to join, but ChrisCross would never be welcome.

The Priestess doesn't respond to his greeting.

That doesn't stop him. "Maybe we could hook up soon… find a room in an inn… like our players did on Earth."

Hmm. There's some history here I'm not privy to.

Entwined around the man's waist, a blue Electric Serpent bares its fangs and hisses at Dylan. The snake's skin shimmers with new growth—after being skinned alive by Rolag, Amarynth's Pseudo Code Dragon.

Rolag isn't with us currently—he's on cool down until 2:00 AM, System time, less than an hour away. I like the little guy. He's cute.

Cute is the opposite of what I'd call ChrisCross, the only avatar we've met of his kindred type—*Elitist*. Even in Khertaan, that's a divisive label—added intentionally by the developers to create conflict. ChrisCross's player chose it as his kindred, and the choice in itself says something about the nature of the player—and thus his avatar. But is that reason enough for me to dislike the avatar? I don't know. I can see arguments either way. Personally, I'll give him the benefit of the doubt until he proves he's a jerk, which might be about to happen.

"Settle down, Lance. This sexy lady might want to spend some time with us." Attired in white Cloth Armor bearing more in common aesthetically with pajamas than protective wear, ChrisCross licks his lips. "Twenty dollars for twenty minutes of your time, Priestess. Or do you charge more than Debra Jones?"

Am I correctly understanding the history between their players?

Mithabel's Battle Axe appears in her hand. From behind the Elitist, the Elf Tank hefts her weapon overhead and aims for ChrisCross's spine.

A dozen armored City Guardsmen materialize as though from nowhere, Spears and Swords in hand, all of them pointing at Mithabel. Their Leader steps close to her, hand outstretched. "Stash it, adventurer, or forfeit a life."

"Fine." The weapon vanishes.

"You even so much as draw a weapon again in our city, you'll forfeit it and spend the rest of the night in a cell." The Guard Leader lowers his arm. "Do I make myself clear?"

"Crystal."

"Tsk, tsk." ChrisCross spins on the ball of a foot to face the Tank. "Christopher Warden has a message for Megan Wright. He says to tell her Debra Jones was the best lay he ever had. He went to her office that evening to ask for a repeat performance. He regrets his choice of language, and would have used different words if he'd known Megan was there. But he didn't say anything that wasn't true. If you pay a woman for sex, she's a whore by definition."

"What are you saying?" Mithabel's eyes bulge. She shoves ChrisCross aside to peer at Dylan. "Is Debra Jones a prostitute?"

Confusion wrinkles Dylan's brow.

ChrisCross chuckles. "I'm surprised Megan didn't fill you in, Mithabel. She was right there and heard everything. Debra tried to get Christopher to shut up, but he spilled all the sordid details. Maybe Megan thought your knowing about it would affect your game." He shrugs. "Let's hope it does. Have a good day." He saunters into the Mystical Magical Shoppe.

With the situation concerning the inter-dimensional invaders, all the PCs should be helping each other. That won't happen with this lot.

Mithabel shakes her head, her gaze locked on Dylan. Eventually, she turns away and catches me watching her. Her countenance droops. "Megan didn't know," she whispers, attenuated low enough for Dylan not to hear.

"Does she know now?" I softly inquire. Though Megan currently lies in a prison cell, she and Mithabel have a mental connection beyond the private communication channels available to the rest of us. Megan Wright is a strange breed. She's not a PC, per se, and she's not an NPC. The awareness of PCs in Khertaan stems from the *subconsciousness* of their players.

Mithabel is Megan's subconsciousness in avatar form. But with Megan, her *consciousness* has been directly implanted into a secondary avatar, like she's interacting with Khertaan through VR gear. But she's not. She's asleep on Earth, and yet her conscious mind is still active, along with her subconscious mind, each one powering an avatar in Khertaan. That is, Megan and Mithabel stem from the same Earthling mind. Can they even keep secrets from each other?

Still shaking her head, Mithabel turns back to Dylan, but she has no words for the Priestess.

"You *act* surprised." Dylan steps close enough to kiss Mithabel, and the Elf Tank's eyes light up. But the Priestess doesn't follow through, doubt lingering in her gaze. "He's right about Debra, Mithabel. But she put that life behind her. Christopher had been one of her clients. *Only once.* Sadly, he couldn't leave it at that, and came asking for more. Megan was there and heard everything. It touched Debra that Megan never once brought up the subject afterward."

The Bikini-clad Elf curls stiff fingers without closing her fist. "Megan was in shock from the first words out of Christopher's mouth, and none of what he said afterward registered with her. But know this... none of what's been revealed here changes how I feel about you, Priestess. None of this changes Megan's feelings for Debra, either, I assure you."

Dylan gives a weak grin. "Thank you, Mithabel."

The Elf Tank nods. "Is Debra okay? I can't imagine how she must feel, finding out the friend she thought didn't mind her past indiscretions didn't even know about them."

Dylan sighs. "Seems they were both confused. But I'm with you. None of this changes any feelings we all have for each other. Hug?"

"Please." Mithabel opens her arms and Dylan slips into her embrace.

Amarynth slides her arms over the shoulders of her comrades. "For what it's worth, Anna Milligan was there too that evening and heard everything. She isn't one to judge, and neither am I. Let's put it all behind us and win this competition."

"I want to hug, too." I can't wrap all three women in my arms, so I wedge myself between Dylan and Amarynth, curling my arms around their waists.

I'm the first to pull away. "I'm dying to tell you all my own news."

Amarynth steps back. "Do tell."

I'm so excited for them to hear, and I can't help but clap and jump. My skirt flies up around my hips. I don't care if people can see my culottes. "I'm a level 6 Shadow Wizard."

Mithabel and Dylan slide out of each other's arms, turning amazed gazes on me as one. They echo each other. "What?"

A giggle wriggles up my throat. "I took Shadow Wizard as my subclass. That million XP bounty put me at level 15 Guide. When I decided on a subclass, I went straight to level 6 in it. I've got *all kinds* of new skills, an extra life, *and* another level in Mental Armor. I got one spell for free, called Shadow Warrior. If we can afford them, I'd love to buy more spells in the magic shop here... and I need an empty Potion Flask." I don't say why I need the Flask. Will they be remotely curious?

Dylan grimaces. "The only Flasks I have in inventory contain Oil. Do you have a pressing need? I'd rather not dump the Oil and waste it unless it's urgent."

I shake my head, swallowing my disappointment. "I don't want you to waste Oil. But maybe it won't cost too much to buy an empty Flask...?"

"We're here to price magic weapons first." Mithabel swings an imaginary Axe. "But we can price Wizard spells, too. Then we're heading to the temple to price Priestess spells. We *all* want something, but there's no way we can afford everything we want... unless you're willing to sell that Shadow Stone you're carrying—you know, that red gem you can change into a Dagger at will and slice through Leather Armor like it's nothing."

So... Mithabel *is* still sore at me for killing Dylan. "The Shadow Stone's curse won't let me part with it. I'm lucky not to be influenced by its curse in other ways, but my level 3 Mental Armor protects me. I thought a Shadow Stone to be a fitting item for a Shadow Wizard, and it's the primary reason I chose the subclass." I didn't need to ask their permission, either, but maybe they think I should have at least asked their advice.

"That's great, Charli." Amarynth pats me on the shoulder. "Your being a Wizard means I don't need to be. I didn't want it, but we all felt the party needed Wizard spell capability. Thank you for taking on that responsibility. So now I'm the only one not to choose a subclass." Her eyes focus on text no one else sees. "I've made up my mind. I'm taking Weapon Specialist - Crossbow. It's skills stack with my Archer class when I use a Crossbow. I can't wait to get into another encounter...."

"Yeah." Dylan opens the door to the Mystical Magical Shoppe. "Let's get our shopping done, so we can start the quest Ezmerelda gave us." The Priestess gazes down the street towards the Red Pegasus Inn, where our party's first quest awaits.

CHAPTER TWO

Charli: Negotiations

We file into the Mystical Magical Shoppe.

I enter last. "I didn't get a System message about the update. Do any of you know what changed?"

"Let me ask Kaleisha." Only the PCs have personal support AIs. Mithabel has described hers as a brown-skinned woman identifying as a Jamaican dancer named Kaleisha. No one else can see or hear a personal support AI except the PC to whom the AI is assigned.

The Elf Tank spends a minute in private conversation with Kaleisha. I look for Wizard Scrolls and Potion Flasks while I wait, and spot a short shelf with a promising display of merchandise.

Mithabel nods at her unseen AI. "There have been a couple skill name changes. A few tweaks to skills and traits have been made, not that we knew exactly how they all worked to begin with.

"The biggest changes were with combat. Encounter resolution has been officially restructured using *combat heartbeats*." She goes into a long spiel about how combat works now. The things that stand out most to me are that we can take one action per second, and individual actions no longer have cool down timers—the cool down timer is for the next combat heartbeat. I'm sure I'll hear more about it during encounters.

Girlish laughter echoes through the expansive showroom. With matching broad smiles plastered across their faces, Dylan and Yuni stand together at a display case for magic Cudgels. Mithabel's attention turns to them, and the jealousy monster contorts her expression. Averting her gaze from the two Priestesses, she heads for a display case of Axes.

A System message appears in my view. *The Top Individual Avatars list has updated.* I call up the list. Mithabel is first, but there's an additional name after hers—ZAngel of party ZAvengers.

ChrisCross shouts across the room. "Hey, MAD Elf woman. How did you get on the Top Avatars list?"

Mithabel inspects an Axe for sale. "Go stick your head in a toilet."

ChrisCross murmurs something and returns to scanning shelves of magical Potions, not far from where some empty Flasks are set out for purchase.

"Does this mean what I think it does?" Dylan asks over our party chat.

Mithabel grits her teeth. "I think so. ZAvengers found Ezmerelda's hut, and she's given ZAngel a Ring like mine. I wonder if we could go back there and get Rings for everyone in our party."

I pick up a Flask and check the price. Oh, my gosh. Guess who won't be adding an empty Flask to their inventory today. I return the Flask to its shelf before I drop and break it. "Each party experiences its own stream of events in Khertaan, Mithabel. The hut where we met Ezmerelda doesn't exist in the same location any longer for MAD, but it's there for any parties who haven't visited it yet. ZAvengers probably has a Guide with them. You're lucky to have me."

"We are indeed." Dylan weighs a magic Cudgel in her grasp with a sigh that says she knows we can't afford everything our party wants, and a Cudgel for her is not likely to make the cut any more than an empty Flask for me. "Are you saying that a Guide is necessary to find Ezmerelda's hut? That's a real disadvantage for all those parties that didn't recruit one. I mean, it's not like we actively recruited you, either. If not for Amarynth's High Social Status trait, we'd never have met you, Charli."

It's nice for someone to recognize my worth. "I can't argue that."

Mithabel looks at the price of the Axe she's been studying. Whistling, she puts the weapon back. "Did you find out what your Wizard spells will cost, Charli?"

"Not yet." I amble over to the counter, where the salesman is leaning on his elbows, hardly paying us any attention, waiting for someone to decide what they're buying. He straightens at my approach. "Yes, little miss?"

The honorific he uses to address me is okay, but the adjective is rude. Just because I'm young doesn't make me *little*. I'm as tall as XStorm's adult male Wizard. Would the salesman call Bradford *little mister*? I don't think so. But I understand the tactic. He's trying to make me *feel* small, so I'm compelled to buy something, *anything*, to make me feel bigger and more important. But I'm onto him.

Granted, the salesman needs to sell his wares to earn experience, and every NPC in Khertaan wants to gain levels— it's the overarching goal for us all—but even if his ploy had worked on me, I don't have any money. I'm relying on the others in party MAD to buy stuff for me. "Where can I find Wizard Scrolls?"

Color drains from his face. "You'll need to go next door for that, miss. I don't sell Scrolls of any kind, only equipment. I do have Potions, if you're in need of magic but unable to afford Scrolls." He returns to leaning on his elbows. "You're that Charli character, aren't you?"

"I am."

"Of all people to win the Last Survivor bounty. You're not even an adult."

"So?"

He sneers. "How old are you? Twelve?"

"I'm officially fourteen, according to the System. But I first became aware twenty-six years ago. When did you first become aware?"

Nearly all NPCs in Khertaan became aware two days ago, when the competition started. So even though the System officially makes this guy an adult and me a minor, I'm technically older than he is.

The sneer hasn't left his face. "I suppose winning a million XP made you terribly happy. I saw you jumping and clapping, your skirt flying up. What would your parents say if they saw you acting like that?"

This conversation is getting way too serious for me. "I don't have parents."

He harrumphs. "No parents. No siblings then, either. No kids, obviously, and never to have any. At least the System gave me a family—other NPCs who care about me and whom I care about. What family do you have? The PCs in your party? Do you think they care about you?"

"Lady Amarynth is like a mother to me." I want to walk away, but I realize, too, that it pays not to get on the bad side of shopkeepers who have the ability to jack up prices even higher than they already are.

He shakes his head. "When the PCs reach level 30, they're all out of here, and you'll still be stuck in Khertaan. Then who will you have in your life? You'll never age—you'll always be fourteen, a minor—unable to do everything adults are allowed to do. Will you still think you're better than us then?"

I look him in the eye. "I'm not better than you. I got lucky. That's all. I'm sure you'll earn lots of XP today, with all the parties coming through town."

He stares back at me. "This shop was designed for PCs who are here for the long term, not short-term competitions like this. I won't be earning much of anything today. I mean, you know how much money your party *doesn't* have. I'll be lucky to sell one item today, and I don't mean just to your party. I mean *one item sold today to anyone, period.*"

"I'm sorry. But I do wish you luck."

"Yeah, thanks. Sorry for venting on you. I'm sure you're a nice girl."

I meander away from the counter, holding onto Hope. I switch to party chat. "Spell Scrolls are sold next door. This store only sells items. But if the price for an empty Flask is any indicator, spells will cost a ton."

Amarynth whimpers. "It's $14,000 for a magical Light Crossbow and $16,000 for a Medium one. For a Heavy one, they want $20,000. How are we supposed to pay for anything when the mooks we kill don't drop loot?"

Mithabel sighs. "We need to do better at harvesting mook body parts."

"And I thought the magic Cudgels were expensive." Dylan picks up one she'd previously examined and double-checks its cost, as though maybe she'd made a mistake in reading it the first time. "A price tag of $500 doesn't seem so bad now. But I want to see what they have at the temple first. Are we ready to mosey over there?"

Amarynth holds up a pair of Boots. "This is what I need — Boots of Silence." One of the disadvantages of her level 2 Increased Movement trait is the excessive noise she makes when using it. "They're only $2,000." With a drawn out exhalation, she carefully sets them back in place on the shelf.

At this rate, like the shopkeeper guessed, we'll be lucky to buy one thing for one person. The one person won't be me.

"We're heading over to the temple," Yuni says over local chat. She raises an eyebrow at the Polynesian Priestess. "You want to come with?"

Dylan brightens. "We were just heading that way ourselves."

Much to the shopkeeper's chagrin, every PC in his store files outside without a single purchase. I leave last, giving the salesman a smile and a wave. He doesn't return my smile, but does nod at me.

We stroll across Main Street in pairs, the PCs oblivious to the traffic jam we're causing. I walk beside Bradford in the back. In front of me are Mithabel and ChrisCross. Lance is wound around the Elitist's waist. The reptile watches me, as though suspecting I might attempt to back stab his PC master.

Mithabel and ChrisCross don't talk to each other. The Elitist keeps glancing her way, but she's lost in her thoughts, her eyes alternately looking down at the road and casting ahead at Dylan and Yuni. A mounted Guardsman curses as he's forced to halt his steed to avoid smacking into the Elf Tank. She pays him no mind.

I pause to let the Guardsman saunter by. He nods at me. "Good girl." That's the phrase programmed into us NPCs for speaking to pets when they behave. I'm nice to him and he insults me. I bet I could take him in a one-on-one fight. Does he know who I am? Is he jealous of my level? Will every NPC I meet be rude to me because I have more XP than any of them? Gee whiz.

The shopkeeper is right. In the long term, what did my winning the million XP bounty really get me? When Lady Amarynth leaves Khertaan—which I know she eventually will—what will become of me?

A group of PCs engaged in an animated discussion stand in a circle near the entrance to a building of stone and wood with a medieval European look—Ye Shoppe of Wizardly Accoutrements—the store selling Wizard Scrolls. I meander in that direction while MAD and XStorm enter Omni Temple, a grand, domed adobe structure.

Concentrating on my level 17 Hide skill, I sneak up close to the PCs, who I identify from local chat logs as party Quantized. Why aren't they using their party chat? Are they not that clever? Maybe they were talking to a Guard or shopkeeper on local chat and forgot to switch back. In any case, I'm able to listen in. I walk right up and stand just outside their circle, holding back a snicker. I doubt any of them have skills or attributes at a level high enough to notice my presence.

"How are we supposed to know how they did it?" Attired in a yellow robe fitted to her small stature, Toxxi the Faerie stands about a foot tall. Violet-skinned, she sports shoulder-length, wavy brown hair and eyes sparkling like gold. Her single purple wing is leathery, like a bat's. Mithabel severed her other wing before the update, while protecting Dylan from the bounty seekers. Mithabel *could* give the Severed Wing back to Toxxi, who could then reattach it, but the Elf Tank wants a magic Axe so badly, I suspect she'll trade the Wing for one. I feel sorry for Toxxi. She's so short, and now must walk everywhere.

The Cheetah in the party, Zip, stands a little over two feet at the shoulder. The spotted cat serves as a mount for Ger-Alt, a green-skinned Goblin shorter than me by half a foot. The Goblin looks a bit large for the cat, but Zip doesn't mind. It would seem a better idea for Toxxi to ride Zip, but Ger-Alt looks too comfortable on her mount to give him up.

A Dust Storm Falcon with the unimaginative name of Falco sits on the asphalt next to Toxxi. Covered with blue, gray, and white feathers, the bird stands a couple inches shorter than the Faerie. In the attempt made by Quantized to win the bounty on Dylan before the update, Falco made things difficult for MAD, stirring up a dust storm that no one could see through except members of Quantized. Fortunately, Amarynth managed to keep shooting the bird out of the sky, limiting his effectiveness against us.

Falco looks around, as though he senses something he can't see—like me.

"I think we need a Guide." Next to the bird stands FepXveq the Dark Elf, attired in a skin-tight royal purple Leather Armor body suit and wearing matching Leather Gloves accentuating her slender fingers. The ebony woman stands about six feet tall. It's impossible to gauge her actual height, because of her bushy black afro. She's not underweight or overweight. She glances my way, and for a moment I feel her eyes settle on me. But then her gaze slides away, searching as though she knows something is there, but doesn't know what. "I think those other parties had Guides with them. I'd wager they found some special place that we didn't find. We should have hired a Guide back in Voorton."

"I don't know what makes you think that." Skeeter is a black-eyed squirrel covered with gray fur. Rising on his hind legs, he stands taller than Falco or Toxxi. Looking at him, it's difficult to see anything other than a wild animal that belongs in the forest.

Briefly closing my eyes, I try to bring his image to mind, and it slips from my mental grasp. He's forgettable, and I think magically so. Or maybe he's exercising a skill or trait. If I had a skill like that, in combination with my Hide skill, I could disappear and no one would even miss me. What am I thinking? That happens already anyway. No one from MAD is looking for me even now or inquiring about my whereabouts over party chat.

Skeeter jumps onto Zip's head and from there to Ger-Alt's shoulder, using it as a perch. He trembles with nervous energy as he looks up at the towering FepXveq. "Do you have skills you're not telling us about?"

"I don't, but the skills and attributes I do have make me think someone is watching us." The Dark Elf woman looks right at me, without her gaze locking on me. She knows I'm here, but can't see me. "Falco, stir up a little dust there, please." She points at me.

"There's no need for that." I cancel the Hide skill, struck by an idea. "I'm sorry. It was rude of me to eavesdrop. But you're right, FepXveq. Your party does need a Guide if you're to find Ezmerelda's hut. I happen to be a Guide, and I can take you there, for a price."

"What's this, you say?" Dressed in a dark brown Leather Bra and Loincloth, the Goblin woman twists in her seat on the Cheetah's back to look my way. The big cat lazily turns to better accommodate his rider. Ger-Alt motions at me. "Go on, young lady. Tell us why we should go to this hut of which you speak."

20

I shrug as I approach them. "Ezmerelda is a granter of quests. She's also the one who gives out the Rings that put their bearers on the Top Individual Avatars list. It seems she only gives out one Ring per party. I don't know what it does other than put you on the list, though it is magical, so if you wear it and punch something with your Bare Hand, you're attacking with a magical weapon."

Falco clacks his Beak. "You're saying that Mithabel and ZAngel both have one of these Ezmerelda Rings?"

I nod. "I know Mithabel does. I assume ZAngel does. And I bet none of you do, or any other PC."

"And you can take us to Ezmerelda's hut?" Skeeter the Squirrel's question draws my attention to him, perched on Ger-Alt's shoulder. His ability isn't like my Hide skill, making him unseen, but rather alters my impression of him, making him an unimportant part of my surroundings.

I nod my reply.

Toxxi twitches her single wing. "What's your price to take us there?"

Heck, if I can't get what I want from MAD, maybe I can get it from Quantized. "One Wizard Scroll and an empty Potion Flask."

The Goblin woman seated on the Cheetah coughs. "We have no money, young one. Scrolls and Flasks, even empty ones, cost more than we have. The only thing of possible value we can afford to part with is a Dirk I carry. I paid $5 for it during character generation."

"Can't you even buy me an empty Flask? They cost $50 each." This is so disheartening.

"*Fifty dollars?*" Falco flutters his wings. "*For an empty Flask?* That's ridiculous."

"I agree, but that's what I priced them at just moments ago."

The Goblin shakes her head. "We have *no* money. As in zero dollars. The mooks don't drop loot."

"Surely you have *something* else you can trade." Though maybe not, if they don't know about harvesting mook body parts.

Toxxi shifts her weight, rustling her one wing. "Why do you think we tried so hard, dying numerous times, to earn that million XP bounty?"

"Did anyone even win the bounty?" Skeeter asks.

"She did." FepXveq motions at me.

Astonishment fills the gazes of all the other Quantized members.

Their amazement at my accomplishment feels good, and coaxes a giggle from me. "I confess. It was me."

Zip the Cheetah speaks for the first time. "What level are you now?" His dispassionate tenor voice touches my soul, as though I'm talking to a long lost friend.

In five minutes, despite their lack of funds, I'm more at ease with this party than I've been with MAD since the update. "I'm level 15 Guide and level 6 Shadow Wizard."

Now even FepXveq looks impressed. "I wish we had something with which to pay you. I think I speak for all of us that we would love to have you guide us to Ezmerelda's hut, regardless of which of us acquires a Ring from her."

"Fine." I hope I don't come to regret what I'm about to do. "I'll lead you to Ezmerelda's hut on the promise of a payment of $50. But our agreement has to be registered with the System, not merely a verbal one. And if you agree to an additional $100, I'll tell you a secret worth far more than that."

The party members look questioningly at each other, talking on their party chat, no doubt.

Ger-Alt delivers the verdict. "We agree to your terms, the full $150."

I nod. "Every party member, even the NPCs, must agree to be held accountable for the money until I'm paid, once I've taken you to Ezmerelda's hut, regardless of whether she gives you a Ring."

Falco flaps his wings. "How do we know you aren't scamming us?"

"She's not." Zip the Cheetah stares into my eyes. "I trust you, Charli."

"That's good enough for me." Ger-Alt pets Zip's head. "How do we register this agreement with the System?"

"I'll have it sent to each of you to be accepted." I formulate it in my mind and send it via the System to each of the five members of party Quantized, including the Companion NPCs. *Make that six.* Can't forget Skeeter the Squirrel. "I won't be with you as a member of your party. I'm still a member of MAD. But I can belong to their party and still travel with you. It's all spelled out in the agreement I just sent you. There's also a clause that forces an automatic transfer of funds from you to me if at any time your party funds accumulate to a total of $200 or more and you haven't yet paid me after I deliver on my part."

"I don't know about this." Falco shakes his Beak.

Ger-Alt swings a foot at the Falcon. "Do it, bird."

Falco looks up at FepXveq as though seeking permission.

FepXveq nods.

"Fine, I'll do it."

Six notifications come in. They've all agreed to my terms. Fabulous! Now we'll see how much party MAD appreciates me when I tell them I'm not going into the dungeon with them to complete Ezmerelda's quest. Mystic Hollow Cornfield, here I come.

Falco raises his Beak. "So what's this $100 secret?"

"All in due time. I'll be back in ten minutes. Wait here for me."

CHAPTER THREE

Megan: Ye Olde Shoppe of the Profane

I can't believe it. She's a sex worker? That's not the Debra I know.

Calm down. Do something constructive. Think about your next move in the competition.

I don't even know Debra.

Get a hold of yourself. Take a deep breath. Stretch. Don't scream—you'll attract the attention of the City Guard, and you don't want them taking you back to prison. They'd double the security and make sure you don't escape again.

Debra was having money problems. I could have helped her, if she'd only confided in me. Shit, I've been living all alone in that big house. She could have moved in with me years ago.

Yeah, well, you can't live with her in the big house now. The Orc Wizard made sure of that. Burned it to the ground, hoping you were in it. You're lucky to be alive.

Don't remind me.

But you need to remember... everything. The competition facility... what was it called?

Fanciful Pegasus.

How did you get there?

Kevin. On his Motorcycle. The Mad Cow Ballista chased us across the desert, firing gigantic Pencils at us all the way. Kevin insisted I call him Kev. A strong black dude... I felt safe with him, though I never told him so.

Did any of the big Pencil missiles hit you in the head?

There. I see it. Ye Olde Shoppe of the Profane. Looks promising.

What do you hope to accomplish in there?

I go inside. "Excuse me, shopkeep. Do you sell magical weapons?"

The proprietor laughs, stroking his gray beard. He gestures about the showroom. "Everything on the shelves is magical. Looking for anything in particular?"

I hold up my Battle Axe. "Something like this, but enchanted."

"Oh, sure. If you have the money, I've got the goods."

"Great." I guess I have to ask. "How much?"

"Depends on how heavy you want the enchantment. Least expensive is $9,000."

"Holy crap. How is anyone supposed to find that kind of money?"

He shrugs. "I don't make the rules. It's my goal to gain levels as a shopkeeper, and I can't do that if I give away my stock. But I'm willing to barter. Got anything to trade?"

I laugh. "Sure. This Battle Axe."

The guy points over my shoulder. "What about that?"

I pluck the duplicated Severed Faerie Wing from its makeshift Rope Holster on my back. "You mean *this*?"

He nods. "Yeah, *that*. It's worth a bit. Give me your Battle Axe, the Faerie Wing, and $200. I'll give you a Magical Battle Axe. Deal?"

Shit. I don't have $200. Mithabel has $50 in inventory she hasn't spent yet, but if I take it, she'll wonder why, and I'll end up having to tell her I escaped my cell. "How much will you give me for this suit of Leather Armor?" I bring it out of inventory onto the counter he's standing behind.

His look of disgust isn't concealed despite his beard. "I can give you $30 for that, and I'm being generous."

"It's worth $60."

"If it were new and you were selling it to an adventurer, I'd agree." The proprietor shook his head. "I can't give you more than it's worth, or I won't earn the XP I need to advance."

This is silly. "Why do you need to advance? You're just an NPC."

"Get out of my store." He stabs a finger towards the exit. "I don't tolerate bigotry."

"No, please. I'm sorry. I wasn't thinking. That was insensitive of me." I need to remember this is his world, and in it his existence has as much meaning to him as mine has to me. Perhaps more so. I'm the one who doesn't belong here, walking around in a secondary avatar body that the City Guards have rightly identified as an illegal entity.

His expression softens. "I'll excuse your bad behavior this once. You'd do well to watch your tongue, not just in my store but everywhere in Khertaan, if you want to get along with its residents. Now, we were discussing a trade, and you're trying to come up with another $170. What else you got of any worth?"

Maybe you could *steal* a magic weapon.

"What other items do you have for sale? Anything less expensive?"

"You're free to look around. The prices are marked on them." The proprietor settles down behind the counter.

I reposition the Faerie Wing on my back. It's an awkward job, even with the benefit of Third Person POV, but if I stashed the thing, Mithabel might see it. Maybe I could have the Wing permanently attached to my shoulder somehow. That could be cool. I stash the Leather Armor.

Uh huh. You don't want Mithabel seeing any of the items the System duplicated during the update. Not the Bow, the Axe, the Wing, the Ring, the Bikini, the Platform Slippers, or the Rope. None of it. Why are you keeping secrets from her?

I forget my reasons, but I'm sure they're good ones.

Of course.

There are no other customers in the place, which is good in some respects, but bad if I'm to try stealing something. The proprietor is watching me like a hawk. I need something to distract the guy.

Maybe you could simply stash one of the items and run out with it.

Maybe I could.

I take a Magical Battle Axe off the shelf. Shit. It won't stash.

The proprietor points at the exit again. "Strike two. One more and you're banned. Best think twice about that. If I ban you here, you'll be banned at every establishment in the city, along with the rest of your party. If you're not in my shop to conduct legitimate business, I suggest you leave now."

Bloody hell. I can't cause trouble for Mithabel—I need to fly straight. "I really want a magical weapon before I leave this city, and I have nothing else of value. Can you suggest a way for me to earn some money?"

The old guy pats his stomach and grins. "Now you're talking. There's a quest I can offer you, and in return for its successful execution, I'll grant you a Magical Battle Axe, or any other weapon in the store with a level one enchantment. Interested?"

"I'm all ears."

Laughter bursts from him, jiggling his belly. "Then that will make this quest super easy for you. All you need do is bring me a Severed Ear from any PC or from an NPC who isn't a citizen of Maron. Do that, and you can keep all your items and your cash. One magical weapon for one Severed Ear. Only one. I don't need two. It can even be your own, if you like. But don't do the severing inside my shop."

Are you listening to this crazy bastard? With all his talk of insensitivity and threatening to ban you for stealing, he wants you to take someone's Ear? That is messed up.

Yeah, it is messed up. "Okay, deal. I'll be back once I have what you want."

"Good luck. Have a nice day. Hope to see you again soon."

He *is* one crazy bastard. But I don't care. I need an Ear. I'm *not* giving him one of mine. I should go find that little bitch Toxxi if she's still around. Mithabel already took her Wing. What's an Ear next to that?

CHAPTER FOUR

Morrow: Mind Spears and Goblins

"Grab my hands, you two." Kylie reaches out to either side. My wife wears a skin-tight black Leather body suit. Her golden blond hair falls in tight curls to frame her pale face. Behind her rise white Angel wings with a span of twelve feet. Slithy and I take her offered hands. She gives us each a knowing glance. "Prepare for lift off."

"Whoa." Slithy giggles as our feet leave the ground. My daughter is scantily clad in fringed attire—a cropped Blouse and a Loincloth crafted from worn beige cloth. Her blond hair cascades in waves onto the black-spotted-red poison-dart-frog skin of her exposed shoulders.

Kylie carries us westward towards the sun, soaring above the Brassy Grassy. We've nothing to fear from those giant metallic spiders if she keeps us airborne.

"Ha ha. Hold up. You're going too fast." Rancor, my Woodpecker Familiar, perches on my shoulder when we pause for him. "Thank you!"

Renee, my sexy personal support AI, flies effortlessly beside me. She goes where I go, not always in sight, but always near.

She keeps out of my way during encounters, but otherwise, it's a thrill having her in view. It's for the best that I can't touch her. I tried once, and my hand passed through her. She wears a strapless red suede top that doesn't cover her navel, a red leather skirt with a hem striking her at mid-thigh, and knee-high red leather boots. Only I can see or hear her, which is a good thing. If Kylie ever saw Renee, I might never hear the end of it. My lady-in-red waves to get my attention. "I have so much to tell you, darling."

"Spill."

Renee goes through a whole spiel about combat heartbeats, cool down timers, action timing, and a few other tidbits of System info. I assume Slithy and Kylie are fed the same information by their support AIs.

Slithy shades her eyes with black-striated red fingers. "I don't see a Cornfield."

"Me neither." I shade my eyes too. It doesn't help. "Charli said she didn't know how far it was, but if we can't even see it from up here, it must be really far away. How far can you carry us like this, Kylie?"

The Angel shakes her head. "Georgie says I can do this indefinitely. One of my traits is Party Flight. If we had more people in the party, I could take everyone, as long as we stay connected in a chain. Let's go a while longer. It can't be a grassy field forever."

I'm in agreement. "Is anyone recovering lost HP, Auni, or Psi points?"

I get replies in the negative all around.

Slithy looks back. "We're leaving the giant spiders behind. Maybe we should set down and rest a while. See if that helps with recovery."

Kylie grunts in disagreement. "We're not hurting *that* much."

Slithy makes a popping sound with her lips. "Oh. Hmm. I just got my expended Psi point back."

I lean out to look past my wife at my daughter. "Any HP or Auni returned… for anyone?"

Kylie shakes her head. "Not me."

Rancor echoes her.

"Well, I'm game to keep flying if everyone else is." I don't see a compelling reason to land, knowing that some restoration is occurring. There's no reason to think HP and Auni won't also recover as we travel.

Renee rocks her head side to side. "I've still more to say, lover boy."

"We have time."

She smiles. "And secrets. Your wife and daughter and their support AIs don't know about ODYSSEY yet, and now might not be a good time to mention they have nanobot collectives in their brains. Let them get used to life in Khertaan first.

"A key thing is to reach level 30 in Khertaan as quickly as you can. That's the threshold where you'll be able to optimally blend your Morrow persona in Khertaan with the Nick persona on Earth, enabling your incarnation on Earth to fight the forces of Seth."

I take a moment to absorb what she's said. "Anything else?"

"Yes, but if ODYSSEY or I attempt to divulge certain information without the proper triggers, it could tip off Fanciful Pegasus to your presence. If the developers discover you, they'll tag all three of you as illegal avatars and do their best to terminate you."

Okay then. Ours is the burden of saving the multiverse with limited information at our disposal. No pressure. "What's this about *blending* my persona with Nick's?"

She raises an eyebrow. "This is how ODYSSEY explained it to me. Your awareness as Morrow is actually Nick's subconsciousness time-shifted to the Khertaan universe. Nick's body is—"

"Wait," I say. "What do you mean *time-shifted to the Khertaan universe*? Khertaan is a virtual world, not its own universe. What kind of *time-shift* happened?"

Renee shakes her head. "I'm only repeating what ODYSSEY told me. If I may finish...?" She pauses. "Nick's body is sleeping in his computer lab, his conscious mind inactive while you're active. When you reach level 30, you'll return to Nick's body, where his conscious mind and his subconscious mind—you—will become interchangeable, one dominant while the other observes. The idea is that all the powers you gain in Khertaan will transfer with you. Whichever of you is dominant should be able to call upon the abilities of either. That's what is meant by *blending* your personae."

"I see." I'm not sure I do, but some things must be experienced to be fully understood. The time will come.

To the east, the army of giant metallic spiders stretches across the horizon. We're outpacing them, but they're still coming. "Is there a more precise term than *giant metallic spiders* for those monsters following us?"

"They are known as *Arachnid Behemoths*."

"What are their vulnerabilities?"

"Unknown. But they've already been tagged as illegal avatars. They have code to keep them active in Khertaan, preventing the developers from simply turning them off. So the devs are taking extreme measures to deal with illegal avatars, empowering designated NPCs to deliver special attacks against them, not only lowering HP instantly to zero, but also draining

Constitution scores to zero with a single blow, stopping the slain target from respawning. If you encounter one of these special NPCs, do *not* let them kill you, because then you'll never respawn to finish your training."

"That's good to know." I'm glad I asked the questions that triggered *that* info.

There's movement below us—a group of six short brown-metal men. "Do you all see that?" I point with my free hand. We've seen this kind of mook before and fought some already—*Brass Goblins*.

"Should we fight them for the XP?" Kylie slows and circles over them.

Slithy tosses her long blond hair. "I have an idea. Take us down to about fifteen feet above them. I'll use my Mind Spear. They won't be able to touch us. I have six Psi points and there are six of them. I'll render them mindless and we can take them as treasure. The more treasure we have, the better equipment we can buy when we find a shop. I'll recover my expended Psi points while we travel."

"That's not a bad idea." I give my Frogkin daughter an approving nod. "But you should keep at least one Psi point in reserve. After you Mind Spear five of them, Rancor and Kylie can take out the last one with a joint attack."

"Let's do it." Kylie descends, stopping about fifteen feet above one.

A silver energy beam shoots from Slithy's forehead, striking the top of her target's bald pate. The Brass Goblin plops onto its butt on the ground. Kylie flies us over the next one. The little men jump at us, but can't get high enough to attack. Slithy picks off five of them one by one with the psychic Spears streaking out of her brain. All five affected mooks sit on the ground, unresponsive.

We set down fifty feet from the last remaining mook and drop hands. My wife and my Woodpecker Familiar charge the last foe. It's too dumb to know it doesn't have a chance, and charges to meet them. They're both far faster than it. Kylie's shimmering Spirit Sword and Rancor's jackhammer Beak make quick work of it, blasting it to bits before it can harm either of them. This is too easy. Renee reports earnings of 120 XP, same as we earned from our first encounter. We're each roughly a quarter of the way to level 2.

Laughing, Slithy collects the five mindless Brass Goblins, stashing them to her inventory. "I only have twenty-four slots available, but multiple Brass Goblins all sit in the same slot, tagged with the number of Goblins it holds. I could load up on these things all day."

I point at the ground. "We should rest a while. See if resting recovers your Psi faster, and maybe Kylie can recover some of her lost Auni. Lost HP will likely take longer to heal, but heal faster for someone inactive, and faster still for those who sleep. When you're flying us around, Kylie, you're active, but Slithy isn't. That may be why she recovered Psi points but you didn't recover Auni."

"Okay." Kylie takes a seat on the ground. "But if those Arachnid Behemoths come too close, everyone promise me we'll take to the skies immediately."

"Ha ha, yeah." Rancor perches on my shoulder. "I'm not liking those Arachnid Behemoths."

CHAPTER FIVE

Morrow: Recovery and Innuendo

"I'm recovering Psi points at the rate of one every five minutes when resting." Slithy jumps to her feet and paces in a circle around me. Ten minutes pass. "Okay, I've just regained another point. Resting definitely helps one recover." Satisfied with the results of her little experiment, she returns to sitting on the grass, her back to mine.

I relax against her, careful not to put all my weight on her back, but giving her sufficient support. "I'm sure sleeping would help even more."

With tucked wings, Kylie lies on the ground, her head in my lap. She's not sleeping, so her Auni recovers at the resting rate. I play with her blond curls, twirling them in my fingers. Her eyes are closed and a contented smile on her lips.

Rancor perches on my shoulder, occasionally sticking his damned Beak in my ear. "Ha ha, I'm making sure it's clean."

"Well, stop it. I'm not an Earth human. I don't get waxy buildup."

"Ha ha, how do you know?"

After thirty minutes of resting, neither Kylie nor Rancor have recovered any HP they lost from our first encounter. We can't afford to take more time. The giant spiders can't travel as fast as Kylie can fly, but their shapes loom ever closer on the horizon.

Back in the air, we soon spot more little brown metal men, darker than the previous ones. "Renee, what are those?"

"They're Iron Goblins, darling, a bit tougher than the Brass kind."

Having seen them too, Slithy points. "Can I try my Mind Spear on one of them?"

Kylie descends. "I'll make a quick pass over them, to see if they produce any missile weapons."

As we zip by overhead, the Iron Goblins look up, but no weapons of any kind materialize in their hands. Kylie hovers over one. It staggers under Slithy's silvery Mind Spear and then swings a fist at a nearby friend. The friend responds with his own fist.

The two Iron Goblins battle it out while Kylie soars upward. We circle and watch the fray. The four not in the fight watch their two friends hurting each other, unsure which they should help, or whether they should help either. In about half a minute, one of the two combatants explodes into a spray of iron shavings. I'm not sure which one died until the victor turns on his nearest buddy.

"Wow." Slithy laughs. "I didn't know I could do that."

Kylie chuckles. "None of us know what all we can do."

It only takes one hit from a healthy Iron Goblin to defeat the already wounded one. Four remain.

Slithy motions for us to descend again. "Let me try hitting one of them twice. Take me to that one." She points to the one furthest from the others.

Once hit by a Mind Spear, the targeted Goblin flails about as though attacking invisible foes. His friends stay away from him.

Slithy waits out her combat heartbeat cool down timer. "Okay, take me down again."

After the second Mind Spear attack on his person, the Iron Goblin plops down on the ground and sits motionless.

"Renee, can you shed any light on the Goblin's condition?"

"Of course, darling. His MP is at zero percent."

"MP?"

"Mental Hit Points. There's SP for Spiritual Hit Points and EP for Emotional Hit Points. With the update, the System instructed us AIs to use these new abbreviations."

The other three Iron Goblins run in separate directions.

"Do we chase them?" Kylie circles over the fallen one. "Or do we grab our treasure and continue west? I vote for the latter."

I nod. "Me, too. We need to stay ahead of those spiders. Renee, do you have any other info on the Arachnid Behemoths?"

My support AI in red leather holds up one finger. "Let me see…. Accessing…. Megan Wright reported an encounter with them… *on Earth*."

Whoa, this is something. "Remind me about Megan Wright."

"She's a *potentially* illegal avatar." Renee pauses, frowning. "She has a legal avatar in Khertaan by name of Mithabel—powered by Megan's *subconscious* mind, the way you're powered by Nick's subconsciousness. But after examining all readily accessible data on the subject, ODYSSEY's best guess is that Megan entered Khertaan with her *conscious* mind, occupying a *secondary* avatar, currently imprisoned in the Maron city jail awaiting confirmation of her legal status—which is not likely to be granted. Oh… listen to this… ODYSSEY postulates that Megan Wright hosts an intelligent nanobot collective of her own—not ODYSSEY nanobots, but something of alien origin that enabled her to interact with inter-dimensional invaders on Earth. If it's true, she might not be aware of her collective, but likely communicates with it, considering it a part of her thought stream."

"An alien nanobot collective? Is that something we should be concerned about?"

"The jury is still out on that, darling."

While we descend, I report the latest information from Renee to my fellow party members.

My daughter reaches down for the sitting Iron Goblin. The motionless monster vanishes under her touch. We head west again.

Renee announces the end of the encounter. "You've received ninety XP. Would you like to give it to me?"

"Huh?" I'm so flustered, I almost lose my grip on Kylie's hand. "Give you what? The XP?"

"What else would I be talking about?"

"I didn't realize I could give you XP."

"You can give me anything you want, you bad boy."

I'm so glad Kylie can't hear this exchange. "You're not being serious, Renee. Please tell me you're joking."

She frowns and crosses her arms. "I'm bored, is what I am. What harm is a little sexual innuendo between friends?"

Slithy shakes a fist in triumph. "A third of the way to second level. That's what I'm talking about."

"Renee, I'd love to give it to you. You don't know how much I'd love to give it to you. But your timing is terrible. Besides, I can't touch you—remember? So *giving it to you* would be rather difficult."

The support AI rolls her eyes. "I thought you'd be more fun than this during down times. Now I see why they're called down times. You really know how to let a girl down."

"Renee, *please*."

"Do you want to see my nipples?"

I don't say a damn word.

She grabs the bottom of her leather top and pulls it up until her nipples pop out. "Do you like them?" She leans over and strokes my cheek with a finger.

I don't feel it. Or do I? Maybe I do. I must be imagining it.

She lowers her top to cover her breasts and then leans over to touch my lips with her insubstantial finger. "Kitty got your tongue?"

I shouldn't feel her finger, but I swear I do. "Renee...."

She plants her ethereal lips on mine. There's electricity. I understand electricity, and this is making my hair stand on end. Okay, so I have a mohawk. It's still electrifying. Oh, God.

"Morrow?" Kylie's voice demands my attention.

With a pout, Renee drifts out of my field of vision.

"Yes, my love?"

"You're thinking about something. Spill."

"I...."

"Mom, watch out!"

Slithy's warning draws our attention towards the ground. A dark mottled-gray metallic serpent large enough to swallow me whole strikes at us.

CHAPTER SIX

Charli: Pantheons

We easily find the spacious lobby of the non-denominational Omni Temple. Dylan and Yuni browse a centrally-located kiosk for Priestess Scrolls. I and the other members of MAD gravitate to the plaques lining the lobby walls. The bulk of XStorm members don't stay, leaving Yuni alone with us.

Mithabel stares holes through XStorm's Priestess.

I tap her on the arm. "Are you all right?"

The Tank doesn't look at me. "Why is Dylan consorting with the enemy?"

Mithabel is *so* obviously jealous. Dylan must be aware of what she's doing to her friend. So the question is, why is our Priestess tormenting our Tank, when she knows Mithabel has romantic feelings for her? But it's not my business to fix their love lives. "Did you see this, Mithabel?" I point at a plaque to distract the Elf. "Dylan's Goddess Scintilla rules over the Exemplar pantheon."

The Tank reads the indicated plaque. I read it in its entirety too.

In addition to Light, Scintilla's domains include Gold, Mentors, and Growth. Does that mean Dylan can invoke spells in those domains too? That could be useful. Does Dylan even know about the other domains? Would a Goddess fail to convey such information to her Priestess?

I move to another plaque, this one taller, and motion for Mithabel to follow me. "Says here there are five pantheons. There's Exemplar, the one Scintilla belongs to. There's also Justiciar, Diabolical, Anodyne, and Disruptor. Exemplar and Diabolical are enemies. Justiciar and Disruptor are enemies. Anodyne doesn't have any enemies, or maybe considers all the others as enemies. I wonder which pantheon Yuni belongs to. It would be something if she serves a Goddess in Diabolical."

I suspect Mithabel would think it fine if the Asian Priestess belongs to Diabolical, and the absolute worst if she belongs to Exemplar, the same as Dylan.

"Did you finding anything, Dylan?" Mithabel asks over party chat.

"Yeah... Advanced Heal." Dylan holds up a Scroll. "Works to restore not only Physical, but Mental, Spiritual, and Emotional damage. I really need to learn this, but it's pricey, as you can imagine. Two thousand bucks."

"What do we have to sell?" Amarynth is also passing time reading wall plaques. "Whatever we have, I can autograph it." The Viking Archer signed three Ferro Serpent scales when she traded them for those three delver's specials upon first entering the city. Because of Lady Amarynth's High Social Status, the salesman had been thrilled to make the exchange, basically giving us $250 in trade for each signed scale, while he balked at giving us more than $1 per scale unsigned.

"I still have seven Ferro Serpent scales to sell or trade." Dylan draws a deep breath as she picks up another Scroll to examine.

"Rolag should have an Electric Serpent skin that might be worth something. He'll be rejoining us in forty-two minutes. Charli has the Shadow Stone, but she's keeping it. Otherwise, we've nothing of significant value."

"Not true." Mithabel brings Toxxi's Severed Faerie Wing from her inventory to hand. "This might fetch a few bucks."

Dylan furrows her brow. "You need to give that back to Toxxi. She's crippled without it, as you proved in front of everyone before the update."

"She was trying to kill you, Dylan, and you want me to give it back to her?" Mithabel's anger is palpable. "She deserves being permanently handicapped."

"Are you listening to yourself, Mithabel?" Dylan tosses a Scroll back onto the shelf. "*No one* deserves being permanently handicapped, whether on Earth on in Khertaan. I expected better of you."

"*Khertaan is just a game.*" Mithabel stashes the Wing. "Faeries aren't real. If they were, of course I'd give it back."

I knew I could count on Mithabel to say something offensive. I punch her in the stomach, hard, doing my best to look furious.

It couldn't have hurt, but the Tank looks taken aback. "Why'd you do that? What did I do now?"

"Fuck you, Mithabel." I stomp out of the temple. One of the others will explain it to her. I invoke my Hide skill and step back inside to hear the aftermath of my little show.

With pained gaze, Mithabel looks to Dylan for answers, but can't find a voice for her questions.

The Polynesian Priestess briefly closes her eyes and exhales before speaking. "My Goddess, Mithabel. You're being a real bitch, you know that? Charli is an NPC. She only exists in

Khertaan, not Earth. Do you understand what you just said about her? That she doesn't matter."

That's true. And yeah, it does hurt.

The Elf Tank huffs. "In the grand scheme of things, Charli *doesn't* matter. Nothing in Khertaan does. You and I don't even matter. We're not real. We're only here as long as the game runs, and that won't be forever. *Megan and Debra* are real. *They're* who matters. We're just here on their behalves, because the System requires it."

Ouch, *that* stings—and totally isn't true. I'm as real as anyone on Earth. So is Mithabel, if she could just see it.

Dylan carries a Scroll to a counter attended by a woman in a hooded gray robe. The Polynesian Priestess places the Scroll on the counter. "I'd like to barter for this, please." She lays the seven Ferro Serpent scales next to the Scroll. "My friend over here is Lady Amarynth, and she'll autograph these."

Blond locks spill out as the attendant draws back her hood to examine the scales. She glances at Amarynth and nods. "I can give you at most $200 per autographed scale. That comes to $1400. The Scroll is priced at $2000. Do you have anything else to trade?"

Ignoring her friend's admonishments, Mithabel strides to the counter and tosses down the Faerie Wing. "How much is this worth?"

The attendant's eyes widen. "I'll grant you an in-store credit of $6000 for this."

Mithabel draws the Wing back into her inventory. "Great." She heads for the door. "I'll be across the street. I have a Magic Battle Axe to buy."

Focusing with all my will on staying Hidden, I squat low as she passes, and then follow her outside.

CHAPTER SEVEN

Charli: Wing

Old-fashioned car horns and tires squeal in protest as Mithabel darts into Main Street. There aren't any crosswalks, so what is one supposed to do? I cross behind her, staying close so as to avoid being hit by someone who can't see me.

Coming to a stop right in the middle of the far lane, Mithabel grumbles as though to herself. Lifting her gaze, she pleads with eyes and hands to some unseen person before turning around to face Omni Temple. Though Hiding, I skirt around her to avoid being caught in her field of vision.

She raises both arms overhead and shouts. "*I'm sorry*. What happens in Khertaan matters. The residents of Khertaan matter. Kaleisha matters. Charli matters. I'm a bitch for saying anything that could be construed otherwise."

It took a scolding from her personal support AI to make Mithabel understand. Good for Kaleisha. I accept Mithabel's apology, but I'll still honor my commitment to Quantized. I hurry over to them, cancel my Hide skill, and wave for Ger-Alt and company to follow me.

Horns squawk and horses neigh. Turning back around, Mithabel rushes out of the road, coming to a stop before the entrance to the Mystical Magical Shoppe. With a brief spin as though catching her bearings, Mithabel spots me. Her eyes widen as she catches sight of Toxxi and the other members of Quantized. As we approach, she stays rooted to the spot.

"Excuse us." I'm pretending to still be angry enough at Mithabel and her insult to have left MAD and join party Quantized. Looking like she has swallowed a fly, Mithabel's eyes briefly focus on invisible text before her—undoubtedly checking her party roster. I'm still on it, of course. I haven't actually switched parties. But maybe this will make her think twice before claiming that NPCs in Khertaan don't matter.

The Tank swallows hard again as she steps aside for us, her lips working but no words escaping.

I hold open the door to the Mystical Magical Shoppe and wave Quantized inside.

Ger-Alt rides up on the back of her pet Cheetah, Zip, who bares his teeth and hisses at Mithabel. Skeeter clings to the Goblin's scalp, nestled in her hair as though it's his nest. He gives Mithabel a coy look of innocence. Ger-Alt glares at Mithabel, doubtlessly recalling how the Tank took her Battle Axe after she broke Mithabel's Longsword. An eye for an eye, as the saying goes. Of course, Mithabel wouldn't have taken anything from Quantized if they'd left us alone. But no, they joined everyone else in trying to slay Dylan for the Longest Survivor bounty. And they paid dearly for their efforts. I can't blame Mithabel for her reaction to them.

FepXveq stands out prominently in her suit of royal purple Leather Armor and Gloves, not to mention her black afro that makes her look six-and-a-half feet tall. Falco rides her armored shoulder. As FepXveq strides past Mithabel, Falco mutters, "Bitch," sounding more human than a bird should.

Bringing up the rear is the violet-skinned Toxxi. Her single wing, translucent with crimson veins but leathery, like a bat's, droops behind her left shoulder. She stops at Mithabel's feet and tosses her wavy brown hair. Without looking up, she resumes her trek into the shop. She wouldn't beg Mithabel to return her Severed Wing, no matter how much she wants it back. But other severed body parts have reattached to their owners in Khertaan, and there's no reason to think her Severed Wing wouldn't do likewise if Mithabel returned it. The loss must be debilitating for the Faerie.

I follow Toxxi inside, not holding the door open for Mithabel. It's a swinging door, hardly mattering whether it's held open. I picture Mithabel hitting the door hard as she enters, but she's remarkably calm. Maybe she really is sorry.

Dismounted, Ger-Alt stands by the shelf of Magical Battle Axes, gripping one by the handle and assessing its balance and weight.

The Tank remains at the doorway and watches while party Quantized shops, expressing their shock at the prices more aggressively than any of us in MAD did. Mithabel continues to watch until negotiations for prices begin with the shopkeeper, at which time she moves closer to the counter, no doubt to eavesdrop. I pretend not to notice.

Toxxi climbs onto the Cheetah and then jumps onto the counter top. She flaps her remaining wing. "I understand this might be worth something. How much will you give us in trade if I were to sever it and hand it over to you?"

The shopkeeper's eyes bug and he waves a hand in protest. "Please don't. I'll have no bloodshed in here."

The Faerie isn't satisfied with that answer. "I can step outside to do the severing. How much?"

"I... please..." The shopkeeper wilts under Toxxi's stare. "Fine. Fine. I'll give you $5000 in store credit for your Severed Wing, provided you step outside first and come back with the stump wrapped so it doesn't drip blood on my shop floor."

"Will you take $5000 for one of those Magical Battle Axes?"

The shopkeeper shakes his head. "They sell for $6000."

I lean on the counter next to the Faerie and turn on my level 9 Negotiate skill. "You know you've undercut my friend here on the value of her wing. And you've marked up your Battle Axes. You can give her a Battle Axe and $1000 in store credit for her wing and still earn a great deal of XP from the trade."

The shopkeeper glares at me. "Oh, it's you." He bows his head. "You're right, of course. Okay, sure. Bring me a Severed Faerie Wing, and I'll give you a Battle Axe with a level one enchantment and an extra $1000 in store credit. Now go on, before I change my mind."

The Faerie claps once, but otherwise doesn't act thrilled. How could she be? She is, after all, sacrificing her wing and giving up on the idea of getting the other one back. Toxxi jumps off the counter onto Zip's back and then to floor. She gestures to Ger-Alt. "I need you to chop my wing off."

"Are you sure you want to go through with this?" Ger-Alt mounts Zip.

Skeeter remains on Ger-Alt's head as the lot quietly passes Mithabel and leaves the shop. FepXveq and Falco stay behind. The Dark Elf's features remain as expressionless as always as she peruses the shelves. Perched on her shoulder, Falco keeps a watch on everything and everyone in the store, occasionally turning that hawkish gaze on me.

The Tank approaches the counter, sidling up to me. I push back my wide-brimmed Hat and look up innocently at Mithabel, saying nothing.

The Tank initiates a private chat with me. I accept.

"I'm sorry, Charli." The Tank places a hand over one of mine on the counter. "I'm such a bitch. Can you forgive me?"

I shrug and say what I suspect she really wants to hear. "You only spoke the truth. What's there to forgive?"

"Charli. I mean it. I'm sorry." Mithabel slides her free arm around my shoulders and squeezes. "Come on. Let's go to the temple and rejoin the rest of MAD. We could really use your Negotiate skill. I'm sorry we didn't ask you to use it before. It's difficult remembering what skills everyone has. And you know you can always offer if we don't ask."

"I think you'll appreciate me more if I take a break from you." I pull my hand free of Mithabel's grasp. "I'm not officially leaving the party. But I'm traveling with Quantized for now. While you go to fulfill your quest at the Red Pegasus Inn, I'm taking Quantized to Ezmerelda's hut, so one of them can get a Ring and get onto the Top Individual Avatars list."

"Are you shitting me, Charli?" Mithabel draws back, her neck turning red. "After they tried to kill Dylan, you're going to help them?"

I laugh at that. "Are you forgetting who *did* kill Dylan?" I turn my back on her and take three steps away. "If you want me back with MAD, you won't try to stop me. This is my decision. I should be back before you finish your quest, and I can join back up with you then."

Sadness permeates Mithabel's voice. "If it's the price I must pay to bring you back to us, then I'll pay it. We need you with us, Charli. You're important to us. You matter. And we like you as a person, too, if that means anything. I'm sorry I took you for granted."

"I believe you." I turn to face her. "I'll plan to meet back up with you after I return to the city. Try to get along without me until then. And don't ask me anything over party chat while I'm gone. My silence on all matters is part of the price you're paying to regain my services."

Mithabel chuckles. "You're using your Negotiate skill on me right now, aren't you?"

I grin as I shrug. "Do I need to?"

"You really are a devil, Charli."

"I know." I bow dramatically. "It's my Complex Personality trait at work, no doubt."

"You can't blame all your quirks on that trait."

"Watch me." So far, I've not discovered any other use for it. The trait might as well be good for something.

The Tank slaps the counter top in a show of bravado. "Okay. So we're good then."

"We're good." I glance at the shop exit. "Guess Toxxi and Ger-Alt will be a while. They have to go outside the city to draw a weapon. I'm glad I won't be watching." I initiate a private chat with Zip the Cheetah. "Hey, buddy. Where are you now?"

"Hi, Charli. I'm thankful for what you're doing for us. We're about halfway to the city gates."

I tell Mithabel where they are.

"I don't think they'll actually do it." Mithabel meanders to the Battle Axe shelf. I can guess her thoughts. With me here, using my Negotiate skill on her behalf, she could maybe get a Magical Battle Axe and a pair of Boots of Silence in trade for the Severed Faerie Wing she carries.

The shop door opens. Dylan and Amarynth enter. Yuni isn't with them. Catching sight of Mithabel, the Polynesian Priestess waves a Scroll in the air. "They gave it to me on credit, Mithabel. Can you believe it?" Her eyes shift towards FepXveq. "Is the rest of Quantized here?" Her gaze moves back to Mithabel. "Did you return the Severed Wing to Toxxi?"

The Tank takes an Axe from the shelf, one she was looking at earlier. "No and no. With Charli's help, I'm going to trade the Wing for a Magical Battle Axe and some Boots of Silence. Toxxi can buy the Severed Wing from the shopkeeper if she wants it back."

"Dammit, Mithabel, we talked about this." Dylan stashes her Scroll. "You're giving it back to Toxxi, or you and I are no longer traveling together. Do you understand me?"

Blinking as though to hold back tears, the Elf nods. "Okay. Okay. But Toxxi isn't here right now. She's gone out of the city to chop off her other wing for money."

"*What?*" Dylan's face contorts as though about to crawl off her head. "Mithabel, I love you, but you are stretching my patience. We're not evil people, and I'm not letting you turn into one. This competition isn't about the prize money. There are inter-dimensional monstrosities invading Earth, and it's our job to train to combat them. Toxxi needs to be included in the training, not shunned for what happened before the update. Contact her on a private channel and tell her you're giving her back the Severed Wing before she severs the other one. *Now*, Mithabel."

I hold out a hand to the Tank. "Don't bother, Mithabel. She doesn't want to talk to you. Give it to me."

Mithabel places the Severed Wing in my hand. "I'm sorry for everything. This whole training-to-combat-invaders situation hasn't sunk into my brain yet. I know—we all need to work together rather than against each other. It's difficult for me to mentally make the switch, but I swear I'll do better. Come back to us safely, Charli."

"I just hope you learn something from this, Mithabel." I hand the Severed Wing to FepXveq. "Go ahead and take this to Toxxi. I'll be right behind you." The Dark Elf and her Dust Storm Falcon Companion leave the shop. I return to the chat with Zip. "Don't let Toxxi chop off her wing."

"Yeah, FepXveq already told us. We're not quite to the gates yet. We'll meet you there."

I fetch an empty Flask from the display and take it to the counter. "Give me this in exchange for a piece of Cornstalk from the hut of the Seeress. My friends and I are going to visit her now, but I need this Flask before I go."

Rattled, the shopkeeper nods. "Yes, fine. It's a deal." He won't realize until I'm gone that I hit him with the full force of a level 9 Negotiate skill. But both he and the System will hold me to the deal I've negotiated, of course.

As I'm leaving the shop, Dylan accosts Mithabel. *"You've driven Charli away."* Their conversation is over party chat, so I'm hearing it even after the door closes behind me.

"She's still on our party roster, Dylan. Check for yourself. She's coming back to us. She just needed a break from me, and for that I'm sorry."

"Hey, ladies," Amarynth says. "I had to autograph all seven Ferro Serpent scales and talk down the price, but I got the Boots I wanted. They threw in this Dirk, too. And a Cudgel for you, Priestess. Sorry it's not magical. It was kind of you to give Yuni's Cudgel back to her, and I'm glad I could replace it for you."

"Dylan," Mithabel says, "can you use your powers of persuasion to convince the shopkeep to give me this Axe on credit?"

"It wasn't like that. I promised to pay for the Scroll at two o'clock, when Rolag returns. He has the Electric Serpent skin, and we're using it to pay for the Scroll. It's already been agreed upon. So it's not long-term credit. Sorry if I misled you."

"So you both get something magical and I don't," Mithabel says. "I don't even get a replacement for the Sword I lost. Great. I guess I deserve this."

Amarynth giggles. "This is unexpected."

No one says anything.

Finally, Amarynth speaks again. "These Boots allow me to operate at level 3 Increased Movement if I want. *Sweet*. If you thought I could run circles around you before, just wait until you see me in action now."

"Well, it will be two o'clock in a few minutes." By her tone, Mithabel isn't happy. "Let's go pay for your Scroll, Priestess. Then we need to start our quest."

I turn down the volume on party chat and hurry for the city gates.

CHAPTER EIGHT

Megan: Orc Wizard

From whom shall I take an ear? Can't be a city resident. Are any of these pedestrians non-residents? Do I go up and ask each of them and then whack off their ear if they say they're from out of town? I can't—not without drawing unwanted attention. The ban on drawing weapons in the city will make this tough.

There goes XStorm now, headed for the city gates. But you can't take them all on.

Maybe I could sneak up behind the one in back once we're outside the city and slice off his ear. Ah, it's ChrisCross. I'd love to take off his ear.

"You there. Halt!"

Ah, shit. They've found me.

The City Guardsmen converge… not on me, but on a red cloaked figure across the street looking my way. Behind him stands a Motorcycle. On Earth, he had banners over his head reading *Orc Wizard* and *HP 100%*. They're gone now, but I swear it's the same guy—or one just like him. I killed a fireball-throwing fellow just like this back on Earth, after he burned down my house and torched my car. How is this guy in Khertaan?

You're in Khertaan. Why can't he be too? Ezmerelda said the invaders would try to stop your training. So here they come. Best keep a lookout for Arachnid Behemoths and Mad Cow Ballista too. You've got six lives between you and Mithabel, and the invaders want them all.

Holy crap. This changes everything.

A fireball blasts into the swarming Guards, and they fall back screaming, arms flailing before they pop out of existence. More Guards rush into the gaps left by their slain comrades, Spears tossing and Swords swinging.

A male voice booms. *"He's an illegal avatar. Take him alive!"*

Spears and Swords disappear as the Guards stash them. Ropes and Nets appear instead—only to be disintegrated by another fireball, along with another half-dozen Guards. But more Guards step up. Their Ropes and Nets fly at the Orc Wizard, lashing around him and dropping over him.

The monster bellows as fire flowers from his body, searing the restraints upon him. More Guardsmen fall and others replace them. Those who die pop back into existence behind their ranks, respawning as soon as they die. How many lives are they willing to lose to fight this monster?

Being Guards, maybe they have infinite lives. More of them are consumed by the Orc's flames. They can't get their Nets on him, but they're intent on taking him alive. How long can this go on?

I count five fireballs. Every time he throws one, a half-dozen Guards vanish from the inner circle surrounding him and reappear on the outer edge. Who will run out of resources first?

The Orc Wizard must be using up his Auni, but the Guards are using up lives.

Ah… where's fireball number six? The Orc Wizard is out of Auni. The Ropes and Nets tighten around him, forcing him to his knees. The Guards don't beat him needlessly, but lift him to his feet once they have his arms pinned to his sides.

"You're coming with us." A Guard slips a Rope loop over the Orc's head, tightens it around his neck, and heads toward the city gates, where the holding cells are located.

They'll expect to find you in your cell.

Yes, I know. Dammit.

Are you staying in the city or leaving?

If I leave, it will have to be over or under the city wall. The Gate Guards would detain me. But I have no skills for climbing or digging.

Mithabel recently went up in level. Have you checked since then whether she picked up any new skills?

No, I haven't. I'll check later. For now, I'll scoot over to the prison house and slip back into my cell. It's the safest bet. The Orc Wizard isn't going without a struggle, which works in my favor.

Without breaking into a run, I hurry along the sidewalk. Sorry, lady, for nearly stepping on the hem of your huge-ass dress. Apologies, sir, for knocking off your top hat.

Maybe if you compressed your body, you wouldn't run into as many people.

The side alley I used when sneaking out lies ahead. I retrace my steps….

The prison entrance stands just across the street. I look both ways. The Orc Wizard approaches, a dozen Guards surrounding him, all their attention on him.

Don't run, or you might attract attention. Walk casually across the street.

This is taking forever. They're bound to spot me.

You don't know that. Take a deep breath and keep walking.

They'll see me go inside.

That's doubtful. You have your Hide skill turned on. It's not likely they'll spot you, being so preoccupied with the Orc.

Right.

You're in.

No Guards are present. The keys are still hanging on the wall, and the cell door is still standing wide open.

They haven't noticed you're gone.

Ha, right.

Get the keys. Close the cell door. Lock it. Put the keys back. Compress your body. There you go, between the bars. Back in your cell. Change back into your Leather Armor. Keep the Bikini on beneath it and the Ring on your finger, but keep your hand out of sight. Throw all the other duplicated stuff under the cot, including the Severed Faerie Wing.

I'd stash some of these things, but I'm not ready for Mithabel to discover them. The cot blanket is flimsy but looks clean. Drape it over the side of the cot to better hide my stuff.

You best hurry—their boots are scuffing the floor in the hallway. Lay on the cot. No… sit up. Act curious.

The sounds of struggle echo along the hall. Guards enter the outer cell area, dragging their prisoner every step of the way.

The Orc Wizard catches sight of me and immediately stops struggling. He grins at me. He has found his quarry, despite his resistance to coming here.

The Guards notice the Orc's change of behavior. "No, you're not going into the cell with the pretty lady." One of the Guards grabs the keys off the wall and opens a cell on the other side of the room. The other Guards push the Orc inside. The first Guard locks the cell door. "If you're legit, you'll be out of here shortly after 8 AM. If you're not legit, as we have reason to believe, you'll be expelled from Khertaan instead. Same as her." He points a thumb at me and then returns the keys to their spot on the wall.

One of his comrades scratches his head. "How are these illegals getting in?"

The first Guard shrugs. "It's not our job to figure that out. We've caught them and locked them up. The System will check them sometime in the next six hours. That's all we need to know. But let's get back out there in case a third illegal pops up. It's rather fun fighting now that we have infinite lives."

"Yeah." A third Guard grabs a bar of the Orc's cell. "Hear that, illegal? We've got *infinite* lives. Your fireballs won't do shit for you. Burn us all day, and we'll keep coming back. We're your worst nightmare. I hope more of your like does show up in Maron. More XP for us."

Not even a glimmer of understanding lights the Orc's gaze, as though he doesn't comprehend one word of what the Guards are saying. His glare is locked on me, like I'm his sole reason for being. I hate to think I am, but there's no doubt this fiend will chase me to all ends of the world — whether that world be Earth or Khertaan. He doesn't speak my language, but he's communicating his intentions loud and clear.

You should ask the Guards about their infinite lives.

"Hey, Guard. Do you really have infinite lives, or just really high Constitution?"

Sneering, the addressed Guard walks over, pressing his face against the bars of my cell. "It's not *high* at all. It's *negative*. If we die, it just goes more negative. It will never hit zero, so we just keep respawning."

"Wow. How did you get that?"

"The update, what else?"

The first Guard smacks the talkative Guard upside the head. "Enough chatting with the prisoners. Move out."

The Guards file out, leaving me and my nemesis alone together, separated only by twenty feet and two rows of metal bars. The Orc clearly has exhausted his Auni, so he can't shoot a fireball at me... but how long before his Auni replenishes sufficiently for him to kill me? I've got to act fast.

You'd think prisons like this would be set up to prevent replenishment of Auni or casting of spells.

Agreed, but they also should prevent the use of skills, and they didn't prevent me from using mine to escape.

The Orc tries the bars of his cell. He's not going anywhere. To him, that means I'm not either. He reclines on his cot, closing his eyes. Sleep *is* the fastest way to restore expended Auni.

Is he sleeping? It will make what I want to do easier.

He's lying very still. Maybe you should go now.

I quietly pull my Battle Axe out from beneath the cot, compress my body, and slip between the bars of my cell.

You're being noisy.

Shh. Let me concentrate. I creep across the room to his cell and slide between the bars. My Goddess, *I'm in his cell.* Voluntarily. He doesn't look peaceful in his sleep, but just as savage as when awake, his fangs jutting over his lower lip. Hard lines etch a fierce mask on his face. Veins bulge from his muscular gray skin. He's all but naked, wearing only a drab Loincloth and hooded red Cloak with gold trim. Before I killed him—or one like him—on Earth, with the heel of my pump through his eye, he'd put a Dirk into my leg. That had hurt like bloody hell. He might be unable to throw fireballs, but he's still a danger.

Why are you in this freak's cell?

I intend to take his Ear. Should I Stun him first? I don't want to kill him, which an indiscriminate swing of the Axe might do. If I kill him, he'll respawn somewhere out there, and I might as well just open his cell door and let him out.

If you try to saw off his Ear with your Axe, he'll wake up before you finish. Stunning him first seems the best tactic. It should be easy with him already being asleep.

Shit. His Dirk is in his hand. He's awake....

He comes at me.

I'm not as afraid of him as I was two days ago on the side of the road on Earth. I Parry. He doesn't know who he's dealing with. I smack him with the dull side of the Axe head, going for the Stun.

He slumps back on the cot. That was too easy. I stash my Axe and take his Dirk. It's easier harvesting his Ear with the smaller bladed weapon. The body part looks strange in my palm, separated from his head. It's not bleeding. I slip out between the bars before the Stun wears off.

Holy crap, that was close. You could have died.

I know. His clawed fingers look as lethal as any Dirk.

He's up. His snarls and bellows are unintelligible.

I laugh at him. "You lose, monster." I fetch the keys off the wall, unlock the door to my cell, and leave it hanging open. Keeping the Leather Boots on, I stash the rest of my Armor. "Can you understand me?" I equip my Axe again.

The Orc Wizard thrashes in his cell, shouting words I don't understand.

"Who do you work for, Orc?" I stuff the Severed Ear into my Bikini top. I'm not stashing it, for fear Mithabel will see it and try to use it for trade herself. It will ride against my chest until I get back to Ye Old Magic Shoppe. I slip the Dirk into the top of my right Boot. The blade presses against my skin, but my Natural Armor is tougher. "If you're not going to say anything useful, could you please shut the hell up?" I loop the Rope around my neck and right shoulder, and set the severed end of the Faerie Wing in the Rope loops, so it juts up, as though it's my own appendage. I wish I had a better way to carry it. "What planet are you from, you raving lunatic? You've been assigned to kill me, right? Why me?"

You haven't figured that out yet? *You* killed him on Earth, where their bullets went right through him. The Khertaan PCs are training to fight the invaders, but you've already proven you're capable—*without the training*. Maybe you shouldn't even be in Khertaan. Maybe you should be back on Earth, fighting the invaders now.

I'm not ready for that. I need more power to fight the invaders effectively, and Khertaan is where I'll get it.

What's left? The Battle Axe, Bow, and Platform Slippers... I don't want to stash any of them, so I wedge the heels of the Slippers in the Rope loops lying over my breast. The Battle Axe and Bow stay in hand. I put the keys back on the wall and leave the incoherent, snarling Orc Wizard behind me.

Yeah, you're not getting any answers from him, just noise.

His bellowing increases in intensity. "You can't avoid death forever, bitch. If I don't kill you, others will."

He can talk my language after all.

Do you want to hang around to talk more, or do you think he's merely trying to delay you?

I have an appointment to keep at Ye Olde Shoppe of the Profane and a Magic Battle Axe to claim. I put the monster behind me. The System clock in the top right corner of my view reads Day 3, 2:00 AM, on the dot.

CHAPTER NINE

Morrow: Class Level Two

A beam of silvery energy blasts from Slithy into the striking Serpent's yawning maw, but to no avail.

Kylie darts aside, her grip strengthening on my hand, but the larger-than-me metallic snake changes course midair. *Damn.* I draw my wand into my free hand… and nearly drop it as fangs sink into my left calf, front and back. Nick's memories of leg pain pale in comparison to the fire charging through me.

My Angel wife maintains her grip on me, but the weight of the Serpent drags us down. Rancor launches from my shoulder and plunges his Beak into a reptilian eye. The Serpent is still very much alive, with the ground fast approaching. Damn. I cast my spell—using 8 of my 10 Auni, plus 1 bonus point from the wand.

Yellow forks of lightning bursts from my tattoo. An unholy shriek escapes the Serpent's clenched jaws, but it doesn't release me. We smack into the ground. Kylie pulls her hand free of mine. The world blurs.

Renee informs me the Ferro Serpent Boss has less than a quarter of its HP remaining, while I'm just above half. I should feel good about that, I suppose, but I'm practically out of offensive juice, while the Serpent still has its fangs in me.

A shadow lashes across my vision. Kylie shouts a familiar war cry, cut abruptly short. The Boss wraps its tail around her and constricts.

The fangs in my leg press in harder, wrenching a scream from my lungs. My life force ebbs....

I can't do another spell in this combat heartbeat, but what else can I do? I bend at the waist, catch sight of scaly skin, open my mouth, and expend my last 2 Auni. I don't get any bonus Auni, because my Lightning Breath is a trait, not a spell.

As I exhale with force, a cone of yellow Lightning bursts past my lips. The fangs in my leg stop squeezing... they're gone. As dark specks of metal swirl into the air, my pain subsides.

With wings fanned above her and her blue Spirit Blade in hand, Kylie stands over me, looking for all the world like an avenging Angel. Admiration fills her gaze, and pride swells my head.

Renee peers into my view. *"Congrats, Morrow. The Boss is defeated. You've earn 1200 XP and have attained level 2. Your Auni has been replenished and is now at 16. You've also gained the skill Lightning Resistance at level 1. Your other skills have increased in level by 1."*

My Frogkin daughter lets loose a croaking whoop. "Woo hoo! Level 2 Mentalist! My Psi points are up to 13—*yay*. And I now have the Levitate skill." Her feet float off the ground. "I can hover in the air above the battle and shoot enemies with my Mind Spear. Hee hee."

Kylie extends a hand to me. "We need to move. Arachnid Behemoths are closing on us. I'll tell you my improvements once we're airborne."

CHAPTER TEN

Morrow: Spider and Snake

With Slithy holding one of Kylie's hands and me holding the other, we fly twice as high as we were before, not wanting another surprise.

Kylie's Auni has increased to 8. She picked up the skill Spirit Resistance—not helpful in physical combat, but should prove useful against possession attempts or other spirit-based attack forms.

Rancor's new skill is Psi-Parry. He can expend Psi points, of which he now has 7, to enhance any Parrying he does.

Unlike expended Auni and Psi points, our lost HP wasn't restored by our recent level gain. I'm lowest at 53%. Kylie is next at 89%. Rancor comes in at 96%, and Slithy is still at 100. It's too bad lost HP doesn't restore on level advancement. Without a healer, we may need to sleep to heal any significant amounts of HP, but we can't do that with the Arachnid Behemoths breathing up our backsides. With each level advancement, we gain raw hit points, but it's impossible to say exactly how many, since all we are privy to are our percentages.

"I see more of those Iron Goblins." Slithy points.

We're far enough ahead of the spiders, we *could* stop to beat up on the Iron Goblins and earn some XP.

Throwing glances at the rest of us and getting nods all around, Kylie descends. "Keep an eye open for Ferrous Serpents." She stops twenty feet above one of the Iron Goblins. "Want to try your Mind Spear on it, kid? Let's see if your improved version can take one of them down."

A silvery Mind Spear streaks downward from Slithy's forehead, striking the Iron Goblin. The mook falls over and lies still on the ground. The Frogkin girl pumps her free fist. "*Yes. Let's swoop down and collect it.*"

The other Iron Goblins run towards their fallen comrade when they see us dropping towards him, but they aren't fast enough. Kylie swings Slithy over the comatose Goblin. The Frogkin Mentalist touches her target and stashes him before the other mooks can close on us.

Kylie shoots upwards. "Are we taking any more of them?"

Slithy giggles. "*Please, please.* It won't take long, they won't hurt us, we'll have more treasure to sell, and I recover Psi points quickly."

I glance over at her. "You should keep more than just 1 Psi point in reserve. But I can expend a few Auni. See how much my lightning strikes affect them."

Kylie gives me a glance. "You need to keep most of your Auni in reserve, honey—just in case another Boss snake takes us by surprise. Your Lightning is our most effective attack against those things."

"Yes, my love."

Rancor pipes up. "Ha ha, let me fight a Goblin. I'd like to try my Psi-Melee Weapon skill."

"Fine, I'll set us down about twenty feet from them. Get ready." Kylie descends. Five Iron Goblins run toward us. Slithy's

Mind Spear drops the first one. I cast a 1-point Lightning Strike spell at another Goblin, which effectively becomes a 2-point spell due to my wand. The attack lowers the mook's HP to almost half. I hurt the Boss more than I hurt this guy.

Rancor's Beak glows silver, looking much like a shimmering dagger, and he drives it into a third Goblin's chest, reducing the mook to just under half its HP. "Ha ha, I'd hoped to drop the mook in one blow, but doesn't my silver Beak look cool?"

Kylie shouts as she charges, her Hypnotic Voice stopping the Goblins in their tracks and preventing them from hitting back. A glowing blue blade appears in her hand, and she lops off a head. Iron Goblin death sparks shower the area.

Slithy takes down an uninjured Goblin with another Mind Spear. I cast a 2-point lightning strike at the Goblin I struck before, and the golden bolt blasts him into bright bits.

There's one Goblin still standing. He runs—not towards us.

"Ha ha, no way, toupee." Rancor speeds after the fleeing Goblin, but isn't going fast enough to catch him. Kylie speeds up beside him and holds out her hand. Rancor latches onto a finger. The Angel flies up and over the running Goblin, dropping from the sky in front of him. Though he makes a fist to attack, he doesn't act as quickly as either of his foes. Rancor's silver Beak connects, and Kylie's blue blade finishes the job, reducing the Goblin to sparkling bits.

We each earn another 180 XP, according to Renee. She gives me a bright smile. "Good job, darling. You're my hero."

"Ah, shucks, Renee. I could kiss you for saying that."

"Oh, goody." She puckers her lips and leans towards me. After a quick glance to make sure no one's watching, I pucker my lips too. I swear I feel something when her insubstantial lips overlap mine.

"You're such a bad boy." Renee flies backwards away from me, her reclining pose showing more leg than if she were upright. If I'm a bad boy, she's an evil woman.

Slithy Jumps twenty feet to one of the comatose Goblins and stashes it. Then she Jumps to the other and stashes it, too. "I've got 6 Brass Goblins and 4 Iron ones in inventory." Her smile is as captivating as always. "I really hope we find somewhere to trade them in for magic items."

Kylie collects us all and carries us again into the sky. To the east, the Arachnid Behemoths have come too close for comfort. "Let's not stop again for a while."

Slithy pouts. "By my calculations, we only need to kill or capture 10 more Iron Goblins to reach level 3."

I'm, however, in agreement with my wife. "Level 3 won't mean much if those giant spiders catch us. They're spiders, so they probably can throw webs, and we don't know how far they can throw them. Being giant-sized, they can probably throw them really far. We should stay well ahead of them."

"But we could fly way way up, backtrack, and go over them." Slithy blinks eyelashes at me, which looks adorable on her masked red face. "If we come down behind them, we can take our time and grind away at Iron Goblins until we reach level 4 or 5. Then we can quickly catch back up, since Mom flies so fast."

Kylie squeezes my hand. "Do we know where the spiders are headed?"

I squeeze back. "No, we don't. They *might* be following us, in which case, nothing would keep them from turning around. If they're not following us, we might want to beat them to wherever they're going, to give a warning to whomever might be in their path."

"Oh, wow, look." Slithy points back to the east.

Kylie turns us around and hovers in place.

A Ferrous Serpent rises up before the lead Arachnid Behemoth. The giant spider drives a pointed leg through the Boss monster, skewering the snake. The Boss monster writhes but can't free itself. It wraps its tail around the spider leg to constrict, with no apparent effect on the spider. The Behemoth lifts its leg to its mouth, bites down on the Serpent's neck, and tears off the Boss monster's head. The Boss evaporates into a cloud of metallic dust. The spider army keeps coming.

Kylie spins around and speeds westward.

Is that the edge of a Cornfield just ahead?

CHAPTER ELEVEN

Charli: To Ezmerelda's Hut

Holding my skirt up to my waist, showing my culottes, I run along the sidewalk, darting around and between citizen NPCs who don't know what to make of a teenage NPC girl in a hurry. Is a boy chasing me? Am I playing a game of tag with other girls? Or am I running away with some stolen object? "Slow down, girl," yells one old man in top hat and tails. "Oh, my Lord," cries a woman in a bustle large enough to conceal two men. I skirt around her without colliding with her clothing.

No Guardsmen are in evidence, as though they've all been called to some other part of the city, so there's no one in a position of authority to tell me to slow down. I make good time, and soon I spot Quantized huddling together.

Toxxi spreads her wings, *both of them*, and rises into the air, waving for me to come over. Her smile welcomes me as I reach the group. "Thank you, Charli."

"Thank Dylan. She insisted, and that's why Mithabel relented."

Ger-Alt nods at me from her seat on Zip. "You're a good person, Charli. How long do you think this trip to the hut will take?"

I could grow accustomed to such accolades. "Going there should be quick. But just so you know… I have something to attend to afterward, so I won't be guiding you all the way back to the city."

The Goblin bobs her head. "What is this something you'll be doing afterward? Not that it's our business, but if we can be of assistance, we're glad to help."

"It's nothing you can help with." I head for the gates. "But there is something you can do for me, and it will relieve you of the necessity of paying me the $50 for my Guide services. When we reach the hut, I intend to take a piece of Cornstalk from it— I'll need you to deliver it on my behalf to the Mystical Magical Shoppe."

Toxxi raises a hand. "I'll do it. It's the least I can do for the part you played in the return of my wing."

The two Guards outside the gates pay us little mind as we pass them. They're too busy looking past us through the gates into the city. I catch a whiff of smoke.

Ger-Alt waves to get my attention. "What's the best way for us to include you in group discussions if you're not in our party? Is global or local chat our only options?"

"I can set up a private chat and invite you all to join." I initiate it and send the invites, all of which are accepted. "Did any of you smell that smoke?"

"I did." FepXveq nods, her afro quivering atop her head. "But I saw no indication of anything having burned. It didn't smell like cigarette smoke. It's befuddling."

Ger-Alt and her Cheetah mount turn their attention away from the city gates. "The cause of the smoke isn't our concern. Which way to Ezmerelda's hut?"

I point across the Grass Bladed Field, which is no longer a field of grass, but bare dirt. "Back that way. But we'll be traveling in a special fashion through the forest."

"You've got my curiosity piqued." Toxxi flutters thirty feet into the air. She shades her eyes and looks around. "No signs of mooks about. We are clear to travel."

We cross the dirt Field without incident, arriving at the edge of the Black Poison Forest. I move into the shadows of the tree cover.

Toxxi hovers above our heads. "What's this special kind of travel we're taking? I'm really not looking forward to fighting the Boss of this territory again. First time was hell. If it hadn't been for Skeeter, we'd never have gotten past it."

Skeeter? Oh, yeah, the Squirrel. I keep forgetting he's with us. "How did you deal with the One Strike Scorpion Boss, Skeeter?"

The Squirrel chatters. Maybe he's laughing? "I put my Mentalist skills to work. The Boss had a Displace ability, so everyone attacking it kept missing. But one hit from me, and it was dead." His voice loses its cheer. "Sad thing was, though, Ger-Alt, FepXveq, and Zip were all hit by it before I defeated it, and they became possessed. We had to kill Ger-Alt, after she killed FepXveq and Zip. I'm with Toxxi on this. I hope we can avoid encountering that thing again."

I double-check my Monster Lore. "After defeating a Boss once, you can enter and leave its territory as much as you like. We don't need to face it again. We'll go from here directly to the Mystic Hollow Cornfield, where Ezmerelda's hut is. But I need everyone to gather in a circle with me and hold hands, paws, talons, or whatever you have for grasping." I hold my hands out to either side.

Toxxi drops from the sky, folding her wings as she lands beside me. "Would it work for me to hug your leg?"

I nod. "As long as everyone has contact with my person directly or indirectly though a chain."

The violet-skinned Faerie grabs my calf. Ger-Alt stays mounted on Zip, who sidles up to me on the right. The Goblin woman grasps my right hand, while Skeeter sits in her hair. FepXveq takes my left hand, with Falco perched on her shoulder. That's everyone.

"Here goes." I concentrate on my Shadow Passage skill. My cheeks warm. This is my first time trying a Shadow Wizard ability.

It isn't working. What's wrong? Do I not understand something? I'm limited to 3 passengers per skill level, but at skill level 2, I should be able to transport a total of 6, not counting myself. What are the other skill limitations? "Is everyone in shadow?"

Falco lowers his head. "Now I am. Sorry, I was catching a few rays."

"Not a problem. I should have said something. Let's try this again."

What color surrounds us drains away. But we lose more than color. Our bodies lose substantialness and definition, becoming silhouettes of our former selves.

Our environment blurs, turning to black and white, light and dark, degrees of brightness and contrast. Weightless, I sense the ground beneath my feet, a tickle rather than pressure. "Hold on." My words echo off distant unseen hills. Exerting my will over the group, we move as one, gray ghosts traveling among the forest shadows.

Calling upon my new Avoidance skill, I skirt the bright spots where sunlight peeks through the treetops. As though by instinct or intuition, my highest ranked skill—Navigation—informs me of the direction to our intended destination. We move faster than if I were running downhill along an empty, paved road. Blurred shapes of trees whiz past us on either side. We dart around clumps of brush and leap over fallen logs without slowing. This is power, and it's my power. And I'm only halfway to level thirty. I can't imagine how powerful I'll be at level thirty. I already feel like a Goddess.

A wall of light appears before us, and I slow, looking for any way forward, any trail of shadow I can follow. But there is none. "Brace yourselves." My voice still echoes like we're in a cave. I take us into the light.

Those of us with feet on the ground stagger as our weight returns, all of us drawn back into our physical bodies by the presence of light. The Black Poison Forest is at our backs. We're on the edge of the Mystic Hollow Cornfield. Ezmerelda's hut awaits straight ahead.

The rows of cornstalks afford some shadow, but nowhere do I see dark patches dense enough for my Shadow Passage skill to work. I drop hands and point. "It's just there. Hurry, and with any luck we'll avoid encounters."

"Yeah, I'd rather not fight the Shadow Protean Boss or any Shadow Amoebae again." Toxxi releases my leg and takes to the sky, along with Falco. "I don't see any hut."

I walk along the furrow between two cornrows. "It's straight ahead. It won't look like a hut, per se. More like a dense group of cornstalks arranged to form four walls, with corn silk used for a thatched roof."

"There it is." Falco streaks ahead, far above us. "Follow me."

"Watch out for the shadow monsters." Ger-Alt rides Zip in a furrow parallel to mine. "Those Shadow Amoebae are hard to fight, and I don't even want to think about fighting another Shadow Protean Boss. I hate how that thing got into everyone's heads. Made us all stupid for hours after the fight. If it hadn't been for Falco, we'd have all succumbed to that thing and probably still be lying on the ground, drooling like rabid dogs."

Falco glances back. "I hadn't expected my Mental Armor trait to be of much use in the game. But was I glad to have it."

I huff. "I was the only one in my party with Mental Armor. It wasn't easy to beat that Boss. I needed magic to be effective against it."

"You'd think psychic skills would work against it, too." Skeeter peers at me from atop Ger-Alt's head.

Ger-Alt laughs. "If only you'd been in your right mind when using them."

FepXveq follows in the furrow behind me. "My Vitals Strike skill seemed to have some effect on the shadow monsters, even though they don't have physical bodies. I wasn't using a magical weapon."

Toxxi swoops down to fly alongside me. "When will you tell us the $100 secret, Charli?"

"After one of you has Ezmerelda's Ring and everyone is out of the hut." I don't want them to come out of her hut without it, so I'm giving them incentive.

We reach the crude hut. They circumnavigate it and find the entrance. I grasp the end of a Cornstalk protruding from the structure. To my relief, it easily tears off. I hand it to Toxxi.

She stashes it. "You can count on me to deliver it for you, Charli."

Ger-Alt dismounts from Zip and holds the tarp up for me. "After you."

Though I've been in Ezmerelda's hut once already, I figure, why not try again? But an invisible barrier stops me. "Seems I'm not allowed in a second time." I stand to one side. "I'll wait here."

"Don't let a shadow monster get you." Toxxi flies in behind Ger-Alt and Zip.

"Try not to be too long. Just make sure one of you gets the Ring. I'll be sitting in the shade at the other end of the hut, waiting for you." I make my way to the east side and settle down, leaning against the wall.

I turn off all my chat channels. The world is quiet. Closing my eyes, I seek my inner self. Who and what am I exactly? I'm Charli, a fourteen-year-old NPC Cowgirl Guide and Shadow Wizard. But who am I beyond those labels?

Mithabel believes she's insignificant except as a training tool for Megan Wright, and that I'm even less significant. But what makes Megan Wright's existence more significant than either Mithabel's or mine?

How does the saying go? *I think, therefore I am.* What am I doing at this very moment if not thinking?

Is Megan Wright significant because she has a soul? But what is a *soul*? Who is to say I don't have one? If it's sentience or awareness or a conscience... I have all three.

Anything you conceive and believe... you can achieve, goes another saying. I can conceive of growing up and becoming a woman, of marrying and having a family. Can I believe it, and if I do, can I truly achieve it? How does that work? Does it only work for Earth humans? Why should that be?

"You can achieve nothing." The voice belongs to Mithabel. But *it isn't her*, because I turned off all my chat channels. The Shadow Protean Boss is nearby, attacking my mind.

It doesn't know who it's dealing with. Opening my eyes, I don't see the Boss because it's twisting my thoughts to make me think I'm not seeing it. It could be standing right in front of me, and I wouldn't know it.

Except, I have new skills and traits to call upon.

Mental Armor level 3... the best defensive trait a person can have against mental attacks like those of the Shadow Protean.

Monster Lore level 20... which informs me of the Boss monster's strengths and weaknesses.

Search level 14... which allows me to notice the Boss standing five feet away in the shade to my left.

Shadow Resistance level 5... which grants a bonus to all my skills and traits used to defend myself against this shadow monster.

Avoidance level 4... which works to help me move away from undesirable phenomena, including attacks of any type. It's like an enhanced Dodge.

Most of all, I'm a level 6 Shadow Wizard, something I wasn't when I encountered this thing before. I have a spell I'm aching to try.

I cast Shadow Warrior. I have 84 Auni, and I put 44 of it into the spell. At my class level and with that amount of Auni pumped into the spell, my Shadow Warrior can deal 50d6 of damage in one attack, or half that in the light. We're in shadow here. That's why I chose to wait on the east side of the hut.

My Shadow Warrior blends into the darkness, but I can ascertain where he is. The dark warrior strikes with a dark blade, not of metal but of shadow, an effective attack against the

Shadow Protean Boss. But the Boss isn't an easy kill, not even for me and my summoned fighter, and its HP only falls to 69%.

The Protean's initial attack against me—when it spoke with Mithabel's voice—failed miserably against my Mental Armor. The Boss will attack me again, ignoring my Shadow Warrior, even though it's dealing all the damage at the moment. The Protean doesn't care about its own existence. Its purpose is to do as much harm as possible to PCs and NPCs, and my Shadow Warrior doesn't qualify as either. If it could, the Boss would go after a PC instead of a less significant NPC, but my prolonged presence in the area has triggered it to spawn, and I'm its only acceptable target.

"You aren't even as significant as an ant." This time the voice belongs to Morrow. Good try on the Protean's part to depress me, but I don't fall for its trick. Morrow isn't here, and would never talk to me like that if he were.

I equip my Shadow Stone and will it into the shape of a blade. Using my Shadow Passage skill, I shadow travel the five feet to the Boss. It's insubstantial, so I move right inside it. Holding up my Shadow Stone knife, I cancel my Shadow Passage skill. The Shadow Stone delivers its attack against the Boss, and the thing's HP falls to 67%. Hmm. I'm not as impressive with my attacks as my Shadow Warrior, who follows my attack with one of its own.

The Boss monster's HP falls to 29%.

"Please don't kill me." The voice remains that of Morrow. It's another mental attack from the Protean, but my MP score holds steady at 100%.

My next attack with the Shadow Stone knife does about the same as the first. Then my Shadow Warrior destroys the mook.

Dark mists swirl as the Boss and my Shadow Warrior vanish. I earn some XP, but it's insignificant compared to what I need to advance to level 16.

A flash of light in my view signals that someone is trying to contact me. It's Amarynth. I accept her private chat invite.

"Charli?"

"Hi, Amarynth."

"Did you just earn some XP?"

"A little bit, yeah. It was nothing."

"I got a noticeable bump towards my next level," she says. "Are you all right? What did you fight? Is everyone in Quantized okay?"

"They're inside Ezmerelda's hut right now. They just went in. I expect they'll be out in fifteen to twenty minutes. I'm waiting outside for them. Don't worry about me. I can handle myself."

"But what did you fight, Charli? Please tell me."

The Viking Archer is the reason I joined MAD. There's no need to keep the information from her. "I killed a Shadow Protean Boss."

"*By yourself?*"

"Yeah. It wasn't a big deal. Not that I want to do it again soon. I put a lot of Auni in the spell I cast. I'm down a bit more than half at the moment."

"Please be careful, Cowgirl."

I laugh. "Sure, I will. Thanks for caring, Lady Amarynth."

"You're welcome, and please, just call me Amarynth, like everyone else in the party does."

"I'll try, *Amarynth*."

"Good. Okay, I need to go. We're entering the dungeon soon. Let me know if you're in any trouble. I can always head hop to you if you need it."

Ah, yes, the ability transfer option we discovered. That's *not* the secret I'm planning to sell to Quantized for $100. Mithabel is already mad enough at me. Revealing that secret should be a party decision, not mine alone. No, the secret I'll sell to Quantized is something that came entirely from me, from exercising my Monster Lore skill. If I want to sell my knowledge and can find a buyer, that's not something I need permission to do. "Thanks, Amarynth. Good luck with the quest."

An additional fifteen minutes and zero encounters later, the hut fades away like smoke in the wind. I turn up the volume on my chat channels. The members of Quantized look around. Their gazes land on me, and they collectively exhale sighs of relief.

Toxxi flies towards me. "We're honored you brought us here, Charli." She turns to face her fellow party members. "Thank you all for allowing me to accept Ezmerelda's Ring."

I bring up the list of Top Individual Avatars, and there's her name on the list. She has what we came for. "Congratulations, Toxxi."

"So." Ger-Alt climbs onto Zip's back. "Do we get to hear the $100 secret now?"

"Yes, ma'am." I rub my hands together like a bank robber planning a job. "Here it is: Mook body parts are valuable to the right buyer. If you want money, you harvest body parts from the mooks that attack you, and sell them. There's a catch, of course."

Toxxi scoffs. "Yeah, a big catch, from what we've seen. Mook bodies explode into nothingness when you kill them. How are we supposed to harvest body parts if the corpses don't hang around?"

"Exactly." I nod. "You must harvest from a living mook, and if it dies as a consequence of the harvesting, whatever was harvested will disappear right along with the mook's corpse. It's best if you harvest the body part, stash it while the mook is still alive, and then kill the mook—if killing it is your intent. You then need to find a buyer for the body part. Some body parts are worth more than others, depending on the mook type and who the buyer is. The body parts are used for spell components. Any PC or NPC Wizard might be able to use them, if one can figure out the right components to use for the right spells."

"Sounds a bit tricky to me." Falco circles above us. "Chopping off an arm might kill the mook, and thus, the arm isn't harvested. How do we go about harvesting a body part from a living mook and not kill it?"

All eyes turn on me. I shrug. "That depends on the mook, how difficult it is to kill, and what opportunities you can avail yourselves of. MAD took some scales from a Ferro Serpent Boss, ripping them off during a fight. They weren't worth much, until the party found a way to make them more desirable. Exactly what they did in that regard is knowledge I don't have the right to sell you. The thing is, as you've already seen, mooks in Khertaan rarely drop loot, and when they do, the loot is just as likely to be cursed as not. And that's pretty much all I have to tell you. I trust you'll put this knowledge to work to earn much more than the $100 you're paying me for it. Are you all ready to return to Maron, or do you want me to leave you to your own devices? I have somewhere to go before I reenter the city, but I'll take you back to the edge of the Grass Bladed Field if you like."

The group share glances. I'm not sure how satisfied they are with the $100 secret I've revealed to them, but they have no other good way of earning money, so it should more than pay for itself if they take it to heart.

Toxxi is first to break the silence. "I vote she takes us back. I for one don't want to risk encountering the Scorpion Boss in the forest. If she takes us to the Field, we can undertake Ezmerelda's quest all the sooner."

The group is in agreement. We march through the Cornfield to the edge of the forest, where we take hands like before. I turn us all to shadow shapes and whiz through the shade of the forest canopy until we reach the other side, where we say our goodbyes. While they head across the Grass Bladed Field for the city, I shadow shift and travel back to the Cornfield.

Using my Hide and Avoidance skills to journey without triggering encounters, I stroll along a furrow, headed for the eastern side of the field, where I hope to find a pile of Ashes lying on the ground, the same pile of Ashes from which I took my Shadow Stone. They're the Ashes of a dead Scarecrow, the only remains I'm aware of left behind by a slain mook. If they can be of use to anyone, they'll be the most use to me, a Shadow Wizard carrying the Shadow Stone originally buried in them. I don't know how I'll put the Ashes to use, but I'll likely never have another opportunity to collect them, so if I want them, I've got to get them now, before I join up again with MAD and head further west. I've got an empty Potion Flask to collect the Ashes in.

CHAPTER TWELVE

Mithabel: Clamoring NPCs

Returning to the party after an undeserved and far too long cool down period, Rolag surrendered the Electric Serpent snakeskin at Amarynth's bidding, and Dylan turned it in at Omni Temple to pay for her Scroll of Advanced Heal, which she then committed to memory, thereby consuming the Scroll, but making the spell one she could cast any time through the expenditure of Auni.

"Thank you, everyone, for supporting me. I can support you even better now. Not only does this spell allow me to heal mental, spiritual, and emotional damage, but the Auni-to-healing ratio for physical damage is better than my original Heal spell." With a grin, she took a deep bow. "Are we all ready to head into the dungeon?"

Mithabel nodded as she lifted off the ground, demonstrating the new Flight Speed skill she'd picked up from her last level gain. "But could we take just a moment to go over our new skills? As you can see, *I* can now fly. Not fast, but I'm assuming the speed will increase as the skill level rises."

The eyes of all party members locked on her, each finding a different way to express their amazement.

Dylan's face scrunched with a grimace. "Um… I can Deflect Shurikens. Like I'll ever need that. Have you seen anyone else throwing Shurikens? I haven't."

"You never know." Amarynth chuckled. "I picked up Deflect Crossbow. I take that to mean I can deflect Crossbow *Bolts*."

Rolag grins. "I'm sure it means you can deflect the Bolts, not the Crossbow itself. *I* just reached level 10 and get to pick a subclass. I know what subclass I want, but of course, it's not my choice."

Amarynth shook her head. "It *is* your choice. You don't need my approval to make that kind of decision about yourself."

"Oh, goody." Rolag settled on the ground, closed his eyes, and folded his wings. "*Oh, yeah.*" He opened his eyes and lifted his wings as his whole body grew. He'd stood a foot tall at the shoulder before, and now stood half that again. His wingspan had been just under five feet before, and now was more like seven feet. He didn't look so much like a pet now. He looked dangerous. His fangs clacked and he gave the group an evil grin. "I'm a Were-Giant." His grin fell. "Oh, crap. I can only make one transformation to and from giant form per day at my current level. Is it okay if I stay big?"

"Please do." Amarynth covered her mouth with a hand. "Until there's a situation where you need to be your smaller size. I think the saying goes, *bigger is better*. What skills come with your new class?"

"Enlarge, as you can see, and Intimidate."

Mithabel set her feet back on the ground. "I can see the effects of both your skills. Good choice of subclass, Rolag. No one will want to mess with you. I can only imagine how big you can become at higher skill levels. Anything else new you want to share?"

"No, but I will remind everyone that most of my skills are aerial in nature, including the last one I picked up a few levels ago, Repulsing Winds, which is now at level 4. I don't know if it will be even more effective at my larger size, but here's hoping."

Dylan turned to each member of the party. "Anyone else have anything you want to mention?"

No one did. It was time to visit the Red Pegasus and begin their quest.

**

The group made their way along the brick sidewalk, passing shops, taverns, and inns busy with NPCs hoping for opportunities to earn their own XPs. Someone shouted about their tavern having the best brew in Maron, inviting the adventurers to come in and savor a cup before continuing their journey. Another person yelled about being the best Guide this side of Voorton, not realizing the party already knew him to be wrong about that. No Guide in Khertaan could be better than Charli.

A line of posing ladies vied for the party's attention, all dressed in red gowns slimmer than the petticoats worn by other women in Maron. "Come on, sugars. We'll show you the best time. Your sexual persuasions don't matter, we'll satisfy you, guaranteed." Their bodies undulated like trained cobras. Dylan slowed to watch until Mithabel grabbed her by the arm and pulled her away. They both had to run to catch up with Amarynth, who was covering ground like an asteroid hurtling through space—fast and silent.

On their left rose the imposing three-story stone building identified as the Maron Ministry of Commerce by letters etched into the stone above the overly tall double doors. A grand feat of architecture, the building sported thick stone columns, dark glass windows, balustrades, and ornate balusters supporting winged stone gargoyles.

On the same side of Main Street as the Ministry of Commerce sat a sprawling two-story structure considerably less grand in design, but still reflecting an upper class aesthetic. A sign over the front door identified the establishment as the Red Pegasus Inn, with an illustration matching the name. Double doors reached only a third as high as the doors for the Ministry, but still stood over eight feet high.

A bulky, tanned male bouncer not wearing a shirt blocked entry to the Red Pegasus. "Three lovely ladies to enter? Come on in."

"And me." Rolag swooped down to land beside Amarynth. "I'm her Magical Companion."

The bouncer frowned at Amarynth. "Pardon, Milady, but you'll need him on a leash and he needs to keep his wings folded while in the lobby. Once you're in the dungeon—where I assume you're headed—he can do whatever you want."

"Not a problem, sir." Amarynth summoned her fifty-foot Rope to hand. "I'd expected to put this to different use." She tied a loop in one end and slipped it over Rolag's neck. "Come along, my pet."

"Keep the leash no longer than six feet, Milady. Head straight across the lobby to find the hallway to the dungeon."

"Thank you kindly, sir. In we go." Amarynth led the way, Rolag on her heels like a wolf pretending to be domesticated.

Low lighting left much of the inn lobby in shadow. The dining area stretched along the right side of the lobby, with a long drink bar to the right of that. Shadows covered everyone, cloaking identities, with only the far wall behind the bar being brightly lit. Tall bottles of whiskey and varnished kegs shimmered under sourceless magical light. Though only minutes after 2:00 AM, the place bustled with whispered conversations, clinking glasses, and patrons making orders. The sun never sat in Khertaan, not moving from its 3:00 PM position since the competition started two days ago. To the residents of Khertaan, the time of day was only as significant as the latest System announcement proclaimed it to be.

Before party MAD traveled halfway across the lobby, a collective gasp rose from the dining area and bar. Leaping from their seats, NPCs shoved each other aside and shouted over each other in their rush to be the first to interact with the adventuring party. *I'm an expert at finding traps. I'll guide you in and out. I'll fight any monster you face. I'll carry any treasure you find.* Everyone had some service to offer. With sufficient money to hire people or the right goods to barter for their services, even a lone adventurer could take on the dungeon quest.

Clamoring NPCs jammed the lobby before the adventuring party could cross it. Pressed from all sides, Mithabel took a deep breath, recalling how NPC residents intent on murdering Dylan on the street outside had similarly surrounded them some two hours ago. Hell, some of these NPCs might well have been among those seeking the bounty placed on the Longest Survivor.

None of that mattered now.

The Polynesian Priestess held her head high with serenity and lifted her hands. "People of Maron, patrons of the Red Pegasus Inn, hear my words. We are without resources with which to pay any of you for services rendered in the dungeon below this establishment. However, we will allow one of you to accompany us and gain XPs to advance your class skills. For your trouble, upon a successful completion of our quest and exit from the dungeon, Lady Amarynth will autograph any one inanimate, non-sentient, non-magical object you own, within reason. I'm sure everyone here realizes how this will increase the value of the autographed item a hundred-fold or more. Under these conditions, who of you is willing to go with us?"

Everyone remained in place—shouting and hands raised. *I'll go. Take me.*

"We can only take one." Dylan lowered her hands in a calming gesture, and the crowd quieted. "The Sun Goddess will make the choice." The Priestess raised her hands again. "Scintilla, please shine your light upon the one you desire to accompany us." Dylan closed her eyes, spun in a circle, and cast her Light spell when she came to a stop. She opened her eyes.

The ray of light emanating from Dylan's hand fell upon a masculine figure of pure white, wings folded behind a frame shorter than Charli's. The only splotches of color about the man were his pink eyes and the pink mouse sitting on his shoulder, a tiny white noose around the rodent's neck, with the other end of the thread hanging loosely around the man's throat like a necklace. Snowy curls cascaded down the man's bare, muscled back and chest, reaching to the white linen Loincloth covering his privates. He bowed to Dylan, his pet scurrying to reposition itself so as not to fall and hang itself. As the light from Dylan's spell faded, the other NPCs stepped away into the darkness of the dining area, murmuring their disappointment at not being chosen, but no longer pressing the party to accompany them. Using her priestly powers, Dylan had resolved a situation that could easily have turned ugly.

The winged man straightened. "I am Zyekt, a fallen Angel of the Psyon class. I thank your Goddess for choosing me." With a thumb he pointed to the hairless pink creature on his shoulder.

"This is Niav, my Faithful Companion, a female Mouse of the Guide class. We are both glad to be at your service."

"We're glad to have you." Dylan gave them a smile as she added Zyekt to the party roster. Companions like Niav and Rolag didn't require a slot. Megan Wright didn't count, either, being a secondary avatar of Mithabel. Each party had six slots available in total. After admitting Zyekt, taking into consideration the slot allotted to the absent Charli, the party still had one empty slot remaining.

Kaleisha danced into Mithabel's view. "Party MAD is contracting the services of the Angel Psyon Zyekt and his Faithful Companion, the Mouse Guide Niav, for a price previously negotiated. Check your chat logs for price details. Price is to be paid upon successful completion of the dungeon quest and return from the dungeon to the Red Pegasus Inn lobby. Do you vote to accept this contract, chief?"

"Um, I think so, but do you have a recommendation, Kaleisha? Do you see any problems with my voting yes?"

The Jamaican dancer's eyes widened. "How thoughtful of you to ask for my opinion, Mithabel. I recommend the contract be accepted. It may prove helpful to have a Guide in the party while Charli is gone, and having an Angel Psyon in the party will give you an opportunity to learn about Angels and Psyons first hand, regardless of how helpful this particular NPC will be on the quest. The price you're paying for both their services won't deplete the party's resources at all."

"Well, then, I vote to accept."

"All present members of party MAD have accepted the contract, chief. Angel Zyekt has officially joined the roster."

"Welcome to MAD, Zyekt. Did I pronounce that right?" Mithabel offered her hand to the Angel.

Beaming, the Angel shook her hand with vigor. "You even emphasized the ending *t*. Very well done, indeed."

The Tank bent down to meet the gaze of the Mouse. "And welcome to you, Niav."

The Mouse wiggled her whiskers and squeaked back a reply. "Thank you for having us."

Amarynth and Rolag took their turns welcoming the new party members. The Mouse showed no fear of the reptilian, though Rolag dwarfed her more than a hundred-fold in mass.

"So...." Dylan strode to the hallway entry and pointed towards the dungeon entrance. "Let's get it on, shall we?"

CHAPTER THIRTEEN

Mithabel: Alcoves

The dungeon door closed of its own accord behind them, casting them into darkness. Mithabel's Dark Sight kicked in, allowing her to see her surroundings in black and white. "Who else can see in here?"

Niav the Mouse squeaked. "I have the Heightened Sense of Smell trait. The open areas, hallways, doorways, etc., all have a distinct odor. I can guide you with my eyes open or closed, with light or in darkness. The hallway before us stretches out for twenty feet before it comes to a T-intersection leading east and west. We're currently facing south. There is something different smelling about the floor in the intersection, so it might be a pressure plate."

"Impressive, Niav." Dylan stood still. "The quest vision we received from Ezmerelda showed us traveling in the dark for ten minutes before we came upon a locked, iron-bound wooden chest bearing the name *Ogaltha*. Indistinct figures moved around the chest. We need to find it, take something from it, and leave the dungeon with what we take."

"Your Goddess did right by you, choosing the two of us to aid you on your quest." Zyekt reached out to either side of him. "Two of you take my hands. Can anyone else see in the dark?"

Mithabel willed her feet off the floor. "It's just me. I can also fly. Not real fast, but I hope that won't be a problem in here."

"Very well. Priestess, take my left hand. Archer, take my right. Dragon, can you fly slowly and hover when necessary?"

Rolag huffed a tiny flame. "No, I need to keep moving when flying. I can circle when I have the space for it, but no hovering."

"Then hold onto Amarynth."

The Viking Archer removed her noose from Rolag's neck, and he clutched her armored shoulders from behind.

Zyekt nodded. "Tank, I'll follow you—Niav will direct me as to where you go, but it would also help if you could give a running description of what you see as we travel. Does anyone have a light source, should we need it for emergency use?"

"That would be me." Dylan laughed. "I've got a Light spell and thirty Torches. I also have three Tinderboxes, six Flasks of Oil, and fifteen Candles."

Amarynth reached across in front of the Angel, snapping her fingers. "Give me a Tinderbox and two Torches, in case we get separated."

"No problem." Dylan produced the items from her unlimited inventory space and blindly handed them over. "Let's go."

Zyekt's feet lifted from the floor. Dylan, Amarynth, and Rolag rose with him, held aloft by the power of his Party Flight trait rather than his physical strength.

Stuck between the much taller Dylan and Amarynth, the undersized albino Angel could pass for a twelve-year-old if not for his muscle tone. Viewed with Mithabel's Dark Sight, Zyekt was a silhouette in white, from his upraised wings to his bare chest to his loincloth to his bare feet, with his flowing hair the starkest white of all. Next to him, his passengers appeared a dingy gray.

With Mithabel out front and the Mouse Guide whispering directions in the Angel's ear, the group flew near to the intersection and paused. Moving ahead and careful not to touch anything, Mithabel examined the floor, calling on her Detect Anomaly skill. "A square portion of the floor is elevated a scarce fraction of an inch, which jibes with Niav's guess there's a pressure plate here. Should we trigger it? It could be a trap… or it might be a switch that unlocks something somewhere—which could be good or bad."

"Normally I'd doubt a deadly trap would be set this early in the dungeon." Ten feet away, Dylan hovered in the grip of the short Angel's left hand. "The quest vision didn't indicate we needed to trigger any trap, so I vote we leave it be."

Amarynth hovered to Zyekt's right. "I'm with Dylan. According to the vision, we're only going ten minutes in. We can always come back and trigger it if it turns out we need to."

"I don't have a vote." Zyekt grimaced, looking in Mithabel's general direction. "Do we have consensus, Tank?"

"Sure." Staying off the ground, Mithabel drifted forward, passing over the pressure plate. "But give me a second." She glanced left and right. "Fifty feet to the east is another intersection, one fork continuing straight while the other one heads south. Fifty feet to the west the hallway bends to the south."

"I smell reptilians to the east." Niav kept her voice lower than Mithabel's, though it wasn't necessary, given that they spoke over party chat. "Dozens, I think, lying in wait for us. To the west, I smell a musty void, like a pit or chasm."

Dylan pointed west. "We had no encounters in the vision quest. Let's go towards the musty void. If it's a pit or chasm, we'll fly across it."

The group headed west. Mithabel glanced back every so often to check whether the reptilians were following. The party neared the bend heading south.

"Wait a second." Mithabel flew forward to check out what lay around the corner. "It's a mud pit trap, fifteen feet deep and twenty feet long, for the entire width of the hallway. Could be quicksand at the bottom." She chuckled at a mental image. "I can picture a party fleeing the reptilians, rounding this corner, and falling in. I vote we fly across."

Everyone agreed, and the Tank led the way. "Beyond the far edge of the pit, the hall continues south, with alcoves lining both sides. I can't make out if anything hides in the alcoves."

Niav sniffed the air. "I smell wood and a hint of metal."

Dylan huffed. "It's already been ten minutes. We must be close to the chest."

"Our time in the dark might have been condensed in the vision," Amarynth said. "Think about it. Ezmerelda wouldn't have kept us in her hut for a day if that's how long the quest took."

"You're right." Dylan grimaced.

"System announcement, chief." Kaleisha abruptly appeared beside Mithabel. "Toxxi the Faerie has landed on the Top Individuals list."

"Wow, that was fast." Mithabel cleared the edge of the pit. "Charli wasted no time leading Quantized to Ezmerelda's hut. They might be back to Maron before we find the Ogaltha chest."

As Mithabel neared the first alcove, Niav spoke up in her squeaky voice. "The smell of wood and iron are stronger now. They're coming from beyond the first alcove."

Mithabel nodded… then caught herself, since none of her companions could see her. "Hold up a moment."

Three alcoves lay to the west side of the hallway and two lay to the east, staggered so that none lay across from another.

The Tank hovered before the nearest one. "The walls of the first alcove are covered with engravings—a jumbled mess except for a centrally-placed one on the back wall—appears to be a manticore—body and mane of a lion and the face of a human, staring at me. Creepy. It's got a scorpion tail and the wings of a bird of prey, like an eagle. The whole thing looks intentionally asymmetrical. A stone bench sits directly below the manticore.

"Other engravings look like flowers—heads of animals surrounded by petals. There are groups of wavy, curved lines… like waterfalls. Other engravings look like the work of a mad chiseler, without rhyme or reason."

"Don't enter that alcove," Dylan said. "Move up to the second one."

The Tank complied. "Ugh, I don't like this one. Lots of pentagrams, stars, horns, and eyes. There's a stone bench against the back wall in here, too. Above it is a large engraved circle with two horns off the top. Inscribed in the circle is a pentagon circumscribing a pentagram, with an eye in the center of that. Ugh, it's like the eye is watching me. I swear it's moving."

Dylan shivered. "I don't like that one, either. Move on to the third one."

The third one was the middle one on the side with three alcoves. Mithabel laughed at the interior decor. "There's a stone bench like in the others, but the walls are bare except for an engraving over the bench—a mug, overflowing with a foaming head."

Zyekt chuckled. "Sounds good to me."

The next alcove was the second of two on the east side of the hallway. "The fourth one has lots of circles with straight lines radiating outward, like suns. A larger sun sits above the stone bench against the back wall. As you might guess, there's an eye in the center of the large sun—watching me, I swear."

The Elf Tank flew to the fifth and last one. "Guess what the main symbol is in here." She paused, but no one ventured to reply. "It's a balance, with both sides at the same height. A sword is engraved above the weighing pan to the right. A shield bearing the visage of a griffin weighs the pan to the left.... I know what these alcoves are."

Dylan knew, too. "The benches are altars to the five pantheons of Khertaan. The one with the symbol of the sun is the one I'd want to interact with, if it's decided we're to interact with any of them."

Mithabel listed them out loud. "The first one, with the manticore, is an alcove for the Disruptor pantheon. The second one is for Diabolical. The third one is Anodyne. Fourth is Exemplar—your pantheon, Priestess. This last one is for Justiciar."

"Do you see any wood or metal items?" Niav paced on the Angel's shoulder, her tail twitching. "I still smell them, but can't say whether they're in the alcoves. If you find them, they might help you decide what to do."

"Let me look further down the hall." Mithabel flew beyond the fifth alcove. "The hallway comes to a dead end. There's a door-shaped outline in the end wall, barely discernible."

"Did you detect any hidden doors in the alcoves?" Niav trembled with intensity.

"Stay calm, Mouse. Let me check."

"I know there's something here."

"Okay, okay." Mithabel flew back to the group. "I'll have to fly inside the alcoves if I'm to get a closer look. I'll try the first one first. Here goes nothing." She flew into the Disruptor alcove—the one with the manticore symbol—careful to touch nothing.

She nearly jumped out of her skin when Kaleisha spoke.

"Do you devote your service to the Disruptor pantheon, Mithabel?"

The Elf Tank backed out of the alcove. "We want to go to the Exemplar one, folks. I was just asked if I devoted my service to the Disruptor pantheon. I didn't answer. I wasn't going to say, *yes*, and I was afraid to say, *no*."

Dylan huffed. "You don't all have to devote yourselves to my pantheon. As long as everyone avoids the Diabolical pantheon, we can still work together. Actually, it might not be a bad idea to have connections with other pantheons. It's entirely up to you all, of course. I just don't want you to make decisions for yourself based on how you think I'll feel about them."

Amarynth scoffed. "*Disruptor* sounds too chaotic. If I'm choosing a pantheon, I'd prefer it to be a lawful one, straight as a Crossbow Bolt. Failing that, I could go with good or neutral."

"What about you, Mithabel?" Dylan's voice trembled with hope.

"If I were to pick one, I'd want it to be the same as yours, Priestess. *Exemplar*."

"I'm pleased to hear that. Rolag, are you in on this too?"

"I'm devoted to Milady Amarynth. No pantheon for me, thanks."

Dylan turned her blind gaze towards the Angel. "Zyekt? Niav? Either of you want to dedicate your service to a pantheon? This is your chance."

The Angel laughed. "We're good."

"Okay then, who's first? Mithabel or Amarynth?"

Mithabel flew down the hallway ahead of the others. "I'll go first. The Exemplar alcove is the closer of the two. You all stay back, but come quick if I call… or if I'm silent for more than ten seconds."

The Tank returned to the last alcove of the two on the east wall and hovered inside.

Kaleisha appeared as expected. "Mithabel, do you devote your service to the Exemplar pantheon?"

Mithabel directed her reply not only to Kaleisha but also to the party chat, so the others could hear her side of the conversation, even though they couldn't hear Kaleisha. "Yes, I devote my service to the Exemplar pantheon."

The sun symbol on the back wall glowed with magical yellow light. Golden rays struck Mithabel, and she raised her hand to shield her eyes.

The alcove expanded. Mithabel occupied the center of a larger space, hovering before a white marble dais supporting a golden throne. On the throne sat a blond black woman dressed in a yellow robe and wearing a golden tiara decorated with glimmering white pearls. The Tank had seen this woman on this throne before—inside Dylan's dreams during the trek from Voorton to Maron.

The black Goddess beckoned for Mithabel. Flying forward, the Tank stopped before the seated deity.

"Welcome, warrior, to the fold of Scintilla, Goddess of Light. My secondary tenets are Mentors, Gold, and Growth." The deity smiled. "Promote my principles and you will receive my blessings."

Mithabel produced her Battle Axe from her inventory and tapped its single-edged blade. "It's not gold, but my metal is at your service, Goddess."

"Hold it forward, warrior, and I will enchant it for you."

"With pleasure." A thrill ran through her as Mithabel extended her arm and Axe towards the Goddess, placing the Axe head within easy reach of the throne.

The seated blond Goddess placed her dark hand upon the flat of the blade. The metal glowed with an orange light. "Go in peace, my Daughter of Orange Metal. Defend the innocent and all those devoted to my precepts."

The light faded from the Axe. The scene collapsed upon itself, the throne and Goddess shrinking into a speck. The sun symbol no longer adorned the back wall of the alcove. The stone bench lay in crumbled pieces. Mithabel still hovered in place. "I'm *good*," she called over party chat as she backed out of the alcove, studying her Axe and seeing no difference in it with her Dark Sight, wishing she could see it in the light.

Niav squeaked. "The metal smell is strong."

Dylan softly called, "What happened, Mithabel?"

There was no use in Mithabel brandishing her Axe for the others to see, but she did so anyway, instinctively. "The Goddess Scintilla blessed me and my Battle Axe. I'm an Exemplar warrior now, dedicated to promoting the tenets of Light, Mentors, Gold, and Growth." She flew back to the others. "I met Scintilla, who dubbed me Daughter of Orange Metal. She put her hand on my Axe blade. It glowed for a moment. Did you see the light coming from the alcove?"

"I didn't see any light." Dylan shook her head.

Mithabel shrugged, a wasted gesture. "I believe it's all right for Amarynth to walk alone into the Justiciar alcove if she chooses. When I left Scintilla's presence, the symbol disappeared from the Exemplar alcove and the stone bench broke to pieces." She stashed her enchanted blade. "I assume each alcove can only be used once."

Niav sniffed the air. "I don't smell metal anymore. I only smell wood."

"Do you smell the wood any stronger now?" Amarynth equipped her Crossbow. "Let's go. I could use a divine enchantment. Who needs to spend money at the store when you can simply sell your soul for a magical weapon?"

Mithabel led the way. The group reached the last alcove, bearing symbols of balance, sword, and shield.

Amarynth loosed her hold on the Angel and dropped to the floor. No trap triggered.

Under Mithabel's guidance, Amarynth walked into the alcove. No noise or light emanated from the alcove, but after about a minute of Amarynth standing still, Crossbow in hand, the stone bench crumbled and the engraving above it vanished from the wall.

Niav nodded with vigor. "The smell of wood is stronger now."

Amarynth backed out of the alcove, holding her Crossbow and grinning broadly. "I met Athlea, Goddess of War, Leaders, Conquests, and Curses. She looks like a Native American chieftainess, complete with a headdress, robes, and all. I've never seen anyone like her up close and personal before.

"She gave me the title, Daughter of True Aim. Yuni is her Priestess. She made my Crossbow glow blue for a few seconds. It's enchanted now—by a *freaking* deity." Laughing, she stashed her weapon.

Niav shook her head. "I don't smell either the metal or the wood anymore. I don't know how it's possible, but I think I was smelling those scents as an indication of what was supposed to happen. Since I don't smell anything else, I think we're done here."

Amarynth took Zyekt's hand and once again was airborne. The party headed south towards what Mithabel hoped was a door leading to the item of their quest.

CHAPTER FOURTEEN

Megan: Ghost Maker

Holy crap, Mithabel can *fly*? That should mean *I can too*. I picture myself in the air… heh heh, my feet just left the floor.

Quickly setting back down, I place the Severed Orc Ear on the counter.

The proprietor of Ye Olde Shoppe of the Profane glances at it and does a double take. He picks it up and studies it for a minute before bringing out a magnifying glass for an even closer inspection. After another couple minutes, he puts away the magnifying glass. Then he brings out a transparent glass jar and drops the Ear into it, screwing on a metal lid. The glass darkens, becoming opaque, and his eyes dilate. He stifles a laugh. "I won't ask how you came by this. Help yourself to *any* of the enchanted Battle Axes." Taking the jar, he hurries to the back of the store.

Slick. I take him at his word and comb the shelves for the Battle Axe with the highest price tag. This one looks good. Wait, this one is priced higher. No, this one is higher—I think it's the one. Don't see any priced higher than $150,000. It's got to be something special. "I've found the one I want, sir. It's called Ghost Maker."

"Yes, yes, an exceptional weapon," the proprietor replies loudly from the back room. "*It's yours*. Take it in good health. It grants a critical hit bonus equal to your class level, and deals *all* domain types of damage—physical, mental, spiritual, and emotional. This Ear you brought me is incredible beyond imagining. Take a magical Bracelet while you're at it, if you like. Choose any one. I recommend a Bracelet of Action. Allows you to prematurely end a combat heartbeat once per super-heartbeat."

"What's a super-heartbeat?"

"What? Oh, sorry—thought you'd know. It's a set of six normal heartbeats, or one minute, by default. There are ways to shorten heartbeats, if one has the right trait, skill, or item—like that Bracelet, just as some debuffs can extend heartbeats."

I find the Bracelet he's talking about and slip it on my left wrist. "Got it. Thank you, sir. Enjoy your Ear."

"Oh, I will, I will." His laughter almost sounds maniacal.

What have I unleashed? Doesn't matter. I'm out of here. "I'm leaving you my non-magical Axe." I don't want to stash it or carry it.

I need to get out of the city, and now I know how to do it—simply fly over the wall. Speaking of flying, maybe I could get the overexcited shopkeeper to give me something else. "Um... sir... would you mind throwing in one more thing for me? It shouldn't be expensive. I just need something to strap this Wing more securely to my back. Got anything like that?"

He comes hobbling out, his hands empty. "I'll not only find something for you, I'll make sure it fits, but in turn you must tell me what type of creature you took that Ear from."

"The guy was an Orc Wizard, not originally from Khertaan. He's been trying to kill me, so I had no qualms taking his Ear. It's quite possible he's an illegal avatar."

"My goodness. That explains a lot." He chuckles, his eyes gleaming. "Very well, let's get you outfitted here." From a shelf he takes a cord Harness. "This is typically used to secure a Sheath for a Sword. I'll make an adjustment or two, and it will work for your Wing. Please remove that coil of Rope you're wearing and hand me the Wing."

I comply, and he disappears into the back room.

For me, the Wing symbolizes craftiness, thinking outside the box, being more than people give you credit for. They'll look at me and wonder *what kind of weirdo has only one Wing*? If they see me flying, and the Wing isn't moving, they'll be even more curious. I won't explain anything to anyone—if they can't figure it out for themselves, let their minds be warped. As though inter-dimensional invaders won't warp their minds enough.

The shopkeeper returns with the Wing, the stump extended. "Here we go. Let's try this on for size."

"Great." Stashing everything in my hands, I stand with arms outstretched to either side, clad only in my Bikini.

He slips the Harness over my left arm and head, so it rests on my right shoulder. With a few adjustments, he sets the Wing so it doesn't flop in my face when I turn or lean forward. Finished, he steps back and assesses his efforts, nodding in satisfaction. "When you equip the Wing and Harness, do them as a unit, and they'll equip like I have them now."

Using Third Person POV, I admire the proprietor's handiwork. Observed from the front, it appears the foot-long, translucent, crimson-veined, leathery, bat-like Faerie Wing is a natural limb, even if a bit small for someone my size. "That looks awesome, shopkeeper."

He grins. "I'm glad you like it. If you ever want another quest, come back again. I'm only allowed to grant you one per day, but come back tomorrow for another if you like."

"I'll keep that in mind." I don't tell him I have plans to be somewhere far from Maron tomorrow. I have no idea where I'm going, but I can't stay here. The City Guards will be on the hunt for me as soon as they discover I'm gone. I can't fight them and hope to win, since they have infinite lives. Leaving the city is my only option. "I do have one more request, sir. Do you have a Map of Khertaan?"

"You're the first adventurer to ask me for one, surprisingly." He shakes his head in bemusement. "You'd think that would be the first thing an adventurer would want. And I'm the only shopkeeper in the city who has them. So I can tell you, none of your competition has one." He unrolls a Map on the counter and points. "See this dotted line? You follow that, and you'll avoid encounters. It's a designated safe route, but only for those traveling by land. If you fly, the route doesn't protect you."

He points at a smaller marking on the Map. "See this city? It's called Minook, meaning *high point*. It's quite a climb, and it's not safe to fly up the outside. There *is* a safe path up, so I understand, but it's not marked on here, I'm afraid." He rolls up the parchment and hands it to me. "The Map is yours, Mithabel. Good luck on your journeys."

Oh, my. *He thinks I'm Mithabel.* I don't correct him, because to do so could set off a trigger in the System alerting the City Guards that I've escaped. I wave the Map and stash it. "Thanks, shopkeeper."

Once outside, I gasp and catch my breath. Oh, Goddess. I can't believe it.

No, really, catch my breath. Wow. Is this freaking awesome or what?

"Halt, there!"

Dammit. A crowd of City Guards spring out of hiding.

How did they know you were here?

"Come with us peacefully, avatar, or forfeit a life. If you die, you'll respawn in our jail, so think twice before attempting to flee." Two dozen Crossbows raise and aim at me.

Crap. I stash my Wing and Harness, not wanting to lose them to these bozos. Holding up my hands, I casually walk forward. I could try flying, but I don't know how fast I can move, and I don't want to unnecessarily cost Mithabel a life. They won't check my legality for another five hours. Maybe the developer friend of Mithabel's—Raphael—will come online before then and get me out of this mess. It will be fun seeing the Orc Wizard again. *Not.* They better have some way to prevent him from casting fireballs.

The Lead Guard grabs my arms and cranks them behind my back to lock my wrists in manacles. One of the manacles is attached to a chain, the other end of which the Leader hands to a nearby underling. He pushes me from behind. "Get moving, avatar. It's time for your evaluation."

I don't stumble from the pressure he applied between my shoulders. But, damn, they're going to evaluate me already? "I thought I had until eight o'clock."

"Due to your being such a flight risk, my special request for a priority evaluation was granted. Soon as you're back in your cell, the evaluation begins. Better hope you're legal. If you're not, you'll be eradicated from the System."

"I'm telling you the truth—I'm a secondary PC avatar granted for testing purposes."

"Really? Then you should pass the evaluation without issue. But if the System determines you're cheating, not only will you be eradicated, but so will your primary avatar. You'll be disqualified from the competition."

Holy crap. I can't let that happen to Mithabel. "May I ask how you knew I was in this store?" The underling holding the other end of the chain tugs me along. I don't resist.

The Leader's grin is evil. "We saw you were gone from your cell. Then we noticed our other captive was missing an Ear. We monitored the transactions in the city shops for any involving a Severed Ear. And... we found one. We City Guards are not as stupid as you PCs might think. If indeed you're illegal—which I've no doubt you are—you made a huge mistake coming to my city. You have about thirty minutes left to live."

Much as I hate to bother Mithabel, I need to let her know what the bloody hell is going on with me. She needs to get in touch with Raphael *pronto*.

Holy crap.

What happened?

I tried to contact Mithabel, and it didn't work. Um... I can't contact anyone. My communications channels aren't functioning. I'm on my own.

But you were just talking to the Guard.

I was. "Guard?"

"Yes?"

"My communications channels...."

"Yeah, they're terminated—except for local chat, with a greatly reduced range. No one is coming to your aid."

"You are one nasty bastard."

He smiles. "I know. Too bad for you."

CHAPTER FIFTEEN

Morrow: Painful Experience

Renee flourishes her arms. "Welcome to Mystic Hollow Cornfield, darling, where even shadows tremble."

Kylie slows. "Do we need to land, or keep going?"

I motion for her to keep flying. "We've got a giant spider army behind us. Let's not dally. If something forces us to land, then we'll land."

Slithy points down. "You mean like that?"

A young girl in a wide-brimmed Hat kneels next to a pile of Ashes, scooping them into a Flask. Could it be…?

"Renee, what can you tell me about that girl?"

"She's the NPC Cowgirl Guide named Charli. You met her before."

Oh my God. "Take us down, Kylie."

We descend, and the Cowgirl looks up as our shadow falls over her.

"Charli?" Though she's who I suspected, I can scarcely believe my eyes.

The Cowgirl Guide corks her Flask and stashes it as we land six feet from her. She flashes a smile. "Morrow? Kylie? Slithy?

What a surprise. How good to see you again. It seems like years and yet only hours ago that we last talked. How are you?"

Slithy hops next to the Cowgirl. "We're still getting the hang of this place. Are you traveling alone?"

Charli shrugs. "I am. I'm glad you all found the Cornfield. I assume you're headed for Maron… I'm traveling that way, and would love your company."

Kylie chuckles. "We don't know where we're headed. Having a Guide to show us the way would be much appreciated. If you'll join our party, we can all fly together. Slithy, send her an invite."

"On it." My Frogkin daughter stares into space for a moment. "Okay, it's sent."

"I can't accept." Charli frowns. "I'm already in party MAD and I promised I'd stay in it. But I can accompany you, like I accompanied Quantized until a few minutes ago. I should take you to see Ezmerelda. One of you should get the magic Ring she offers."

"We'd like to have you with us whether you're officially in the party or not." I glance over my shoulder. "But there's an army of Arachnid Behemoths on our tail, and they'll catch us if we travel by land. Can you fly?"

Charli strokes a cornstalk. "No, but that's not the problem you might think it is. I'm not familiar with Arachnid Behemoths, but they can't enter the Cornfield until they kill the Boss monster for the Brassy Grassy, so until that happens, we have time."

Slithy grimaces. "Um… they already killed a Boss monster. We saw them do it."

The Cowgirl mouths the word, *oh*. "I'm sorry to say, flying across the Cornfield won't be like flying across the Grassy Brassy. The Cornfield mooks can fly, so it's not like you'll avoid encounters by traveling by air. And since I have to walk, maybe you could walk with me?" Heading west, she beckons for us to follow. "Do any of you have Mental Armor or any mental-based attacks? Any Psi-based skills? Any magic items or spells?"

I fall in behind her, gesturing for the rest of my party to follow suit. "I have Mental Armor, though I haven't used it and don't know how. I also have Lightning spells."

"Good." Charli moves quickly along the furrow between two rows of cornstalks. "If you need the Mental Armor, it will kick in automatically. The Lightning spells might come in handy. Any one else?"

Slithy Jumps along a parallel furrow. "I'm a Mentalist. I have Mind Spear and Mind Shield powers and a few skills."

"Nice." Charli glances over at my leaping Frogkin daughter. "Your powers will be quite useful against any mook in the Cornfield. What about you, Kylie?"

Bringing up the rear, my Angel wife flies with her head above the cornstalks, glancing about as we move forward. "My Spirit Blade deals physical and spiritual damage. I also have Spirit Shield."

"Spirit-based attacks and defenses won't be useful in the Cornfield, though physical attacks might. You have anything else?"

"I have the Angel traits of Hypnotic Voice and Hypnotic Gaze."

"I'm not familiar with those, but they sound promising."

"I'll be glad to demonstrate when I have a chance."

Perched on my shoulder, my Woodpecker Familiar flaps his wings. "Ha ha, me, me."

Charli looks back with a smile. "What are your abilities, little guy?"

"Call me Rancor. I'm a Psi-Warrior. I have Power Strike to multiply my Beak Attack, which I can boost as a Psi-Melee Weapon, to do both physical and mental damage. I also have the skills Psi-Armor and Psi-Parry."

The Cowgirl guffaws. "Wow. Your party is highly geared towards surviving the Cornfield. We're getting close to Ezmerelda's hut now. Hopefully we won't run into any mooks before we reach it."

With a giggle, Slithy Jumps over Charli's head to land in the furrow to the Cowgirl's right. "How long will we be in the hut?"

"Gee whiz, that's some jump." Charli doesn't slow. "You can't rush Ezmerelda. It could be anywhere from twenty to thirty minutes."

I glance back, grateful not to see any Behemoths. "I doubt we'll have that long."

"You'll be safe from all mooks while you're in the hut." Charli gives me a thumbs up. "Maybe these Arachnid Behemoths you mentioned will pass by while you're with Ezmerelda, and then we'll be behind them. I'm curious. Exactly how big are these Behemoths?"

Slithy Jumps out ahead of Charli. "They're the size of houses. Two or three stories."

"Oh, my gosh." Charli coughs. "I wonder why I don't know about them. My Monster Lore skill is level 20."

"They're inter-dimensional invaders." I'm the slowest moving of the group and struggle to keep up. "They aren't native to Khertaan. They're here to destroy all PCs before they can reach level 30."

"That doesn't sound good." Charli glances over her shoulder at me, slowing as she realizes she's leaving me behind. "Does that include you three?"

I shrug. "I imagine so."

Kylie grabs my left hand. "Need a lift, stranger?"

"Oh, thank you, yes, my love."

"Oh, thank you, yes, my love," mimics Renee, flying along beside me, though she appears to be lying on her side, resting her head on her elbow. "You want to see my boobs again? Your wife won't mind, right, *my love*?"

"Stop being a tease, Renee." I'm careful not to vocalize the words on local or party chat.

"How about I go topless for you?" Renee waves her free hand, and her red top disappears. "Hell, I'll even go bottomless." She waves her hand again, and her skirt disappears. She's not wearing panties. All she's wearing is her red leather knee-high boots. She lifts one leg, showing a thin line of blond hair marking her crotch. "I'm so fucking bored, Morrow. Won't you do anything about it?"

"Renee, *put on your clothes*."

She pouts. "Fine." She doesn't wave her hand this time, but her clothing reappears on her body. "You're no fun at all."

Kylie squeezes my hand. "Penny for your thoughts."

"Sorry, but they're not even worth a penny at the moment, I'm afraid."

"We're here." Charli comes to a stop before a dense patch of cornstalks standing taller than the others, a layer of corn silk decorating the top. Our Guide leads us around to the west side.

The dense patch covers a rectangular plot of land. On the west side, the stalks noticeably lean in at the top. A black tarp hangs from the top of the slanted wall, reaching the ground. Charli motions at the tarp. "Go on in."

Kylie lands beside the Cowgirl, releasing me and taking hold of Charli's arm. "We'll go in last together. It's not that I don't trust you. It's that I'm distrustful of Khertaan in general, and we don't want to lose your company."

Charli frowns. "I'm not allowed to go in a second time."

Kylie frowns back. "We'll see about that."

"You should go in first, Dad." Slithy gives me a nudge.

"Sure." I lift the tarp and head in.

Twenty feet from me, crimson flames crackle to life inside the hut, like a burning campfire, but doing little to illuminate its surroundings. An aged female voice from beyond the flames wheezes in greeting. "Enter if you must."

"Thanks, we will."

The others follow me in, with Kylie hugging Charli and carrying her in, dropping her to the ground once they clear the tarp.

I incline my head in the direction of the voice. "I'm Morrow. This is my daughter, Slithy; my wife, Kylie; and my Magical Familiar, Rancor. I think you might already know our Guide, Charli."

The old voice coughs, hacking like someone who has smoked cigarettes all her life and yet lived to be ninety. "What do you want with Ezmerelda?"

My eyes adjust to the darkness. A hulking figure sits on the floor near the far wall, cloaked in shadow. The crackling fire sits halfway between her and us. The hut had looked to be maybe ten feet square on the outside, but in here it's like forty feet square. "I believe you might have a Ring to bestow upon us."

"Do you, now?" Hoarse laughter escapes the old woman. "And what do you have for me?"

I shrug. "Information."

She laughs again. "*You* have information for *me*? Very well, tell me this information you have. If it's a significant truth and I don't already know it, I will grant everyone here a Ring."

I point to the exit. "There are Arachnid Behemoths in Khertaan. They'll be here any minute. You know what Arachnid Behemoths are? They're giant metallic spiders standing two stories tall. They killed a Ferro Serpent by spearing it with a pointed leg and then biting its head off. We need to warn people in Maron, and to do that, we need to be ahead of the spiders. So as much as we'd like to sit and chat with you, and while Charli has warned us we can't rush you, we would appreciate any expediency you can afford us."

"I see." Ezmerelda leans forward. "What you have told me bears the mark of truth and is significant. I admit I did not already know it. You have each earned a Ring." She extends an arm that elongates to reach the flames in the middle of the room. From the tips of her thumb and elongated, bony fingers each hangs a Ring, shimmering golden in the firelight—five Rings in total. "Any of you may come forward and take from me what you take."

Slithy nudges me. "You go first, Dad." She likes volunteering me for tasks.

My Boots stir up dust as I cross to the edge of the fire. The Rings hang suspended over the flames. I reach for a Ring... and flames flare up, licking my fingers. I jerk my hand back with a yelp. "What the hell, old woman. This wasn't our deal."

"I am offering five Rings to you. Take what you take."

"You weren't damaged, darling." Renee thrusts her head into view. She scowls. "Why didn't you take the Rings?"

I reach again, and again the flames lick my flesh, but this time they're hotter than before. I yank my hand away, holding my tongue.

Renee scoffs. "Still not taking damage, tough guy. Just take the Rings. What's wrong with you?"

I glare at the old bitch. She's doing some kind of mind magic on me, making me feel pain that isn't there. I swipe at the Rings.

The flames are faster than I am. They burn me on the outside and the inside. I stumble backwards, losing my balance.

Strong arms catch me. "I'll do it." Kylie helps me regain my balance and then strides up to the fire. She reaches for the Rings, and the flames erupt, swallowing her arm. But Kylie doesn't flinch. One by one she removes all five Rings from the old woman's fingers. She steps back and bows to the old woman. "Thank you for your gifts, Ezmerelda." Kylie turns to me and hands me a Ring. "This is yours, I believe, Wizard." Her hand is black as charcoal from the flames.

My AI whistles. "Kylie *did* take damage from that. She's at 85% HP now."

"My God, Kylie. How did you do that?" I slip on my newly acquired Ring. "The pain must have been unbearable."

My Angelic wife faces me. "I have the Pain Tolerant trait. So what if I'm down some HP? We have our Rings." She hands one to Slithy and one to Charli before slipping one onto her own hand. "What do these Rings do for us, Ezmerelda?"

"Do you have time for such questions?"

Slithy studies her Ring. "Not really."

Charli puts hers on, emotions battling for control of her face. "Aren't you going to show them a quest?"

"Do you have time for visions?"

"Not really." Slithy fidgets. "Can you enter the quest into our player logs and let us be on our way?"

"What else do you have to give me?"

I might have something. "More information you're lacking."

Ezmerelda pauses. "Very well. Tell me another significant truth I don't know, and I will give you a quest in expedient fashion."

"Do you know the name Seth?"

The old woman levitates off the floor, leaning even closer. "How do *you* know that name?"

"My player, Nick, encountered him on Earth. I suspect Seth has an avatar in Khertaan." I consider mentioning Gondra, but hold back his name for the moment.

Ezmerelda drops her chin and clenches her bony fists. She slowly raises her head. "Your quest has been added to your character logs. You must reach level 30 before Seth does, and trust me, it won't take him long to reach it. What levels are you?"

I point at Kylie, Slithy, and the Woodpecker riding my shoulder. "We're all level 2."

Charli's skirt rustles. "I'm level 15."

Ezmerelda points at Kylie. "Because of you, Angel, the four in your party will be at level 5 when you leave this hut. But you've still a long way to go. Defeat the Boss for the Cornfield and leave the territory as fast as you can. Let's hope the Arachnid Behemoths have trouble killing Shadow Proteans. That could buy you some time." She turns to Charli. "You also need to reach level 30 as soon as possible. These PCs you travel with are special. They have the ability to alter the laws of Khertaan, perhaps even to allow you to join their party while you remain in your current one. If they succeed, you could earn XP from both parties. Through you, both parties could earn the XP earned by either party. It may be the only way any of you will reach level 30 before Seth's avatar does. Now begone, all of you. Find a Shadow Protean to kill and then leave the Cornfield in all haste."

"We will." Kylie bows. "Thank you for your help, Ezmerelda."

"Yeah," says Slithy, "thanks for your help."

Charli tips her Hat at the old woman. "Later, Seeress. Thanks for the Ring."

Grabbing Charli by the hand, Kylie exits the hut, the Cowgirl in tow. Slithy exits behind them.

I turn to face the old woman. "Thank you, Ezmerelda. Sorry for the rush." I push the tarp aside.

Something whistles through the air, striking me in the back of the head. On the dirt floor lies a coin glinting silver in the firelight. I bend down, pick it up, and stash it. I'll look at it later. "Thank you again, whoever you really are. Do you know Gondra?"

The old woman nods. "We're related. I'm not telling you how."

"I wondered." I leave the hut.

Glancing over my shoulder, I find the hut has vanished.

"Congratulations, you're level 5 Wizard, darling." Renee blows me a kiss. "Your Auni has replenished. Your new maximum is 34."

"Do your programming thing, Morrow." Kylie lightly punches my shoulder. "Let's get Charli into our party."

"Yeah, um, about that. You and Slithy need to help. I need to tell you something else, too." I pause in my uncertainty.

Slithy taps her forehead. "I already know, Dad."

Kylie looks at both of us like we're talking a foreign language.

I exhale and meet my wife's gaze. "Right. We all have nanobots in our brains. Our Khertaan program is running on them. So... to make the change to Khertaan that will allow Charli to be in two parties simultaneously, we all three may need to concentrate on influencing those nanobots to make the mod."

"Back up... we *what?*" Kylie stares at me like I'm an alien from outer space.

Slithy nods knowingly. "That's what I thought. It's not a big deal, mom. But... um... we need to move."

I shake my head. "This will take full concentration. Let's give it one minute and see if it works."

Kylie throws up her hands. "I can't believe this."

"One minute, and not one second more. Charli, keep a watch for us. If you see any sign of giant spiders, interrupt us." Slithy closes her eyes. "Let's do this."

"The name for the nanobot collective is ODYSSEY. You can talk to him if you try. Tell him what we need. He'll make the actual mod." I close my eyes and direct my next words inward, not aloud. "ODYSSEY, if you can hear me, I need you to make an alteration to the Khertaan program."

There's no response. My nanobots are still in silent mode.

Slithy croaks, like an actual frog, following it with a laugh. "The program is altered. A new invitation for Charli to join our party has been sent."

Damn. My daughter is good at this. Better than I am. I'm jealous and proud at the same time.

Renee sidles up to me and whispers in my ear. "Charli has been invited to party TimeTrippers, darling. She has accepted and is now a member of your party."

"TimeTrippers is a cool name." The Cowgirl Guide tips her hat. "Thank you for allowing me to be in your party while not breaking my promise to MAD."

Kylie grabs my hand. "Slithy, you hold onto Charli. Let's fly."

"That's curious." Charli pauses, distracted. "I just gained 200K XP, and I don't know why. Did you all gain a bunch of XP just now?"

Renee nods at me. "Congratulations, darling, you are level 11 Wizard. You may now choose a subclass."

What the hell? Where did those 200,000 XP come from?

On the periphery of my vision, two feminine figures waver like mirages. I don't turn to look. I know better. The two ghosts Nick loves the most have found his avatar, even in Khertaan. Lady ghost and child ghost.

"Wrong." The larger of the two ghosts swings a glowing silver blade—not of metal, but of pure energy. I move aside with but a thought, and the blade misses. My attacker isn't a ghost, but *Tabbie*—Nick's girlfriend in a timeline he occupied not so long ago. She's accompanied by her daughter, Samantha. They're both dressed in green bikinis and swinging glowing silver swords.

Samantha cries out as she swings her weapon. "You were supposed to marry Momma."

I try to dodge, but the blade connects, stinging like a son of a bitch.

Where's Kylie? She'd taken my hand, and then vanished. Where's Slithy and Charli?

Tabbie charges, swinging her blade again. "You miss me, don't you, Nick? You want me. So why didn't you marry me instead of her?"

I manage to avoid her blade again. What is going on here? I'm still in Khertaan, I think. I'm still Morrow, not Nick....

Samantha stabs me, leaning on the hilt of her weapon to drive her blade in deeper.

It doesn't hurt, though it does restrain. I try to pull away, but I'm stuck. Tabbie raises her sword and aims for my neck, like she's going to behead me.

"Tabbie, please."

A shout rings out. It's *Kylie*, my wife.

Tabbie, a girlfriend from another time line, freezes where she stands. So does Samantha.

Charli's voice comes from all around. "Use your Lightning, Morrow. The Shadow Protean is attacking you, messing with your mind. This is the Boss encounter. Hit it with your Lighting attack. Hurry, while it's Hypnotized."

I hate to attack Tabbie and Samantha, but I have to trust Charli. *It's not really them.* It can't be. I summon my Auni, step close to the two paralyzed figments of my imagination, and breathe Lightning on them both, pouring all my Auni into the attack. All 34. Oh… that's not true. I had 34 Auni at level 5. Only a moment ago I hit level 11, and my maximum Auni doubled. I just poured 70 Auni into my Lightning Breath attack. I seriously hope it's overkill.

The vista before me clears like fog dispersing. Tabbie and Samantha drift away with the fog. I'm holding Kylie's hand. No cornstalks stand before me within five feet. They've been obliterated, leaving only a few scorched husks behind.

Renee sways her hips. "You've gained 2400 XP, darling. You're at zero Auni. You landed some serious critical damage against the Shadow Protean. *Your* HP stands at 78%. All other health ratings are still 100%. You took no damage to MP at all."

Charli's eyes are wide. "Wow. The battle that MAD had with one of these things dragged on forever. You three killed that Boss within twenty seconds. That thing you did with your voice, Kylie, really made a big difference."

Kylie squeezes my hand. "I think this means we can leave the Cornfield. Is that right, Charli? Are you holding Slithy's hand?"

"Yes and yes, ma'am."

"Good. Hold on tight." She takes to the air, lifting the rest of us with her as though we were feathers. Once airborne, the Angel I call wife looks east to search for the Behemoths. I look, too.

Damn. They're on top of us.

Metallic webbing shoots across the Cornfield at us.

CHAPTER SIXTEEN

Mithabel: Lizardman Savages

Kaleisha danced into sight, her eyes questioning. "Congratulations, chief, you are level 12 Tank and level 3 Anjai. You have acquired the Hide skill as a new Anjai skill. You have a free trait level to assign."

"That's cool. Assign it to my Natural Armor trait."

"*By the Gods.*" The short albino Angel grimaced in embarrassment at his outburst. "Apologies, but I've just earned 200,000 XP. I'm level 11 Psyon and am eligible for a subclass." His eyes glistened in the dark, his welling tears visible only to Mithabel. "Fortune shone its light upon me and Niav when your Goddess chose us to accompany you. I need no alcove to tempt me to pledge my soul to her service. Praises to Scintilla, Goddess of Light."

Niav squeaked an echo of the sentiment. "Praises to Scintilla."

"How did we earn so many XP?" Dylan cast her unseeing gaze around, as though searching for anyone who could explain what happened. "Did we earn all that from the alcoves?"

"Kaleisha, why did we receive the 200K XP?"

"You also earned another 2400 XP just now, chief." Kaleisha smiled. "The 200K XP are a reward granted by the proprietor of Ye Olde Shoppe of the Profane for completion of a quest. The quest required your party to deliver a Severed Ear to him. He received one, of such a special nature he awarded the maximum XP he could."

"And who delivered this Severed Ear to him?" Mithabel had a bad feeling about this. It had to be one of two people, either Charli or Megan Wright, and she doubted it was Charli.

"The quest logs show that you turned in the Severed Ear, Mithabel."

"*What?*" No, it had to have been Megan Wright. Had she been freed from jail or had she escaped? Mithabel bet it was the latter. If Megan had been freed, she'd have notified her party of the good news.

"How did you complete a quest for a shopkeeper while you're in a dungeon, Mithabel?" Dylan had received the same info from her support AI. "*Oh. It wasn't you. It was Megan Wright. She must be out of prison. Did you know?*"

"No, I didn't. But let's contact her now, shall we?"

Amarynth interjected. "I already tried. She's incommunicado."

Mithabel gritted her teeth. "I have another way of contacting her. Give me a minute." She focused on the internal private connection she shared with Megan Wright due to their being different aspects of the same person. "Megan, tell me what's happening with you."

There was no response.

"Dammit, Megan, speak to me."

Still nothing. It was as though Megan Wright didn't exist.

"Kaleisha, locate Megan Wright."

"Accessing…. She is in custody of the City Guards."

"Are you shitting me, Kaleisha? If she's still in custody, how the hell did we earn that 200K XP? I certainly didn't do that quest."

"That's all the info I have, chief."

"It bothers me that I can't contact her through our private channel."

Kaleisha shrugged. "Sorry."

Mithabel shrugged too. "Fine. Let me know if she becomes available for chat via *any* method. Keep trying to contact Raphael, too." She directed her next words to the party. "Let's continue our dungeon quest. I can't reach Megan, but she's still in custody. It's nearly 3:00 AM, so we have another five hours before they evaluate her to determine whether she's legal or not. Let's finish up this quest and then see what we can do to get her out of prison, if Raphael, our developer friend, hasn't sprung her by then."

Keeping everyone else aloft, the dwarfish Angel inched forward. "We're right behind you, Tank."

At the end of the hall, the Elf Tank searched for anomalies. Nothing evidenced other than the rectangular outline she'd noticed before. "Stay back. I'm going to try opening this door." She waited until Zyekt had sufficiently backed away before placing her hands on the wall inside the outline and pushing.

Nothing happened.

She tried pushing on the wall from various angles. Nothing. *Whoosh.*

Her Danger Sense activating, Mithabel whirled around, equipping her Magical Battle Axe and throwing a warning over party chat. *"Enemies behind you."*

The scuttling of large creatures drew close enough for all to hear.

"Reptilians," squeaked Niav. "Several."

No one in the party aside from Mithabel could fight in the dark....

Dylan shouted for Light, illuminating the smooth stone walls of the hallway. A half dozen skulking reptilian-humanoid creatures sprang into action as the light revealed them. Loincloths covered green and black spotted scaly skin. The mooks bared fangs and brandished claws, waving tails thick as clubs behind them.

A Crossbow Bolt struck the closest one in the eye, but didn't faze the creature.

Kaleisha pirouetted out of view. "Lizardman Savages, chief. Amarynth's Bolt dealt 20% damage."

They were up against some tough opponents.

Mithabel flew towards the enemy, activating her new Hide skill. It would cancel once she attacked, but provide some protection until then. She raised her newly enchanted Battle Axe.

Rolag sprang towards the enemy, buffeting his wings. The Lizardman Savages staggered under the force of his Repulsing Winds. Two of them lost their footing and went down. The other four struggled to stay upright, and kept to their feet.

Another Crossbow Bolt struck Amarynth's previous target, but still didn't drop him.

Snarling their frustration with Rolag's windy defense, the standing Savages dropped to the floor, crawling forward on their bellies.

Yet another Crossbow Bolt struck home. This time, the targeted Lizardman blasted apart, his death sparks caught in the Dragon's wing buffet. Amarynth had landed a critical hit.

Dylan raised her hands and cried out. "Scintilla, grant us your blessing in this battle."

Mithabel's muscles hardened.

Yet another Crossbow Bolt sped through the air, striking the head of the Lizardman next closest to Mithabel. No critical hit this time.

The Tank slammed her Battle Axe into the wounded mook's head, going for a Stun, to give Amarynth automatic critical hits on him. To the Tank's surprise, the Savage laughed off her attempt with a gravelly voice and slashed at her with dirty claws, slicing through her Leather Armor as though she wore nothing. Pain burned in her stomach.

Kaleisha groaned. "Ouch, critical hit on you, chief. Your HP is down by a quarter. MP, SP, and EP have all dipped. And... you're poisoned. Anticipate continuing health losses across all damage domains."

Dylan shouted over the tumult. "They're servants of pantheon Anodyne. They're enchanted, so be careful."

Mithabel shouted back. "They're poisonous, too... and they deal all four types of damage." Nasty foes, indeed.

The nearest one gnashed his fangs in an attempt to bite her face, but Mithabel successfully Parried. He struck her leg with his bludgeoning tail, but not being a critical hit, it didn't hurt.

Yet another Crossbow Bolt slammed into Mithabel's attacker, obliterating him. Damn, the Archer didn't need her targets to be stunned, dealing a high proportion of critical hits and firing three or four times as fast as Mithabel could attack.

Rolag lifted into the air, angling his Repulsing Winds attack. The enemies on the floor hid their faces with their arms, bringing them to a halt. Mithabel silently thanked the party's Dragon. If not for him, she'd have another three of these nasty mooks on her.

From Zyekt's pointing finger sprang a beam of black energy. It struck one of the struggling Savages on the floor. The mook shrieked. The wind lifted his body and tossed him over his buddies, depositing him on the floor near the Exemplar alcove. Rolling onto his back, he clawed at his eyes.

Mithabel's stomach burned. "Sweet mother, Zyekt."

Amarynth fired again, her target one of the Savages crawling across the floor. Kaleisha reported another critical hit, but not enough to kill outright.

The wounded mook launched himself at his closest target— Mithabel. His claws scraped her Armor without penetrating the Leather. His bite clamped on empty air and his battering tail failed to matter. Mithabel's defenses protected her against anything less than a critical hit—how it was meant to be.

The other two Lizardman Savages scrambled towards Mithabel. Beyond them, Zyekt's victim, albeit unable to hurt himself, still gouged at his own eyes.

Her Danger Sense triggered again. "We have more company coming, folks. I have a feeling they'll keep coming until we get through that door behind us."

"I'm on it." One end of Niav's leash fell loose, the other still attached to Zyekt. Mithabel caught sight of the Mouse Guide scrabbling across the ceiling towards the end of the hallway. "Buy me some time."

Another missile struck the Savage threatening Mithabel, but he didn't fall.

Dylan sang. "Scintilla, Light my Shurikens."

Mithabel sang, too, under her breath. "Goddess, put this blade where you want it." Her Battle Axe connected with the Lizardman's neck and took off his head. Pixels scattered across the hallway floor.

Pain slammed her in the belly and clawed at her brain, the poison taking its toll.

Rolag continued his wing buffet—an effective deterrent. The newly arrived Savages plowed into the wall of wind. Beyond them, countless more Lizardmen streamed into sight.

"How's that door coming, Niav?" Mithabel glanced back. The door, if indeed it was such, remained closed.

A Crossbow Bolt whizzed through the air, striking one of the two crawling Lizardmen. He howled in agony. A glowing Shuriken struck him, and he blasted apart in a shower of pixels.

Zyekt cupped his hands around his mouth as though about to shout, but he waited. His actions came much slower than those of everyone else. Was he purposefully holding back?

The last remaining Savage from the original six took a Crossbow Bolt in the face, but shrugged it off. With a loud grunt, he propelled himself at Mithabel. She sidestepped his bite, knocked his claw attack aside, and let the tail smack her, scarcely feeling it. Then she planted her Axe blade in his gut and sent his molecules spinning to the ceiling.

A spike of pain drove through her skull and reamed her spine. She gasped and staggered, tears welling in her eyes. "Priestess, a little help, please. This poison...."

Amarynth put a Crossbow Bolt into one of the approaching newcomers, a staggering hit, but not a fatal one.

A Shuriken followed in the missile's wake, and the Lizardman's electric atoms went whining back to the hell from which they'd sprung. "Be right there, Mithabel."

The Tank glanced over her shoulder. "Door, Niav?"

"Almost through." The Mouse flung dirt and stone chips from a hole forming beneath the door.

Amarynth called out. "Be careful, Niav. We don't know what might be on the other side."

"I'm hoping for a door handle."

The suicidal Lizardman still lay on the floor attempting to pluck out his own eyes. He wasn't dead, but he was out of commission. Mithabel averted her gaze from the horrid sight.

The female Viking Archer, a machine pumping out Bolt after Bolt, sent another one down the hallway. Its target staggered. Rolag's wind buffet knocked him off his feet, and he fell in front of a line of companions, who parted left and right to avoid trouncing their fallen friend.

Over twenty Lizardmen pressed toward them, those in the back pushing those in front, closing the distance to the party of adventurers.

It wouldn't do for the mooks to attack any of Mithabel's comrades. Grunting against her internal anguish, the Elf Tank flew to the center of the hallway, out in front of Rolag, hoping to draw all the mook attacks. The Pseudo Code Dragon's Repulsing Winds didn't affect her, blasting around her.

A hand fell on Mithabel's shoulder. "May Scintilla relieve your pain, sister." Soothing energy flowed from the Polynesian Priestess into the Elf Tank, but did little to dissolve the spike in her brain, which hammered even deeper into her body and psyche.

Dylan's voice trembled. "Damn, Mithabel. Is this from just one hit?"

"A critical hit, yeah."

Another Crossbow Bolt shot between the oncoming Lizardmen and finished the wounded one on the floor.

Three Lizardmen closed on Mithabel, clawed hands raised and jaws clacking. Two others headed past the Tank, one to either side.

A hair-raising shout shook the walls. "*Stop!*"

Every Lizardman froze in mid-action.

The short Angel gasped. "Did I do that?"

A Bolt from Amarynth struck a Lizardman at pointblank range. Mithabel's Axe ripped open the gut of a paralyzed assailant. Rolag stopped his wind buffet to breathe fire, catching three foes halted before Mithabel, finishing the one with a gut wound and scorching the other two.

Niav squeaked with excitement. "*I'm through*. There *is* a door here. It's barred on the inside. There's a catch that needs to be held back while the bar is lifted. I can't do it myself."

"I'll be right there." Dylan pushed more healing energy into Mithabel. "That will have to hold you, Tank."

Niav muttered. "You'll never fit through, Dylan."

"No, but I might." Mithabel glanced back. "Zyekt, can you keep our foes stunned with that shout of yours?"

"I don't know, Tank. This is all new to me."

The Lizardman directly in front of Amarynth exploded from a missile to his chest.

"Well, you need to try, and try to act quicker than you have been." Mithabel turned her back on two singed and motionless Lizardmen, their arms drooping at their sides.

Dylan paced the Tank. "I can't cure the poison, Mithabel. Sorry."

Pain speared the Elf's chest, but she gritted her teeth and tried to conceal the hurt. "How do I stop this poison, Kaleisha?"

"It must run its course, chief."

One of the two burned Lizardmen popped like a balloon, punctured by another Crossbow Bolt. The other one snapped out of his paralysis and charged after Mithabel, while another Savage dove for Dylan. Mithabel moved to impose herself between the Priestess and both assailants as best she could, blocking a claw attack from the right. "*Use your voice, Angel.*"

More Savages charged in to fill the void left by their slain companions.

The Lizardman attempting to attack Dylan staggered back under a Stunning blow from Mithabel's Axe. The burned Savage swiped at Mithabel, but his claws failed to pierce her Armor. His jaws clamped on air and his tail missed by six inches. A Crossbow Bolt to his head sent him to pixel limbo.

The Priestess flung a Shuriken into the Stunned Savage before her. It wasn't enough to kill him, but Rolag moved in with a Claw attack to finish the job.

"Angel, *use your voice*." Mithabel grabbed Dylan by the arm and pulled her away.

Foes still flooded the hallway, three headed for Zyekt, towering over him.

"Fall back, Angel, if you can't use your voice again." Dragging Dylan along, Mithabel hurried toward the Mouse and the door.

As they left the illuminated area, the Priestess stumbled.

"Steady, Dylan."

Light blossomed around them as Dylan uttered another spell.

The Angel shouted, commanding the enemy to halt.

The Mouse poked her head through the hole in the floor. "You can't fit through here, Mithabel."

"Watch me." The Tank stashed everything except her Bikini and Ezmerelda's Ring. Dropping to the floor beside the hole, she concentrated on shrinking, hoping her level 3 Compress Body skill would suffice.

Bending her body to follow the dip of the tunnel with some difficulty, she squirmed her way through, and came up in a chamber—twenty feet square and empty, another door in the east wall, also barred. Turning to the door she'd just squirmed under, she noted the catch Niav had mentioned. It would have been impossible for the Mouse to hold it back and lift the bar, but was incredibly easy for the Elf. The door swung into the chamber. "Come on, folks."

Niav scurried off to one side to avoid being trampled. Dylan rushed through, casting another Light spell. Seconds later, the Angel shouted again, and seconds after that he came rushing into the chamber, followed by Rolag and then by Amarynth. Mithabel pushed the door closed and dropped the bar back in place. Everyone waited, listening. Ten seconds later, the door shook as their assailants slammed their bodies against it.

"There's another door over there." Mithabel pointed to the door leading east. "But I think we're safe enough here for at least another minute. I'm going to scan the room for anomalies." She flew alongside the wall.

The Angel flew towards the other exit. "We need to leave this chamber *right now*."

Mithabel paused, hovering. "How are you so sure?"

"I invoked my Foresight power." He pointed at the barred door. "They're coming through any moment."

Another wave of pain savaged Mithabel from within. "Sweet mother, this poison is *still* killing me. Can't you do something, Priestess?"

Dylan followed Zyekt to the east exit. "Hold it together until we get out of here." She unbarred the door, and it swung into the chamber. The darkness of another twenty-feet-wide hallway beckoned to them.

"Take my hands." Zyekt reached out for Dylan and Amarynth. Niav jumped onto his shoulder and slipped her head into the loop at the end of her leash. Rolag shrunk to his puppy dog size and perched on Amarynth's shoulder. He'd been nearly three times his normal height, looking even more ferocious than when he'd first gained the Were-Giant subclass. What level was his subclass now, and how much larger could he expect to get?

The Angel took to the air, towing everyone but Mithabel. The Tank left the room last.

As she made to close the east door, the floor trembled. The Lizardman Savages cried in triumph as the north door broke under their might. Damn, what could she do? Quickly invoking her Hide skill, she warned the others over party chat. "They've breached the chamber."

Niav moaned. "We can't see where we're going, Tank. My sense of smell is off with all this dirt in my nostrils. Either you join us or we need a light."

Dylan huffed. "We've already corrupted the quest anyway. In our vision, there was *no light or battle*. We did something wrong. Maybe we shouldn't have accepted the magic items from the alcoves."

Mithabel hovered near the door. "We can limit how many attack us by holding them here. Rolag, come stand next to me. Amarynth and Dylan, take them out with your missiles. Zyekt, use your voice whenever you can. *Hurry, everyone.* This is our only chance." She brandished her Battle Axe.

Rolag settled beside her, bulking up again.

Mithabel grunted as poisonous pain rocked her once more. "I take the right, you take the left. Go for the Stun. Dylan, make sure we have the blessing of the Goddess still upon us. It makes it easier to Stun these mooks."

"It's still in effect, Tank, and will be until the encounter is officially over."

Clawed Lizardman fingers grasped the edge of the door.

CHAPTER SEVENTEEN

Megan: Executioner's Axe

How do I get out of this? These Guards are about to do what the Orc Wizard has been trying to do all along and failing. Mithabel won't even know what hit her. If the Orc Wizard killed me, at least she and I could respawn. There's no coming back from what these goons aim to do.

I follow them down the hall to the jail cell, past all the photos of me plastered on both walls. Why are these photos here?

There's your red 2015 Mustang GT convertible you love so much.

I *did* love that car—until I crashed it trying to flee that stupid Orc. Taking his Ear was not payment enough for the loss of that sweet ride.

I slow as we pass the photo and imagine the car being here. Half expecting it to materialize, I'm disappointed that it doesn't.

Maybe the photos are reflective of what you want to see.

We're back to the cell area. The Orc Wizard is still here. He laughs when he sees me. I try not to react. Six Guards are already stationed in the room. Were they afraid the Orc would attempt an escape too? Hell, why hasn't he broken out? Have they nullified his magic? Maybe they have something that dampens or prevents Auni and Psi use. I'm betting so. I'm strongly hoping so.

My Anjai subclass is based on Earth's Ninjas, a fact known in Khertaan only by us Anjai, verified by our support AIs. I don't *feel* like a Ninja, and I doubt I come off as one to others, but I love my Anjai skills, especially since they don't require a source of power. The Guards can block Auni and Psi use all day, and they won't affect any of my traits or skills—either the Tank-based ones or the Anjai ones. In fact, last I checked, both my Auni and Psi scores were zero, and I don't expect they'll ever be otherwise.

"Into your cell." The Leader holds the door open. "Lie on your back on the cot. The evaluation begins shortly."

You ought to have some skill or trait to get you out of this. The ability to fly, neat as it is, won't do much for you while you're in this cell. Compressing your body allowed you to slip between the bars before, but pulling the same trick now won't get you far with all these Guards watching your every move. Big deal that you can detect anomalies, see in the dark, sense danger, or be especially alert. Your fighting skills will only be useful if you try to fight your way out, and that's not likely to go well. There seems to be nothing you can do.

I'm not so sure about that. I'll bide my time and see what develops. An opportunity will come knocking, and I'll be ready.

I lie on my back on the cot and stare up at the ceiling, my manacled wrists a miserable lump in the middle of my back. The chain attached to my manacles stretches across the floor.

You can at least slip out of the manacles anytime you want.

Now is not the time.

I have no sense of anything happening, other than my wrists growing increasingly more sore. I compress them enough so the manacles cease digging into my flesh.

"We have ourselves an illegal avatar, boys. Termination to be carried out forthwith. Send out a notification *to city residents only* that a public execution will occur in thirty minutes near the city gates." The Guard Leader opens the door to my cell. "Get up, illegal." He picks up the chain and gives it a yank, dragging me off the cot. Using my flight ability only enough to keep me from crashing to the floor, I get my feet beneath me and stumble forward. I don't want them knowing I can fly. I still might be able to escape them—all the more likely if I can catch them by surprise.

The Leader hands my chain off to another Guard, who leads me out of the cell area. The Orc Wizard laughs as they take me away. He knows they intend to do what he's failed to do, and more thoroughly and expediently than he could have managed. He would have needed to kill me over and over until my Constitution hit zero.

Up the hallway of photos we go, and then we're outside. The Guard leads me along the street. I don't falter, don't fall behind, because if I did, the taut chain would spin me around backwards, what with the chain attached to my wrists behind my back.

He'd probably love to be seen dragging you down the road in your Bikini.

I won't give him that satisfaction.

The city residents pour out of their homes and shops, staring at the illegal avatar. Guards walk in lines to either side of me, some with Swords drawn, some with Spears pointing at me, and others with loaded Bows trained on me. Ha. If they killed me with their weapons, that wouldn't eradicate me from the game.

I'd respawn, effectively escaping their grasp. Their weapons are symbolic, something to visually demonstrate the degree of power they hold over me.

That might be your way out of this. Compress your wrists to slip out of the manacles and then fight the Guards until they kill you. You'll lose a life, which means so does Mithabel, but at least you won't both be eliminated from the competition.

But, damn, I'm too curious. I want to know how they plan to eradicate me. The only way to learn is for my execution to proceed. At the last second, after I've learned as much as I can, I'll slip free of my manacles and fight.

Keep in mind… if you die without being eradicated, the Guard claimed you would respawn in prison.

Yeah, there is that.

We approach a man wearing a black Hood and wielding a Double-Bladed Axe, each blade twice as wide and long as the blade on my single-bladed weapon. Silver edges sparkle in the eternal sunshine, outlining black metal blades. The Executioner rests his foot on a chopping block.

They intend to take off my head.

That can't be all there is to eradicating me. The beheading must be symbolic. I concentrate on the Axe, the chopping block, and the Executioner, scanning for anomalies.

We reach the chopping block. Guards turn me to face the gathered crowd while the Leader postures for show, waiting for more people to gather before speaking. He wants as many residents to see this as possible. Maybe he earns more XP for a larger audience.

"Citizens of Maron." He's finally satisfied with the crowd size. "We have among us today a person come to this world through illegal means. Such contamination of our environment cannot—*will not*—go unpunished. After careful scanning, analysis, and verification by the System that the woman before you is indeed illegal, she is to be eradicated from this universe. It is imperative we maintain a purity of character and ethics. Look upon this face. Study it well, for there is another among us with a similar appearance who must also be brought to justice.

"Other outsiders are infiltrating our universe illegally. We have another suspect imprisoned. The truth of his illegality will be verified within the hour. We already know the outcome, but believe in due process, and are not here to promote arbitrary executions. The System will inform us, and we will act strictly in accordance with its findings.

"A process exists by which validated PCs may enter our world, and those who violate the rules must be dealt with harshly. We will set an example with the eradication of this illegal. Spread the word of what you see here today, especially to any PCs you encounter. Make sure they know not to break the rules in our beloved city. Make sure they know we will not tolerate such behavior. My name is Guard Leader Howard. Remember it. If you have any information about other illegals in Maron or Khertaan at large, do not hesitate to send it straight to me. XP will be awarded for actionable information according to its degree of veracity and utility."

Excited murmurs rise amongst the crowd. "I saw her look-alike," shouts one man. "She went into the dungeon under the Red Pegasus Inn with Lady Amarynth. They haven't come back out yet."

The murmurs become lively conversations.

Guard Leader Howard raises his hands, and the crowd quiets. "No one is to touch anyone in their party or anyone accompanying them. That especially goes for Lady Amarynth. Anyone who touches her against her will may forfeit XP, or a life if you have no XP to give. If you see the fugitive, report her location immediately to me. Again, my name is Guard Leader Howard. Send me a DM. I will redirect resources as required to remand the perpetrator into our custody."

Goddess, he's so full of himself.

He strides over to me, his grin evil. "I'll hold you down myself." He takes the free end of the chain from his underling. Tugging on the chain, he leads me to the chopping block. "On your knees, illegal."

If I'm to learn anything, I need to do as ordered. I drop to my knees before the chopping block.

Moving around me so he's facing the bulk of the crowd, Guard Leader Howard places a palm at the base of my skull and pushes, shoving my face against the top of the block. I switch to Third Person POV and watch the scene like a bystander. It's a weird sensation, observing the Guard Leader mistreat my body and simultaneously feeling the pain of his mistreatment. He plants a knee across my back and yanks up on the chain, stretching my arms backwards and above me. The opposing downward and upward pressure locks me in position, my face smashed against the wood of the chopping block.

This is surreal.

The consequences of the Executioner removing your head will be all too real. Is it time to escape?

In a minute. There must be more to this execution than meets the eye.

You're a brave one. Or foolish.

I might be both.

The Executioner positions himself by my head. He raises his Axe to examine an edge, running a thumb along the sharpness. A thin line of red appears down the length of his thumb. He licks it, savors it, and nods. It's all for show, because avatars don't bleed in Khertaan. He raises the Axe over his head and looks to Guard Leader Howard for the signal.

I'll compress my body at the last second. Slip out of the manacles. Give myself room to maneuver my head off that block. I'll have to fight, and might be killed, but not by the Executioner's Axe.

You think there's something special about the Axe?

It's the Axe, the Executioner, or the chopping block. The Axe looks the most impressive.

Guard Leader Howard raises a fist. The crowd cheers. The Guard Leader shakes his fist. One edge of the Executioner's Axe glows blue. The crowd roars.

If you're escaping, now might be a good time.

Yeah, I agree.

If only you could Hide, like Charli.

I can only imagine myself not being on the chopping block.

Guard Leader Howard slams his fist down on my back—except, my back is gone. *I'm gone.* The Executioner hesitates, not knowing whether to swing or not, his grip on the Axe handle relaxing.

I'm invisible, still on the block. Guard Leader Howard's fist pummels me again. The chain is still stretched between my wrists and his fist.

The Guard Leader brings up his fist, motioning at the Executioner to do his duty. "Strike, strike, strike."

Are you going to compress your body now?

Yes, I believe I will.

My wrists slip free of the manacles and my face retracts from the chopping block. The pressure of Guard Leader Howard's knee in my back pushes me down, but I tuck my chin and twist beneath him. The top of my head slams into the chopping block, but glances off without pain—my Natural Armor at work. I roll away from the Guard Leader as the Executioner's Axe bites into wood. Still watching with Third Person POV, it's like I'm playing a video game, controlling the moves of my avatar as I watch her antics play out before me.

Since you're invisible, you could fly away and no one would know.

Switching to First Person POV as I rise, I watch Guard Leader Howard motioning for the Guards in the wings to rush forward, tightening the circle around the chopping block. I fly as high as I can as fast as I can, which isn't as fast as I've seen Rolag fly, but, hey, I'll take it. I'm out of their reach.

I fly to the city gates while the Guards mill about in an attempt to find and recapture me.

Wait. Listen. Do you hear that?

A Motorcycle approaches from beyond the walls. I can't identify the rider at this distance, but I don't see a red robe flapping.

The same kind of engine growl emanates from behind me. Crap. Another Motorcycle comes from the vicinity of the prison, carrying a red robed rider. The Orc Wizard has escaped from his cell and is coming to make sure I'm dead.

I'll deal with the rider approaching from beyond the gates as I must, but I'm not staying inside these walls another moment. Once I fly over those gates, I'll feel *so* much better.

CHAPTER EIGHTEEN

Charli: Shadow Traveling

Kylie flies backwards to avoid the giant metallic mesh arching across the sky. But it's coming too fast and it's so darn big. It wraps us and drags us down. Kylie's Party Flight trait doesn't extend to enemy webbing, and the Angel isn't physically strong enough to carry such a load. I try to stash the web, on the off-chance I can, but the attempt fails.

"No worries." Kylie is strong enough to influence the direction we fall, and we land as far from the Behemoths as possible, behind a thicket of cornstalks dense enough to provide some resistance to the Behemoth's pull. She releases her passengers and disappears, reappearing outside the webbing. "Watch out." A glowing blue Sword appears in her hand, and she hacks at the webbing until it separates.

Slithy and I slip out through the slit. With Rancor gripping his shoulder, Morrow clears the opening just as the Behemoth gives a powerful yank on the webbing, ripping it through the thicket.

The Angel dismisses her Sword, we all grab hold of each other in an expedient if haphazard fashion, and we're airborne once more.

"Stay low until we're clear." I base my guidance on my Monster Lore skill. If we head for the sky while in range of the webs, we'll be easier targets.

Kylie flies just above the tops of the cornstalks.

Until the Behemoths kill a Shadow Protean Boss, they can't leave the Cornfield. "The Black Poison Forest shouldn't be far. We'll be safer there."

I have a grip on Kylie's right wrist, and Morrow's left hand is in my right. Slithy is on Kylie's left. Rancor still clutches Morrow's shoulder.

A wad of webbing flattens a swath of cornstalks directly behind us.

The spiders are too close. "We have to lose them or the Forest won't manifest for us...."

Slithy points. "I see treetops."

"Yikes, that's not good." I see the forest, too. "That means the spiders have already killed a Cornfield Boss and can enter the forest too. So... listen. Once we get to the forest, let me take over. Shadow traveling will be faster through the woods. Kylie, land in a shaded area, and everyone keep hold of each other."

Kylie flies at an upward angle. "Can't I simply fly over the forest?"

I grimace. "The forest Boss monster is on the ground. We need to kill it before the Behemoths do, if we want to reach Maron first, and we can't do that unless we're on the ground."

Slithy bobs her black-spotted, red-skinned blond head. "Listen to her, Mom. She knows this place better than we do."

"You're right." The Angel solemnly nods and descends as we reach the edge of the forest. She flies further, until the shadows deepen, and then sets down. Still keeping hold of each other, we all glance back as a unit. The Arachnid Behemoths tower above the horizon, too close for comfort.

"Everyone switch to Third Person POV and scan the ground for a Scorpion." I shift my grip from Kylie's wrist to her hand. She returns my squeeze.

At my mental command, our bodies dissolve and day turns to night. The world becomes darkness and then a blur of motion.

"I can't see squat." There's an absence of physicality to give breath to Morrow's statement. His voice is an echo absent the original utterance.

My reply has the same echoing quality. "We need distance first."

None of us speak for a time. The world rushes past as we zigzag between trees and skirt even the smallest clearing where sunlight would interrupt our journey.

I bring down our traveling speed. "Remember... look for a Scorpion. Nothing else matters."

We continue moving forward, not wanting the Behemoths to catch us. Are they slowed by the trees, some of which are taller than the Behemoths? The spiders can't simply walk over them.

"Still moving too fast." The frustration is clear in Morrow's voice.

Slithy and Kylie echo agreement with him.

I slow more, not mentioning that I have a level 14 Search skill. I don't want them to feel like I'm doing everything for them. "It's small, fast, blinks in and out, and is never where it seems to be."

"*Stop, Charli.*"

I come to a halt as Slithy demands.

She lets go of Kylie, becoming physical, while the rest of us remain in the shadow realm. Did she see the Boss? Why are her eyes closed? I Search the ground in front of her, and my combat heartbeat starts, indicating we're in an encounter.

A Scorpion appears nearby, its tail striking at Slithy's foot, the stinger penetrating the Frogkin woman's red flesh.

The shock of the sight extends my combat heartbeat five seconds.

But the Frogkin woman doesn't flinch. A silver beam of energy springs from her forehead... hitting a dead leaf.... She missed her target....

Yet the Scorpion's body goes limp. Her eyes still closed, Slithy bends down as though to touch the motionless Boss, but is off by several inches. The Scorpion vanishes. Opening her eyes, Slithy punches the air with a fist in triumph. In the next moment, without taking a step, she stands a foot closer to me, laughing. "I faked it out with its own ability. We should get moving again."

The encounter has ended as abruptly as it started. I shift out of shadow so we can collect the Frogkin Mentalist.

"How did you manage that, kid?" Morrow asks what we're all wondering.

"Charli told me all I needed to know. I realized it could Displace, but it didn't know I could. So it struck where it thought I was, and while it might have thought it hit, it didn't. I used my Anticipate skill to guide my attack—rather than relying on my eyes. I knew I'd only get one shot, so I put all my Psi points into a Mind Spear. The Boss—a One Strike Scorpion—is a vegetable now, in my inventory with the Goblins I stashed." Giggles shake Slithy's shoulders as she puts a hand over her mouth.

I can't help but giggle with her. I can't imagine anyone else even attempting to stash a Boss monster, mindless or not, big or little.

Kylie reaches a hand towards her daughter. "I hate to think what would have happened if it had gotten one strike on you. You should be more careful."

Slithy dismisses her mother's concerns with a toss of her blond hair. "I wonder how much we can get for it in trade." She squeals. "Oh, my goodness."

The System informs me I've earned 30K XP. Not enough to put me to level 16 by a long shot. And since when was the Scorpion Boss worth 30K XP?

Morrow gasps. "Nice work, Slithy. I'm up another level. We'll catch up to you yet, Charli."

I shake my head. "The One Strike Scorpion was only worth 3K XP when MAD defeated it. Maybe you earned more for taking it alive. We'll have to remember that... earn ten times the XP for Boss monsters by taking them alive."

Kylie grabs Slithy's hand. "Let's hope those damned Behemoths don't kill a Scorpion anytime soon."

I take us all back into the shadow realm and head west. The trees whiz by fast. In short order, we reach the edge of the forest, and I shift us back to the physical realm.

"Welcome to the Grass Bladed Field." I use air quotes around the name of the field, now a plot of bare dirt. I point across it. "There lies the city of Maron. Follow me. And don't worry about the Boss for this new territory. MAD cleared it once for everyone."

"Does that mean we can fly across?" Kylie holds out her hands to either side.

"Yeah, sure." I don't think there's a problem with it. We all grasp hands once more.

Ears perked, Kylie glances over her shoulder, tucking her wings. "Um, guys."

I hear it too. A crashing sound. I don't want to look, but I do.

A pathway forms in the Black Poison Forest like Moses parting the Red Sea. An Arachnid Behemoth looms into sight.

If ever I were allowed to use a curse word, now would be the appropriate time. "Gosh, they've already killed a Scorpion Boss. Probably stepped on one without even knowing it."

"Time to fly," Kylie says, and we're airborne.

CHAPTER NINETEEN

Mithabel: Orc Children

Kaleisha spoke in a rush. "Congratulations, chief. You just gained level 13 Tank, level 4 Anjai. Not sure why. This encounter is not over."

Rolag braced himself. "Hold your attacks, Mithabel. Let me try something first."

The Lizardman Savage pulled the door wide open.

Being invisible—or so she hoped, Mithabel didn't move, but stood poised to attack with her Magical Battle Axe.

Rolag raised the scales on his back and bared his fangs, making himself as Intimidating as possible. The Lizardman caught sight of him and froze, his gaze locked on Rolag's. A battle of wills played out on the faces of the Lizardman and Rolag, and the Lizardman lost. He slowly pushed the door closed as he carefully backed away. Rolag's Intimidate skill had won the day.

The Tank led the way back to the rest of the party. She collapsed against Dylan as poison rocked her body again. "Help me, Priestess. I can't function this way anymore. I just want to die."

"I'm here, Tank." Dylan brushed Mithabel's cheek.

Broken on the inside, the Elf melted under the Polynesian's touch. A calmness settled in Mithabel's mind, followed by a gentle flowing of energy into her veins. She closed her eyes as the energy continued to fill her, lifting her thoughts, her spirits, her emotions from the depression into which the poison had dragged them. She drew a deep breath and straightened, looking into Dylan's eyes. "You grow more Beautiful all the time, Priestess. Even in the dark. It's amazing how gorgeous you are."

Dylan made a purring sound. "I know. You look lovely, too, Tank. Even in the dark." She chuckled.

Kaleisha cleared her throat. "Ahem…. You've gained 25K XP for the encounter with the Lizardman Savages, chief. The encounter is officially over. The poison has subsided, and Dylan has restored all your health stats to full. You're good as new."

The Tank exhaled loudly. "Glad that's over."

Amarynth clucked her tongue. "We should go… before those Savages change their minds and decide to start another encounter with us."

"You're right." Mithabel once again took point while the others followed. Since her party members couldn't see her anyway, she activated her Hide skill to make it less likely potential foes with Dark Sight would notice her before she noticed them.

"I'm not picking up your scent, Mithabel," Niav said over party chat. "Hold on…. I've got it now. What did you do?"

"Sorry. I'm using my Hide skill, just in case. I forgot it affected scent as well as sight."

"It helps that I know you're there," Niav said. "We're good now."

They traveled due east along a hallway with blank walls, floor, and ceiling. It was a perfect stretch of hallway for floor traps, but Mithabel didn't spot any anomalies to give them away.

An end to the hallway came into sight. "Wait here, please. Dead end up ahead. I'll go check it out."

She studied the side walls and then turned her attention to the end wall. "I see outlines of two doors, one large enough to walk through and the other one small, like the door to a safe. I don't see anything else. Should we shine a Light?"

"No." Dylan shook her head in the dark. "Our quest vision didn't show us using any Light, so the less we use, the closer we stay true to the vision. I'll have Light ready in case we're attacked, but let's try to proceed without it. See if you can open the doors, Mithabel."

Amarynth suggested opening the smaller door first. "Maybe it contains the opening mechanism for the big door. If you try opening the big door the wrong way, maybe it summons mooks… like Lizardman Savages."

Dylan echoed her agreement.

"Good idea." The Elf Tank focused on the smaller door, located shoulder height from the floor. One side of the outline gapped more. She pushed her fingernails into the gap and pulled. A stone plate fell from the wall into her hands, exposing a compartment one foot high, wide, and deep. "I found a lever, people, pointing straight up. Looks like it can go left or right. Which way do I push it?"

"Left," said everyone but Dylan and Zyekt, and then Dylan changed her mind, too.

The Angel, however, persisted. "I've got a strong hunch it should go to the right."

"What's everyone's Intuition scores?" Mithabel checked hers. "Mine is 10... average."

Amarynth's was 11 and Niav's 12. Dylan and Rolag each had 8. They all felt strongly the lever should be pushed to the left.

Zyekt's was 16. "I feel it in my bones, it should be pulled to the right."

On hearing the Angel's Intuition value, everyone else murmured consent.

"To the right it is." Mithabel readied herself. "Rolag, would you join me, please? Wait by the larger door and use your Intimidate skill on anything that might be waiting for us when it opens. Ready?"

The Dragon moved into place. "Ready."

Mithabel pushed down the lever.

A click sounded as the lever locked in place. The larger door swung inward, revealing a chamber measuring fifty feet square.

High pitched howls echoed from the room, like puppies excited for feeding time. Humanoid figures varying from two to four feet tall rushed at the opened door. Mithabel positioned herself beside Rolag and prepared to strike with her Battle Axe, still concentrating on her Hide skill. Rolag bared his fangs and arched his back in preparation to Intimidate.

"Oh, Goddess." Mithabel shuddered at the sight of disfigured children—some shambling, some running, some dancing, and others approaching with caution.

Kaleisha appeared beside Mithabel. "The System has auto-identified these creatures as Orc children and has automatically enabled language translation."

"Look at the Dragon." The nearest child ran up to Rolag and touched his reptilian snout with a tentative finger. "Are you here to play with us, Dragon?" Tiny fangs protruded from the child's mouth, pointing up. A male, he wore only a ragged loincloth. His dark hair was closely cropped.

A female child dancing nearby admonished the first child. "Watch out, stupid. He'll bite your hand off." She wore a loincloth as well, but also a ragged top covering her flat chest. Her fangs weren't as long as the boy's, but her gnarled hair hung past her shoulders.

Another boy ran over, looking not much different from the first boy. "No, he won't. Dragons don't like the taste of Orcs, only Humans. But he might breathe fire and burn off your hair."

"He better not burn off my hair," said the dancing Orc girl, making no effort to put more distance between her and the Dragon.

One of the cautious children—a girl—peered at Rolag from behind the others. "He looks mean. He might bite your hand off just to spit it out."

The dancing girl looked straight at Mithabel. "What about the Elf next to him?"

The first boy huffed. "Are you calling me an Elf?"

Tossing her dark hair, the dancer spun in place. After making a complete rotation, she pointed at Mithabel. "No, dummy. Standing *beside* him, not in front of him."

"There's no one standing *beside* him. You're trying to scare me."

"Who opened the door?" An adult Orc woman strolled into sight. "Close it back and leave the nice Dragon alone."

The dancer spun to face the adult, her dark hair swirling. "It opened by itself. Or maybe the Elf opened it."

The first kid stamped his foot. "There's *no* Elf."

The Orc woman approached the door, her eyes scanning the area. Mithabel didn't move. The woman's gaze passed over the Elf Tank without focusing on her.

Over party chat, Dylan asked, "What are we doing here? Don't tell me the chest we're looking for is in that chamber."

"We have to check it out. I'll fly in and take a look." Mithabel folded her legs against her chest and then drifted like a balloon over the heads of the Orcs.

The dancer tracked the Tank with an extended finger. "*The Elf is coming in.* She's flying over our heads, all curled up in a ball."

The adult and kids looked up, trying to spot what their little friend saw. As long as the woman didn't see Mithabel, all should be fine. The Tank floated around the room, hugging her knees and careful not to fly too low.

The dancer ran beneath Mithabel, constantly pointing up at her. "There she is. Don't you see her?"

Against the south wall sat an iron-bound wooden chest, locked with a padlock. A plate on the face of the chest under the padlock bore an engraving—the name, *Ogaltha*. "I found the chest. It's definitely the right one. And it's locked. What's our plan to unlock it?"

Niav offered her services. "If it's made of wood, I can gnaw through it."

Dylan huffed. "I didn't realize the object of our quest would be in a chamber where children lived. We can't steal from children."

Mithabel involuntarily rolled her eyes, thankful Dylan couldn't see her. "It's not like they're using whatever is inside the chest. It's locked and doesn't look like it's been opened in years. Of course, Charli would remind us that nothing we see in Khertaan is the actual age it appears to be. She's a teenager—and has been for over two decades. She could have been created to be any age. It's the same here. The developers didn't have to populate this room with children. They could have made them adults, and we could have had to fight them to get to the chest."

"Well, we're *not* killing children." Dylan's tone was firm. "It doesn't matter that they're NPCs. We're *not* killing them."

"*Right there.*" The dancer stood directly below Mithabel, arm sticking straight up. "*She's... right... there.*"

The adult Orc woman moved up beside the dancer, her eyes staring through Mithabel. "I swear I don't see anything, child. How big is the Elf? How is she dressed?"

"She's almost naked. She wears a black Bikini and carries an Axe."

The adult shook her head in dismissal and turned away. "Children, I told you to leave the Dragon alone. Go on and close that door."

Mithabel didn't like the sound of that. "Rolag, don't let them close that door. Come inside a bit."

The Pseudo Code Dragon took a step forward. Smoke puffed from his nostrils.

The children backed away, screaming.

The Orc woman stopped in her tracks. "You mustn't come in, Dragon. There's a curse on this place. If you come inside, you can't leave without the Ring. You can't take the Ring without opening the Chest. The Chest won't open unless you kill one of the children. You appear to have Morals and a Conscience, and aren't one to kill a child. So, I beg of you, turn around and leave us be."

Dylan gasped. "Oh, my Goddess, Mithabel. Get out of there now. We're *not* killing a child. Just fly out without doing anything or touching anything. Maybe the curse won't affect you if you haven't touched the ground. Let's hope."

Mithabel stayed put. "And abandon the quest? What if Orc lady here is lying?"

"Promise me you won't kill any of the children, Mithabel. *Promise me.*"

"Sorry, Dylan, but I can't make that promise."

"*Promise me*, or I'm never speaking to you again.... Amarynth, what are you...?"

A lit torch flew into the room.

A Crossbow Bolt whizzed past Rolag, striking the first boy. The child exploded into tiny glowing bits, swirling like a small tornado, flowing upward and fading from sight.

Against the south wall, the lock on the Chest came undone and fell to the floor. The lid popped up. The interior was empty except for a single golden band.

The Orc woman clapped her hands on her face. "*No.* My poor Urgook."

Amarynth peered into the room. "Get the Ring and get out of there, Mithabel."

Dylan clapped a hand on Amarynth's shoulder and yanked her back. "You damned *bitch*. You heard me say we weren't killing any kids."

The Archer scoffed. "You didn't hear me agree to that. Besides which—*they aren't kids*. They're arrangements of pixels like any other mooks we kill in this game."

"Don't let Charli hear you say that. Besides, we were supposed to do this quest without any Light."

"You already violated that rule—if it is a rule. We've been kept in the dark about so much in this game, it's time to make our own rules."

The second Orc boy stomped on the torch and put it out.

Mithabel dropped towards the chest, arm outstretched.

Shouting and pointing, the dancer jumped up and down. "The Elf is going for the Ring."

"No." The Orc woman rushed towards Mithabel.

The Tank snatched the Ring from the bottom of the Chest.

The world went dark. Mithabel crashed to the floor beside the Chest, her flight ability failing her. Pain shot up her spine.

The Orc woman towered over Mithabel, her gaze locked on the Tank, and her words came in the form of a private message. "So there was an Elf here after all. Not an Elf anymore. You made a bad choice taking that Ring. But it's yours now, and no way to be rid of it. My name is Okguul. Hope you enjoy your life as one of my wards. You'll remain here until someone kills you." She leaned over the Chest and dropped another Ring inside before closing the lid and replacing the lock. Then she offered a hand to the fallen Tank. "Rise, Ogaltha."

CHAPTER TWENTY

Ogaltha: Shut In

With every muscle aching, Ogaltha stood, dressed in a ragged top and loincloth. She held no weapon, and none lay on the floor. "Kaleisha, where is my Battle Axe?"

Remaining out of sight, the support AI made no reply.

The Ring from the Chest had slipped onto one of her fingers.

The dark-haired dancing Orc girl came to a stop in front of her. "You're one of us now, Ogaltha." The girl was Ogaltha's height. "I'm Ullullu. It's nice of you to come and replace that awful Urgook. Will you dance with me?"

Ogaltha glanced around, her mind racing too fast for anything to fully register. "This isn't happening. This is only in my mind. Dylan, can you hear me?"

The Polynesian Priestess didn't reply.

"Amarynth? Rolag? Zyekt? Niav? Someone say something, *please*."

Okguul clucked her tongue. "They don't know what you're saying, Ogaltha. Your outgoing chat channels are being mistranslated to everyone but us Orcs. Your incoming channels still function properly, however, for the most part."

Ogaltha's friends still waited for her at the open door. Rolag spoke. "I don't know, Dylan. The Orc woman just closed the Chest and locked it back. I don't see Ogaltha anywhere. I don't know if she got the Ring. All I know is, this place is freaking me out. I'm not going in. *Ogaltha, where are you?*"

Ogaltha waved. "I'm here." She ran to Rolag and waved her hand in his face. "It's me…. Ogaltha." That name wasn't right. What was the right one? Why couldn't she remember?

Rolag's mouth bent up in a grin, looking a bit evil on his reptilian face. "Aw. I like you, too, little one. Just look at them, Milady. For Orcs, they're so cute. I feel bad you killed one of them."

Dylan bristled at his words. "No one is killing any more of them. The Goddess help me, Amarynth, if you shoot one more child in this game, I'll have nothing more to do with you. I'm serious. It doesn't matter what they're made of. It's the *principle* of it. Promise me, or we can part ways right here."

Ullullu danced over and grabbed Ogaltha by the hand. "Come, sister. Dance with me."

Amarynth huffed. "Fine. I promise not to kill any more children in the game."

"No, don't make that promise." Ogaltha jerked her hand from Ullullu. "I need to rejoin my friends. I'm only imagining this. My MP has been lowered so dramatically, I'm hallucinating. Dylan can heal me."

The dancer giggled. "Don't be silly, Ogaltha. You're not hallucinating. Come on, I'll show you." She skipped over to the door and pointed down the hallway. "Go on. Leave."

"I will." Ogaltha brushed past Ullullu. As she attempted to pass through the doorway, electricity filled it, knocking her back. Rolag jerked back from the door.

Ullullu swung the door closed. "There. Told you. You're stuck with us."

"Open the door again." Dylan's voice betrayed her panic. "*Ogaltha*, where are you? Please answer me."

Ogaltha banged on the door. "I'm still inside. *Get me out.*"

Rolag spoke again, his voice clear over party chat though he was on the other side of the door. "The compartment closed, too. I don't see either door now."

Niav squeaked. "Let me burrow into the room. I'll find her."

"We can't ask that of you," said Amarynth.

"The hell we can't," said Dylan. "We're not leaving without Ogaltha. *Tank, answer me.*"

"I'm in here, Dylan. I'm in here." Ogaltha banged again on the door.

Okguul tapped her foot on the stone floor. "They really don't know you're speaking to them, Ogaltha. Besides which, *they* can't enter now. The entrance no longer exists for them. Your place is here with us until *another* party arrives to fulfill this quest and chooses to kill you."

"This can't be." Ogaltha's fist fell by her side. Pounding on the door produced no satisfactory results. "I can't stay here. I need to be with Dylan. I *need* her. You have to let me out. Where's my Battle Axe? If I need to die to leave, I'll kill myself."

Ullullu laughed.

Okguul shook her head. "Suicide isn't possible in Khertaan. None of us will oblige you, either—and even if we did, you'd respawn in this chamber as you are now. Settle in and get comfortable. I recommend dancing and making friends with the other children. It will help keep your mind off things. And who knows? Perhaps you'll come to enjoy your life here."

The Tank-turned-Orc-child glared at Okguul. "I'll find a way out of here, old woman. Just watch me."

Dylan shouted over party chat. "*Ogaltha*, this wasn't funny to begin with and it still isn't funny. *Say something*, dammit."

Pain ripped through Ogaltha like a ball of Lightning flowering in her gut. Clutching her stomach, she dropped to her knees, gasping for breath.

CHAPTER TWENTY-ONE

Megan: Escape

A bolt of Lightning zaps me as I fly over the gates. Pain flowers in my gut and courses through me. Clutching my stomach, I keep flying by force of will. "Mithabel, are you there? Kaleisha? Dylan? Amarynth? Charli? Rolag? *Anyone?*"

Dammit. I'm so tired of being completely cut off from my party. Hell, at this point, I'd welcome *any* familiar friendly face.

Guardsmen on the ground shout alarms, aiming their polearms at the top of the gates behind me. They don't see me flying away.

My health is down and I don't know by how much, only that it's not zero. Mithabel has taken the same damage I just took, with no understanding of why, and no way to ask me about it. But when Dylan heals her, I'll be healed, too.

The Motorcycle approaching from the west slows to a stop on the Grass Bladed Field — which no longer consists of blades or grass. The rider shouts my name. *"Megan?"* He's hoping for an answer but has low expectations for receiving the one he hopes for. "I know you're there. Show yourself."

My spine tingles. I recognize that voice. *Kevin.*

He's my hero—the young black man who on Earth had pretended to the cops to be my boyfriend and then saved me from Arachnid Behemoths when they attacked an ambulance I rode in. I had the Orc Wizard's dagger stuck in my leg at the time. How can *Kevin* be here? Is he in Khertaan as a PC?

If I want to speak with him, I need to be closer, due to the modifications made to my ability to communicate. I fly to him, hovering six feet away, but hesitate to reveal myself.

His eyes scan the air between us, like he knows I'm near but not exactly where. "Megan?" His voice is conversational. "I know you're close. Get on the Bike."

His license plate reads HOWLER, the same as it did on Earth. I study his Bike and his face for anomalies—discrepancies. I see none. This is the same Kevin who drove me across the desert, headed for the Fanciful Pegasus facility—the site of the gaming competition.

We rode his Bike. Dr. Splat and his computerized assistant, Nigel, accompanied us in their van. The four of us stopped at a gas station. Dr. Splat and Nigel left before we did. A Mad Cow Ballista burst into the store and started shooting up the place, trying to kill me.

Drawing my attention back to the present, Kev shouts at me. "Get on the Bike, Megan. *Now.*"

Something bellows behind me, and I turn in place to look. Splinters shower the area as a bovine charges through a freshly created hole in the Maron city gates. The cow carries a large Crossbow mounted on its back. An over-sized, sharpened Pencil materializes in the Crossbow's flight groove, the pointy end aimed at me.

A crashing sound emanates from the east. A female Angel approaches, holding hands with the crew she carries: a blond woman with black-spotted red skin; a white man sporting a green mohawk, on whose shoulder is perched a red-crested bird; and a white teenage girl with cowboy hat and pigtails—the Cowgirl I know as Charli. Behind them comes the source of the crashing, *one of those damned Arachnid Behemoths.*

Bloody hell, it's not just *one* Behemoth—*it's a whole freaking army.*

I don't drop my Hide skill, but shout out. *"Charli."* I'm not sure if I'm close enough for her to hear me, or if the shouting will help.

"I knew it." Kev's voice swells with conviction. "You *are* here. *Get on the damn Bike.* Those things are here for *you.* We need to get out of here, *now. Come on,* Megan."

"I need to talk to Charli."

A giant Pencil strikes the ground below where I'm hovering, spraying Kev with dirt. If the missile had been aimed three feet higher, it would have punctured my leg… or maybe his tire.

I fly up. "I won't be long, Kev. Don't get shot. I'll be right back."

Coming behind the Mad Cow Ballista, the Orc Wizard rides his Motorcycle through the hole in the gates. Arrows and Spears fly at him, but if he's hit, it's not evident.

Kev speaks into a radio transceiver. "I've located her, Nigel, but I don't have her on the Bike. She's invisible, and my locator isn't precise. Enemies are in pursuit—an Orc Wizard, a Mad Cow Ballista, and an army of Arachnid Behemoths, number too great to estimate. She needs to talk to someone before she'll come with me. I'll report again shortly."

Nigel's voice crackles over a speaker. "Try not to let her die, Kevin. Get her to Minook as soon as possible."

"Megan?" Charli must have heard me. She and her friends head my way.

"Yes, it's me." I'm still shouting.

Crew in tow, the Angel draws close. "Whoever you are, show yourself. If you want to talk, you'll need to come with us. We have to warn the city."

A Pencil zips past, two feet behind me.

Kev shouts, his tone desperate. *"Megan."*

I'm not about to terminate my Hide skill. "Those Behemoths are here for me, not the city. Follow my voice, stay close, and I'll explain later." I fly towards Kev. "Who are your friends, Charli?"

The black-spotted, red-skinned blond speaks up. "I'm Slithy, a Frogkin Mentalist and Martial Artist. My Mom here is Kylie the Angel, a Spirit Warrior and Barbarian. The Lightning Wizard-Warrior here is my Dad, Morrow. His Psi-Warrior Tank Familiar is Rancor. Glad to make your acquaintance, Megan. Any friend of Charli's is a friend of ours. If she trusts you, so do we. Right, Mom?"

"Of course." The Angel doesn't sound too sure.

An adventuring family… sounds nice.

"Charli," I ask loudly, "are you able to contact Mithabel?"

The Cowgirl grimaces. "Lately, I can't. You?"

"No. My chat channels are completely messed up." I lower myself onto the Bike behind Kev as another giant Pencil strikes the dirt near his back tire. He revs the engine and takes off. A fireball splashes down where we'd been. "I can only talk on local chat at near proximity, so stay close, please, Charli."

Kev holds the radio transceiver to his mouth as he races across the bare dirt of the so-called Grass Bladed Field. "I have her, Nigel. Enemies remain in pursuit. We're headed for Minook, accompanied by an Angel female, a Frogkin female, a Punk male, a Woodpecker, and a Cowgirl. Megan knows them, so I'm operating under the assumption they're allies. Kevin out."

Nigel acknowledges and the line goes quiet.

Another huge Pencil launches from the Mad Cow Ballista.

I duck and yell. "*Swerve*, Kev."

He leans left, darting aside as the Pencil grazes my back. "*Again.*"

He leans further left. A fireball scorches the dirt to our right.

Kylie's voice booms. "*Stop.*"

Kev ignores her and so do our pursuers.

The Angel curses. "My Hypnotic Voice doesn't work on *any of them*?"

A silver beam of energy descends on the Mad Cow Ballista, emanating from Slithy's forehead. The Mad Cow ignores the attack and keeps coming, much to the voiced chagrin of the Frogkin.

Kylie points. "Everyone, look."

I can't look yet. "Veer to the left, Kev."

"What is it?" Kev asks as he evades another five-foot Pencil.

The Angel shakes her head. "There's another Behemoth army west of us, coming this way."

The Frogkin girl groans. "Is this Cow *mindless*?"

Charli calls over to me. "I didn't think you were getting out of prison until eight o'clock, Megan. How did you get out early?"

"Long story. *Incoming, Kev.* Pull right."

He leans into an evasive maneuver, averting another catastrophe. The Bike leaves the dirt of the Grass Bladed Field and plows into sand.

I expect the sand to drag at the bike's tires, like on Earth, but the bike doesn't slow. "Charli, is this a new territory?"

"Yup. We've entered the Dunes of Doom."

I equip my game map and wave it at the Cowgirl. "Take this, kid. We're going to Minook and need to follow the dotted line. It's a safe route…. *Incoming, Kev, pull left.*" I pause as we dodge another fireball. "Now slow down a hair."

"Not with the Ballista and Wizard breathing down our necks."

A Lightning bolt streaks down from the Punk Wizard in the sky and obliterates the Mad Cow. The Punk guffaws. He shouts at Kev. "Take a moment to slow down now, man, while the Orc is on cool down."

Kev slows, and the Angel brings her crew low over us. Charli reaches down, and I stuff the map into her grasping hand. Kev speeds up, skirting a dune. I assume hitting one would bring the bike to a stop. Now we have even more things to worry about avoiding.

"*Pull left, Kev.*"

He does. Another fireball explodes off to our right.

I shout to Charli over the Motorcycle roar. "The route is only safe for those traveling by land, not by air. It obviously doesn't protect against the invaders. But it should keep random mooks away from us."

Charli glances at the map, then at the land laying before us. "The safe route goes through the middle of the Arachnid army up ahead. Hang to the left of the dune in front of you and then head straight towards the sun."

Another fireball blasts the sand behind our back tire.

Kev shouts at me over his shoulder. "Tell your friends to deal with that damned Orc Wizard on our tail."

Morrow yells. "Why are the invaders after you, Megan? We thought they were after us."

I yell back. "That Orc Wizard attacked me on Earth and has been following me ever since. If you can deal with him, I'd appreciate it."

Slithy points at the Orc. "Drop me in front of him."

She's either very brave or very foolish....

"Come on, Mom. Drop me in front of him. I'll be okay."

I crane my neck to watch. Kylie stays high in the sky to give herself plenty of time to dodge should a fireball come her way. Staying ahead of the Orc Wizard, she dips low of a sudden. As she arcs back up, Slithy continues descending. She lands in a crouch twenty feet ahead of the Orc Wizard and his Motorcycle. A beam of silver energy springs from her forehead, and though the Orc tries to avoid it, the beam strikes him. Sadly, whatever it was meant to do, it doesn't work, because he's still coming.

He veers to avoid hitting the Frogkin, tossing a fireball her way. Slithy doesn't even try to dodge. The fireball hits her. No, it goes right through her. The Bike speeds by to one side of her.

She Jumps like a frog. She's apparently aiming for him, but goes wide. And yet, he's knocked off balance, and his Bike goes down on its side, sending up a plume of sand. Then she's pounding the ground with her fists, but the Orc's head is bouncing as though she were clobbering him. A Dagger appears in his hand, and he thrusts it up, where Slithy isn't, but where she would be if she were striking him.

The Dagger is knocked aside by some invisible force.

Slithy continues pounding the ground. She looks to be five feet away from the Orc, but his head continues to bob as though it's feeling the impact.

The Orc Wizard stabs upward with his weapon, but once again it is knocked aside.

Kylie whimpers. "I can't take this. He's going to hurt her."

A bolt of Lightning streaks down from Morrow, slamming into the Orc Wizard. The invader *pops*, his electrons scattering in the air.

"Are you okay, kiddo?"

"I'm fine, Dad. Not a scratch on me."

"Set me down, Kylie. You and Charli go ahead and give directions to Kev and Megan. Slithy and I will follow on the invader's Bike. Rancor, you're with me and Slithy."

"Oh, so only Charli and I can be attacked by random mooks now, is that it?" Despite the protest, Kylie puts Morrow on the ground next to the Orc's fallen Bike. Slithy jumps on behind him and Rancor perches on his shoulder. Morrow starts it up... and here they come, barely close enough for me to hear them.

Kev waves to get Charli's attention. "Are we still going straight west?"

"For a ways. In a mile or so, you'll turn right." Charli pauses before adding, "Just so everyone knows, the city of Minook—where we're headed—is located atop a spire. There are a few paths leading up the spire, but only one of them is safe, on the west side. If we try to fly to the city, there are guardians. I'm not sure what kind. That's all the info I can currently get with my Landmarks skill."

Kev slows enough for the others to catch up. Kylie and Charli stay in the air so Charli can determine our path, while the rest of us ride the Bikes through the dunes.

Do you remember?

I don't want to.

It was just you and Kev. On his Bike, just like now. Racing across the desert sands, just like you are now. What happened?

I *don't* want to remember.

It was after dark. Kev had the headlights on. The Mad Cow Ballista was after you. You evaded one missile and then another.

I said, I don't want to remember.

Come on. What happened next?

CHAPTER TWENTY-TWO

Megan Flashback: Bloodless

We're on the road to Fanciful Pegasus. Night has swallowed us, but our headlights illuminate asphalt.

A super-sized Pencil brushes my hair as it shoots by. "They're going to hit us. Turn off the headlights." They'll have a harder time hitting us if they can't see us.

Kev flips off the lights. He drives like he can still see, but I'm blind. He leans left again, and another missile plows the sand next to us. He comes to an abrupt stop. "Shit. Double shit." The bike bounces as it rides off the shoulder. "Arachnid Behemoths on the road ahead." The bike groans from the effort of moving over unpaved terrain.

"How many?" I don't like our chances trying to outrun our enemies on a bike in the sand. Not if they were keeping up with us when we were on the asphalt.

"Two."

A missile crashes into the bike. The motorcycle flips, throwing me onto the sand. I straighten my limbs. Nothing is broken. "*Kev?*"

He groans from nearby but says nothing.

I crawl to him as hooves clomp on the road behind us, drawing closer. "*Kev*? You okay?"

He doesn't even groan.

My fingers find him. There's no blood, so I hold onto hope. Groping, I find the projectile, thicker than a Spear, piercing his stomach just below the ribcage. The missile is shattered. "No, Kev, you can't die on me."

He pushes something at me, and I take it. My heart races with the hope he'll survive.

"Put them on. Save yourself." His hand falls limp on my leg.

"*Kev, no.*" I grab his wrist, seeking a pulse. I can't find one. "Kevin, you bastard, don't you leave me."

The spiders skitter on the road yards away.

He'd given me a pair of goggles. I drop them in place over my eyes. I see in the dark now, though everything is black and white.

My pretend boyfriend lies crumpled on the sand. I'd felt and now see two feet of a six-inch thick shattered Spear protruding from his abdomen. There's no sign of blood. It must be draining out beneath him, seeping into the sand… with that kind of injury, he's got to be bleeding.

The bike, HOWLER, lies silent on its side, its keys still in the ignition.

The two spiders stop a dozen feet away. Noisy hoof-clomping on the road behind me announces the arrival of the Mad Cow Ballista.

The sand between me and the spiders rises, dome shaped, to fall away as a figure with a masculine build rises out of the ground. He's cloaked and hooded, obscuring his facial features. "Megan Wright. My name is Seth. You are a hard one to kill. So I've decided to stop trying, on one condition. I ask you to join me. Will you consider it?"

"Whatever it is you want, there's no way I'll give it to you if this man dies." I climb to my feet and step back. "Have one of your spiders web him. It could keep him from bleeding out." I don't want to sound desperate, but I am.

"Why should I do that?" The hooded man called Seth glides over the sand without bending a knee, stopping five feet from me. "Of what value is his life to anyone?"

"He has knowledge about the game. Knowledge you don't have because it isn't on a computer anywhere." I have no reason to believe that's true, but I don't have much else to go with.

Seth laughs, a hollow sound. "Admit it, you love him."

"If that's what it takes for you to help him, I'll say it." I haven't said I loved any man in years. "I love him."

"You don't mean it."

I want to scream. "Please help him, dammit. I'll do anything you want, just help him while he still has blood in his body."

A spider scurries forward and throws a metallic web, wrapping Kev in a mass of chains.

Goddess, I hope it staunches his bleeding, though I still haven't seen any blood from him. "Thank you." I run over to the downed bike. Where's the radio transceiver Kev used earlier? There. I push the button and get static. "Nigel, are you there? This is Megan. If you can hear me, please bring Dr. Splat. Kev is hurt."

"You're being presumptuous." Seth glides across the sand to stand beside Kev. "What makes you think Dr. Splat can help your boyfriend?"

"Where are you?" Nigel's voice emits from a speaker. "Is it safe where you are?"

"Better tell him, *no*." Seth glides to me, reaching for the transceiver. "Let me speak to him."

I hand him the transceiver.

"Hello, Nigel. My name is Seth. Inform Dr. Splat his services are not needed. There is nothing he can do for the young man. And tell your boss, Franklin Freeman, that the contestant, Megan Wright, will not be making it to the competition."

Kev's lips tremble. "I love you, too, Megan. I'm sorry."

"You have nothing to be sorry about, Kev."

"Get ready to ride as fast as you can."

Seth hands the transceiver back to me. "Don't listen to him. You're going nowhere. You'll either pledge loyalty to me or die where you stand. Which will it be?"

Kev's body explodes. Millions of brilliant particles turn the night sky to daylight. Seth throws up an arm to shield his eyes, staggering back. Mad Cow Ballista moos frantically. The spiders reel.

Kev is gone, dammit.

I'm not blinded, my eyes protected by the goggles. He has sacrificed himself to save me, and I can't disappoint him. Pushing my grief deep into my gut, I right the bike and push it, my knees wobbly.

Seth stammers before crying out. *"Stop her."*

A Pencil whizzes past me. I continue to push the bike across the sand towards the road—towards the spiders, but not straight for them.

Their webs strike Seth instead of me. He flails against the chains. *"You fools!"*

I get the bike's wheels onto the pavement. Jumping on, I start it up and ride the hell out of there before their eyes can adjust.

"Get her!"

I speak into the radio transceiver. "Nigel, this is Megan. Kev is dead. I'm on the road, headed in the same direction Kev was taking me, which I assume is towards you. I've got four enemies behind me. I need your help to deal with them. Also, I don't know where I'm going."

"We're heading your way in the van. Keep driving the way you're headed until we meet you. Sorry about Kevin. He was a good man."

"But he wasn't a man, was he? He was a hologram, just like the invaders. Tell me it's not true."

"It's not true. The invaders aren't holograms. Neither is Kev. He's like you."

"What do you mean, *he's like me*?"

"He's from Destin, just like your father."

"Where the hell is Destin?" How convenient for Nigel that I can't ask my father, who died years ago.

"Go to the right around the dune straight ahead." Charli's voice draws me out of my flashback. "Get ready for the Behemoths."

"I see them." Kev seems remarkably capable for someone who supposedly died on the road to Fanciful Pegasus a few days ago.

It's good that you finally remembered. The true enemy is Seth.

I really need to stop talking to myself in second person.

Oh, that's rich. You think you're talking to yourself.

How else do I explain this back-and-forth conversation in my head?

Do you need an explanation? For now, you might want to pay attention to what lies before you.

Arachnid Behemoths fill the horizon—their only goal being my total destruction. I'm *so* special.

CHAPTER TWENTY-THREE

Morrow: Shadow Warrior

"How many XP did we get for those two kills?" I inquire of Renee as I race after Kev and Megan.

"I'm really sorry, darling, but you didn't get any."

"*Why not?*"

"The System doesn't recognize the Mad Cow Ballista or Orc Wizard as mooks, Bosses, NPCs, or PCs. So there's no award for killing them."

This doesn't sit right with me. "Slithy, can you ask ODYSSEY to modify the Khertaan program to recognize those things we just killed as mooks? Do the same thing for the Arachnid Behemoths, too, in case we end up killing some of them. I'm thinking since these things are immune to your Mom's Hypnotic Voice and your Mind Spear, they ought to be worth more XP than your typical mooks, like maybe 10K each at least, and way more for one of those Behemoths."

"Yeah, I noticed we didn't get any XP for those kills. I'm with you—we deserved some. Let me see what I can persuade ODYSSEY to do for us."

Okay, so I'm thinking 10K minimum for the cow, twice that for the Bike-riding Wizard, and… I don't know… 500K each for the Arachnid Behemoths.

We're sandwiched between two armies of those giant metallic spiders. I can't imagine how we'll defeat even one of those things, if they're immune to Kylie's Hypnotic Voice and Slithy's Mind Spear. How many HP will one of those things have, and how much armor? They're likely worse than any Boss in the game. How many XP is the worst Boss in the game worth? That should be a guideline for establishing the XP value for a Behemoth.

Slithy taps my shoulder. "It's done. I pushed for as many XP as I could."

Renee lays across the handlebars. The wind ruffles her hair and miniskirt. "Congrats, my darling Punk. You've earned 40K XP for the defeat of the Mad Cow Ballista and 60K XP for the death of the Orc Wizard, for a total of 100K XP."

"Good job, kiddo."

Kylie echoes me. "Proud of you, Slithy."

My daughter squeezes me around the waist. "Thanks, Mom and Dad."

I can't imagine Nick being on such an adventure as this with his family when married to Jean in his original timeline. His kid Mel might have been down with it, but Jean? No way. Something like this would have been akin to Satan worship for her. Kylie seems to be getting into it, and Slithy definitely is. Even with the fate of the world hanging in the balance, doing this together is like the family vacation Nick never had. Yes, it's scary to think any of us could die, but we can respawn, even if only a limited number of times. Moreover, we're avatars in Khertaan, but we have associated Earth bodies. While I'm kicking it with the family in Khertaan, Nick is lying unconscious in his computer lab on Earth, waiting for me to either die or reach level thirty.

On both Earth and Khertaan, I love being husband to the super-intelligent, hottest woman on the planet and being father to the smartest girl, who's also a beautiful woman, a gamer, and a time traveler. Throw in a powerhouse Woodpecker for a Familiar, and I'm the luckiest man alive. "I love you both so much. You're a cool pet, too, Rancor. And you're the best Guide ever, Charli. I just want you all to know that." I make sure to only talk on party chat, so Megan and her friend Kev won't hear and feel slighted. But, hey, I don't really know them.

Kylie flashes a smile my way. "Your green mohawk is growing on me."

Rancor rubs his head against my neck. "Ha ha."

Slithy squeezes me harder. "I love you all, too."

Charli wipes a tear. "I don't know what to say. You've all made me feel more like family in just a short time than MAD ever did. Granted, I joined MAD less than three days ago. But in all my lives, I've never felt as close to anyone as I feel to you all now."

Slithy sniffles. "You can be my sister. I've always wished I wasn't an only child."

"Are you sure?" Charli's voice quavers.

"I'd love to have another daughter." Kylie strokes one of Charli's pigtails.

I'm getting emotional, myself. "Me, too. Welcome to the family, Charli."

"Ha ha." Rancor lightly pecks my neck. "Can I be part of the family, too?"

Slithy pats his head. "But Rancor, you're already part of the family. You're the family pet."

"Ha ha. Nice."

Kevin shouts. *"Which way, Charli?"* He's headed straight for an Arachnid Behemoth. We're almost in range of their webs. Will the route on Megan's map protect us against their attacks? A minute ago, they weren't recognized by the System as mooks, but now they are. Does that mean the System will block their perception of us, provided we stay on the safe path?

Charli refers to the map. "The path goes straight ahead. Unless you want to leave it, you'll need to go directly under the Behemoth in front of you."

I've got additional concerns. "Kylie, be sure to fly *really* high. You and Charli aren't protected, and we can't be sure how far those webs can reach."

Slithy digs her chin in my back. "I want to fight one of those Behemoths so bad."

"*No,*" both Kylie and I say at the same time.

"After we get past them, I want to shoot one with my Mind Spear, just to verify whether it works."

She does have a point. "Once we're past them… I suppose it won't hurt to try. You could try your Voice on them, too, Kylie. Just so we know. I'm sure this won't be the last we see of them."

Kev and Megan ride into the shadow of a Behemoth. The giant metal spider hesitates. The whole line of them stops moving. A web fires from the spider directly ahead. Kev and Megan duck as the webbing flies over their heads and strikes the ground behind them.

I veer to avoid the webbing.

Charli's shout is panicked. "Morrow, *you're off the path.*"

Shit. But does it matter? Kev and Megan were attacked, so the safe route didn't protect them from the spiders.

Metallic webs from either side shoot towards us. I gun the Motorcycle, but it's not enough. The webs hit us, and the Bike stops dead. Slithy and I are wrapped up in them, our momentum pressing our flesh against the metal strands.

"*Stop.*" Kylie tries using her Hypnotic Voice. I hope it works.

"Listen, Dad. I'm stashing the Bike and teleporting out. Then you're going to teleport out."

"Ha ha." Being small enough, my Woodpecker Familiar wriggles his way out.

The Bike is crushing my right leg. It's abruptly gone, stashed in my daughter's inventory. "I can't teleport."

She squeezes my hand. "You will. You'll see."

The Behemoths are still moving. "Your mother's Voice didn't work on them."

I spot Kylie overhead. "We're coming to help."

"No, Mom. We'll be okay. Keep Charli and yourself out of web range."

Still far above us, Kylie hovers, her Spirit Blade in one hand and Charli gripped in the other.

Slithy leaves—one moment there and the next not.

Renee sits on the sand in front of my face. "Your daughter requests a head hop."

"A *what?*"

"Just accept it, Dad."

"I accept."

A mental image of Slithy appears in my brain space. "I'm lending you my Teleport Self skill, Dad. Take it, and let me have momentary control of your mind and body."

"Sure, just get me out of here."

A Behemoth towers over me, raising a leg, the end of it sharp as a spike. It descends, fast, aiming for my head.

In the next moment, the leg vanishes. I'm free of the webs—and standing in shadow. I look up... and wish I hadn't. *I'm directly under the thorax of a Behemoth.* Slithy's prone form lies at my feet.

Rancor sits on her motionless arm. "Ha ha, glad you got away, Morrow." He flies up to take his regular perch on my shoulder.

Slithy's mental image leaves my brain space. Her prone form stirs, and she jumps to her feet. "We're on the safe path here. Maybe it won't protect us, but the spider we're under can't see us, so I want to try and bring it down. How much Auni do you have left, Dad?"

I'm not processing what she's saying, but answer her question. "It's fully restored now."

"Good. Charli will head hop to you, just like I did. Let her in. She has a spell that we think can take down these Behemoths, and she needs to be in the head of someone who has the Auni to cast it. That's you. Are you with me on this?"

"Do I have a choice?"

"Not really."

Renee pops her head into my field of vision. "Charli requests a head hop to you, darling. Do you accept?"

"I do."

"And do you take me as your lawful wedded support AI?"

"Sure, Renee. Why not?"

"Oh, you're making me blush."

A mental incarnation of Charli appears in my head. "Hi, Morrow. I'm lending you my Shadow Warrior spell and Shadow Passage skill. You'll only have them while I'm in your head. Do you accept?"

"Yes, ma'am."

"Great. Cast Shadow Warrior first, with all the Auni you can spare. Invoke Shadow Passage right after."

New knowledge enters my brain, as though I learned it long ago but am only now remembering it. I have the spell, Shadow Warrior, and the skill, Shadow Passage. I cast Shadow Warrior, throwing 60 of my 76 Auni into it.

A silhouette appears before me, sporting a black mohawk. He brandishes a black blade, crafted of shadow. Silently, he rushes at the nearest Behemoth leg, swinging his weapon. The blade connects, amputating the lower quarter of the Behemoth's limb.

"Behemoth is at 94% HP," says Renee. "Damage to monster is limited by attack location."

"Grab Slithy's hand and do the Shadow Passage skill," Charli urges me.

I do as I'm told.

The Shadow Warrior runs for another of the spider's legs.

"Take us up, Dad. I want to see if I can attack it."

I find I can fly within the spider's shadow.

As we rise, a silvery energy beam shoots from Slithy's shadowy head, striking the underside of the Behemoth. "Drats, my Mind Spear doesn't affect any of the invaders."

We come within striking range, and Slithy strikes the chitinous underbelly with her Bare Hands.

Renee bats her eyelashes. "That's a shame. Negligible damage was dealt by your daughter's attack, despite her ability to Ignore Armor when attacking with her Bare Hands."

"Ha ha, let me help."

Both Slithy and Rancor slip free of my hold, their shadow forms returning to their normal physical bodies. Slithy levitates next to the Behemoth's underside while Rancor flies up beside her to join the attack.

Hell, I might as well get in on this, too. I summon my Lightning Blade.

Rancor drives a Beak against the metallic skin of the Behemoth. A clang echoes beneath the monster.

Renee sighs. "No damage dealt by poor little Rancor's attack."

As the Shadow Warrior continues to slice and dice Behemoth legs, Slithy tries her Mind Spear and Bare Hands attacks again, thinking they might be more effective when she's not in shadow form. Renee tells me they're not.

The Behemoth reaches beneath itself in an attempt to spear Slithy. Not if I can help it. I'm not close enough to attack with my Blade, so I fire a Lightning Strike spell with all my remaining Auni.

"Your enemy's overall HP has fallen to 90%, darling. Front leg HP is at 44%."

My missile wasn't enough to destroy the leg, but enough to give the spider pause.

The Shadow Warrior amputates a leg, and the Behemoth slumps on that side, two of its legs shortened.

My Frogkin daughter bangs her fist against the enemy again. "*Ow*. I'm done. My Bare Hands don't sufficiently Ignore Armor at my level."

After a second futile attempt, Rancor declares he's giving up, too.

I discover my Lightning Blade does next to nothing against the Behemoth, as well. Our most effective weapon is the Shadow Warrior. I grab Slithy and Rancor and pull them back into the shadow realm. Then I switch to Third Person POV to watch the Shadow Warrior at work.

With the spider down on one side, its underside is within reach of the Shadow Warrior's blade, who just keeps hacking away. The spider stabs at the Shadow Warrior, and this time the sharpened end of the leg is on target. Yet, it goes right through the Shadow Warrior's torso, not fazing him in the slightest. That's convenient.

Kev shouts from where he's waiting with Megan. "Where do we go, Charli? I can't evade these things forever."

"One more minute." Charli is on a private chat channel with Kevin, but their conversation isn't hidden from me while she's in my head.

"We might be dead in a minute."

It takes only another thirty-some seconds. Four more strikes from the Shadow Warrior's black blade... and the Behemoth is defeated.

A small sun erupts into existence where the Behemoth had once stood, shedding brilliance for miles.

The sudden light rips us out of the shadow domain, shoving us back into our physical bodies. The heat melts the skin from my bones and then consumes the bones. My Third Person POV shuts down and all goes black.

CHAPTER TWENTY-FOUR

Ogaltha: Dance With Us

Had Megan Wright taken damage? Ogaltha had no other explanation for the sudden onset of pain.

Shit. She couldn't even *think* her right name. *Ogaltha* was the *wrong* one.

As much as the two of them needed to conserve the number of respawns they had remaining, Ogaltha held out hope that Megan would die and release Ogaltha from this unholy condition she found herself in.

Since Ogaltha still lived, that had to mean Megan did too. But something had happened to her. "Megan, can you hear me? Kaleisha? Dylan? Charli? *Anyone?*"

No one answered her.

But she could hear voices… from the other side of the door….

Niav squealed in protest. "I can't dig through the floor, the door, or the wall. I don't think we're getting back in there."

"*You have to.* We're going nowhere until Ogaltha is back with us."

Hearing Dylan speak her wrong name drove a stake through Ogaltha's heart.

Niav quieted. "Shh. Someone's coming—from the same way we came. It's not Lizardmen... might be another party. There, see their torches. What do we do?"

Amarynth grumbled. "There's nowhere to hide. I guess we fight them."

"Let's not. Maybe they can find the door and get Ogaltha out."

Ogaltha agreed with Dylan.

Ullullu twirled on the dungeon floor. "Dance with me, Ogaltha."

The young Orc Tank waved the dancer away. "Can't you see I'm trying to listen?" She pressed her ear tighter against the door, as though the act might improve her ability to hear her friends.

"Well, well." The masculine voice from beyond the door was an unfamiliar one. "You're MAD, aren't you?" He chuckled at his own pun, as though no one else had ever thought of it. "Isn't Ogaltha in your party? Where is she? Did the Guards take her already?"

"Hello. Yes, we're party MAD. I'm Dylan, Priestess to Scintilla, the Sun Goddess. This is Amarynth, our Archer, and Rolag, her Dragon Companion. The Angel here is our hired help, Zyekt, and the little lady on his shoulder is our Guide Mouse, Niav. May I ask who you are?"

"Oh, forgive my manners. My name is ZAngel. We're party ZAvengers. My kindred goes without saying. This is TehnKhar, an Elitist, which is more terrible than it sounds. He might as well be called a Narcissist, ha. This is TorEye, the Robot member of our party. And, last but definitely not least—nor will she let you forget it—is VeraCity, our resident Flame Demoness. Yeah, I know—an Angel and a Demoness in the same party. But we get along very well. So... the Guards already got Ogaltha, it appears."

"What are you talking about?" Amarynth asked.

ZAngel chuckled. "Your absent party member—Ogaltha. Come on. She's number one on the Top Individual Players list, and MAD is number one on the Top Parties list. She's gotta be in your party, but she's not here. So I assume the Guards collected her already. Or she's invisible."

That wasn't an answer. Ogaltha imagined Dylan's beautifully sincere face as she pressed for one. "No, seriously, *what are you talking about?*"

"You don't know? There was a System announcement. Ogaltha is a wanted person. There's an XP award to anyone who gives Guard Leader Howard information he can use to find and apprehend her. Something about her being an illegal avatar and needing to be expelled from Khertaan. It's too bad, really. But, hey, her expulsion should put me number one on the Top Individuals list.

"So... no Ogaltha here. We would have appreciated earning XP from this chance encounter between our parties. I suppose we still could. You might not be too difficult to kill without her to help. I'd wager I'm better with Hypnotic Voice than your NPC Angel here, and the fight would be over before it began. Shall we test my theory? Whoever wins will get a boatload of XP for killing the other party."

Dylan huffed. "Let's not fight. Let's see if your party can get past that dead end wall. Ogaltha found a door and went through. Then the door closed and we can't get it open again. If you can, then you'll get to collect XP for finding her."

"Tell me the truth." ZAngel spoke in a lower register.

The Polynesian Priestess made no reply for a moment— probably gritting her teeth at the Angel's attempt to hypnotize her. "I *am* telling you the truth. She's inside that room, and we can't get her out."

"Then stand aside and let the pros do the work."

Yes, Ogaltha thought. Let the ZAvengers get the hell in here and kill me.

It was disconcerting that the City Guards had put a bounty on her. They must have already evaluated Megan, ahead of schedule, determined her to be an illegal avatar, and taken it upon themselves to oust her legal avatar, too. But Megan wasn't dead yet—not if Ogaltha was alive. It was doubtful she'd been expelled from Khertaan—it seemed that would have expelled Ogaltha, too.

The Elf Tank turned Orc child mentally reached out again for Megan, for Dylan—hell, she even tried to start a private chat with ZAngel—but her communications with anyone outside this cursed room were severed.

A tapping repeatedly sounded on the door.

"Found it." The new voice was feminine and husky. "There's a lever inside, standing straight up. Looks like it can go either left or right. Which way do I push it?"

"To the right." That was Zyekt. He would know.

"You wouldn't lie to a lady, would you?"

"No. Push it to the right, VeraCity."

"Pushing to the right."

The door swung open and light spilled into the room. Ogaltha jumped back to avoid being hit.

In the open doorway stood a winged woman with burnt red skin. Charcoal black hair flowed over her shoulders. VeraCity, obviously. Having a lean form, she stood more than a foot taller than Ogaltha's childish form, close to Dylan's height. Her bat wings, though currently folded, looked sufficiently large to span ten feet.

Behind VeraCity stood a pale winged man, his shoulder-length hair pure white in the light of the torch he carried. Not overweight, but heavyset and muscular, he stood half a foot taller than the woman, with a wingspan similar to hers. That must be ZAngel.

To the Angel's right stood a bald man with metallic silver skin and pure black eyes. Fit and trim, he stood taller than VeraCity and shorter than ZAngel. Obviously this was the Robot member of party ZAvengers—TorEye.

That meant the fourth member of ZAvengers, who stood to the Angel's left, was TehnKhar, a man with olive skin and trimmed black hair. The second tallest member of the group, he also appeared to be second heaviest. A sneer seemed a permanent fixture on his face. Ogaltha found herself simultaneously disliking him and in awe of him. She fought the urge to kneel before him as she might do if he were a monarch, disgusted at the very idea.

Regaining her wits, Ogaltha threw her arms wide. "Here I am. Shoot me. Kill me."

"Oh, how cute." VeraCity eyed the small Tank. "The little Orc girl wants a hug. Give her a hug, TorEye."

The Robot stepped forward.

"Stop." Okguul, the Orc adult woman, held up a hand as she strode towards the door. "You mustn't come in, Robot. There's a curse on this place. If you come inside, you can't leave without the Ring. You can't take the Ring without opening the Chest. The Chest won't open unless you kill one of the children. You appear to have Morals and a Conscience, and aren't one to kill a child. So, I beg of you, turn around and leave us be."

It was the same wretchedly incomplete warning Okguul had given to Rolag when he'd started to enter the room. But would her warning be heeded?

Dylan pushed past the Robot, stopping shy of entering the room. "Orc woman, I am Dylan, Priestess of Scintilla, Goddess of the Sun. My friend Ogaltha entered this room. I believe you are holding her captive, and I ask that you return her to us. As you may recall, our Archer killed one of your children, as disturbing as it may be. You told us a child had to die for anyone who enters to leave. We fulfilled that unpleasant requirement, and I ask that you release to me my dearest friend in all the world, that she may return to the competition."

Ogaltha couldn't simply barge out—she'd tried and been shocked for her efforts. She hopped in place while pointing at herself. "Dylan, it's me. Tell ZAngel to kill me."

As though he understood, the Angel cleared his throat. "Allow me." The Robot stepped back, and the Angel took his place. "Come here, Orc woman." He beckoned.

She walked towards him. "I beg you not to enter this place." She stood next to Ogaltha, facing down the Angel. "Please back away and let us close the door."

"No." Dylan stuck a foot in the doorway, enough to block it from shutting. "Not until Ogaltha is back with us." She turned to ZAngel. "Don't go in or let any of your people go. They won't come out, even if you kill one of the children."

The Angel leaned forward and stared into the Orc woman's eyes. "Tell me your name."

"I am Okguul, Watcher of the Children."

"Tell me, Okguul, is Ogaltha in there with you?"

"She is."

The Tank pointed both her index fingers at herself as she repeatedly jumped in place. "It's *me*. I'm Ogaltha." But no one paid her any attention.

"Where is she?"

"I told you. She's in the room."

"*Where* in the room?"

Okguul shook her head. "I cannot help it if you cannot see her."

Dylan scanned the room. "Ogaltha has the Hide skill. Makes it more difficult to see her, but not impossible."

ZAngel rubbed his hands together. His voice dropped into its lower register. "Ogaltha, make yourself visible."

His soothing baritone voice coaxed Ogaltha to obey— except... she wasn't invisible. She wasn't using her Hide skill. They didn't see her because she inhabited a form they didn't expect of her. Looking directly at her, they saw an Orc child, and dismissed her as unimportant.

She waved her arms with as much energy as she could draw from her small Orc girl form.

A voice spoke inside the Tank's head. "We are Ogaltha. We are Orc. We are children. We belong in this room, not outside it. Do not struggle against your fate. Celebrate your belonging with us. Dance with us. *Dance with Ullullu*. She is your friend." The inner voice overwhelmed that of ZAngel. Against her will, the young Orc Tank turned the waving of her arms into a dance move.

She wanted to cry. "*No*. I'm not Ogaltha."

"We *are* Ogaltha."

ZAngel spoke again, but his words were muffled, unintelligible.

Ogaltha willed for her magical Battle Axe to come to hand, but it would not. She tried to equip her Self Bow, but it also refused. She tried to draw her Rope out of inventory, but it did not materialize. All she had to work with besides her childish Orc body were the rags covering her, her Bracelet of Action, and the two Rings on her fingers—Ogaltha's and Ezmerelda's.

She tugged at the jewelry, and they refused to come off. Fine. She grabbed the ragged top covering her childish torso, and lifted it free of her shoulders, baring her undeveloped breasts. Wadding the ragged garment into a ball, she threw it at Dylan.

The Priestess batted the rag aside, glaring at Ogaltha. This was the little Orc Tank's only chance to be seen. She held up the hand bearing Ogaltha's Ring and pointed at it. "Ogaltha." The word passed her lips without resistance. She spoke it again. "Ogaltha." She pointed at Ezmerelda's Ring and the Bracelet. Then she pointed back at Ogaltha's Ring and then at her head. If anyone could understand, Dylan would.

Comprehension lit Dylan's eyes and she raised her hands for casting a spell. "In the name of Scintilla, Goddess of the Sun, of Light, Mentors, Gold, and Growth, I hereby *Excise* the spirit possessing my friend. Ye spirit by name of Ogaltha, I command you through the power of Light to leave the body you occupy and return to the Ring upon her hand, its Metal to be your prison. Through the power of Scintilla, I command you, Ogaltha, to transform back to the Elf you are, and to come to me."

Okguul and the Orc children cried out as one. "*No.*"

The Orc woman continued. "You cannot have her. Not this way. You must kill her to free her. It is the Law."

The Flame Demoness pointed at Ogaltha. "I'm happy to oblige." A missile of flame sprang from her finger, striking the young Orc Tank in the middle of her naked chest.

Ogaltha screamed as she was forced back into her magical prison—the Ring upon her hand. Her Orc child's body exploded into shimmering particles.

In the same instant, a tremendous heat enveloped Mithabel, and a miniature sun blinded her. Then the void took her, and everything was nothing.

CHAPTER TWENTY-FIVE

Megan: Fairest in the Land

You died.

I know, dammit.

I'm lying in bed, wearing my black Bikini, Ezmerelda's Ring, and my Bracelet of Action. The bedroom is the same one where I started out in Khertaan. My dying caused Mithabel to die, too.

Do you know that for certain?

It's my understanding that when one of us dies, the other dies, too.

What if you both died of separate causes in the exact same moment?

That seems a stretch, but I suppose it's possible. I don't see why it matters. We're both dead. I wish I could talk with her. I wish I could talk with *anyone* I know.

Maybe you can. You should try.

I jump out of bed. The mirror and pocket watch lie on the floor near the wall, where I threw them during a tantrum last time I was awake. Other items lie on the floor where I swept them off the end table.

I put everything back in place except the mirror and the wand for controlling the crystal ball. Maybe I can talk to Ezmerelda again and get more info from her. But first, I look into the reflective device, hoping it will work like before. "Mirror, mirror, in my hand, who's the fairest in the land?"

An image of Dylan appears in the glass. She gasps, briefly covering her mouth. "Megan? Oh, Goddess, is that really you? Did you die? Is Mithabel okay?"

"Dylan, are you a sight for sore eyes. I'm *so glad* I reached you. I've not been able to freely communicate with *anyone* until now, and it's been driving me out of my freaking mind. Sorry if Mithabel's absence is putting you in a bind on your quest. I'll go to sleep shortly, which I *hope* will allow both Mithabel and me to respawn. But there's something I need to tell you...."

The Priestess nods, waiting for me to continue.

I take a deep breath. "I was evaluated for legal status ahead of schedule. They said I was illegal and that both me and Mithabel had to be expelled from Khertaan. They turned off all my communication channels so I couldn't ask you for help. I could only talk on local chat with limited range. It's been *unbearable*. Then there was this Executioner with a bad ass Axe trying to behead me. He didn't, thank the Goddess. That's *not* how I died. Mithabel had skills I didn't know about but accidentally triggered, and they saved my ass.

"But I digress... Charli showed up and said she was blocked from talking with you, too. She was with another party. They were being chased by metal spiders larger than houses — Arachnid Behemoths. Actually, turns out they were after me.... Anyway, I was fleeing on a Motorcycle with Kev — you don't know him, but he saved me on Earth before... a story for some other time — and then the spiders closed in on us from both sides.

I gave Charli my map of safe routes, and she was directing us to the city of Minook, but then Slithy and Morrow—two of Charli's new friends—decided they wanted to try killing one of the Behemoths. They succeeded... unfortunately. When it died, it exploded... like Khertaan mooks normally do... but this one released a *ton* of heat. *That's* what killed me. So... if you see any giant metal spiders, be careful if you go to kill them, and stay far back, like over a hundred yards.

"One more thing... you should go to Ye Olde Shoppe of the Profane and get one of the safe route maps. Tell the shopkeeper you're in Mithabel's party and he might give you one for free... maybe other equipment, too. I'm sorry if I'm rambling. It's been really difficult not being with you and Mithabel. How are you doing?"

Dylan tosses her hands. "I'm beside myself, Megan. Unexplained XP keep piling on us. First it was a couple hundred thousand and then a few thousand more. When Mithabel died, a *million* XP dumped on us, for no apparent good reason. I'm a level 15 Priestess, level 6 Shuriken Specialist. It's crazy. We have a couple of hired NPCs in the party, and they're level 15 now, too. They are out of their minds with excitement. We're not telling ZAvengers about our gains. ZAngel thinks he's hot stuff and thinks he's better than our hired Angel, but even though Zyekt isn't even as tall as Charli, he could easily put ZAngel down in a fight. Our hired Guide, Niav, is Zyekt's pet Mouse, and she could probably even take ZAngel in a fight. Did *you* get the million XP?"

I shrug. "I wouldn't know. I can't see Mithabel's character sheet *or* talk to her support AI. If she gained levels, I can only guess what her new abilities are. How far are you in Ezmerelda's quest?"

193

"Mithabel got the Ring from the Ogaltha chest. It turned her into an Orc child who couldn't leave the room until she was killed. One of the ZAvengers—a Flame Demoness called VeraCity—killed her, or so we thought. You say you died, too, so I'm wondering whether you or Mithabel died first. Either way, we have assurances Mithabel has been freed from the curse. So we'll be leaving the dungeon soon, and we're hoping Mithabel will respawn before we reach the exit. Will you be sleeping soon?"

"Yeah, but I want to see if I can learn anything new from the crystal ball here first."

Dylan nods. "We helped ZAvengers with Ezmerelda's quest. Their Robot went in to open the chest and get the Ring. He turned into an Orc child, and Amarynth shot him. Now we're waiting to see if he respawns. If you want to hold this channel open for a bit, I'll let you know if he does."

"I'd appreciate that."

"Oh… he's back already. Good. Can't wait to see Mithabel back with us. Um… we're going to work with ZAvengers to get out of the dungeon, and everyone is ready to go. Call me again if you learn anything new."

"Will do."

Dylan's face fades from the glass, and I'm looking at my own reflection, cast red by the light filtering through the overhead curtain.

There's something else I'm dying to try. "Show me Mom."

There's no response.

I try it another way. "Mirror, mirror, on my palm, where in the world is my mom?"

The glass frosts over. I get it. It won't work to contact anyone not involved with Khertaan. I place the mirror on the table.

Before turning on the crystal ball, I check the closet where I found all my equipment last time. There's the Faerie Wing and its Harness. There's Ghost Maker, my newly acquired magical Battle Axe. There's another Battle Axe—like the one I had before I acquired Ghost Maker—but looking far sharper than I remember. Its edge is practically glowing.

What else? Two Bows. Two pairs of high-heeled Platform Slippers. A suit of Leather Armor. A duplicate of Ezmerelda's Ring, exactly like the one I'm wearing. Another Ring with a thinner band—the Ogaltha Ring. After hearing what Dylan said about that Ring, I'm not putting it on—no way. I don't relish the idea of becoming an Orc child. I touch it lightly and stash it immediately, before it can slip onto my finger.

I'll leave some items behind this time. The Leather Armor isn't needed. I only want one pair of Slippers and one Bow. I pile everything I want onto the bed. I take both Ezmerelda Rings—the one I'm wearing and the duplicate. Maybe someone in the party can take advantage of the duplicate.

Testing the exit door, I find it still locked. I bet it will unlock when I reach level 30 in Khertaan.

I should be hungry or thirsty, but I'm not. Has so little time passed on Earth? For that matter, *am I on Earth*? I'm so freaking confused.

Are you going to turn on the crystal ball?

Yes. I tap the ball with the wand.

The crystal interior lights up with 3D images. A man not wearing a shirt kneels before a brunette woman. Dressed in black leather and holding a cat of nine tails, she silently rears back to strike him. I don't want to watch, so I wave the wand, and the scene changes.

Waves break and wash onto a sandy beach. Wind whistles. Gulls cry as they soar above the beach. Footprints in the sand are gradually erased by the waves.

A metal Spear so tall as to extend off the top of the scene jabs into one of the footprints. Blood spills from some unseen victim. The waves wipe away the blood stains. Ugh. Wave the wand again.

Screaming gray-skinned people—too disproportionately thin to be human—flee before ravaging Arachnid Behemoths. Bulbous buildings of wood, clay, and plaster collapse under the crushing blows of giant, metallic spider legs. Sharpened limbs skewer robe-wearing residents, pulling them from their abodes and flinging them off-scene.

A hooded masculine figure glides rather than walks into view. His face is hidden by his dark hood. He isn't fat, but fills out his full-length brown cloak enough to prove he's not skinny like the others.

The view centers on his shaded face. "Look upon the means of your destruction. The multiverse will be destroyed. Every member of every sentient race on every planet in every timeline will die. Even I, Seth the Destroyer, will die by my own hand after all else is destroyed. All who can hear me, prepare for your end. My armies will find you, and they will infiltrate and destroy your worlds and shelters. You may attempt to hide in dimensional pockets, far flung timelines, or game worlds, but you cannot hide, and you cannot destroy me before my time. The only method at your disposal to avoid destruction at my hand is to destroy yourselves before I find you. You have been informed." The hooded figure glides off-screen.

Holy crap.

This battle I'm in is bigger than I thought. It's not just Earth at stake. It's the whole freaking universe. No, it's even bigger than that. Seth mentioned a multiverse and timelines, dimensional pockets, and game worlds. He called himself the Destroyer, and that's what he intends to do, destroy it all, down to the last living sentient thing, including himself. How can someone like that be reasoned with? They can't. Our only hope is to stop him, and he claims that isn't possible until he's done destroying us.

No, he said we can't destroy him before his time. We need to avoid dying until his time comes, whenever that is.

He could be lying… or exaggerating….

I keep waving the wand, changing channels, looking for Ezmerelda. Dammit, she's not showing up. Come on, bitch, show your face. Dammit.

Maybe you should respawn in Khertaan. You need to reach level 30, pronto, and you're at best only half way there. The next 15 levels are going to be hell, especially if between you and Mithabel you only have 5 respawns left. You might even be down to 4, if both of you dying caused her Constitution score to drop by 2. If that's the case, you can only die twice more, and then you're both out of Khertaan forever.

I know. *Fuck.* I turn off the crystal ball, toss the wand on the end table, and get in the damn bed.

But how can I sleep now?

CHAPTER TWENTY-SIX

Megan: Gondra

I *can't* sleep.

I get out of bed, go to the exit door, and try it. I know it won't open, and it doesn't. I fetch my Ghost Maker Battle Axe from the bed and take a swing at the door. Damn. It goes right through the door… as I knew it would. How is my weapon substantial in my hands or when I lay it on the floor or bed, but not when I try to hit something with it? That's messed up.

I'm messed up.

I throw the Axe on the bed. It lies there, taunting me.

Do some push ups. Do some sit ups. Do some jumping jacks. Dammit. Still not tired.

What is wrong with you?

I don't know. I'm not tired, hungry, or thirsty.

How long have you been in this room?

It feels like days. The pocket watch still reads three o'clock. Is time seriously not moving? Then how am *I* moving?

I turn on the crystal ball again with a tap of the wand. A female human reporter talks with a random human male on a busy sidewalk. "How are you preparing for the alien invasion, sir?"

The interviewee gives the reporter a dismissive wave. "There's no invasion. It's all a hoax. The government wants us to be afraid so they can appropriate more money to the military. You can't believe everything you see on TV or read on the internet."

The reporter shakes her head. "I've seen what these things can do personally. I can tell you it's not a hoax. The invaders are on this planet. It's only a matter of time before they'll be here. You need to prepare."

"Bah." The man walks away. He turns back to face the reporter. "You should be ashamed of yourself, spreading lies. Get a real life, and stop your scaremongering."

"I've seen people killed by these things, sir. You need to take this seriously."

"*Get a life.*" This time, he doesn't look back.

An Arachnid Behemoth leg comes down into the scene. People scream and scatter. The reporter runs towards the camera. "Get in the truck, Ed."

As the cameraman backs away, he catches the last interviewed man in frame. The man continues to walk calmly away, oblivious to the Behemoth behind him. The giant spider stabs a fleeing woman, cutting her scream short. This doesn't faze the man walking away, who doesn't turn around to see what the commotion is about. He gets into a car and slowly drives away, as chaos ensues behind him.

"*Get in the truck, Ed.*"

The cameraman does as he's told, his camera still capturing the slaughter as the reporter drives. Then he points his camera off to the side. A line of Behemoths stretches to the horizon. The reporter turns onto a road leading towards the Behemoths.

I can't watch this. Change the channel.

"Ezmerelda, please talk to me." I wave the wand to go to the next channel, and then wave it again. "Ezmerelda. *Please.*"

I wave the wand again. A man in a hooded cloak comes into view. His stance is different than Seth's, and he's a bit taller. As with Seth, this fellow's face is masked in shadow. He speaks. "Megan Wright?"

"You're not Ezmerelda."

"No." He pulls his hood back, revealing a face covered in scales and having slits for nostrils, like a mix between a reptile and a human. "I am Gondra. I want to help you. The invaders know you're special and want you dead, along with everyone else training in Khertaan. If they find you on Earth before you finish training, your Earth is lost, among other worlds. Seth and his armies have already destroyed many planets across many timelines, including some alternate Earths. It's my goal to stop him from destroying yours and to save as many others as possible. You must go back into Khertaan immediately and continue your training."

"Hello, Mr. Gondra, sir. I hear you, but you look a lot like this Seth fellow who says he's destroying everything. And I don't feel like I'm training at all in the game. I mean, I'm gaining XP for things I had no part in. How is that training?"

"Seth and I can take many forms, not always of our own choosing. It is unfortunate you find it confusing. As for your training, it's not training in the sense you think. You're absorbing energy of the type needed to transform yourself and your weapons to be the most effective against the invaders. The XP you earn reflects the amount of energy you absorb. It doesn't matter *how* you get it, it only matters that you do.

"Being in Khertaan is the mechanism by which the energy is transferred to you. It's practically a fluke that this mechanism exists at all, and there's nothing I can do directly to change how it works. Nick and Kendra McKenzie discovered how to access the mechanism and exploit it, but even they do not fully understand what Khertaan is. Someone—I'm not sure who—has found a way to exploit the mechanism to the degree you're seeing, allowing you to earn XP through the exploits of others. Be glad for it. It will help you reach level 30 quickly with a lower risk of losing all your lives.

"So… please… return to Khertaan while you can. Your Earth, your universe, and what remains of the rest of existence needs you."

I shake my head. "Yeah, well, all this responsibility laid on my shoulders is keeping me awake. What you're saying doesn't help."

Gondra closes his eyes and pulls his hood back over his head. "I can't do it for you." He backs away, gliding across the ground like Seth did, until he's off screen.

What the bloody hell am I supposed to do?

I keep waving the wand until I find a channel showing some landscapes untouched by humans or invaders, with soothing background instrumentals playing. Tossing the wand onto the table, I hop back into bed, pull all my items against my body, lie on my back, and fold my arms over my chest.

Take a deep breath and exhale slowly.

I close my eyes and focus on the music. Let it carry me away to the place called Khertaan—the Subconscious World, where only sleeping freaks may enter.

Unless you're an NPC, mook, or invader, right?

Shut the hell up.

CHAPTER TWENTY-SEVEN

Nick: Low Energy

After enduring an explosion of heat like that, how am I still alive? Hell, I'm not hurting at all.

Ah, but the explosion happened to Morrow, not me. I'm Nick... and I'm awake....

But why am I in bed? I should be lying on the floor of my computer lab.... Has someone moved me? Wait... this place is familiar. I'm not on a bed... it's a folding couch.... But I can't be here... I don't belong here....

Bodies press against me from either side, the one to my left smaller than the one to my right. The one to my left shifts positions.

"*Nick?*" The voice is familiar. "*How...?*"

I face the speaker. "Charli?" She's wearing her typical outfit with the Skirt, Culottes, and wide-brimmed Hat. I'm in agreement with her... *how* is this possible?

The body to my right stirs and sits up. "Who the hell are you?"

I know that voice, too—and am at a loss as to how I've come to be with her now. This isn't the Fanciful Pegasus timeline I occupied when I entered Khertaan. I time-shifted while unconscious. Bloody hell.

Charli blushes as she scrambles out of bed backwards. "I'm not…. I'm sorry…." She glances around. *"Where* am I?"

Tabbie—my girlfriend in this timeline—shoves my shoulder. *"Who is this girl,* Nick?"

The Cowgirl tips her Hat. "My name is Charli. I'm a Cowgirl Guide—"

My mind whirls, reaching for something plausible. "She's a distant cousin. At the moment, she's homeless and orphaned. I offered to help her out. Charli, this is my… friend…, Tabbie."

"All this overnight, Nick, while I'm asleep?" Tabbie pushes me again. "And you bring her into *my* bed?"

The Cowgirl heads for the door.

"Charli, don't leave. Please. You have nowhere to go." I roll to face my girlfriend.

Tabbie studies my face. Her pinched lips relax. "Okay, Nick. I believe you. But she *can't* be here. She has to stay at your place, even when you spend the night here." She rolls on top of me. Fortunately, she's in pajamas. *"Especially* when you spend the night here."

"Hmm." Charli takes a step towards us. "I've never seen the act of copulation before."

Tabbie laughs. "Now ain't the time either, sweetheart. Could you step outside a moment? I'm sure five minutes will be enough."

Hanging her head, Charli grabs the door knob and fiddles with it. The door isn't opening.

"You have to turn the deadbolt."

"Charli, no, don't leave." I grimace at Tabbie.

With an exasperated sigh, Tabbie rolls off me and off the bed. She turns the deadbolt and opens the door. "You don't need to go far. We won't be long."

The girl walks out on the second story walkway. She glances down at the parking lot and then looks back over her shoulder at me.

I roll off the bed. I'm wearing bike shorts and a t-shirt. Unexpected, but I'm glad not to be in only my underwear. "Charli, you can't be out there alone. If anything were to happen to you, I'd never forgive myself." I grab my shoes and put them on while speaking to Tabbie. "I'll make it up to you. But for now, Charli and I need to figure out her living arrangements. We'll go to my place and hash it out there." I slip past Tabbie and join Charli on the walkway.

Tabbie can lose her cool, but she seldom shows it beyond pinching her lips. Hell, she can be downright nice in situations that might significantly upset other people. "Well, the least you can do is have some breakfast with me before you go. Both of you get back in here, and I'll get you some toaster pastries. What kind do you like, Charli?"

"I don't eat."

"We're not hungry, Tabbie. Sorry, but we really need to take care of this situation." I'm still wearing my grimace.

My girlfriend in this timeline sighs. "You don't have to leave now. It's my day off. We had plans. My kids are expecting us to pick them up today. Bring Charli along. She'll like Samantha. You ever been to the ocean, Charli?"

The Cowgirl's eyes grow wide. "No." She looks to me. "I wouldn't mind seeing the ocean, Nick."

Tabbie holds the door open wide, standing aside for us to come back in.

If Tabbie says I had plans with her and her kids, I believe her. I don't know my immediate past in this timeline, but planning a special day for her and her family is something I'd have readily done. They all deserve some goodness in their lives. I motion for Charli to go ahead of me. "We'll go see the ocean."

The Cowgirl jumps and claps her hands. "Oh, goody, wait until I tell all my friends back in…. Oh." Her face falls and she stops jumping. "I'm never going back to Voorton." Her gaze turns serious. "We aren't in Khertaan anymore." She points at the parking lot. "I've never seen or heard of anything remotely like a paved field before. And those horseless carriages look like they're from the future."

I wait until she's through the door and then follow. "You're right. This isn't Khertaan. This is not a virtual world. This is reality."

Tabbie's brow furrows, but she doesn't pry.

I tell her anyway. "Charli was spending all her time playing video games. Virtual reality stuff. She has a hard time distinguishing the real world from the virtual sometimes, because the virtual one is so immersive."

"No." Charli plops down on the edge of the bed. "I can distinguish this place from Khertaan. And I don't agree with your assessment that my home is a virtual world. If it's virtual, then so am I, and look at me. Am I virtual to you?" She faces Tabbie, arms spread. "What about it, Tabbie? Do you think I'm virtual?"

With a sigh as much confusion as relief, Tabbie closes the door and heads for the cupboard. "Toaster pastry, Nick?"

"Thanks, but I'm really not hungry." It isn't a lie. Normally I'd be starving after a night's sleep. But now, I'm neither hungry nor thirsty.

Charli looks around the room. "Is all this stuff yours, Milady Tabbie?"

My girlfriend guffaws. If she'd had a bite of pastry in her mouth, she'd have spewed it across the room. "*Who* you calling *what*?"

"I'm sorry." Charli drops her chin and peers from under a fallen brow at my girlfriend. "Did I pronounce your name wrong?"

"No, you said my name right." Tabbie laughs. "But I ain't no *Milady*. Just call me Tabbie." She sinks her teeth into her breakfast and chews for a moment before speaking again. "Mm. Sure you don't want one of these?"

"No, thank you." Charli glances at me. "How do we get back to Khertaan?"

I bite my lower lip. "I don't know if we can, Charli." I want to carry the topic further, but don't want Tabbie thinking I'm insane. On instinct, I attempt to converse with the Cowgirl on the TimeTrippers party chat channel, but as far as I can tell, no such channel exists. It only works in Khertaan.

I'm flabbergasted that *Charli* exists here. Hell, I'm confused as to why *I'm* here, in *this* timeline with Tabbie as my girlfriend, and not in the timeline where I'm married to Kendra. In *this* timeline, I don't have a lab. Does Fanciful Pegasus even exist in this timeline? Does the Khertaan program exist in this timeline? This predicament smacks of interference from Seth. He's diverted me to a timeline where I can't get back into the game. Is it his doing that Charli is here, too? Does he not want Charli in the game, either?

A crazy thought... maybe ODYSSEY diverted me here. "ODYSSEY?" I direct the question inward. "What's your status? Can you talk to me?"

Charli gasps. "Oh, Goddess. I'm level 16."

I give her a sharp look. "How do you know?"

"I can access my character sheet. Honestly. I thought about it and it popped into view. I earned a million XP for that Behemoth kill, even though it killed us. Can we use our skills here?"

Tabbie looks from me to Charli and back again, but doesn't say a damned thing.

If Charli can summon her character sheet, maybe I can too. I concentrate, but no stats appear before me. What about my support AI? "Renee?" I don't say it aloud, because that would really confuse Tabbie. "Can you hear me?"

No response. It's as I expected. But Charli's very presence is an enigma, and her ability to summon her character sheet even more of one. Can her skills work here, or her Shadow Warrior spell? "How much Auni do you have?"

"Full up at 90. Guess what? I picked up a Critical Hit - Shadow skill on my Wizard subclass. I wonder if that will work for my Shadow Warrior."

"I'm going to take a shower while you two talk about your game." Tabbie leaves the room.

I wait until a distant door closes. "Tabbie doesn't understand about Khertaan.... Try a skill. What's a good one that we'll know for sure whether it works when you try it?"

Charli vanishes.

"Holy shit." I laugh out loud. "You disappeared. You *are* still here, right?"

There's no way I imagined her... is there? I'm freaking out.

Someone taps my shoulder. A grinning Charli kneels on the bed behind me. "I can shadow travel here. Let me try something else. Close your eyes for three seconds."

Trepidation chills my spine, but I close my eyes, slowly count to three, and then open them. She's nowhere in the room. "Okay, Charli, you can come out of the shadows now."

She doesn't reappear. On an impulse, I swing an arm at the space where I last saw her, and strike unseen flesh. Feels like a shoulder.

"My Hide skill works. Next time Tabbie wants me to make myself scarce, I don't have to leave the room." She reappears where she'd been before I closed my eyes. Mischievous notions lift the corners of her mouth and spark her eyes.

I raise my eyebrows. "Not if she's wanting a certain thing from me. To be honest, I don't want you out of my sight until we're safely back in Khertaan. I hope that's sooner than later. Promise me you won't use your Hide skill until we're back in Khertaan, and you won't travel the shadows without me."

"I promise… unless there's an emergency."

"I can live with that."

One more time, I try contacting ODYSSEY. No luck. I try Renee. Still no luck.

"You don't have a respawn chamber." Charli says it as a matter of fact.

I nod. "I thought the lab where you first appeared to me would be my respawn chamber. I don't know why I didn't wake up there. I also don't know why you're with me now."

She shrugs. "Could it be because we died while I was head hopped into your mind? To be honest, I don't know if my body died from the explosion. I was pretty far up in the air with Kylie. *I think* you dragged my mind with you when you died, and I gained a physical presence here to house my awareness. Do you have a more plausible explanation?"

"Can't say I do." I pace as I think. Rather, I pace as I attempt to calm the chaos in my head.

The Cowgirl scoots to the edge of the bed and sits there, swinging her legs. "So what's the plan? You don't have a respawn chamber and I'm not even sure what I am." She pauses. "If my body is still alive in Khertaan, maybe I can will myself back into it. Should I try?"

I consider her idea. "It's better for one of us to return to the game than neither of us. If it works, then try head hopping back to me. If you don't return within ten minutes, I'll take it to mean you can't. Either way, you can inform Kylie, Slithy, and the others about my situation. If I figure out a way to come back to the game, I will, as soon as possible. Or if you figure out how to bring me back to Khertaan, then do it."

"Could you do me a favor, Nick?"

"What's that?"

"Stop referring to Khertaan as a game or a virtual world. It's my home. It's real to me. You're basically saying I'm not real—that I'm... *disposable*. Mithabel said as much, too, and I didn't like her saying it, either."

"I'm sorry. It's just... I *invented* Khertaan. It doesn't feel real to me."

She glares at me. "So... you're saying you're God of Khertaan? Should I fall on my knees and worship you?"

"I...."

"Face it. You didn't *invent* Khertaan. You found a way to access my world and to stir my consciousness. Khertaan might not have the same laws of nature as your Earth, and maybe you can influence the laws of nature in Khertaan with your computer programs, but you're far from all-powerful there."

"I.... Yes. I'll watch what I say."

"Good. Then... I guess this is goodbye, for now." Her head twitches. She frowns. "Ugh. It didn't work." She closes her eyes for several seconds. "Nope, it's not working. We're both stuck here."

Surprisingly, I'm relieved. If she returns and I don't, I'll feel so alone, even though I'm back with Tabbie. No one else in this timeline other than Charli shares knowledge of Khertaan or inter-dimensional invaders. To be the only one on the planet with that knowledge and not be able to do anything about it would be devastating. It wasn't that long ago in this timeline that I tried to commit suicide. That's how I ended up meeting Tabbie in a mental health facility. I'm not feeling my most emotionally or mentally stable right now, and losing Charli would make it worse.

Wait a damned second. It was in the mental health facility that I met Susie—not realizing she was my kid. Now I'm super confused. Susie is my daughter with Kendra. But in this timeline, I didn't marry Kendra. So how did Susie exist in this timeline? She must have time-shifted from her original timeline to this one. I've time-shifted between alternate timelines before. *That's the obvious answer.* Duh. I need to time-shift from this timeline to the Fanciful Pegasus one, where I married Kendra and had my computer lab. Then I can use the lab to respawn.

I really have not been thinking clearly today. I've never been a morning person.

If only I could get ODYSSEY to send me to the right timeline. But he's too low on energy reserves to even speak to me.

Charli swings a foot in my direction. "I see the wheels turning. What are you thinking?"

"It's a long story, but I have this nanobot collective called ODYSSEY in my head. He can shift me to other timelines. He doesn't have the energy for it at the moment, so we need to find a way to energize him. Then he can send us to the timeline where my lab exists, and we can respawn in Khertaan."

"How do you energize him?"

ODYSSEY had mentioned a couple times how something I'd done helped boost his energy level. "My eating sugary foods or drinks might help, like sweet buns and soda. Maybe caffeine helps. And there was one other thing...."

The Cowgirl leans towards me, kicking the bed with her heels. "*What*?"

"Not something I want to say."

"Sex?" She laughs. "Want me to wait here while you visit Tabbie in the shower?"

My girlfriend returns to the living room. "Did I hear my name mentioned?" She glances at Charli and then me. "I'm ready to go. Are either of you getting a shower first?"

"Guess you missed your chance." Charli winks at me.

"Stop it, Charli."

Tabbie squints with one eye. "What am I missing?"

"It's nothing." I glare at the Cowgirl.

Charli can't stay quiet. "I was suggesting Nick join you in the shower while I stayed out here."

Tabbie frowns and points her chin at me. "Yup, you missed your chance, buster. If neither of you are having breakfast, then let's go pick up my kids."

"Maybe I'll have one of those toaster pastries after all." I go to the cupboard and pull out the box. It's half full. How many of these must I eat to energize ODYSSEY? And what if toaster pastries don't contain the actual catalyst? Perhaps I should stick to sweet buns and soda. I know that combination works. I put the box back. "Let's stop at a convenience store. I've got a certain craving." I find a pair of jeans, my wallet in the back pocket, and slip them on over the bike shorts. I have a pair of tennis shoes here, too. "Okay, I'm ready."

Tabbie puts a hand on the Cowgirl's shoulder. "You're going to love the ocean."

Charli's grin widens as she hops off the foldout couch. "I can't wait."

CHAPTER TWENTY-EIGHT

Charli: Thunderbolt Chocolate

Nick drives us on the freeway in his minivan.

I'm sitting on a bench seat behind him and Tabbie. I say nothing, because Nick already knows where he's going, but each turn he'll be taking pops into my head before he takes it. My Navigation skill works just fine.

My Landmarks skill triggers an abrupt alert. I grab the back of Nick's seat. "Turn off here."

"We never go this way." But he takes the exit.

Tabbie glances over her shoulder at me. "You know this area?"

"I'm a *Guide*. It's my job to know about Landmarks, and there's one this way."

At my direction, Nick pulls into the packed parking lot of a Twirled Delight restaurant. Lines of parents and children stand twenty feet long at two windows. A glass door leads inside.

He glances back at me. "Why are we here?"

"All I know is it's a Landmark. I suggest we go inside."

Tabbie punches Nick's arm. "Let's get my kids and come back. If we're having ice cream, I want to enjoy it with them."

Nick looks to me. "Will that work?"

I shrug. "I don't know. There could be a dimensional portal to hell inside. Like I said, all I know is it's a Landmark. I don't know it's purpose. You want me to go look?"

Tabbie glances at the ceiling but says nothing. She's probably wondering why Nick is giving any credence to what I say, but she's also not opposed to getting her kids ice cream.

"I'll take a quick look." Despite not being familiar with minivan door handles, I figure it out and slide the side door open, jumping out before Nick can argue.

Kids mill around tables, while others sit with their parents. I see nothing dangerous or out of the ordinary. It's just another ice cream parlor. The only standout thing about it is the size of the crowd. People love the place.

Nick climbs out of the van and heads my way. I head back, and he stops, glaring at me like I've done something horrible and deserve punishment.

I get in the minivan. "I see nothing terrible inside. No gateways to the seven hells. I think we're okay to go inside for ice cream."

With my direction, it's only a few minutes before we arrive at the townhouse belonging to Tabbie's mom, Elsa. We walk up the short flight of steps and knock on the door. A boy of maybe eight years answers the door. Tabbie addresses him as Leonard. He runs away without speaking. The three of us go inside.

Inside, the aroma of sausage and eggs hangs on the air. An older woman I assume to be Elsa, Tabbie's mom, hobbles into the living room. "Come in, come in. Anyone hungry?"

A shriek precedes the running figure of little Samantha, a girl of maybe ten years. She doesn't run for her mother, but for Nick. She leaps, and throws all four limbs around him, her arms around his waist, her legs around his thighs. She presses the side of her face against his stomach. It's so touching. If it were just the two of them in the room, I'm betting he'd let her hug him for as long as she liked, but his cheeks flush with us others present. He's self-conscious.

"Come away from the nice man." Elsa doesn't use Nick's name. They're not on a first name basis as far as she's concerned. She takes hold of Samantha's arm and pulls the girl free.

Samantha beams at Nick. "When are you and Mom getting married?"

Tabbie guffaws. "Stop it, Sam. Get your brother. We're going for ice cream and then the beach."

The ten-year-old's mouth gapes. "Really?" She hugs Tabbie and then runs after Leonard.

Nick turns to me, pinching his lips between his teeth as he shakes his head. Something happened that he doesn't want to talk about in front of Tabbie and her mom. Did that hug from Samantha help to energize ODYSSEY? It doesn't require sex or sweets. It requires *emotion*. That has to be it. And I'm betting the stronger the emotion, the more it energizes ODYSSEY. Is Nick realizing this?

Elsa touches her daughter's chin. "I suppose you'll be marrying soon, now that you're both legally divorced."

"Wait." Nick looks around, searching the walls for something. "I'm sorry, but I've suddenly forgotten what year it is."

Tabbie throws him a confused glance. "We'll tell you when we've decided, Mom. You'll be the first to know."

A teen boy strolls into the room. He's a little older than me....

How old am I? Some might say three days. Some might say forty years. Nah, no one but me would say I'm forty. The System says I'm fourteen, so I'm fourteen. I bet this guy is sixteen. He looks sixteen. He's a bit on the heavy side, but he's got muscles.

"Hey, Mister Nick." The teen's eyes drift to me. He raises a hand in greeting. "Hey."

Tabbie taps his shoulder with a fist. "Don't you have anything to say to your mother?"

He grins at her. "Hey, Mom. Aren't *you* going to introduce me?"

"I'm Charli." I curtsy. "I'm a Guide and a Wizard."

The teen's eyes light up. "You play Tunnels and Troglodytes? I have a Rogue named Ronnie I've been dying to play again."

"I don't know what that is." I take a step closer to him. "But you could teach me. What's your name?"

His smile is warm. "Oh, yeah, sorry. I'm Ulric." He looks to Nick. "Maybe she can join our game? Whenever we play next...."

Nick nods, though he looks confused. "Is it really Tunnels and *Troglodytes*? I thought.... Hell, I can't remember what I thought."

Whatever is going on with him must be a side effect from switching timelines.

"Charli is Nick's niece." Tabbie has a strange look on her face. I can't tell if she's angry or amused.

"Distant cousin." Nick remembers his lie, and I think Tabbie was testing him. "Her parents are missing and considered dead. Their will gave everything to charity. Charli was left with nothing. It's all very suspicious, but until the courts can decipher it all, Charli is under my custody."

Ulric casts his gaze downward. "Sorry about your parents. That's rough."

I grimace. "It's like I never had any parents at all, honestly. Sometimes I feel like I don't have any family. I'm alone in the world. But I appreciate everything Nick is doing for me." Thing is, I really don't have any parents. I mean, Nick and Kendra brought me into their world years ago with the help of their computer programs, but they aren't my parents, and I'm not their daughter, no matter whether they're willing to claim me as one.

Samantha returns to the living room with Leonard in tow. "We're ready for ice cream."

Leonard doesn't look at all excited.

We pile into the minivan. Ulric sits with me on the rearmost bench seat while Samantha and Leonard occupy the other one. We all buckle up, and a few minutes later, with me shouting directions at Nick, we pull into the parking lot of the Twirled Delight.

Filing inside the parlor, we grab a table.

Nick collects our orders. "I'll never remember all this."

"I will." Samantha jumps from her seat and takes his hand. Those two have a special bond, the likes of which I don't have with Nick. She's more daughter to him than I am. He doesn't treat me the way he treats her. She excites his emotions in ways I don't. Despite our age difference, he and I are more equals than he and Tabbie. Tabbie will never understand Nick's troubles, no matter how many she has of her own. She'll never understand Khertaan, head hopping, timelines, or ODYSSEY. Not that I fully understand them myself, but I understand them about as much as Nick does.

Samantha relates the orders for everyone at our table to the cashier and then squeezes Nick's hand. "What do you want, Mister Nick?"

"I'll have three scoops of Thunderbolt Chocolate on a waffle cone, please."

Samantha nods eagerly. "I want the same thing."

The cashier chuckles. "That flavor packs a real wallop. Have you tried it before?"

Samantha shakes her head. "First time for everything, Grandma says."

The other orders are brought out first, and Nick delivers them to our table. I'm not having anything. Samantha brings the two Thunderbolt Chocolate cones over and hands one to Nick. She licks hers. "*Oh, my gosh.*" She takes another lick. "I've never had anything like this." Without speaking further, she loses herself in devouring her cone.

Nick takes a lick of his. "Oh, my God." He throws a glance at me, like he's trying to tell me something. I understand. The ice cream is hitting the spot and energizing ODYSSEY. Nick closes his eyes and leans his head back, savoring each taste. He's so enamored with the flavor, all he can do is take the next lick and then the next one.

Tabbie harrumphs. "That went fast."

Nick returns to the counter. "Another three scoops of Thunderbolt Chocolate on waffle, please." He drops some bills into the tip jar.

The server exudes pride as she hands him another cone. He doesn't wait to be seated, but starts licking immediately. Everyone else, including Samantha, is roughly halfway finished with their first cone. He sits and devours his, finishing about the same time as Tabbie, the slowest eater of the bunch.

It's not just any emotion that energizes ODYSSEY. It's *pleasure.*

Thunderbolt Chocolate is what makes this place a Landmark. I don't know how much energy ODYSSEY requires, but this should have been a significant boost. "Looks like you could use another one, Nick."

He buys and eats two more.

Finished, the man buries his face in his empty hands.

We all wait to see if he'll eat another.

He looks up with sorrow. "I'm too full. Another cone wouldn't be nearly as satisfying. The law of diminishing returns... the first two were powerful. The third one... still good. But that last one... not so much." He glances at me and shakes his head. It's not enough.

Any given source of pleasure can only energize ODYSSEY so much, and then another source must be sought. Variety isn't only the spice of life, but a necessity for energizing nanobots.

As Tabbie takes her last bite, she points at Nick's right hand. "Nice tattoo. I never noticed it before. When did you have it done?"

A yellow lightning bolt struck through a white cloud is inked on the back of his right hand.

"It's a temporary one." He rubs at it. It's not coming off. Is this also an effect of the Thunderbolt Chocolate? If not, then I'm as befuddled as Tabbie as to where it came from, because this is the first time I've seen it, too. I hope it's a good thing.

"Doesn't look so temporary." Tabbie leans closer to study it. "Looks permanent to me."

"I'm sure it will come off eventually." He stands. "Who's ready for the beach?"

Back in the minivan, I again shout directions from the back seat. Tabbie mutters something about how she lived for years in this area and never took some of these roads. "Well," she says as Nick pulls into the beach parking lot, "that route saved us some time. You kids, be sure to put on suntan lotion before you go in the water."

Only Samantha and Leonard have bathing suits. The rest of us watch from a pier while the two youngest play in the water.

"Don't go too far out," Tabbie shouts when Samantha heads for deep waters.

Ulric and I walk the beach. The waves wash over my feet, tickling them. My laughter comes easily. He doesn't laugh at anything.

Tabbie and Nick stand at the end of the pier, leaning against the wooden guard rails. She drapes an arm around his neck. They don't talk, but simply take in the beauty and serenity of the place.

The sun climbs. Gulls cry. Waves relentlessly lap the beach. Samantha laughs and so do I. Nick gives Tabbie a kiss, and she laughs.

After Samantha and Leonard come in from the water, the adults decide it's time to go. Samantha wants more ice cream, but Tabbie shoots down the idea. Nick drops off the two youngest kids at Elsa's townhouse. Ulric stays in the minivan and rides with us. Nick agrees to take him to Paul's house. I inquire further, and Ulric tells me Paul is his uncle, Tabbie's brother. Ulric often stays at Paul's.

We arrive at Paul's with no directions needed from me.

"Stay for dinner." Paul's wife, Ingrid, invites us. Ulric looks hopeful. Tabbie agrees.

While the meal cooks, Ulric finds a card table and asks Nick to continue the Tunnels and Troglodytes scenario they'd started some time ago. Nick says *yes*. They ask me, and, yeah, I want to see what it's all about. So the three of us grab chairs and sit in the backyard, playing T&T. It's funny to have paper character sheets. The wind is calm, not disturbing our papers.

First Nick walks me through the character generation phase. I choose a kindred from a list in the rules book and Nick tells me not to reveal it to Ulric. He assigns my character some basic equipment. Then he writes some notes for me, also to be withheld for now from Ulric, and we get started.

CHAPTER TWENTY-NINE

T&T: Meeting New People

Fauna perks her ears. "Hark. I hear the footsteps of another traveler upon our path. Perhaps this is the adventure of which the Riders spoke."

An Elf woman strides into sight. She carries a Sword and wears Leather Armor. "Hail," she calls as the pair of travelers comes within hearing range. "I am Emma the Mystical. Who be you, and what brings you this way?"

"I be Ronnie, a Rogue, and my companion is Fauna, a one-quarter goat, three-quarters human lady. We have come this way looking for adventure. Do you know of any?"

"I just fought some Goblins off the road back there." Emma points with her thumb over her shoulder. "Nasty creatures. They are probably more adventure than you're looking for. I'd stay away from them. For adventurers, you lack weapons. What's that you're carrying?"

Fauna pushes out her chest, where she's carrying her lot of fungi. "They're Mushrooms. We plan to feed them to any monsters we meet and try to parley. We're not the type to carry weapons. They did us little good, so we traded them to Riders for information."

"Would you like some Mushrooms?" Ronnie points his chin at the white caps resting against his chest. "They're quite good."

"I'll take them all." Emma shakes out a bag large enough to contain everything the pair is carrying. She holds it under Ronnie's arms. "Go ahead. Dump them in. If it helps, consider me a monster that needs feeding."

"No problem." Ronnie lets the Mushrooms drop into the open bag. He nods at Fauna. "Go ahead. Give them to Emma. We can get more."

The goat-lady does as directed.

Emma closes the bag with a twisting motion and ties the end into a knot. "Thank you very much, gentleman and goat-lady. I will be on my way, as I look for adventure in a different direction than you. Pay heed to stay away from the Goblins. Farewell." She resumes her journey.

Ronnie huffs and calls after Emma. "I thought you would join us in our adventures."

Emma says nothing as she continues walking away.

"Come on." Fauna takes Ronnie's hand and leads him off the path. "We need to find more Mushrooms for the next monster."

But Ronnie is distracted. "Why didn't she join us?"

"Don't fret about it." Fauna finds some Mushrooms. "Come on. Load up."

It takes them longer to collect armfuls of Mushrooms than before, but soon they're back on the road, walking towards adventure.

Fauna stops. "Listen. Is that someone crying?" The two walk a little further. "It *is* someone crying, in the woods to our left. Shall we investigate? It might be an adventure."

Ronnie nods. "Either someone truly needs help or they are pretending to, but in either case, an adventure could be had. Be prepared for deception, but be nice no matter what."

Moments later, they spy a barefoot, green-skinned, green-haired young woman, dressed in dirty, ragged top and loincloth, sitting on a fallen log. She sobs, her head in her hands. She jumps up as the two adventure-seekers approach. "I don't want any trouble. Please go away."

"We will respect your wishes. But we'll leave some Mushrooms for you, should you find yourself hungry." He drops all the Mushrooms he carries in a pile near the log and motions for Fauna to do the same. "If there is anything we can do to help you, please let us know. We'll be on the road over there, seeking adventure."

The green-skinned woman dries her tears. "You two are different than the others. All the other adventurers I've met only wanted to kill me, but I've always managed to get away. All the rest of my family was killed for XP. Yet you two give me food. Is there any XP in that?"

Fauna scratches an ear. "What's XP?"

The green woman stands. "I'm Greelia the Goblin. I'm a Warrior, but my weapons were stolen by an Elf named Emma. She pretended to be my friend, but then attacked me. I hope that is not what you plan to do. You both seem nice. I'd like to be your friend. I could travel with you, if you like. That is, if you don't mind a Goblin tagging along."

Fauna narrows her eyes. "We met Emma the Elf. She seemed nice to us. She warned us about nearby Goblins. Told us not to trust them. Come on, Ronnie, let's be going."

"You met Emma the Elf?" Greelia looks hopeful. "Will you help me get my equipment back from her? I would be ever so grateful."

"No." Ronnie shakes his head. "What's done is done. You can join us, but we press onward, not backward. Won't you have some Mushrooms before we go? They are quite tasty."

"Okay." Greelia's voice sounds more feminine than before and quite cheerful. "Did I surprise you who I am? Did you think I was the Elf?"

Ronnie nods. "I did. You really had me fooled. I didn't think you'd be playing a Goblin."

Fauna eats one of the Mushrooms. "What are you two on about? What do you mean, *playing a Goblin*?"

Ronnie grimaces. "Oh, sorry. We're supposed to stay in character. Welcome to our group, Greelia the Goblin Warrior. Help us carry the Mushrooms. It's time to look for more adventure."

CHAPTER THIRTY

T&T/Nick: Horse Thieves

The three companions stride along the road, cradling loads of Mushrooms in their arms.

Greelia laughs. "This is fun—pretending to be someone you're not."

Fauna sprints ahead two steps and then walks backwards, facing Greelia. "Who are you pretending to be?"

The Goblin girl turns down one corner of her mouth. "Sorry. It's not easy staying in character."

"Someone is coming." Fauna spins around. "On Horses, I think. Should we hide? I don't want to give Mushrooms to Riders. They aren't needy, just greedy."

Greelia chuckles. "I can hide really well. You two hide behind the trees. I'll stay out here and gather information as they pass. Might overhear something important."

"You can't hide out in the open like that." Fauna grabs at Greelia's arm but misses. "Come over here with us." She and Ronnie duck behind some bushes.

"I'll be fine." Greelia bobs her head side to side.

Ronnie gasps as Greelia vanishes. "*Charli?*"

Fauna huffs. "Um, Goblin girl... you aren't supposed to Hide *in real life*. You're supposed to say what you want Greelia to do, and we roll dice to see if it succeeds. Just because you're good at hiding in real life doesn't mean Greelia is."

"Sorry." Greelia reappears, but she doesn't run off the road to hide.

"After the game... you need to tell me how you did that." Ronnie's jaw still hangs low.

Fauna kicks him with a hoof. "What *game*? You two talk strangely. I'm concerned about you."

Greelia scuffs a bare, green foot on the dirt road. "Staying in character is hard."

Four Riders come into view, looking very much like the first group of four Riders Ronnie and Fauna met earlier.

The Leader calls out. "Hail, Goblin girl. This road is only for Humans and those of Human heritage." He dismounts, waving a whip. "It's forty lashes for those who defy the rules."

"Don't harm her." Ronnie stands, revealing himself and his load of Mushrooms. "She's with us."

"Yeah, she's with us." Fauna stands, too. "So leave her alone."

"I'm afraid it's not only forty lashes for your friend, the Goblin, then, but twenty apiece for each of you, for consorting with Goblins."

Greelia wrinkles her nose. "They aren't *consorting* with me."

"Now it's sixty lashes for you, Goblin lass, for talking back."

"But...." Greelia looks confused. "We're simply traveling together, looking for adventure."

"Well, you've found adventure, and it comes in the form of lashes. Kneel and take your punishment." The Leader motions for Greelia to kneel.

Ronnie steps forward. "No. Put your whip away and ride on. This is not the kind of adventure we're looking for."

"And who are you to choose what adventure comes your way?" The Leader steps next to Greelia and places a hand on her shoulder. He pushes down. She resists, but he's stronger, and she drops on her knees, spilling most of her Mushrooms.

Greelia's eyes grow moist. "I don't like this."

"Then don't take it." Fauna runs into the road, throwing a Mushroom at the head of the whip-wielding Leader.

The Leader ducks, but the Mushroom hits his scalp, knocking lose the wig he's wearing. The other Riders laugh at him, and he fumbles with the hairpiece to put it back in place.

"*Come on.*" Fauna runs into the woods, losing most of her Mushrooms.

"I'm coming." Greelia runs after the goat-lady, dropping her last Mushroom.

Ronnie waits until the women pass him, and then follows, bringing up the rear, still carrying most of his fungal goodies.

"Don't just sit there." The Rider Leader gestures at his mounted companions. "Get after them. They must be brought to justice."

The other three horsemen ride crashing through the woods, muttering about how they must do all the dirty work and clean up their boss's messes. "I've never liked Goblins much, though," says one. "They're scum and all deserve to die."

"No, we don't." Greelia climbs into a tree and waits for them to pass by.

Ronnie stops below and looks up at her. "What are you doing?"

Fauna scoffs. "Keep going, or you'll give away her position."

"She'll get herself hurt." Ronnie hides behind the tree Greelia is in and drops his Mushrooms. Fauna sighs and joins him, hiding behind him.

The three Riders pass single file below Greelia. She waits for the last one, and then drops on him.

With a scream, he swipes at her like she's a disgusting bug.

She grabs hold of his hair and pulls—his wig comes off in her hands. Laughing, she jumps to the ground and runs off with the hairpiece.

"You come back with that." The Rider spurs his Horse.

Ronnie jumps out of hiding and cries, "Boo," at the Horse, who rears up and throws his Rider off the back.

Fauna grabs the Horse's reins and jumps into the saddle. "Giddy up." The Horse breaks into a gallop.

The other two Riders give chase. The goat-lady leads them in a circle. Greelia gets up in another tree, and at the Riders' approach she throws the stolen wig at the enemy Rider out front. It hits him in the face, covering his eyes. With him following closely and blindly, Fauna rides under a low branch, which strikes him across the bridge of his nose and tears him from the saddle.

Running to intercept the riderless Horse, Ronnie catches its reins, pulling it aside as the last Rider rushes by, still chasing the goat-lady. Calming the Horse, Ronnie climbs on its back. "Go, horsey." The Horse joins the chase.

Fauna brings her Horse to a sudden stop. The Rider chasing her veers aside to avoid a collision, but he's still close enough for the goat-lady to plant a hoof in his ribs. He teeters, off balance. Ronnie rides past him on the other side and grabs an arm to help him fall.

With a laugh, Greelia runs over and hops on the third Horse. *"Let's go.* That will teach them to pick on people less fortunate than them."

Ronnie grits his teeth. "I don't want to be a Horse Thief."

"Tough. You already are." Greelia rides away through the woods.

Fauna shrugs. "It's an adventure, Ronnie. And you're a Rogue, right? Rogues are basically thieves. If you didn't want to be a thief, you should have been a Warrior or a Wizard."

The dismounted Riders collect themselves and charge at Ronnie.

"Fine." The Rogue shakes the reins. "Giddy up, horsey."

"Dinner is served," Tabbie shouts. "Come and get it."

The three companions groan in disappointment, but return to the road, riding towards more adventure, the nature of which is to be discovered at some other time.

**

"That was *so* fun." Charli's cheeks are flushed. "I really liked throwing the wig in that guy's face."

"You both played well." I pack up my dice and game booklets. "It would be nice to continue the campaign some time."

Ulric folds up the table and takes it away.

"That boosted my energy," says ODYSSEY. "Not as much as the Thunderbolt Chocolate, but you seemed to really enjoy yourself. Keep it up, and I'll eventually be strong enough to shift us out of this timeline."

As necessary as it is, I'll be sad to leave this timeline behind. While I'm in it, I'll do my best to enjoy it. Ironically, the more I enjoy it, the sooner I'll be leaving it.

CHAPTER THIRTY-ONE

Susie: Isolation

Slithy hadn't expected that giant metal spider to blow up. But it did, and the explosion was devastating. She died, and now I'm awake.

"Marta? Are you here?" Slithy's personal support AI doesn't respond. I shouldn't be surprised—*I'm not Slithy*.

It's like I was Slithy in a dream, and now I'm awake.

My skin tingles and my hair stands up, like I'm in a field of static electricity.

Okay, so I'm not in Khertaan, but... *where am I*?

It *looks* like I'm in isolation at the Spring Green Medical Health Facility. I'd recognize the light blue padded walls anywhere. Memories of this place haunt me—memories from when I was still confused about my time travel and teleport abilities. Three years ago, at the age of 17, I went to sleep in my own bed at home one night and woke the next morning in a room at Spring Green. I didn't wake in this room, but I spent time here for bad behavior.

So, knowing where I am, the question becomes *why* am I here?

I also wouldn't mind knowing what year it is. Have I time-jumped?

I suppose the more important question is *how do I get back to where I belong?*

Ha. I've been asking myself where—and when—I belong since I was five years old. In my best estimation, that's the first time I time-jumped. Lightning kept flashing. Electric digits flowed like a circular waterfall with me standing in the void at the center. Then I wasn't in my parents' house anymore, but seated at the edge of a lake, swishing my feet in the water, laughing at frogs leaping away in fright, wondering what it must be like to be one of them.

It makes sense why my avatar in Khertaan would be a Frogkin.

The ceiling glows, but not from overhead fluorescent lights as one might expect. The ceiling itself is luminescent, like it's coated with glowing paint. I don't remember it being that way when I was held in isolation here before.

I wave at the camera over the door. The people in charge are no doubt wondering how I got in here, not only in isolation, but in the facility. *I'm not supposed to be here.*

I was saying that to everyone when I was here before.

Dad was here then, too. When he told me it was 1991, I thought either he was out of his mind or he was trying to gaslight me. I couldn't believe Dad would hurt me like that. To my mind, the year was 2008, I was 17, and the year 1991 was 17 years in the past, when I was born. In 2008, I was dating Timmy Landers—before I came to the full realization I wasn't into boys.

But Dad was right. I had jumped back in time to 1991. I don't know why. It wasn't intentional. It's like I was drawn to Dad when he was going through his midlife crisis. Have I been drawn to him again? Is he a patient here now? When is *now*? Having celebrated 20 years of birthdays, I should by rights be in the year 2011.

If I had to wager, I'd bet I'm not in my proper time.

So... what's my priority here? Is escaping this room necessary? Respawning in Khertaan as Slithy should be high if not top priority, as that's where the action is, and where I feel the most needed. How do I get back?

Rather, how does Slithy get back?

Part of the Khertaan program runs on the nanobot collective parked in my brain. "ODYSSEY, how do I get back into Khertaan?"

A faint masculine voice replies in my head. "Need more energy."

"What kind of energy?"

He gives no response. Lovely. He needs more energy, but I don't know what kind or how to give it to him. Do I insert my finger in a light socket? Drink gasoline? Sunbathe in the nude to collect solar power? Maybe I energize him by energizing myself. Running. Riding a bike. I like bikes. I *love* coasting downhill, ha ha. I like swimming, too. Or maybe he gets energy from nutrients. A certain mineral supplement or herb. What if he needs some kind of drug? A steroid or hormone. Maybe stimulants would do the trick. Caffeine. Mm, I could go for some chocolate. Like Dad, I never cared much for coffee or tea.

So many options to try, and no good feeling that any of them will work.

Okay, then, I'll experiment. Test some of my ideas.

I run in place. "Getting anything from this, ODYSSEY?"

He doesn't say anything.

I go a while longer. Maybe it takes a certain minimal amount to register with him. I don't particularly enjoy running, but if it's the only way for me to give him energy, what choice do I have? "Anything at all, ODYSSEY?"

He's apparently conserving what energy he has, and thus avoids giving me an answer. I run in place another few minutes. He still doesn't respond when I ask again. It must not be helping. Fine. I stop. Now I'm all sweaty. Yuck.

No one has given any indication they've noticed me in isolation. Maybe the camera over the door isn't turned on, because they aren't expecting anyone to be in here. I figured someone would be busting the door down by now, demanding to know who I was and how I got here.

The door is locked from the outside. They keep the doors to isolation locked whether or not anyone occupies the room. But it shouldn't matter to me, not if I still have *my* abilities—the time travel and teleport abilities I've had since I was a child. I will myself to the other side of the door.

Heh, heh, I've still got it.

Other rooms hang off this hallway, many with open doors. The ceiling glows like in the isolation chamber. My skin still tingles and my hair is still statically charged.

This is disturbing yet dope. It's disturbing because it's unreal. It's dope because it's surreal. I know this place—and yet I don't.

It's so quiet. I head for the great room, knowing exactly where it lies. I turn the first of three bends in the hallway. It's eerie that I don't yet hear any signs of life from up ahead—no talking, no crying, no laughing, nothing. I round the second bend, and still hear nothing. Is a fire drill underway? The ceiling glow is brighter here and the tingling on my skin more intense.

A wind carrying the scent of ash warms my face. I reach the third bend. The ceiling glow is nearly blinding. The tingling on my skin has become a constant shock. My blond tresses rise off my ears.

I round the bend… and draw up short before colliding with a wall of light.

Gingerly, I put a finger to it. It's *not* light, but solid, like a force field. It's not letting me pass.

Heh, it can't stop me. I'll teleport to the other side—except I can't focus.

Mentally marking the spot, I backtrack. The shocking diminishes and my hair lowers enough to touch my ears.

I picture the mentally marked location and extrapolate a position beyond the wall of light, assuming the wall isn't more than three feet thick. Maybe I should go for six feet. Ten feet? Make it twenty feet.

Teleport.

The natural light of day falls upon me. The tingling on my skin and electric shocks are gone. My hair falls onto my shoulders.

I'm surrounded by rubble under an open sky. What happened here?

Blackened skeletons lie broken amongst the debris, the flesh burned from their bones. Are they undead? They don't look it, but how does one tell?

Is Timmy still a Ring Ghoul? I have a harder time believing in Ghouls than in time travel or teleporting. But I saw Timmy in that casket, and he was *dead*. Then I saw him climb out of the casket, after I dug him up with the help of his and my future selves. *That* was in 2008. His future self, who went by the name Marvin, had a magical Ring. Marvin put it on Timmy's finger, and later my dead boyfriend crawled out of his casket. As long as he wears the Ring, he's undead.

I'm not climbing over the rubble and skeletons. Why should I? Teleporting is so much more convenient, and more fun than crawling over skeletons. So I teleport outside the ruined walls for a better look at my surroundings.

Um....

Leafless trees tower over fields of scorched earth, blackened branches reaching towards the sky. Banks of smoke drift by like low hanging clouds. Buildings everywhere lie in ruin, demolished and burned like the facility behind me. The scent of ash saturates the air, enough to make me gag. Wrecked and incinerated vehicles clog the road, the charred remains of passengers still seated inside, scorched fragments of seat belts hanging above their shoulders. Vehicles lie on their sides, on their tops, or on their ends, leaning against other vehicles or ruined walls.

Seared skeletons clutter the Spring Green parking lot. Some vehicles in the lot are untouched—and empty of passengers. Someone or something waged war against *life* on this planet— and won. Not a blade of grass stands. No blossoms bloom. Not a single green leaf remains on any tree. It's like this everywhere I look... I wouldn't be surprised if I'm the only living thing on the planet.

In Ezmerelda's hut, Morrow mentioned someone named Seth. Ezmerelda didn't like hearing the name, and said we were ruined if he was in Khertaan. Slithy had asked Marta and ODYSSEY about Seth, and was told he was an enemy attempting to destroy all living things—not only in Khertaan, but every world across all timelines. He has accomplished his task here. I hope this isn't my original timeline, although some version of Mom and Dad could easily have lived here. If they did, they're dead now.

It's depressing to think about.

For that matter, some version of me could have been here, too. But a version of me could have survived the attacks that took place here—assuming she could time travel and teleport. If I could find her, I could get answers. Where would I be if I'd survived this, and no one else did?

Even at my lowest, I've never seriously considered committing suicide. But if I were the *last and only* person alive on Earth, suicide might rank on my list of options. Any version of me who called this timeline home might have done it—but if she's at all like me, she'd explore all other options first.

Marta and ODYSSEY had also mentioned someone named Gondra, who opposed Seth. The two sounded like rival Gods... Good vs Evil or Balance vs Chaos—that sort of thing. Seth wants to destroy every living thing, and Gondra wants to stop him. I'm rooting for Gondra.

Whoever sent me here, I'm betting it was either Seth or Gondra. Who else could do it or want to? I still need to figure out *why*.

Looking over my shoulder, I discover another curiosity. A dome of electric energy shields a portion of the Spring Green Mental Health Facility. The area under the dome isn't demolished or burned. That's where the isolation ward lies.

Someone intended for me to awaken on this world in this timeline. The dome was meant to protect me... or be my prison... for how long... until I starved to death? There's a pleasant thought.

Fortunately, I'm not feeling hungry or thirsty, but I'm bound to eventually. Is there *any* food on the planet? If all the shops have been demolished and burned, and all the vegetation and creatures across the world have been destroyed, then I'm screwed for food. What if food is needed to energize ODYSSEY?

Whoever sent me here doesn't want me leaving, and is doing their best to kill me without outright murdering me. Between Seth and Gondra, Seth has the stronger motivation for not wanting Slithy to respawn in Khertaan. While I'm here, Slithy isn't training. If Gondra is the good one, why would he want to isolate me on a destroyed planet?

For me to escape this place, do I need to know who sent me here or the reason behind it? I need to focus on energizing ODYSSEY. For that, I think I need to find food, because if he doesn't need it, I will. Won't I?

The one person who doesn't need food is Timmy, assuming he wasn't destroyed. And why would he have been? He's not living, he's undead. If he survived, he'll have information that could help me. I should pay him a visit. I have to assume he still lives where he used to. I've never purposefully tried teleporting that far before, but there's a first time for everything.

CHAPTER THIRTY-TWO

Susie: Glynda

Assuming Timmy was still residing at the address I last recall for him, his apartment has been demolished. It had housed other people in addition to Timmy—*living* people—and so Seth destroyed it. I still can't believe Timmy was destroyed too. He's undead. He came back from being killed once already. As long as he's wearing that Ring, he's basically immortal.

I'm making an assumption about what timeline this is—that either it's my original one or events happened the same way in this timeline as they did in my original one.... That might not be true, but if it is....

I was still learning about my powers—driving my old Thunderbird, racing to the scene of an accident I'd thought had killed Timmy, trying to prevent him from being killed. But I'd accidentally struck *myself—a time-traveling version of me*—and killed myself. That's Timmy's story and Marvin's too.

Marvin showed up with the Ghoul Ring and put it on *my* finger. He told Timmy to sacrifice himself to save me from becoming a servant to the Ring. They did some kind of ritual that Marvin knew. A ritual like that shouldn't be more unbelievable than time travel, I guess. Timmy took the Ring himself, and his spirit came to my body to serve as an anchor to my fleeing spirit. I ended up with both our spirits in my body, or so Marvin claimed. His theory goes that's why I started liking girls over boys. As a Ghoul, Timmy lost interest in sex and romance. So we were no longer girlfriend/boyfriend, but it's not like we disliked each other, either. I mean, I owe my life to him. And in a way, he's always with me.

That's if I believe their story....

Not knowing what timeline I'm in, I can't know whether Timmy ever existed here, or whether he became a Ghoul. In any case, he doesn't appear to be here. Where else might he be? I can't give up just because his old apartment building is destroyed.

What if he's trapped under rubble, just lying there, existing, but unable to free himself? How morbid the thought—an immortal undead trapped under a girder on a dead planet... forever.

I should check the debris.

I teleport into the mess.

Using my teleportation to maneuver, I systematically search the entire building as much as I can, softly calling his name. No Timmy.

Some piles of rubble stand as high as I am tall, large enough to conceal a body. I push the top stones off each pile until I'm convinced there's no body below. It's hard work, but I stay calm, patient, and persistent.

I've spent what feels like hours at the task with no luck. I don't think Timmy is here. *Good*.

Holy crap, I just realized.... The shadows haven't changed angle or length. The sun is stuck at the same spot in the sky...

like in Khertaan. Am I *in* Khertaan? It can't be. I'd be Slithy if I were in Khertaan. I can't *be* Susie in Khertaan, can I?

Wouldn't Slithy's support AI Marta be with me if I were in Khertaan?

I'm not fatigued, hungry, or thirsty, even after hours of hard work. That's not like me—not like *Susie*. I could expect it of Slithy. But as Susie, I should be worn out and ravenous with hunger.

I hold my breath and put two fingers on my wrist.

I'm still holding my breath and I have no pulse.

Oh, my... I'm *still* holding my breath and *still* have no pulse.

Unless I'm dreaming, I can't be Susie. But dammit, I'm not Slithy either. My skin isn't red and black like a poison dart frog's.

What does it all mean? This world doesn't look or feel like Khertaan and I don't look or feel like Slithy, but aspects of the place and my body behave as though I'm in Khertaan. Am I in some hybrid timeline, partially Khertaan and partially Earth?

I could go back in time and witness what happened on this planet.

First, I should go home and check on my parents.

I can't bear the thought, but it nags at my brain.

They're probably dead.

That's why I haven't already gone there. If I find anything, it will be scorched skeletons.

But I have to check, don't I?

I visualize the street outside our house and will myself there.

The building has been razed to the ground, its masonry pulverized to dust and pebbles. There's nowhere a living body could hide. Blackened bones lie scattered among the ashes. Refrigerators and other appliances are scarcely recognizable, rent to shreds—thick and twisted metal fingers groping at an ambivalent gray sky.

It's how I'd destroy a place I utterly hated.

"*Mom.*" My lungs ache as they force the word out of me. The emptiness swallows my shout, not allowing it to echo. My gut grows cold and heavy. Tears well in my eyes but refuse to fall. I try to shout again, but don't have enough air inside me. I inhale deeply. "*Mom.*"

The void is still hungry and eats my cry.

An idea strikes, and I act on it without thinking twice, teleporting into the sky far above our demolished house. As I fall, the wind whipping my hair and stinging my eyes, I look down on the ruined vista. There's not a building standing in sight, except the portion of the Spring Green Mental Health Facility under the electric dome. Every tree stands crooked, burned, and bare, or lies on the ground as ashen logs. Not a hint of green vegetation catches my eye. Everything outside the dome is black and white, charcoal and ash. Soot coats the surfaces of retention ponds.

Wait… there's movement… silhouettes against the horizon… the occasional glint of reflected sunlight….

Giant metallic spiders on patrol….

A growling hum sounds in the distance. The hum reaches me even up here. There's more movement below. A Motorcycle and its cloaked rider cruises the ruins. It passes directly below me, driving through the spot where I'd stood a minute ago. I'm falling straight at him. But he's not looking for flying humans. What *is* he looking for?

What could he possibly expect to find amid all this devastation?

He's searching for me.

All he needs to do is look up, and he'll see me.

On an impulse, I twist in the air and look up.

Holy shit.

I've heard the stories of UFO sightings. An unidentified flying object could be anything—it's *unidentified*. But this has to be an alien spaceship. The part I can see—the bottom—is like the underside of an enormous saucer. How big *is* that sucker? It's way up there, maybe not even in the atmosphere. Taking a deep breath just in case I need to speak, I teleport up near it.

Someone else flies above me, below the craft. No, it's not *someone*—it's *me*. Is she the version of me that belongs to this timeline, or is she me-me from my future? She's dressed *exactly* like me, with a dark blue blouse and a black skirt. I bet she's future-me, time-jumped from seconds or minutes ahead back to now for some reason.

Any time I encounter myself from the future, I refer to her as Glynda and she refers to me as Suze. It's Glynda above me, because I'd remember this if it were Suze up there.

Glynda isn't flying. Like me, she's falling.

She disappears—teleporting, I presume. Where did she go?

If she really is future-me, I'll find out in time where she went. I teleport as far up as I can, higher than she was.

I'm right beneath the craft, and prove it with a swipe, stroking the slick metal before I fall away. I'm not light as a feather, but I'm not feeling my weight so much.

Metal sleeves part and slide away from each other like mechanical eyelids, opening a portal in the bottom of the craft. Green light flashes in the portal.

Reacting on instinct, I travel back in time a few seconds, to a time when I know I'm safe.

Glancing down, I see Suze looking up at me. I'm Glynda to her now.

Sucking in another deep breath, I teleport inside the ship.

CHAPTER THIRTY-THREE

Kylie: Dunes Boss Fight

I never imagined I'd be grateful for the company of a telepathic clown whose existence is all in my head. Georgie says Morrow and Slithy should have respawned by now, and has no idea why neither of them have. The Motorcycle couple haven't respawned in my location, either.

After Charli head hopped to Morrow and went limp in my grip, everyone but she and I went kablooey—and she might as well have. The Cowgirl hasn't snapped out of her self-induced coma since, and nothing I do can wake her. When Morrow died from the Behemoth's death blast, he took Charli's mind with him, according to Georgie. So now I'm stuck carting around her unconscious body, presumably until Morrow respawns, at which time we can only hope Charli's mind will be restored.

I've been flying in circles for half an hour, high over the spot where the Behemoth exploded. Why did they have to kill it? They should have stayed with the plan, sticking to the safe route and constantly moving west. But, no, my daughter let her curiosity get the better of her. She needed to know if we *could* kill the Behemoths, and how difficult it would be. Now all my companions except an intangible clown and a Cowgirl rag doll are gone.

Georgie stays by my side without effort, as though he's metal and I'm magnetic. His bulbous nose bobs as he juggles four apples as red as his schnoz. "Maybe you should press on, pumpkin. When the others are ready to respawn, they can join you wherever you are. You can stay high in the sky to avoid the Arachnids and Orcs."

He doesn't voice my main concern, so I ask him pointblank. "What if the others don't respawn?"

His bright red lips exaggerate his frown on his painted white face as he tilts his head towards me and glowers. "Then the fate of the world rests on your shoulders, pumpkin. You've got to reach level 30 on your own. If anyone can do it, you can."

"Thanks for the pep talk, but... *are you crazy*? I've only recently allowed myself to accept that I'm not Kendra. I didn't come to Khertaan of my own free will, and the timing sucked for Kendra to suddenly lose consciousness. Her five-year-old daughter is missing. Her husband is suffering from a concussion. All three of us fell asleep... and the two of them are awake but I... Kendra... isn't. I'm basically her dream self—as long as I'm active, she can't be. Am I to kill myself so Kendra can awaken and be with her family?

"But oh no... there's this nonsense about training to level 30. *It's important for all of existence.* And I'm left to do it with no one to help me but you, Georgie. God help me if you leave."

The clown's frown turns upside down. "You're stuck with me as long as you're in Khertaan, pumpkin. Circle this spot as long as you like, but think how proud Morrow will be when he does respawn and you've made progress without him. It would be nice if you had the map, but Charli stashed it, sadly.

"At some point, TimeTrippers will need to defeat a Boss. If you can do it, that's one less hurdle for the party when the others respawn."

Now he's talking about me taking down a Boss by myself. Fantastic.

Something is happening below. Damn. The giant metal spiders congregate below, crawling on top of each other, building a Behemoth-pyramid in an attempt to reach me. So they're after *me* now? Is there no one else in Khertaan to activate their spider senses? I fly higher, heading west. "You're right, of course, Georgie. I should make as much progress as I can. We're headed for a city atop a spire—*Minook*. It should be easy to spot once we defeat the Boss for the Dunes of Doom."

Georgie throws the apples over his left shoulder, one by one, but rather than fall to the desert below, they loop beneath him and come back to his hands so he can continue juggling them. "Remember, Charli said there was a safe path on the west side of the spire that leads to Minook, once you reach the spire."

The Behemoths at the bottom of the pyramid move to follow me west, and many spiders topple from the top. They aren't thinking machines. They can't learn. They have a task, and they're on autopilot. There's only one way they'll change their behavior, and it isn't of their own volition.

Oh, there's a wild thought. "Georgie, I understand I have a nanobot collective named ODYSSEY in my brain. Is that true?"

"Yeah."

"And it's running the Khertaan program, right?"

My clown AI nods with vigor. "Yup."

"And ODYSSEY can reprogram certain aspects of Khertaan, right?"

Georgie keeps nodding. "That's why you earned a million XP when the Arachnid Behemoth was defeated."

"Okay, so can ODYSSEY reprogram the *behavior* of the Arachnid Behemoths?"

The clown raises an eyebrow. "You could ask him."

I shake my head. "I've tried talking to him. The process doesn't click in my head. Maybe it will eventually, but if you can communicate with him, would you ask, please?"

I slow down so as not to leave the spider army too far behind.

The sky darkens, as though storm clouds are passing overhead. I look up.

A swarm of Pteranodon silhouettes descends upon me. They're fast. Faster than me, I think.

I've seen Slithy stash mindless mooks, so I try to stash Charli's unconscious body. It doesn't work. Is that because she's an NPC instead of a mook? I pull her against my ribcage and hug her with my left arm while I wield my Spirit Blade in my right hand. I present my right side to the flying foes, protecting Charli as much as I can with my interposing body.

As a level six Barbarian, I've got a Scute Armor skill I haven't tried yet. I will it to activate. White bony plates encase my body like an exoskeleton. Each feather in my wings grows a protective plate as well. Unfortunately, Charli isn't covered by the Scute Armor. I shift her into the crook of my elbow and equip my Spirit Shield in my left grip, positioning it to provide her cover.

The Pteranodons draw closer, two distinct groups of dark brown fliers, one a bit further from me than the other. Instead of dive-bombing me as I'd expected, the first group pulls up shy of me, turning their Beaks towards me as they pass. Cones of black liquid spray from their mouths. Hoping my new exoskeleton will protect me, I fold my wings over my face.

I'm splattered with... oil?

No, it's *acid*, and some of it gets past the Scute Armor. If I didn't have the Pain Tolerant trait, I'd be feeling it, I'm sure, but I can shrug off the pain of attacks like this all day. I don't bother to check my HP percentage. I've got to do my best to triumph, and fretting over lost HP is only a distraction.

Georgie waves to get my attention. "How do you want the Arachnid Behemoths reprogrammed?"

I fly towards the ground to avoid the acid attacks of the second flock. "Was Charli damaged?"

"Charli was not hit."

Oh, good. "Ask ODYSSEY if he can reprogram the spiders to protect her." I land, out of range of the spider webs, but the spiders continue their approach. The two flocks of Pteranodons circle and then swoop towards me. "Tell him to hurry, Georgie."

My clown AI doesn't answer. I fly along the ground, putting more distance between me and those damned spiders. If only I knew where the safe path was.

Can my Hypnotic Voice trait work against the Pteranodons? It can't hurt to try.

Between catches of juggled apples, Georgie honks his bulbous red nose. "ODYSSEY says he can reprogram *one* Arachnid to join your party, compelling it to help you. It's the best he can do. If you want him to do it, you need to choose a name and gender for the spider."

I don't think hard about it. "Name: Spyder, with a *y*. Gender: Female."

The first flock of Pteranodons makes a sweep above me. I shout, "*Halt*," as they open their mouths in unison to expel acid. Without releasing their toxic loads, the six flying dinosaurs freeze and then plummet, plowing into the desert sand.

The second flock closes the gap. I need to wait for my current combat heartbeat to end before I can use Hypnotic Voice again. I've not tried using Hypnotic Gaze before, and now seems a good time. I stare at the Lead Pteranodon, striving to meet his gaze. "Pull up."

He obeys.

But the other five Pteranodons in his flock don't follow him as I'd hoped, and keep coming at me.

"Arachnid Behemoth name and gender accepted." Georgie gives me a thumbs up. "You need to officially invite Spyder to your party."

The five Pteranodons swoop down, opening their mouths to exhale. Stashing my Spirit Blade and folding my wings, I present my back to the dinosaurs, pulling Charli against my armored stomach and bending over to shelter her, cranking my left arm over my left shoulder to provide added protection with the Spirit Shield.

Acid melts the sand around me. I sense the acid rending at my flesh, but it doesn't hurt.

Georgie informs me Charli wasn't hit.

The second flock of Pteranodons aim skyward to join their Leader. If only I didn't have to protect Charli, I could deal with these damned dinosaurs. "Invite Spyder to party TimeTrippers, Georgie."

"Invite issued."

The first flock of Pteranodons pull themselves free of the dunes. Shaking the sand from their bodies and wings, they turn my way, locking their reptilian eyes on me. With a flap of their wings, they leap into the sky and speed towards me.

"Invite accepted. Spyder has joined TimeTrippers." The name *Spyder* appears on the party roster.

I shout, *"Halt,"* again at the flock as they open their mouths to breathe, and once more they plummet to the earth, the closest of them hitting the sand only ten feet away. The second flock descends, aimed straight at me. I present my back and my Spirit Shield to them again, kneeling to make myself as small a target as possible. Their acid burns the sand, while I feel nothing.

Georgie informs me neither I nor Charli took any damage from the second flock's attack this time around, but my HP has fallen to 88% from sustained damage from the previous attacks. Their acid is continuing to burn me, even though I don't feel it.

The Arachnid Behemoths grow too near for comfort. "Georgie, which one is Spyder?" But then I see the answer.

The closest Behemoth has changed colors, turning a brilliant green. "I am Spyder. You wish me to protect the Cowgirl. Lay her down and move away."

Every nerve in my body rebels at the thought of turning Charli over to this monstrosity, but this is *my* plan in motion. I do as I'm told, flying away backwards to watch what transpires.

Spyder fires a web. A mass of slender metal lines spreads over Charli. The green spider reels in her web, dragging Charli with it.

Flapping wings signal the recovery of the first flock of six. I throw them a wicked smile and shout at them, bringing them to a halt before they can get off the ground. "Take Charli westward, Spyder."

I speed towards the closest hypnotized Pteranodon. Equipping my Spirit Blade, I drive the glowing blue weapon into the reptilian bird's skull. The mook erupts, spewing rainbow-colored pixels. With the Blade now on cool down, I trade it for my Spirit Dart and fling the missile at the next closest enemy, striking it in its left eye. Landing a blow in a sensitive spot on a hypnotized target greatly increases the chances for dealing a Critical Hit. The second of six Pteranodons goes bye bye.

I'm not done yet. Calling upon my Spirit Noose skill to conjure a Rope of glowing blue energy, I lasso the long neck of one grounded Pteranodon and tie off the free end of the conjured Rope around the neck of another. Still hypnotized by my shout, they don't resist. Let's see them fly now.

Spyder passes behind me. Other Behemoths grow near, and they aren't allies. I've got to move.

The second Pteranodon flock swoops by overhead. I curl up in my shell. The acid bath washes over me. I'm unfazed, but still lose a few percentage points of HP to sustained damage. It's not much, but the damage will keep adding up until this encounter ends, and I have no way to heal quickly. Every percentage point of HP is precious, knowing that what I have left needs to take me all the way to Minook.

The sky grows black.

The silhouette of another Pteranodon appears directly overhead. It's not flying, but has its wings spread wide to both sides. It falls at me, not dive bombing, but flat, like it's doing a belly flop on me. As it drops from the sky, it gets bigger and bigger, the wind moaning around it.

I fly westward, following Spyder. The Boss above corrects its course to stay above me, and it's faster than I am. It's also the size of a football field. It will crush me and Spyder, too, if I stay my current course. I backtrack to the east, leading the monstrosity away from my fellow party members. Thank goodness, it follows me. Spyder and Charli are safe from it for the moment.

The Boss means to slam me against the ground. Even with my Scute Armor exoskeleton, I won't survive such a crushing attack. I'm limited to how many times a day I can switch to Spirit

Form, and I used it earlier to get us free of webbing, but now seems a good time to use it again. I still have seven uses left today.

The moaning wind dies to a whisper. The world turns stark black and white, with only a few intermediate shades of gray. I'm pure white and so is the sand. The huge falling Pteranodon is pure black. With Spirit Blade raised, I fly up to engage the enemy.

My body enters its body, like a ghost flying through a wall. In Spirit Form, I'm insubstantial—a spirit.

Within the bounds of the Giant Pteranodon's body, I swing my Spirit Blade in a circle around me, sensing the damage I inflict on the mook's spiritual being. Is it enough?

I hover in place, unharmed, watching what transpires below me. Filling my field of vision, the Boss continues its descent, making no attempt to pull up.

It lands on the first flock with a slam that visibly shakes the desert floor, giving the Behemoths pause. "Keep going, Spyder." Even on party chat, my voice sounds faint.

The second flock swoops by, showering me with acid, but it passes right through me. I don't even take sustained damage. Ha.

The Behemoths nearest me fire their webs, some at me and some at the Boss. The ones aimed at me go right through me, falling to the ground without their intended captive. The webs aimed at the Boss land on his head and wings, snagging different parts of him. But the Boss is strong. Easily the size of four Behemoths, he rises on his feet, tearing the strands connecting him to them, and breathes at the oncoming Arachnid army.

Four of the Behemoths explode with a force that reshapes the dunes. The light of their blasts rips through the Boss... and through me.

I'm still alive. In Spirit Form, physical attacks can't affect me.

The Giant Pteranodon is still alive, too. Damn, it's tough.

"Boss is at 60% HP and 0% SP, pumpkin. With its spirit crushed to nothing, it has gone berserk. It smashed four Pteranodons beneath it, and they're gone. The second flock is incoming."

"Let them bloody well come." I fly towards the head of the Boss. The second flock follows me. I settle onto the skull of the Giant Pteranodon as the flock swoops down and opens their mouths to breathe at me.

Acid harmlessly passes through me but burns the top of the Boss's scalp. He whips up his head and breathes at the flock in return. When his acid spray is done, the second flock is gone from the sky.

More Behemoths march into range for tossing webs. A mass of strands fall over me and the Boss Pteranodon. I float upward, passing through the webbing. My Spirit Form skill is a saving grace.

The massive winged dinosaur screeches, what would be beyond deafening if my ears were physical, especially since I have a Heightened Sense of Hearing. In my Spirit Form, I only hear echoes of what I'd hear in the physical realm.

A half-dozen Behemoths shatter like glass from the sonic boom, their shards sailing across the dunes, some of them sailing through me without harm. A quick glance proves Spyder is already out of range, thank God.

"Boss is at 11% HP, pumpkin. Seven Arachnid Behemoths were slain by his screech."

"Georgie, do I need to deliver the killing blow to the Boss for me to be allowed to leave its territory, or is being involved good enough?"

"You only need to be involved, pumpkin, but the Boss needs to be dead, not merely berserk."

"Good." I fly down in front of the Boss. "Hey, big guy." I head in the direction of an isolated Behemoth. The Boss breathes at me. His acid doesn't hurt me, and none of the Behemoths are in range of it currently, though a number of them are closing in.

I'm still alive and closer to him than anything else, so he lurches after me and shrieks.

The closest Behemoths shatter. How many? Their shards fly through me and all around, many striking the Boss. His body lights up like a fireworks display. He's *dead*.

"That did it, pumpkin. Now you only need to put enough distance between you and the Arachnid Behemoths for this encounter to be considered officially over."

Staying in Spirit Form, I speed after Spyder. I'm not quite to her when Georgie declares an end to the encounter.

"So, clown, what's my status?"

"The System has deemed you sufficiently involved in the defeat of the Boss, pumpkin. Its death allows both your party and the Arachnid Behemoth army to exit the Dunes of Doom. TimeTrippers gains XP for defeating the Boss. Moreover, the System has determined you to be instrumental in the defeat of twelve Pteranodons and fourteen Arachnid Behemoths. TimeTrippers gains a total of seventeen million, nine-hundred-sixty thousand XP. Sadly, only you and Charli are present and qualified to earn those XP. But, hey, *congratulations*, you are level 21 Spirit Warrior, level 12 Barbarian. Your HP now stands at 89%."

"That sounds good." I—that is, Kendra—wasn't involved so much in the game aspect of programming Khertaan. Kendra was interested in finding a way to make Khertaan objects and beings interact with Earth objects and beings, since that's what Franklin was paying for. Between Kendra and Nick, it was Nick who had the most interest in the gaming aspects of Khertaan. So, all these levels and percentages don't mean much to me. I only know we're supposed to reach level 30, and level 21 is a lot closer than level 15. So I'm doing something right.

A glance over my shoulder proves the Arachnid Behemoths aren't following me. They're headed for Maron. What are their intentions? Something in the city or between me and the city is drawing them. Do I follow them to investigate, or do I press on towards Minook?

I don't know what's *best*, but I like the idea of making forward progress, so, Minook, here I come. If I don't need to worry about giant spiders on my tail, then all the better.

CHAPTER THIRTY-FOUR

Megan: Escaping the City... Again

I'm in the jail cell. I wouldn't have chosen this place to respawn, but I wasn't asked. At least there aren't any Guards present. If one were to enter, I wouldn't want to be seen, so I concentrate on being invisible. I don't know whether it's working... looking down, I still see myself.

I switch to Third Person POV. Ah... interesting. When I go invisible, if I use First Person POV, I can see myself and my equipped items, but if using Third Person POV, I'm invisible to myself. I switch back to First.

Okay... take stock of what I have. In addition to what I *should* have, I have a number of duplicated items. It's really quite some glitch creating these duplicates, but it works great for me.

A number of items I don't want to wear or carry, and I stash them in the inventory I share with Mithabel. She'll wonder about the duplicate Ogaltha Ring if she notices it, but I sure as hell am not wearing it.

I try mentally contacting Mithabel again by various channels, to no avail. The only communication I can avail myself of is close proximity local chat. I'd like to know my full skills list so I can operate at my full potential, but I can't access a character sheet, talk to Mithabel, or talk to Kaleisha, so I'm screwed.

Wait…. I have an idea.

Double check I'm not leaving any equipment on the cot. Compress my body and slip between the cell bars. *Oh, Goddess, this is weird.* My perspective is all off. My brain can't unscramble the images my eyes are sending it. I switch to Third Person POV.

That's better. No wonder my perspective was off. My flattened body is three inches thin, with my eyeballs on opposite sides of my profile. Next time I'll compress along a different axis, so my eyes can cooperate.

I slip through the bars and decompress. Then I fly across the room, moving at the pace of a brisk walk—faster than I could fly before. Cool stuff. I'm feeling more like a Ninja now, or—as they call it in Khertaan—an Anjai.

Since I can compress more and fly faster, my abilities to turn invisible and detect anomalies will have improved. Mithabel has gained levels and thus more skills I don't know about. Oh, goody… more abilities for me to discover by accident.

What kinds of things could Ninjas historically do? I imagine a Shuriken in my grip, but one doesn't materialize. I imagine myself turning to smoke, and that doesn't happen, either. I don't know what to try…. The skills I know about will have to do me for now.

If I go now without leaving any sign I was here, the City Guard will be none the wiser. The space under the exit door measures less than an inch. I can't compress enough to go under it. Fortunately, it's unlocked, so I leave the old fashioned way, careful to close the door behind me.

I fly along the hallway, passing framed photos of me taken on Earth. What *is* their significance? I try and fail to take down the one depicting me in my Mustang. I'll never forgive that damned Orc Wizard for frying my car. That vehicle was my last solid connection to my departed dad.

At the end of the hallway, concentrating on being invisible, I quickly open the door, slip out, and shut it behind me, before making my way to Ye Olde Shoppe of the Profane. Visiting this place seems so long ago. How long has it actually been? I don't know. The System clock isn't working for me.

The proprietor stares in my direction as I enter, his gaze never quite focusing on me. "I know you're there, adventurer. Show yourself if you want to do any business. If thoughts of theft are on your mind, know that the System protects this shoppe against thieves."

I close the door behind me and cancel my invisibility. "Sorry. I can't take a chance of being seen out there. Please don't call the Guards."

Recognition lights his gaze. "You lied to me. You led me to believe you were Mithabel, but instead you're an illegal avatar. I'm sorry, but I must turn you in. If I don't, I'll be stripped of my station and thrown in jail."

I wave him off. "Delay your report just a moment, please. I need some paper and something to write with. How much would that cost?"

He strolls to a display stand and picks up a black feather about nine inches long. "If I were allowed to trade with you now—which I'm not—I'd give this to you as a bonus item for the trade we made earlier. It's an Endless Writing Quill. You could use it to write on the back of the map you received from me earlier." He holds the Quill aloft. "But like I said, I can't trade with you. The Guards, in fact, have already been notified of your presence here. You may wish to leave my shop before they arrive." He fusses with something behind the counter.

"Yeah, about that map…." I'm too embarrassed to finish that sentence. Closing my eyes, I put my hands together as though in prayer. "Please, sir. I'm not an illegal, but the developer who knows otherwise is offline. I've been cut off from nearly all communications, which makes it all but impossible to prove my innocence. But I could get a written message to Mithabel, if I only had a way to write one." I drop my hands and meet his gaze as I walk to him. "Please, kind sir. Help me."

He shakes his head, sorrow or maybe pity in his eyes. "I can't." He goes to another stand and grabs a piece of Parchment. "Please leave. If you could turn the Closed sign for me on your way out, I'm going to take a break out back." Circumnavigating the counter, he disappears through a doorway leading to the back of the building.

It takes a second for it to sink in what he's doing. I call after him. "Very well, sir. I'm sorry I tried to involve you in anything remotely illegal." Turning invisible, I flip the Open/Closed sign and head out the way I came in.

A *whoosh* alerts me, my Danger Sense trait putting me on notice as a contingent of City Guards approaches. Shouting garbled and angry words, they point at me and break into a run, drawing Bows to hand. Either they see through my invisibility or they have some other way to sense me. I fly straight up.

Arrows strike the exterior wall beneath me as I fly over the roof. More arrows speed by overhead, way off target. I descend behind the building.

The proprietor leans against the back wall of his shoppe. I land next to him, stirring up dust. He squats, letting the Parchment and Quill fall. "Oops, how clumsy of me."

The System won't stop me from stealing outside the shoppe, especially when the items aren't in anyone's possession. I snatch up the dropped items and stash them. Hmm. He has given me another Map as well as the Parchment and Quill. "What's your name, friend?"

His smile is priceless. "Thank you for asking, but I'm not deemed important enough to have a name. You may refer to me as the proprietor of Ye Olde Shoppe of the Profane. I suppose you could shorten that to the Profane Proprietor. And by what name may I call you?"

"I'm Megan Wright." I drop my invisibility and offer him my hand to shake. "I'm Mithabel's secondary avatar. Completely legal, I assure you, despite any ideas the City Guards have about me."

He gives me a knowing glance as he takes my hand with a strong grip. "Guards! I have the illegal avatar. Hurry and come!"

I smile. "I seriously hope you don't get in trouble over me, Proprietor Profane." Then I turn on my invisibility again, compress my body, slip my thinned hand free of his, and fly away.

Last time I flew over the city gates, I was shot by a magical lightning bolt. So I'll avoid doing that again. But flying anywhere over the walls might result in my being hit. Yet what choice do I have? The Guards certainly won't open the gates for me, and they'll detect me if I hang around there waiting for the gates to be opened....

So the hell with it. I pick an isolated stretch of wall and fly over with an increased altitude. The additional height doesn't help. Electricity fries me inside and out. Ugh. The attack is brief but the sensation of being slammed by a freight train lingers.

The important thing is I'm still alive, and thus so is Mithabel.

I hurry to land. Equipping the Quill and Parchment, I write in small letters at the top of the page. Space is a premium, if this is to be the only way I can talk to my primary avatar.

Mithabel, this is Megan. Wish we had a better way to talk. What skills do we have now? How many lives do we have left?

I stash both items and hope Mithabel gets the message.

My pain flees. Dylan just healed Mithabel of the lightning damage. Checking inventory, I see the Parchment is still there. Come on, Mithabel. Take stock of what you have. You might be surprised.

I turn my attention to the Map. If only there were a way I could tell where I was in relation to the safe path. Wait… there, next to the line representing the city wall, is a tiny red dot that wasn't there before.

Assuming the dot represents my location, I use it as a guide to fly towards the path. As I recall, I'll need to stay in contact with the ground for the safe path to protect me from random encounters. Stashing my Platform Slippers, I drag my bare toes in the sand as I fly towards Minook at the pace of a brisk walk.

CHAPTER THIRTY-FIVE

Mithabel: Among Friends

Dim magical light illuminated a heavy wooden door at the end of a stone hallway. Dylan and Amarynth sat on the floor, backs to the wall. Having returned to his original small size, Rolag paced nearby. Beyond the Dragon, the dwarfish Angel Zyekt stood with his back to the group as he watched the stretch of corridor leading away from the door. His lady Mouse, Niav, perched on his shoulder, the tiny support leash around her neck. A T-intersection lay ten feet beyond the Angel.

"Congratulations, chief." Kaleisha danced into view. "You are now level 15 Tank, level 6 Anjai. You have gained an attribute point. Nice to see you again."

"Mithabel, you're back." Dylan sprang to her feet, a glowing Cudgel in hand—the only source of light in the hallway. "Took you long enough." More gorgeous than the Elf Tank remembered, the Polynesian Priestess wrestled Mithabel's attention away from everything else.

The black-haired Elf gasped for breath, her gaze scanning Dylan up and down. *"By the Goddess, Dylan.* You are *the... most... beautiful... woman...* ever to grace any world. You... take my breath away.... Your skin is... so smooth... so perfect... so *chocolaty*, I just want to eat you. Your hair... such luscious royal purple curls... I want to twine them around my fingers... and rub them on my cheeks." She met the Polynesian's gaze. "And your soulful brown eyes... I could lose myself in them... forever... and ever."

Amarynth chuckled. "She makes me wish I were a lesbian."

"It helps to look away from her." The Angel wasn't merely standing watch. He was actively looking away from the Priestess so as not to be affected by her appearance.

Tearing her gaze away from Dylan's startling beauty with a concerted mental effort, Mithabel assessed herself. She wore her black leather Bikini, showing off her long, Elven legs—not the short, Orc-child kind. "What a relief. How long was I gone?" She pointed her chin at the door. "What's in there?"

"That's the dungeon exit." Amarynth stood. "We debated whether to leave the dungeon before or after you respawned, but sorta had the decision made for us. On the other side of that door are a bunch of City Guards wanting to take you into custody. If we go out there without you, they'll detain us. We decided it was better to sit here than to sit elsewhere."

"Why do they...?" Mithabel let her words trail off. "Oh, I get it. What has Megan done?"

"They didn't wait to evaluate her." Dylan stepped close and drew Mithabel into a hug. "I spoke with her. They claim she's an illegal avatar and are holding you responsible. So they've put a bounty on you. Megan got away from them, but was killed by an exploding Behemoth. Some of us got XP for the kill." She kept the Tank in her embrace.

"That's not all the XP we got." Rolag snorted, and smoke puffed from his nostrils. "What level are you now, Mithabel?"

The Tank glanced over Dylan's shoulder at her other companions, relishing the press of the Polynesian's body. "I'm level 15 Tank, level 6 Anjai. Why, what level are you all?"

Dylan gave Mithabel a final squeeze and then withdrew. "We're all level 21 in our main classes and level 12 in our subclasses."

Mithabel's jaw dropped. She tried to find words, but all that came out was, "How?"

Rolag snorted again. "When you popped in, Mithabel, you saw what we were doing. That's exactly what we were doing ten minutes ago—when 17 million XP just fell on us for no reason."

"It was most amazing." Peering back from her perch on the Angel's shoulder, Niav waved a tiny paw. "Zyekt and I were most fortunate to have been selected to accompany you on this quest."

"I really wish you'd been here, Mithabel." Dylan took the Tank's hand. "It happened after I talked to Megan, not long after you died. If she'd gone to sleep right away, you'd have been here. But minutes kept passing and you weren't back. I think she was watching the news or something. I suppose you have no memory of what transpired in her room while she was awake...?"

Mithabel shook her head. "I'm still completely cut off from her. It's maddening."

"Sorry...." Dylan grimaced. "So... while you were out, ZAvengers finished Ezmerelda's quest, and we were headed out of the dungeon with them when we ran into Quantized. They told us about the City Guards waiting in the inn lobby. We told them what to expect with the Orc room. They haven't come back yet. ZAvengers left the dungeon. We told Zyekt and Niav they could go, too, but fortunately for them they decided to stay with us."

"We went from level 1 to level 21 on just one quest." Niav gave a squeaky laugh.

Dylan lifted Mithabel's hand. "Is that the Ogaltha Ring?"

The Tank raised her other hand and glanced between the two. She wore an Ezmerelda Ring on her right hand and an Ogaltha Ring on her left. "That's it."

Amarynth grimaced. "Did you forget? Ezmerelda said no one was to wear it."

"I didn't do it on purpose." Mithabel tried to pull the Ogaltha Ring off, but it wouldn't come free. "It slipped onto my finger of its own accord, like it was cursed." She glanced around. "Where's Charli? Is she still with Quantized? I said I was sorry. I didn't intend to insult her. I swear I won't do it again."

"She's incommunicado." Amarynth's tone was tinged with disappointment. "According to Quantized, she dropped them off at the edge of the forest and then went back in for some unknown reason. I've continued trying to reach her over any channel possible, with no luck. I can't even get a response from a direct message."

Dylan released Mithabel's hand. "When I talked to Megan, she told me Charli was with her and some *other* party. I think Charli is responsible for all this XP we've been getting. She's still in our party, so whatever XP she earns, we earn, and vice versa. The party she's with killed a Behemoth. It exploded—not just a display of pixels like most defeated mooks, but a real gut buster.

"The XP Charli and Megan earned us for the Behemoth kill pushed you up to level 15. Unfortunately, Megan died in the blast. I'm guessing Charli *didn't*, and is still earning XP. I just can't imagine what she did to earn 17 million in one encounter.

That's like defeating 17 Behemoths. Megan did mention there were a ton of those big metal spiders after her."

Mithabel grabbed Dylan's arm to catch her balance. "This is blowing my mind." She'd thought she was doing great to be at level 15, and here her companions—including the two NPCs they'd hired for this particular quest—were level 21. She was 17 million XP behind them. It didn't feel right. "Are we wasting our time with this quest? If our ultimate goal is to reach level 30, we should be out there with Charli, out there where the real action is. This quest we're on was designed for PCs who play by the rules. If it were just a game—a competition for a million dollar prize—then we'd of course want to adhere to the rules, not to be disqualified. But we're no longer in this for the prize money. Whatever we need to do to reach level 30 quickly, if it's to cheat and steal and break all the rules, then that's what we do. We need to get out there, find Charli, and help her with whatever she's doing that is bringing in the amounts of XP she's bringing in."

The Mouse waved a paw for attention. "If I may interject...."

Dylan inclined her head. "Please do."

"As a level 21 Guide, I've gained much information. The quests were designed as stepping stones. Assuming you finish the quests correctly, the completion of each one opens opportunities for exponentially increasing amounts of XP. This is how you're meant to reach level 30 in a matter of days instead of weeks or months. It takes a total of over 1.3 billion XP to reach level 30. That will take 80 encounters like the one that earned us 17 million XP. If you progress through the quests in the manner intended, that number might be cut to 20 or even less."

"But have we wasted our time *on this one*?" Mithabel thrust out her left hand, wiggling the finger bearing the Ogaltha Ring.

"I wasn't supposed to wear this. But as soon as I picked it up, it slipped onto my finger. I couldn't stop it. There was no way for me to complete the quest correctly."

"I might know a way." Zyekt still faced away from the group. "Is there anything stopping us from trying it again?"

Dylan raised an eyebrow. "I don't think so. What do you have in mind, Angel?"

"It would mean I'd have to go with you to deliver the Ogaltha Ring to Ezmerelda."

Mithabel shrugged, even though the Angel wasn't looking her way. "That wouldn't be a problem for us if it's okay with you."

Niav eagerly answered before Zyekt could. "Yes, yes, wherever you need to go, we'll go, too."

"Well, then." Dylan nodded. "Tell us your idea, Angel."

"Let's get on the move, and I'll explain it on the way." Zyekt held his hands out to either side. "Grab hold like before, and then extinguish your light, Priestess. We're doing this exactly as you described it—in total darkness, straight there, with no delays or encounters. Mithabel, if you would take the lead, please. We're following the same path as before. But when we reach the spot where Niav tunneled under the door, search the wall again for a hidden compartment like we found at the Orc's room. My Intuition says there's one there, even though you didn't find it before. There will be a lever inside, which you'll push to your left instead of your right."

Dylan chuckled. "We trust your Intuition."

The Elf flew ahead of the others, noting her speed had increased two-fold. She'd also gained an unassigned attribute point. "How many free points did you all gain?"

"Two attribute points," replied Dylan, "and one trait point. Guess what I added my trait point to."

"You didn't...." But it all clicked in Mithabel's head. "You raised your Beauty trait *again*?"

Dylan laughed. "Yeah. I don't know if I should raise it any further after this. I'll have everyone wanting to jump my bones, no matter what their sexual preference."

Mithabel returned the laugh, leading the way to the intersection and turning right. "You are so freaking vain, Priestess. But I love you for it. Have I told you that lately? I do. I freaking love you."

"I love you, too, Tank."

"What are your skills like now?"

The others followed the Elf Tank, everyone holding onto the Angel as he flew right behind her. The Mouse whispered directions to the Angel as needed to keep him on course, using her Heightened Sense of Smell to follow Mithabel in the dark dungeon.

Dylan rattled off her new skill levels, after which Amarynth and the others told theirs as well. Notably, Dylan's Morale skill could give everyone in the group a +26 bonus to all their actions, and she had a new skill called Blinding. Amarynth had greatly increased her skills with the Crossbow, with extra shots per combat heartbeat and the ability to decrease her heartbeat duration. The cool down time for Rolag's combat heartbeat had been halved, meaning all his actions would reset twice as quickly as before. He had increased his Accelerated Healing trait, so that he could heal naturally at a greatly increased rate, and he'd picked up a new Killing Winds skill. But what really stood out about Rolag was his improved ability to Enlarge, which he could now do 16 times a day, able to grow as high at the shoulder as Mithabel was tall. His Intimidate skill had increased to level 14, and he'd gained a bunch of small area attacks and a Mass Block skill he'd not had the chance to try out yet.

Niav listed her changes as they passed the alcoves. Her Guide skills had all greatly improved, including her Monster Lore. For her Mentalist subclass, she had several skills still yet to try: Mislead, Anticipate, Levitate, Displace, Inspect Character, and Teleport Self.

By the time she'd finished, the group had passed the alcoves, entering the area where the Lizardman Savages attacked before. Mithabel planned to use her level 6 Detect Anomaly skill to look for the secret door. Niav offered to assist with her improved Search skill—at level 26.

"Of course, you can help." Mithabel extended her arm, and the Mouse jumped onto it, behaving like she could clearly see in the dark, though it was her sense of smell that guided her. The Tank flew to the wall, spotting the main door immediately. The makeshift tunnel Niav had earlier burrowed under the door was gone.

Niav's ability to Levitate allowed her to move up and down next to the wall of her own accord while Mithabel hovered and scanned for anomalies.

"You may as well go ahead and boast, too, Zyekt." Mithabel continued scanning the wall, despite feeling inadequate with her level 6 skill pitted against the Mouse's level 26.

The Angel didn't downplay his boosts. "I put all my attribute points against Intuition and raised it to 19, which puts it in the super-human range."

Mithabel's cheeks flushed. "Well, hell, then. Can you use your Intuition and tell us where we need to look?"

"It doesn't always work that way. My Intuition in this case is that one of you will find the secret compartment."

Niav pointed. "It's in the ceiling. That's why you didn't find it before, Mithabel."

The Tank flew up next to the Mouse. "Good job, Niav." She looked to the Angel. "Does your Intuition tell us how we should open it?"

Zyekt huffed. "Please, Mithabel. My Intuition can't be invoked on command, or it would be called Knowledge instead. An idea comes to me or it doesn't. And even though the attribute is in the super-human range, that doesn't mean it's always right. Do you think any less of me for my decision to raise it?"

"No, of course not." Mithabel pushed up on the discovered door. It raised and slid aside to rest inside the compartment space. A lever pointed down from where it was anchored in the top of the compartment. She pushed it up to her left.

The large door opened. The party passed through into an empty room. As expected, another door occupied the center of the wall to their left and opened easily. Passing through, they continued down the hallway towards the Ogaltha room.

Zyekt had more to tell. He'd raised his Meditative Focus trait. "For every combat heartbeat I spend not engaged in strenuous activity, I gain a bonus of +1 per trait level to the next action I take, up to a maximum number of heartbeats not to exceed my character level. Thus, with rank 2 in Meditative Focus, if I'm not overly active for at least 21 combat heartbeats, which for me is three and a half minutes, I can apply a maximum of +42 to my next action. Right now, in fact, I have a +42 bonus just waiting to be applied."

Something clicked for Mithabel. "That's why you were always delaying between actions when we were fighting those Lizardman Savages. You don't have to use that trait for every action, do you?"

"No, but during that particular encounter, my Intuition told me I needed the extra boost. I listened to my Intuition."

They were nearly to the Ogaltha room.

Zyekt hurried through his skill list. One of his skills allowed him to summon a glowing silver Sword, Dagger, or Shuriken at will, able to deal both physical and mental damage. He also had three Psi powers: Foresight, Telekinesis, and Projections. The latter power was for projecting illusions. His maximum Psi points, used when invoking his powers, were 168.

That seemed a lot to Mithabel.

Moreover, the male Angel had two Life-Stealer spells—Dark and Harm—and skills that allowed him to cast his spells at targets up to 30 feet away. His Dark spell could enchant a non-magical weapon—though not nearly as effectively as Dylan's Light spell could. Still, Mithabel was super impressed and swallowed a ton of jealousy.

She stopped before the door to the Ogaltha room. "We're here."

Dylan sighed with relief. "You haven't told us your new skills, Mithabel, or where you put your latest free attribute point."

"I haven't bothered with it yet. Listening to you all makes me feel… unnecessary. But… yeah… I should assign my attribute point." Mithabel willed her character sheet to appear. "Ugh. I'm at 4 Constitution—only 4 lives left. Um… hold on… I was at 6 before I died…. Oh, Goddess. It's because of Megan. She dies when I die… and each of our deaths lowers my Constitution…. That does not seem fair…. I guess I'm assigning every free attribute point I earn from now on to Constitution."

With a sigh, she scanned her skills list. "Oh. Sweet mother. I have a new skill—level 2 Shapeshift Siamese Cat."

Dylan, Niav, and Rolag laughed.

The Dragon clenched his fangs to squelch the laughter. "It specifically says, *Siamese Cat?*"

Zyekt huffed. "We didn't run into Quantized. Either they went out a different way than we came in, or they were all killed."

Dylan agreed. "Lizardman Savages, most likely."

"Let's not worry about Quantized." Amarynth shook her head. "What's the plan, Zyekt?"

"I can guess." Dylan raised an eyebrow. "Telekinesis, right?"

"That's right." Zyekt lowered to the floor and released the others. "As long as we don't touch it, the Ring can't very well slip onto a finger. I'll transport it all the way to where we next meet Ezmerelda."

"Sounds like a plan. Okay, then. Rolag, position yourself here, please." Mithabel guided the Dragon to the unopened hidden entrance. She quickly found and opened the compartment wherein lay the lever for opening the door. "Remember, we're doing this in total darkness." Reaching in, she grabbed the lever. "Are we ready?"

Everyone mumbled their agreement.

Mithabel pushed the lever.

The door opened. Mithabel peered through, the only one with the Dark Sight to see what lay beyond. She didn't see what she'd expected.

"Am I glad to see you." The voice belonged to Ger-Alt, the Goblin leader of Quantized, mounted on her Cheetah. The Goblin turned to her companions, most of whom likely didn't have the Dark Sight trait. "It's MAD. We're saved." She turned again to face Mithabel, and her feline mount trod forward. Ger-Alt's gaze met the Tank's. "We thought we were locked in here forever." She and the rest of Quantized filed out of the room.

"It's rough not being able to kill yourself or your party members. We were considering dissolving our party long enough to kill each other, but decided to give it another ten minutes. Glad we waited."

Mithabel stuck her foot in the doorway to prevent the door from shutting. Beyond the Quantized party members, the room lay all but empty. "You've killed all the children."

Okguul, the Orc woman, stood at the back of the room, facing away from the door, her hands on her cheeks, her body trembling.

Toxxi the Faerie sighed. "After Dylan told us about their situation, we felt morally obligated to release them from their sad fates."

Dylan sucked in a breath but said nothing.

Amarynth spoke with clipped voice. "Is there still a Ring in the Chest?"

"No. We took…." The Goblin woman looked Dylan up and down. "By the Goddess, Priestess, how did you come to be so pretty?"

Mithabel watched Okguul. "The Orc woman didn't put another Ring back in place of the one you took?"

"Not that I saw." Ger-Alt's eyes remained glued to Dylan. "Any of the rest of you see her put a Ring back in the Chest?"

The others in Quantized said they hadn't.

FepXveq the Dark Elf—one of the few present able to see in the dark—stepped up to admire Dylan. The woman with the large afro said nothing, but merely looked.

"Which of you has the Ring you took from the Chest?" The Priestess showed no hint of knowing she was being studied so closely—like a piece of art.

"Zip has it in his inventory." Ger-Alt had yet to avert her gaze from the Polynesian Priestess.

Dylan pressed. "Did he put it on?"

"No. Ezmerelda told us not to."

Mithabel gritted her teeth. "Did the Ring try to slip onto Zip's finger...? Oh... he's a Cheetah. He has no fingers." Was it really that simple?

"Oh, it tried, fingers or no fingers. But I resisted long enough to stash it." The Cheetah wasn't riveted by Dylan's appearance. He probably couldn't see in the dark.

Mithabel grumbled. "How the hell did you manage that? I didn't have a chance to resist."

"I have Auni Resistance—what you might think of as Magic Resistance, and I pumped it up using Meditative Focus. I kept the Ring off my digits long enough for me to stash it.... Toxxi came up with the idea. I simply executed it."

"Great." Mithabel focused on her extraordinary Temperance to keep her cool. "So there's no way for us to finish the quest ourselves."

Toxxi said something.

Mithabel didn't hear. Pain rocked her body, like an overload of electricity shooting through every nerve. Gasping, she staggered back.

Kaleisha leaned into view. "You've taken 52% damage, chief, source unknown."

"Holy sweet mother."

"Oh, my Goddess." Dylan flailed about until Mithabel caught her by the wrist. "What just happened to you, Tank?" She laid her hands on Mithabel's shoulders. "May the Sun Goddess heal your wounds."

"You've been healed by Dylan for 16%, chief." Kaleisha bobbed her head to soft background music. "Your HP now stands at 64%."

Dylan swore. "You really took a hit, woman. I need to put a bit more Auni into my spell. May the Sun Goddess *Heal* your wounds."

"What *did* happen?" Ger-Alt finally took her eyes off Dylan to assess Mithabel. "Maybe we should put this place behind us."

"It had to be Megan." Mithabel spoke on party chat so Quantized wouldn't hear. "She just took a wallop from something. If she's in a jam, I might lose more HP. Stay ready to heal me, just in case. If I die suddenly, don't be surprised. If she's in a situation where one attack can deal 52% damage, it will only need two attacks like that in a row to take her out, and me with her."

Another attempt to mentally contact Megan failed. There was no way to know what trouble the blond player had found for herself.

CHAPTER THIRTY-SIX

Nick: Shadow Lover

After dinner, we return to Tabbie's apartment.

My girlfriend in this timeline holds up a blanket. "If Charli stays here tonight, she'll have to sleep on the floor. Here's a blanket she can use."

"I don't need to sleep." Charli paces. "My HP is full. But I would like a blanket. I do get cold sometimes. Do you want me to sit in the bathroom for a few minutes while you two have sex?"

"No, that's okay." Tabbie grimaces. "Sex is off the table for me tonight."

"Sex would be the fastest way to increase my energy," ODYSSEY says in my head. "I believe it's not only pleasure that works, but anything that increases your endorphins. Exercise could work—if you enjoyed any kind of exercise other than sex. Otherwise, at the current rate of increase, it will be weeks or even months before my energy reaches a sufficiently high level. I suspect we don't have months. You need to do what you can as often as you can to build my energy. If sex is not an option for you tonight, then I suggest you find some other enjoyable means of exercise."

"I'm going for a walk." It's the best form of exercise I can muster at the moment. "You two want to come with?"

"I'm out. But maybe I'll have a cigarette while you're gone." Tabbie knows cigarette smoke bothers my sinuses, and always takes her smokes outside.

Charli volunteers to go with me, as I knew she would. We walk in silence for the first couple of minutes.

She speaks first. "How's it coming along—energizing your nanobot collective?"

"I need to keep stoking my pleasure center. Everything we've been doing today has helped, but it's too slow. ODYSSEY recommends I have a lot of you-know-what to speed up the process. Otherwise, we could be stuck here for months. I don't think the rest of the multiverse has months. Hell, this timeline might not have months before the invaders find it."

"You mean sex." She says it without any hint of embarrassment. It's too dark out for me to see whether she's blushing, which I hope means she can't see that I am.

It feels wrong to be having this conversation with a teenage girl, but who else is there to discuss it with? ODYSSEY would be ideal, but he's conserving energy. No one else on this planet understands my dilemma, and I need to bounce ideas off someone. "Yes, I'm talking about sex. But Tabbie isn't in the mood tonight. What am I supposed to do? Find a prostitute? I could get thrown in the slammer for that, which could delay our leaving this timeline even longer."

Charli doesn't break stride. "You could have sex with me."

I try not to break stride, either. "That's not going to happen, Charli. If you were eighteen, I might say *yes*, but you aren't. What are you, sixteen at the most?"

"I first met you in 1996, Nick. Twenty-six years ago."

"You're obviously not twenty-six...."

"My character sheet says I'm fourteen—like it *always* has. It said it in 1996—so one could say I'm forty years old now. In any case, *I'm not from Earth* and it's laws shouldn't apply to me. If my character sheet said I was eighteen, would you have a problem having sex with me?"

"Yes, I'd still have a problem, Charli, because your body is that of a minor. If you told me you were eighteen, I wouldn't believe you, no matter what your character sheet says."

"Khertaan NPCs can't willingly lie, Nick. If my character sheet said I was eighteen and I looked the part, would you have sex with me?"

God, I can't believe I'm having this conversation. "Under the circumstances we find ourselves in, sure, Charli. But you're not eighteen and you have the body of someone too young, so it's out of the question."

"What if a strange woman approached you on the street who was obviously old enough and asked you to have sex with her for no money? Would you do it?"

"What, just right here in the street?"

She shrugs. "Yeah...." She looks about and points her chin. "It's really dark over there."

"Tell me you're not thinking what I think you're thinking." I'm pretty sure I know what she's thinking, and it's brilliant, as far as the logic of it is concerned. Executing the plan is another question entirely.

"I'd have to stay in line of sight."

"I don't want to have sex in the street. We'll go to my place. You can conjure a Shadow Warrior woman for me in the privacy of my bedroom. Do you have to watch, or simply be in your conjuration's line of sight? I wouldn't feel comfortable with you watching, and I need to enjoy what I'm doing or it doesn't help."

"I don't have to watch. The shadow woman would need to be able to see me if she looks my way, but I don't have to meet her gaze or anything. I could sit with my back to you."

What other options do I have? With this idea in my head, I can't think of more. "Do you know for sure you can cast the spell in this timeline? And does your spell work that way? Your Shadow Warrior woman won't try to kill me, will she?"

"Let's find out." Charli gestures. A shadowy feminine figure appears, looking more like a silhouette than a three-dimensional person. I can't discern her facial features, but she's shapely enough to not leave any doubt as to whether she's an adult. She stands straight and unmoving, facing me. If she's wearing any clothes, they're skin tight. Her chest doesn't rise and fall with each breath, because she isn't breathing.

Charli points at me. "Pleasure him."

The Shadow Warrior steps close, tilts her head, and places her cold lips on mine. Her chilly tongue enters my mouth. She pushes me back, into deep shadow, and pulls my t-shirt off over my head.

I try to object, but she's persistent. It's so dark, I can't see a damned thing. There's no way Charli can be watching, or so I tell myself. The Shadow Warrior pulls down my pants. If I tried to stop her, I think she'd fight me.

She's not wearing any clothes. Her skin, pure ebony, chills mine as she presses her body against me. She takes my erection in her cold hand and guides me into her. It's cold inside and not moist. The experience being a new one for me makes it exciting, and I orgasm inside her, but sex with a Shadow Warrior isn't something I want to repeat, and I seriously doubt one session of love making will be enough to recharge ODYSSEY to the required power level.

The shadowy woman dissolves into nothingness.

"That was good," says ODYSSEY. "Brought me up from 35% MJCL to 40%. Do that another dozen times, and we could attempt a jump to another timeline. Would greatly improve our odds of success if I were charged more than the minimum, though."

I pull up my pants and find my t-shirt, pulling it on as I emerge from the shadows. "What's MJCL?"

"*Minimum jump charge level*—the least amount of energy needed to attempt a time-jump. It's not enough to guarantee success, but anything less wouldn't suffice to pierce the timeline membrane, automatically failing."

Charli smiles at me. "Was she any good? Did it help?"

"It helped, but it won't work again. Damned cold."

"It won't help to have sex with her again?" Charli pouts.

"It *might* help *some*, but nowhere near as much as the first time. Did I mention she was damned cold?"

"I'd be warm, but you don't want me."

"Give it up, Charli. But thanks for helping what you could. It was a brilliant idea. From what ODYSSEY just told me, we should resolve to being here for another week or two, at least, and that's assuming I can find willing partners who I'm also willing to do it with. I'll be one worn out man when it's all done."

We head back for Tabbie's apartment, in step with each other.

CHAPTER THIRTY-SEVEN

Nick: TENS Unit and Other Efforts

Sunday morning finds me in Tabbie's bed. Charli nudges me awake. She's wrapped in a blanket. The shower is running. Charli winks at me and tilts her head towards the bathroom.

Tabbie is accommodating, but the pressing need to enjoy it dilutes the pleasure factor for me. ODYSSEY doesn't waste any of the meager energy obtained from the love making session to tell me how little it boosted his MJCL, if any. Damn. This won't be easy.

I consider running another T&T session for Ulric and Charli, but I'm not in the mood for that, either. I've never felt so blasé. The memory of Thunderbolt Chocolate doesn't excite. The only appealing things today are sweet buns and soda. "Where's the nearest place to buy snacks, Tabbie?"

"About a quarter mile south. You going? I'll go too."

Charli jumps up. "Me too."

Fortunately, the place has sweet buns and fountain sodas. I buy two dozen of the sweet buns and two super-sized fountain sodas.

Tabbie raises both eyebrows. "Are you feeding an army?"

"I've got a craving."

"I'll say." She buys a pack of cigarettes.

Charli stares at items on the shelves, but doesn't buy anything. She has no money.

"If you want something, Charli, I'll buy it for you."

She holds up a twelve-pack of batteries in one hand and a box containing an electrical device in the other. "Could this be of help? It's called a TENS unit. Says it delivers electrical current to targeted parts of the body and is meant to help with pain. I'm just wondering if it would have the same effect on your body that sex does."

A half dozen nearby customers give me harsh glances.

I don't care what they think. I'm trying to save their world, and they don't even know it's in danger. "How much does it cost?"

"Two hundred dollars."

"I can afford it. Bring it to the counter. I'll give it a try." I'm admittedly desperate.

Having made our purchases, we head back to Tabbie's place. I fold the bed into a couch and have a seat—the sweet buns and sodas arranged at my feet. Charli sits beside me while Tabbie goes outside for a smoke. The Cowgirl opens the TENS unit box while I gulp soda and stuff sweet buns down my throat. It actually feels pretty great. ODYSSEY has to be getting *something* from this.

"I am."

Charli reads the directions and installs the batteries needed by the unit. It takes six of the twelve we bought. She holds up two wires. They have sticky pads on the ends. "Does anything hurt?"

"Try it on my right leg."

She attaches one sticky pad to my right thigh and the other to my right shin. "Get ready. I'm turning it on. I'm starting on low power and turning it up. Tell me when it's at a level you like."

It's a tingling, pulsing sensation that causes the toes on my right foot to curl. My calf muscles spasm. This is supposed to soothe pain? It's *causing* it.

Charli keeps cranking up the power. I don't tell her to stop. It's like my brain needs to know just how bad this can get, and the thirst for that knowledge is greater than any logic calling for the pain to cease. The depth of the pain is a pleasure of a different type, an experience shiny and new. Finally Charli stops, having reached maximum power.

My leg is on fire, but I don't ask to quench the flames. It's like inviting a torturer to flay the top layer of skin from my body, and then watching him do it because I've never seen it done before.

ODYSSEY grows excited. "Ah, yes. Keep it coming. This is the best yet."

Charli leaves the unit at maximum power until it automatically shuts off.

My leg feels like it's been run over by the proverbial bus. I won't be doing that again anytime soon. I gasp as the pain eases. "How did we do, ODYSSEY?"

"Fantastic. I'm now at 65% MJCL. It's apparently not only your pleasure center that can increase my energy levels, but your pain receptors as well. Any extreme emotion or feeling might do the trick. Perhaps you should try watching a scary movie."

Tabbie returns from her smoke. She glances at the wires attached to my leg and shakes her head.

My laugh is tempered by the lingering pain. "How about we go see a scary movie? We can pick up Ulric too."

"Sounds fun to me." Charli's head bobs.

Tabbie gives me a dubious look. "Okay. But nothing gory."

I nod my agreement, and we pile into my minivan once more. We stop at Paul and Ingrid's house for Ulric. He's not the most thrilled about seeing a scary movie, preferring to play more T&T, but he goes along anyway, probably because Charli is going.

Ulric and Charli sit in the front row next to each other. Tabbie and I sit in the fourth row, so we don't have to crane our necks. The person behind Charli asks her to remove her Hat. Charli apologizes and complies, making her pigtails more prominent from behind.

The movie is rather lame to me, but I hear Charli squeal on occasion. She grabs onto Ulric each time.

"Not even a 1% increase," ODYSSEY reports after the movie ends. "Watch something more scary next time."

I have a feeling it won't help. "It's difficult being scared when one is wanting it. I need to be scared when I'm not expecting it. That might crank up your charge level."

He stays quiet, so as not to use up the meager charge earned from the not-so-scary movie.

We drop off Ulric and head back to Tabbie's. There's nothing to do at her place, especially with Charli hanging around. But I'm responsible for the Cowgirl being on Earth and in this timeline—I'd never forgive myself if anything happened to her. In Khertaan, she can take care of herself, but on Earth I'm concerned she'll do or say something to get the police involved, and then who knows where things will go.

Sitting on the couch, I ask Charli to hook me up to the TENS unit again, but on the other leg. It worked so well before. Maybe it will work well again.

She sticks the pads to my left thigh and shin. "Ready?" She doesn't wait for my reply, but gradually cranks it up like before.

Knowing what to expect dilutes the experience. Electricity shooting through my flesh and nerves still hurts, but doesn't cause the same rush. Damn. We leave it on until the unit automatically shuts off.

"Another 1% increase. I'm at 66% total." There's no reason for ODYSSEY to say more. This time was nothing like the previous one. I suspect the next time I use the TENS unit, we'll be lucky if it generates even a 1% charge.

Having more sex would help, especially if I consider the woman hot and she isn't physically cold as ice—if only I didn't have Charli to worry about. Aside from sex, I need to seek new experiences. "Anyone want to go bungee jumping or sky diving?"

Tabbie's look is more dubious than before. "No thanks. But I'll watch if you go."

Charli jumps up and down. "I'll do it. What is it?"

Tabbie clears her throat. "Falling… off a bridge or from an airplane."

Charli turns to me and whispers. "What's an airplane?"

"You don't know what an airplane is?" Tabbie rubs her forehead as though she has a headache.

I chuckle at Tabbie's disbelieve that Charli could have lived such a sheltered life. "It's a metal machine with wings and flies through the air. It's hollow, and people sit inside. It takes them from one city to another."

"They should have those in Khertaan." Charli claps. "But since they don't, let's do that. Let's go skydiving!"

Tabbie shakes her head. "Do you even know a skydiving place?"

"I do." Charli laughs. "I'm a Guide, remember. I have a level 24 Navigation skill and level 12 Landmarks skill. I can find my way around almost anywhere."

My girlfriend shuts her eyes. "It isn't the same in the real world as it is in your game, Charli."

The Cowgirl bats one of her pigtails. "Khertaan *isn't a game*, and so far all my skills work here like they do there. Maybe it's my high average Optimism talking, but I'm betting all my skills will work here. My Cowgirl kindred trait is Stubbornness, so…. You can call it luck if you want, but you can't make me doubt my own abilities or realness."

Tabbie stiffens.

I don't want my girlfriend to feel offended. "Charli, let's cool it on the Khertaan stuff while you're here, okay? Let's keep it between you and me. Now, you say you can direct us to a skydiving place, and if you say so, I believe you. Let's all go then."

"You two go ahead." Tabbie pulls out a pack of cigarettes. "I'll sit this one out. Will you be staying at your place tonight, Nick? You have work tomorrow, right?"

Bloody hell, I hadn't thought about my job in this timeline. I work at NSA. If I don't show up or call in, they'll send someone to look for me. I don't need that. "I suppose I should. If anything changes, I'll give you a call."

Tabbie walks us out to the minivan. Charli hops into the front passenger seat. I don't yet have the driver's side door open.

My girlfriend leans in for a kiss. As she pulls away, she whispers to me. "Have fun with your little girlfriend."

I laugh, but keep my voice low, too. "Don't tell me you're jealous of my cousin."

"If she's your cousin, I'll eat this cigarette. I don't know who she really is, but I see how she looks at you. She doesn't look at Ulric the way she looks at you. She's trouble, Nick. Be careful when you're in bed tonight. I wouldn't be surprised if she tried crawling in with you... naked."

"Not going to happen." I open the van door and climb in. I don't close it hard. I'm not angry at Tabbie. I understand her jealousy. But she's not telling me anything I haven't already considered. Charli has already offered her body to me. She knows what's at stake. It's in her best interests for ODYSSEY to reach MJCL as soon as possible. And she's not *actually* a minor child. She's not even human. But I don't think that would matter to the court of public opinion or especially a court of law. Her manifestation is that of a minor.

Charli fidgets in her seat. "Are we going?"

"Sure." I back the minivan out of its parking spot. "Tell me which way."

I follow her directions and find myself pulling into a bank parking lot. I start to ask why we've come here, but then realize.... We need money to go sky diving. "I have no idea how much we might need."

"Well, don't ask me."

"I'll see what's in my account. Climb out. You're sticking with me."

The pin number for my ATM card is the same one I've always used. Some things don't change across timelines.

I have over $30,000 in my savings. I try to take out $2,000, but the machine only lets me take $500 per day. So I take the $500 and go inside the lobby to take out more. I have a driver's license in my wallet, with my photo and signature. I sign the withdrawal slip and take out another $1500. With $2,000 in cash in my wallet, I return with Charli to the minivan. I hope sky diving doesn't cost the full $2,000 for the two of us to take one dive. We might want to do more than one dive. I just want to be prepared in case this experience boosts ODYSSEY's energy levels a lot and I want to repeat it.

Back on the road, Charli and I chat about things. We talk about Kylie and Slithy being Kendra and Susie on Earth. How I'm married to Kendra, and Susie is our daughter—but not in this timeline. Susie has visited this timeline before, so she must have the ability to time-shift. Whether she knows it or knows how to control it is another question. It's reasonable to think she died from the Behemoth's death explosion like I did. Where might Susie be right now?

I suspect Rancor died too. As Morrow's Familiar, Rancor should automatically respawn in Khertaan when Morrow does.

Charli changes the subject. "You and Ezmerelda were talking about someone named Seth. Sounds like a bad guy."

"He is." How much should I tell her? "His only agenda seems to be the destruction of all life in all timelines. Then there's this fellow named Gondra who opposes Seth. I've met them both. Either of them could have redirected us to this timeline, and neither of them would be inclined to explain why."

"What about ODYSSEY?"

"The thought did cross my mind, but he's as eager to leave this timeline as we are. As for Gondra, I can't conceive of any reason he'd redirect us away from my respawn lab. He wants us to reach level 30 as quickly as possible, and that ain't happening in this timeline. But Seth... he has motivation to delay our training while he continues his."

"Or maybe our redirection here was a totally random occurrence...." Charli points at an approaching driveway. "Turn in here."

I pull into a parking lot for an establishment called Outta the Sky. We scarcely get inside before we're asked when we'd like to schedule our jumps and are told the earliest open dates are three weeks from today. There are other considerations as well before we can make our first jump. Dammit. I don't want to wait that long. "There's got to be something else we can do to recharge ODYSSEY in the short term."

"We need to go to West Virginia."

I look askance at Charli. "What's in West Virginia?"

She shrugs. "A Landmark."

So we head for West Virginia, with Charli navigating.

Hours pass, during which a coagulation in my stomach grows heavier by the minute. A mixture of Thunderbolt Chocolate, sweet buns, and soda wafts up my throat like an odor. It's no longer sweet, but pungent, like food that's been left sitting out for days. I stop the minivan at a roadside park, instruct Charli to stay put, and leave her behind against my better judgment while I go to the public bathroom and vomit. Everything I've consumed — food or drink — since coming to this timeline floats in the toilet, including the peas, mashed potatoes, and steak served to me at Paul and Ingrid's house. A dozen sweet buns are now a gooey mash. The soda I drank turns the toilet water brown. Looks like a bad case of diarrhea.

"Increased to 69% MJCL."

It's laughable my misery sufficed to recharge ODYSSEY by more than a scary movie could.

My body didn't digest any of the food or drink I've consumed recently. It all tasted good going down, but I didn't need it for nourishment. I've not felt hungry or thirsty. I've only eaten for the enjoyment of it. My body is changing. I'm not human anymore. This is the effect of the Khertaan training. I'm transforming, but into what? Is this what I want? As if I have a choice. This is what Gondra says needs to be done. I trust him as much as I trust ODYSSEY. Perhaps I'm a fool to trust either of

them. But if I trust them, then I have to believe the world—no…
the multiverse—is coming to an end if I don't transform into the
type of warrior needed to effectively fight the invaders.

After washing my face and rinsing my mouth, I rush outside.
Charli is still sitting in the minivan. I'm so worried she'll vanish
on me, and I'll be at a loss as to how to find her.

Another hour, and we cross the state line into West Virginia.
I keep following Charli's directions, and we arrive at a
courthouse. It's closed, as is its parking lot. Signs along the street
inform us there's no parking after 6:00 PM on Sundays.
According to the clock in the minivan, it's shortly after 8:00.
What now? "I'm not sure *why* we're here, but now we're here.
We'll find out why tomorrow. Tonight, we'll find a hotel and get
a room with two beds. Promise me you'll behave yourself."

"I wouldn't dream of misbehaving." Charli gives me a wink
I find unsettling. "There's a hotel just down the street."

I drive the short distance and park in the hotel lot.

"Maybe you should use your Hide skill until we're inside the
room, to avoid any questions."

"I can do that." She vanishes.

I hop out of the van and hurry around to her side, opening
her door and holding out my hand for her to take. When both
her feet are on the pavement, I tuck her fingers inside my belt.
"I'll need both my hands at the counter. Don't let go of me for
any reason while you're hiding. I need to know you're with me
every second."

"Yes, Mister Nick."

"You like being mischievous, don't you?"

I picture her evil grin.

We go inside, hurrying through the revolving door so it doesn't separate us. Staying hidden, Charli keeps tight hold of my belt.

The desk clerk gives me no trouble checking in. I rent the room for one night. I show my driver's license for id and a credit card for payment. Then I sign a paper and he gives me a room key.

Charli and I enter the room without mishap. Once I close the door, she stops hiding. Relief at seeing her physical presence again eases muscles I hadn't realized were tensed.

"Increased to 70% MJCL."

Had my stress been *that* great? I'm so worried about losing her.

"I'm taking this bed." Charli plops on the edge of the bed furthest from the entrance. "Not that I need to sleep."

"I don't feel that tired, either. I should. But I should also feel hungry and thirsty, and I don't feel either. I'm becoming a virtual entity, I think. I don't have any other explanation."

She frowns, but refrains from entering a discussion about the term *virtual*, and how it doesn't apply to Khertaan the way I think it does. The Cowgirl has other things on her mind. "So what will we do all night?" She sets her wide-brimmed Hat on the pillow at the head of her bed. "So many hours until morning... it's too bad we can't take advantage of them to recharge ODYSSEY."

"You promised to behave, Charli."

"Fine, Mister Nick, I'll behave." She reclines and stares at the ceiling. "Let me know when it's time to go. I'll be right here, looking for patterns in the ceiling tiles."

I set the radio alarm clock for 8:00 AM, lie back, and look for patterns in the ceiling tiles too, leaving the light on, afraid to turn it off and plunge the room into total darkness.

It's a long, wakeful, quiet night.

CHAPTER THIRTY-EIGHT

Charli: Courthouse Grounds

I'm grateful for the alarm when it goes off ten hours later. Lying awake thinking useless thoughts is not my favorite activity.

We exchange good morning pleasantries, but otherwise say next to nothing until we've checked out of the hotel and are outside, where I'm allowed to become visible again. We walk arm-in-arm to the courthouse. It's a nice feeling.

Nick finally speaks. "Why are we here?"

"I'm not sure. The Landmark isn't the building, but a room inside."

The courthouse isn't open yet, and won't be for another ninety minutes. We stroll around the grounds to bide the time. I love the flowers, the butterflies, the hummingbirds, and tree frogs. One tree frog pokes its head out of a birdhouse. It's so funny. With a giggle, I lean towards it, puckering my lips. It croaks—a sound I've never heard before—and I jump back with a soft yelp. Nick chuckles. The sound of his pleasure thrills me.

As we continue our walk, I put my weight on his arm, leaning my head against his shoulder. He doesn't draw away from me.

Electric feelings pulse through my chest. "I love you, Mister Nick."

"I love you, too, Miss Charli."

I pull him to a stop. "Do you mean that?"

"I admit I do. Your appearance is that of a teen, but your mind is as sharp as any adult's, and sharper than most. You have a sense of humor I appreciate. You know how to handle yourself, though I'm sick with worry any time we're apart. If you were eighteen, things could be different between us in this timeline, for however much longer we're here. When we go back to Khertaan, Morrow belongs to Kylie, so there can't be anything between you and him. But while we're here, my soul belongs to you, Charli, not to Tabbie, and she knows it. I won't try to deny it."

My insides quiver. "I feel the same way about you, Nick." I loosen my grip on him and turn away. "I tried to like Ulric. I think he likes me. But I can't stop thinking about you."

"I'm sorry, Charli. Life is unfair. But laws are laws, and I don't relish spending the rest of my days inside a prison cell in this timeline. The laws here dictate our behavior, and that's that."

"Laws suck." I turn back to him, but I'm looking down, not up at him. I've never felt so miserable. "Can I at least hug you?"

"Of course." He extends an arm and I fall into his embrace. He pulls me against his stomach and doesn't push me away as I cry on his t-shirt. He strokes my hair. "I didn't know NPCs could cry."

I sniffle and look up to meet his gaze. I'm having difficulty functioning. My eyes grow moist. "We're as functional as PCs, and we're as functional as Earth humans in many respects." I wipe away a tear. "Like PCs, we don't digest food, and we only sleep when we need healing. But also like PCs, we're like Earth humans in many other respects. We live, we laugh, we love, we hate, we cry, we die. Okay, we have multiple lives, which Earth humans don't, but aside from that.... There might be a few other differences. I don't know if we can procreate, but we can certainly go through the exercise of trying. I want to try, so badly—but only with you." I've only spoken the truth, and he knows it. I lean against him again. Goddess, the tears are streaming down my cheeks.

We stand under an oak tree and I cry until the courthouse opens. I can't turn off the tears. Why do I have to be stuck at age fourteen? Am I to *never* know love? Am I to be fourteen for eternity, or until I lose my last life, whichever comes first?

Nick claps me on the back. "Brave face, Charli. Let's find this Landmark."

CHAPTER THIRTY-NINE

Charli: Ceremony

The courthouse halls are all but empty. I navigate them with no trouble. "This is the place." I step up to a window with an *Open* sign.

The old lady clerk peers at Nick over her glasses, then turns her gaze on me. "How old are you, sweetheart?"

"Fourteen."

"Is this man your father?"

"No."

"Is he your intended groom?"

I don't give Nick the chance to interject. "Yes."

He's too stunned to speak. Fine by me.

The clerk frowns. "Your parents need to be here."

"I don't have any parents."

"A legal guardian?"

"Don't have one of those, either."

"Are you emancipated?"

"Yes."

The clerk nods solemnly. "I see. And what is your state of residence?"

"I'm homeless. I don't have a state of residence."

"Oh, my. Do you have any identification?"

"No."

"You poor girl. Emancipation hasn't worked out for you, has it? Are you sure marrying this man is what you wish to do?"

"He promises to take care of me, but is hesitant to have me living with him. I don't want a legal guardian. But I would take him as a husband, if the judge will order it." I lean against Nick, gripping his forearm. I'm exercising the hell out of my Negotiate skill.

Nick is silent. Good for him. I can handle this.

The clerk hasn't given up questioning me. "Wouldn't you rather go back to your parents?"

Is she not listening to me? "Like I said, *I don't have any parents.* If I did, I wouldn't know where they are. They certainly aren't in my life. I have no one but this man. He's good to me, and he'll keep being good to me if we're married. The difference will be I can live with him in his house and people can't tell us we can't."

The clerk frowns and turns her steely gaze on Nick. "And what is your state of residence, sir?"

"Maryland." He pulls out his driver's license. "Here's my id." He slides it through the window opening. I can scarcely believe he's going along with this. He knows exactly what I'm doing.

The clerk glances at his license. "You can't marry an underage girl in West Virginia if you live in Maryland."

No, this can't be. We're so close. This old lady feels sorry for me. She wants to help me. My Negotiate skill can't sway her if she feels compelled by the law. Electricity surges, rising from my gut into my throat. If I had food in my stomach, it would come up. Tears well in my eyes. I can't stop them. I press my head against Nick, my Hat tipping almost to the point of falling off. Isn't there anything I can say to change this situation?

I focus hard on my level 9 Negotiate skill, and the words roll out of me. "Can't the judge order it if he thinks it's what's best for me? I don't want to go to a shelter or live on the street." She's got to be affected by my tears, because they're real.

"It would be best if you went back to live with your parents."

I whirl on the stupid clerk. *"I don't have any parents.* I don't have *anyone* or *anything* except this man." I'm speaking the truth. I have no other words that can be more compelling.

"Wait here." The clerk leaves the window.

I wipe my eyes. Nick puts a hand to the back of my neck and massages me. Goddess, it feels good. I want his hands doing that to me elsewhere, everywhere.

The clerk returns. "The judge asks you to fill out this form, sir." She pushes a sheet of paper at Nick. "The judge is willing to expedite this matter given the girl's plight, even though you're from out of state." She points at one field near the bottom. "You need to place a figure in this box. The amount you place in the box will determine the judge's efficiency in expediting the matter, if you get my drift." She points at the very bottom of the form. "You'll sign and date down here. Make sure you fill in everything truthfully. If anything is later found to be false, your marriage will be rendered illegal and invalid. If that happens and the two of you engage in intercourse, even if both give consent…." She looks Nick straight in the eye. "You would be guilty of third degree sexual abuse. You could be fined up to $500, spend up to 90 days in jail, and be placed in the sex offenders registry."

Except for the part about being registered as a sex offender, those penalties seem woefully inadequate for statutory rape of a minor, even if the sex is consensual on both sides. Even I know that. Nick fills out the form. He gets to the *Expediting Fee* field.

I call upon my Negotiate skill again. "Start with $300."

He writes $300 in the field, signs, and pushes the form back to the clerk.

She pushes the form to me. "Please sign and date on the line below his."

I gladly comply.

The clerk takes the form and leaves the window.

She returns and pushes the form at Nick. "The judge has a lot on his docket. If you want this to happen today, you'll need to increase the Expediting Fee."

"Go to $400." I know the form will come back again, no matter what we offer. If we don't increase it by at least $100, it might be rejected out of hand. When the form comes back, we'll have to increase it again by the same amount we increase it by now.

Nick marks out the $300, writes $400, and passes the form back to the clerk. She leaves the window with it and returns a moment later.

"Judge says that figure is close, but not quite sufficient to bring him to reschedule someone else in order to work you in today."

"Final offer, $500." I'm positive that amount will do the trick.

Nick makes the change. The clerk leaves and returns. "That figure is acceptable. In addition to the regular fees, your total comes to $557. We prefer cash."

Nick counts out six hundred dollars. "Keep the change."

"The judge will be pleased. Come this way."

She leads us to another room. An old geezer ushers us in. He performs the wedding ceremony. He says a few words that pass right through me. He asks if Nick takes me as his wife. Nick says, "I do."

I can't believe this is happening. Things are fluttering inside me I never knew could flutter.

The old geezer asks if I take Nick as my husband, and I say, "I do." Electricity snaps, crackles, and pops all through me until he says, "I now pronounce you man and wife. You may kiss the bride."

With a shriek, I throw my arms around Nick's neck, pulling his head down to my level. I plant my lips on his. He returns the kiss and doesn't try to draw away until I'm done.

He mutters under his breath about 76% MJCL. I'll do my best to raise it to a hundred… or more.

The clerk is our witness. She hands Nick our marriage certificate and other papers, including an official court document ordering our marriage. She turns her gaze on me. "Congratulations, young lady. I hope everything works out for you. You might want to set up residence in West Virginia. I recommend exercising caution in Maryland."

We return to the hotel. Nick walks like a man in a daze. I didn't give him a chance to think or object.

I skip and dance around him. "Can we rent the hotel room for another night, please, my husband? Now that we're legally married, we can have all the sex we want, especially if we stay in the state." I can't wait for him to be inside me. It's legal now. He can't have any valid objections.

He stops walking. "I need to call into work." His voice has next to no inflection, like he's become a zombie.

"If we rent a room, you can use the room phone."

His gaze is unfocused. "You're right. We'll rent a room, I'll call into work, and then we can sit and discuss our next moves."

Sit and discuss our next moves? I know what our next moves are. What is there to discuss? But I know not to pressure him. "Works for me." I grab his hand and pull him towards the hotel. Oops. Slow down, girl. Goddess, I'm so anxious. He isn't. What's wrong with him?

I don't bother using my Hide skill. The clerk gives us a questioning look. I smile broadly at him. "We're just married. We have papers if you want to see."

The clerk gives a single, slow nod. "Congratulations."

Nick signs a form. The clerk hands him two keys to our second floor room, and Nick passes one to me. I'm pleasantly surprised he trusts me to have it. It's a card, not a key. How does it work?

I dance along the hallway, reaching the door before Nick does, and wait for him. He slips his key card in a slot and opens the door. So that's how it works.

He steps through the doorway, while I stay put. Turning back, he gives me a glance, and I return it with raised eyebrows. Is he forgetting what is expected of the groom?

"Right. Give me one second to put these papers down." He goes in and comes back paper free. "Very well, my young bride. Jump into my arms."

With a laugh that bubbles up my throat unbidden, I throw my arms around his neck and haul myself up. He catches me under my thighs and cradles me in his strong arms. I'm so happy. I don't know how I can be any happier, but I hope to find out. I put my head on his shoulder, tears falling uncontrolled, as he carries me over the threshold.

He lays me on the king-size bed, the only bed in the room. I laugh while I cry, looking up at him with pleading eyes, begging him to do to me what I've wanted for two decades.

Nick wipes away my tears, leans over me, and presses his lips to mine. We kiss like the newlyweds we are. My hands explore his body and his explore me. Goddess, it's happening. I throw my Hat onto the floor.

He stops and steps away from the bed, looking about, until his eyes land on a phone. "I need to make a call."

I've never seen a phone before, but knowledge of the device is in my brain. He picks up the receiver and dials a number.

The electricity inside me sputters. How can he draw away from me like this? For a phone call? Can't it wait another hour? My breathing is heavy. My head and heart ache like hell. "If you love me, Nick McKenzie, hang up that damned phone *now*."

He hangs up the phone, but doesn't return to bed.

I close my eyes and wait in silence, holding back the tears, hoping for what I know won't happen.

"I'm sorry, Charli." His voice cracks. "I can't. I know it's legal now, but I can't. You're still *too young*. I don't feel right about it. I'm sorry, but I can't help how I feel, and how I feel has everything to do with how much we'll recharge ODYSSEY."

For him, this whole situation is only about recharging ODYSSEY, not about us and our feelings for each other. But I really don't care—if I can only change his mind.

My Temperance is extraordinary, and my Passion only average, but my pent up Passion erupts, and my Temperance filter can't dampen it. I sit up and face him, letting the tears flow. My Temperance does prevent me from screaming. My voice is soft but trembling. "I'm *not* a child, Nick. I'm not even *human*." I slap my face. "Why can't you see past this facade? I have parts inside me that can do to you what no human woman can. Sex with me will be like nothing you've ever experienced. *I'm your wife*. Let me give you everything I've been programmed to give.

Because *someone* programmed me this way... and I think it was you. Tell me it wasn't."

His face is grim. "It wasn't *me*, Charli. It was alternate-me. The me who occupied his timeline before I took his place. I admit, I've always had a thing for younger women, but not *that* young. You need to be eighteen. And I know that's just a number on your character sheet and you're not human, but you also need to *look* eighteen if I'm to be with you in that way. I'm sorry, but with that girlie smile and those pigtails of yours, you look fourteen, and I can't get past it. Maybe alternate-me could have, but I'm not him. I know how much you want it, but I can't do it, Charli. I'm really sorry."

"Girlie smile, Nick? *Pigtails?*" Anger builds inside me until something snaps.

Glowing white text appears before my gaze.

Complex Personality trait engaged. Switch Persona?

"Yes." I whisper through clenched teeth, as knowledge frees inside my Khertaan brain.

Submit desired configuration information.

I say it loud, so Nick can hear me. "Make me eighteen, blond, and sexy as hell."

My body morphs. I grow taller. My breasts, hips, and thighs enlarge. My waist stays slim. My brown pigtails unwind, transforming into straight blond strands cascading onto my chest and down my back. My crotch vibrates, emitting a humming sound. My character sheet appears in my view. The number 14 in the *Age* field is replaced by the number 18 before the sheet fades from my sight.

Requested persona activated.

"Come here, big boy." I beckon for him with an index finger.

"Charli, *what did you do?*"

"Does it matter? I'm now officially eighteen on my character sheet. No girlie smile or pigtails. Come and give it to your new bride." I unbutton my blouse, slip it off, and toss it on the floor. I'm not wearing a bra, because Khertaan females, no matter the age, don't need the support.

He can't resist me. His shirt comes off, followed by his shoes and pants. I help him with his underpants.

I've never seen a penis before. Watching it stiffen sends an electric thrill through my heart. I know where it goes—into the part of me that's quivering in anticipation of his entry. He doesn't know what he's in store for.

He pulls off my shoes. I slip off my skirt and culottes. I'm wearing nothing else.

I fall back onto the bed, my legs spread for him. He climbs on top of me, his erection teasing my stomach. His lips press against mine, soft and gentle, the way I want them. Then he pulls his head away and kisses my nipples, first one and then the other, still so damned soft and gentle. A moan tears from my throat.

He shifts position, putting his face at my vagina.

"That's not necessary. I'm not human, remember? I don't want your tongue on me. I want your penis inside me."

"You're my kind of woman." He crawls up the length of my body and settles onto me. "Would you guide me in, Guide?"

I'm happy to oblige, cradling his erection with my fingers, and aiming it in the right direction. He gradually pushes it into me. When he's all the way in, I activate my internal suction sleeve, shrink fit it to his penis, and start my internal agitator, moving the sleeve up and down on him, slowly at first, but gradually increasing the speed, based on sensor readings assessing his degree of arousal. I don't want him to achieve orgasm immediately.

His eyes widen and he rests on top of me, kissing me with all his high average Passion. I switch on vibrating massage mode. He gasps, then moans, then groans. He's so erect inside me. He pushes in deeper. He's ready. The agitator increases its rhythm.

He can't take it any longer. His head jerks up and he rises onto his arms like he's trying to push the bed through the floor. His penis throbs inside me.

Ooh, something is happening with me, too. The moans come involuntarily, and I don't want them to stop. My external and internal temperatures both rise a degree higher than normal. My Khertaan heart pounds hard—Nick must be able to hear it. My attribute filters turn off—all of them. They might as well be zero except Passion, which heightens to a super-human level. Electrical sensations flower inside me, rippling from my center outward. I'm trembling all over as though my whole body is on vibrate.

I'm shouting to the Goddess.

This is what I've yearned for—sex and children. Can he give them to me? He's giving me his sperm. Can I use it to procreate? I don't know if or how it works for a Khertaan avatar mating with another Khertaan avatar, much less with an Earth human.

I squeeze his erection as tight as I can with my suction sleeve, feeling his every pulse as he squirts into me.

White text flashes before my eyes.

DNA captured. Activate pregnancy cycle, store sperm for later, or dispose of it?

"Activate... the... cycle." I keep moaning and keep the agitator going.

Nanobot intrusion detected. Destroying foreign bodies.

"No." A portion of ODYSSEY is inside me too. That might be a good thing. I'll figure it out later....

Nick still throbs. He gasps. "Please, Charli... please... I can't... take... please... stop... Charli... please...."

But I can't stop. My Willpower filter is off. My agitator continues its rhythm. If anything, my suction sleeve tightens on him more, as difficult as it is to believe. I want to feel every throbbing of his penis to the last one, until he's completely drained into me, not only his sperm, but his Auni, his life, his soul. I want to pull him—his entire body—inside me, to give birth to him tomorrow.

Too soon my attribute filters turn on again. My average Empathy tells me he's not hurting, but his pleasure center is still firing, nearing sensory overload.

I stop moaning and allow the agitator to slow. He stops throbbing and goes limp. I turn off the agitator and release the suction sleeve. He gasps for breath while pressing his face into the crook of my neck like he's trying to pin me down with his chin.

Finally he lets up on the pressure at my neck, but his body grows heavy on me, crushing me into the bed.

Is he sleeping?

I've never experienced anything like this. I can't imagine I ever will again—not to the same degree. There will never be another *first time*. Before this, I was a virgin. Now I'm not. But I will forever have this experience etched in my Khertaan brain, ready to be called up and felt all over again any time I wish. I might never do anything else. I'm tempted to replay it now, but I'd probably wake Nick. Should I let him sleep?

White text flashes before my eyes. *Two million XP earned. Congratulations, you are level 18 Guide, level 9 Shadow Wizard.*

I will never go back to being fourteen again.

CHAPTER FORTY

Susie: Planet Drain

Under the grip of altered gravity, I collapse on a warm metal floor. The darkness suffocates me. My heart races. The heat is uncomfortable, and if I weren't partially of a Khertaan nature, my human self couldn't tolerate it. I'm Earth human enough to sweat. Is it possible for me to dehydrate?

I sit up, a wall to my back. The wall is cooler than the floor, and I turn my face against it to cool down.

Machinery groans and metal screeches. A speck of light flares to life to my left, becoming a glowing basketball-sized sphere. The wall I'm leaning against trembles as it lowers. I rock away from it and turn to face it.

Gigantic metallic eyelids open before me, not stopping until I can see out, and I look upon a cloudy gray world, barely able to discern the North American continent. Suze falls towards the clouds. She doesn't see me.

A brown metal bowl large enough to hold a basketball drops into place directly behind the glowing sphere and moves forward to shield the interior of the spaceship from its illumination. Rays of light explode from the glowing ball, shooting outward, towards the planet… towards past-me, but she's already gone.

Suze is following the path of what I've already done. That's how it goes with time travel. Some scientists say it isn't possible for two different versions of the same person to exist in the same moment of time, but they know nothing. There's no paradox here. We're both following the exact same script and merely observing the other do it.

The light rays focus into a beam and penetrate the gray clouds, searing them. The beam is only a foot in diameter. It hits the ground where I stood earlier—okay, I don't know that for sure, but I feel in my gut the beam targeted me. There's no other explanation. The beam cuts off and the eyelid slowly closes. Darkness envelops me.

What the hell am I doing here?

Light floods the area from above, casting everything in a brown hue. Footsteps approach, multiple pairs, running. Where can I hide?

Tossed strands of brown-tinted blond hair catch my attention, and I spin to face… myself… from my future.

"Come on, Suze." Glynda grabs my hand and tugs. "Start counting the seconds and follow me."

We race across the floor of a chamber with nowhere to hide under its vast brown metal dome. The approaching footsteps grow louder, but no one is yet in sight. There's a lit hallway to the right from which the footsteps emanate. Ahead of us, cloaked in shadow on the other side of the chamber, an empty hallway comes into view. I'm at a count of seven.

"The hallway ahead of us, Suze. Teleport there, *now*." Glynda vanishes.

I follow suit.

I materialize next to her. She's squatting against the wall to her left, peering around the corner. I squat beside her.

She glances at me with a knowing grin on her face.

A hand falls on my shoulder and I stifle a scream.

"It's me." The person behind me speaks in my voice....

My panic subsides as quickly as it rose. Glynda and I look over our shoulders at Super Glynda—the Glynda to my Glynda. My Glynda knew Super Glynda was coming and didn't warn me, the bitch.

Burn marks encircle Super Glynda's neck. Shushing me before I can inquire, she points across the chamber. "Super Suze, jump back in time twenty seconds and then teleport to your Suze over by the eyelid. You know what to do then. Remember, seven seconds. Get her over here. *Go.*"

I do as I'm told and jump back in time twenty seconds. The focused beam of light is shining on the planet. It cuts off, the eyelid closes, and darkness falls, exactly as I remember.

Overhead lights come on, tinted brown.

Suze sits at the far edge of the chamber. She's not aware of it, but she's rocking back and forth in shock. Watching her while I wait for the right moment, my heart aches for her.

Footsteps approach from the hallway to my left. Brown light springs to life within the hallway.

Suze snaps out of it and jumps to her feet.

I teleport beside her. "Come on, Suze." I grab her hand and tug. "Start counting the seconds and follow me."

We race for the shaded hallway at the back of the chamber as the footsteps grow louder. I'm counting, too. I reach seven. "The hallway ahead of us, Suze. Teleport there, *now.*" I do it.

I squat next to the wall at the mouth of the shaded hallway and peer out. Suze teleports over and squats beside me. My

Glynda—Super Glynda to my Suze—is about to pop in. She'll tell Suze what to do, and then I expect she'll tell me what to do.

I glance at Suze in anticipation. The look on her face is priceless when my Glynda lays a hand on her shoulder. I know she's ready to scream, but I also know she won't.

Suze time jumps at my Glynda's direction. I peek around the corner again. Footsteps echo in the chamber as four brown-tinted humanoids rush out of the lit hallway. I can't guess what color their skin truly is. Roughly six feet tall, they're like emaciated humans, thinner than any human could be and survive. They don't wear clothing, but they have no sign of genitals, either. Tiny wrinkles cover their bodies. Their fingers are disproportionately long, their fingernails adding another six inches to their reach. Their bald heads are almost human... except for the heavy wrinkling, making them all look ancient. They remind me of Ezmerelda....

There's no way....

My Glynda kneels beside me and whispers. "Don't be afraid. I've learned what I need to, but only because you go with them now. A metal collar will be placed around your neck, nullifying your powers. But it eventually comes off. As soon as it does, teleport here, and then time jump back twenty-four hours. At that point, you'll be me, and you'll know what to do next. Sorry... no questions. I gotta go. Good luck!" She vanishes, leaving me alone again.

I might be in shock....

Aliens grab my arms and pull me to my feet. They chirp and squeak as they point at the hallway from whence they came. Releasing me, they nudge me in that direction. I walk behind two of them and ahead of the other two, my hands raised, as though the aliens are Earth police. For all I know, in their culture, raising my hands is like flipping them the bird.

Other than the initial grab and nudge, they don't touch me. I don't give them a reason to, following the lead couple closely. We traverse a hallway formed of smooth metal, the ceiling aglow with brown light. The hallway extends straight for as far as I can see. We near an intersection, and three emaciated aliens cross in front of us. Beyond them, other aliens crowd our hallway. As we press on, none of them pay any attention to my escort and the prisoner in their midst, as though the presence of an Earthling is an everyday occurrence.

After five minutes of brisk walking, the end of the hallway comes into sight. We've been walking at a pace of maybe three miles an hour. I can do the math—we've walked a quarter of a mile. Assuming we started at the center, the entire craft is at least half a mile in diameter—more than the length of eight football fields, over three-quarters of a kilometer. Even if we were only walking at two miles an hour, the craft would still be at least a third of a mile across, over half a kilometer—pretty damn big.

An automatic door slides open before us. We enter a room full of aliens seated at consoles of blinking lights, gauges, switches, dials, digital readouts, and screens. The light in this room is orange rather than brown. At the far end of the room is a large screen displaying a picture of the American continents, devoid of clouds, but covered with red dots, on land and on sea. A dozen red X's also mark spots on land.

Someone wearing a hooded cloak sits on a pedestal chair facing the screen. They swivel side to side as we approach from behind. The two aliens ahead of me stop five feet from the hooded figure.

The hooded one swivels in a one-eighty turn, face hidden by shadow. "Welcome, Susie McKenzie." The voice is masculine and honeyed. "My name is Seth. I'm so pleased to meet you. You've arrived in time to join me in watching the end of your world. Would you care for popcorn?" He gestures with elongated fingers, his nails as long as those of the other aliens, but the exposed skin of his hands wrinkle-free. My alien escorts leave.

The orange light dims, and everyone else in the busy room blurs like the background of a photo taken with heavy depth of field. The large screen in the distance remains in sharp focus, as does Seth. At his gesture, a stool rises from the floor next to him. "Please. Have a seat."

In the orange light, his skin isn't as pale as mine.

I take the offered seat. A whirring sounds above me. A painted white robot arm descends, holding a hinged silvery band, hanging open, sized to fit my throat. I suppress the urge to resist, letting the arm snap the collar in place around my neck. Glynda damn well better be right about this.

With upraised clapped hands, Seth leans towards me. "The suppression band around your throat is just a precaution, mind you. I know you have powers, and I don't want you using them to escape. It will be nice having company who gives a damn — about anything, really. My minions have no cares, no opinions, no will of their own. They blindly follow my every desire, and it can get *so* boring. There's no stimulating conversation — no external displays of emotion. But with you… I expect breath-taking demonstrations of your true human nature."

An alien minion approaches with a paper bag full of popcorn and holds it toward me.

Seth points at the bag. "Go on. I know your kind enjoys munching on snacks while viewing moving pictures on large screens. I don't see the joy in it, but I wouldn't be a proper host to deny you the pleasure. Eat up."

"I'm not hungry, but thanks."

"We're all hungry for something." He dismisses the minion. Then he makes another gesture, drawing a circle in the air, and darkness descends across the room.

Only the large screen can still be seen, like I'm watching a movie in a darkened theater.

"Here we go, Susie. Are you as excited as I am?"

Dimly glowing green lines of liquid flow across the ceiling from the edges of the room, moving towards a central point, where they seep into a glassy domed shell, collecting in its interior, coloring the room with a dark green hue.

Green liquid swirls and swells. It's hypnotic.

The glassy dome empties of green light abruptly, robbing the room of illumination.

On screen, a thick beam of green light blasts towards the planet surface. It strikes, splattering liquid green lightning across land and sea.

The beam stops firing.

Beneath a sparking shell of green, the planet melts, losing its spherical shape, collapsing in on itself. Dark energy flows toward the ship, reversing the path taken by the light beam. The ship vibrates as it sips the soul of Mother Earth.

I can't think straight.

How long does it go on for?

The last dregs of the planet's body and soul are siphoned, the flow of energy ending.

Seth inhales heavily. "I'm winning."

The screen goes blank. Dim orange light returns to illuminate the room.

The hooded one turns to face me, lifting an elongated clawed finger towards my face, halting before touching my cheek. "You're not crying. I was so hoping for tears. Disappointing, really. I thought I knew Earthlings better than this. First you decline the popcorn, and next you fail to show emotions. You might as well be one of my crew."

I shrug. "I was down there, and as far as I could tell, the planet was already dead."

He nods. "I see. Well, then." He lifts a hand, and a Wooden Staff appears in his grasp. He taps it on the floor twice.

Stars whiz by on the screen for perhaps twenty seconds. When they stop, the screen displays an image of a green planet.

Seth chuckles. "Ah, yes, here we go. Would you care for popcorn while I destroy *this* world? It's another planet inhabited by sentient beings, and so of course is high on my list of planets in need of destruction."

I don't look his way, but can't keep from gritting my teeth. "What kind of monster are you?"

"I'm not a monster. I'm a tenet. A force of nature. A Godling, if you wish. You may call me a God if you like. Perhaps you could be my Goddess. Would you like that?" He pauses, as though expecting an answer. "It would only be until I've destroyed everything else. I'd have to kill you before I kill myself, naturally. But you can accompany me to the end, if you like. What do you say?"

An alien approaches with a tablet.

Seth takes the device and views its small screen. "Oh, my. We picked up an Earthling survivor, a young man identified as Timmy Landers. He evidently has powers, not to have been destroyed by my Planet Buster." He returns the tablet to the waiting alien, who takes his leave at Seth's dismissive gesture.

I don't say a word and don't change my expression, doing my best to give no sign of recognition at Seth's mention of my ex-boyfriend.

The hooded one clacks his nails. "We'll wait for him to join us. He'll be here in a few minutes. He put up more of a fight than you did—not cooperating at all. They are en route with his unconscious body. I hope you don't mind if I have him sitting next to me opposite you."

"Would it matter if I did mind?"

He laughs. "I thought it polite to ask."

"Technically…." I still don't look at him. "You didn't ask. You're not being as polite as you thought."

"Oh…." He sounds disappointed. "I must try harder next time. Do you agree?" He laughs. "There, I asked a question. Now I'm being polite."

I'm unsure whether he's serious.

Glynda didn't mention anything about Timmy being aboard. I hope that doesn't mean Seth destroys him in front of me. I could *not* bear that.

CHAPTER FORTY-ONE

Kylie: Watching Charli

I catch up to Spyder in short order. My heart breaks at the sight of Charli's limp body wrapped in webbing.

"Georgie, my character sheet says I have level 18 Spirit Form. How does the skill improve at higher levels?"

The clown honks his nose. "For that skill, the level is the number of switches you can make per day from your physical form to your spiritual form. The count resets daily at 8:00 AM System time. It also resets whenever you gain a character level."

"What's the System time now?"

"5:04 AM."

Trading my spiritual presence for a physical one, I invoke Hypnotic Voice. "Wake up, Charli."

It's to no avail. The girl remains asleep.

She looks different. Her breasts are fuller. A moan escapes her lips, an utterance full of desire. Is she having a wet dream? I slap her cheek. *"Wake up."* It doesn't work.

Fine.

I fly into the sky again for a better view of where we're headed.

A spire rises through the haze. Atop the spire stands a city, its skyscrapers silhouetted against the bright sky. That's Minook, where I'm headed for reasons I don't fully understand. I wish Morrow and Slithy would respawn. They gave off this vibe that what's happening in Khertaan is important to what's happening on Earth. I have the distinct feeling Earth's fate lies entirely in my hands—that answers to questions no one has yet asked wait discovery in Minook, and finding those answers is all on me.

The Earth-bound Nick, Kendra, and Susie are all relying on me. For me to ask the necessary questions and get the necessary answers, I feel I need to reach Minook without dying. If I die, I feel I won't respawn.

Why can't Charli wake up and help me?

The spire looms taller and more distinct with each passing minute. When it blocks a portion of the sun, I know we're getting close. Recalling Charli's warning about flying guardians, I descend, land next to her, and take a seat on the Behemoth's back.

More minutes pass, until the spire completely blocks the sun. On Earth, one could expect a temperature drop within the spire's shadow, but I don't sense any, reminding me this world isn't Earth.

A woman cries in the distance. My Heightened Sense of Hearing picks up the sound without my spotting her. It's a plaintive cry, like a mother who's lost her child and is calling her name, if the name consisted only of vowels. *O-a-ooh.* As soon as she finishes the last prolonged syllable, she calls again. *O-a-ooh.*

The sound originates in the sky and its source isn't stationary. My Intuition is only average, but my Logic, Understanding, and Insight values are all high average, and they tell me I'm listening to the call of a flying guardian. Her voice is haunting, more chilling than a temperature drop would be. If I were of a certain

sexual orientation, I might find the voice alluring, seductive —
but rather I hear an anguished proclamation of loss.

I should lend assistance in the search for what was lost.

The knowledge rises from the core of my being, as though
from my breast rather than my brain, that the call is deceitful,
intended to delay my journey indefinitely while I search for
something that never even existed. Anyone who succumbs to the
siren call would spend the rest of their days searching the sands
surrounding the spire. In a world where avatars have no need to
eat or drink, no one affected by the call would ever starve to
death or die of thirst. Unless something attacked and killed
them, they'd be stranded for eternity, continually searching for
something they couldn't describe and would never find.

Spyder hasn't reacted to the call. Perhaps she has yet to hear
it.

"Georgie, what type of mook is making that call, and how am
I able to resist it?"

"Identification of the creature is not forthcoming, pumpkin.
Nor can I ascertain with certainty the type of attack it is making,
but in scanning your character sheet, in addition to your overall
impressive mental, spiritual, and emotional attributes, you have
level 29 Spirit Resistance and level 16 Auni Resistance. My guess
is those skills are protecting you from the siren call.

"You also have level 1 Party Spirit Resistance, which allows
you to lend Spirit Resistance to those in your party.

"I would suggest that as a precaution, you activate the party
resistance for Spyder and Charli. It might not be necessary for
either of them, since Spyder seems to be impervious to spiritual
attacks and Charli is unconscious, but better to take an
unnecessary precaution than to not take a precaution when you
could have and regret the omission later."

"Agreed." I focus on extending a Spirit Resistance buff to my party. To Spyder, I say, "Let's go around the spire to the right."

The Behemoth gives no verbal reply, but makes the course adjustment.

The haunting cries increase in volume as we trek closer to our destination.

"Oh, Nick, give it to me." The Cowgirl writhes within the restraining webbing. Her lips pucker and make kissing sounds. "Harder. *Harder*. I love you."

What the hell? "Georgie, am I hallucinating?"

"I'm not aware of any debuffs in effect on your person, pumpkin."

If I'm hallucinating, his reply might not be real. I might have only imagined I asked him my question. But if I'm not hallucinating, why would Charli be having a wet dream about Kendra's husband.

Charli whispers. "I won't tell her. I promise. She doesn't need to know."

It's like I'm listening to one side of a two-sided conversation, and Nick is who I'm not hearing. But the flow of thought is jumbled, too. One moment she's behaving like she's making love to Nick, and the next moment she's trying to convince him it's all right if they do.

"I promise I won't even flirt with you in front of her. It will be our secret. Please, Nick. Please. Oh, yes. *Yes*. Do you like that? Can she do *that* for you? I didn't think so." The Cowgirl's sentences are all over the place.

The only thing certain is that she's got a thing for Kendra's husband. I better not hear Morrow's name come from her mouth.... So help me....

"DNA captured. Nanobot intrusion detected. Destroy...." Her body spasms.

A voyeur, perhaps, but I'm compelled to watch.

Charli whispers with a tone of defiance. "Agitator, continue. Tighten suction sleeve. Feel… every throb… to the last… completely drain him… into me… his sperm… his Auni… his life… his soul. Pull him… all of him… into me. Give birth… to him." Her body relaxes, but her lips continue to kiss her unseen lover. Eventually her lips relax, too. Her eyes dart side to side beneath her eyelids, indicative of REM sleep—if she were an Earth human, which she isn't. Her lips part once more, and she whispers, "Pregnancy cycle… activated." Her eyes stop moving. She's completely motionless.

I don't know what I've witnessed, but I wasn't hallucinating. I also don't believe what Charli uttered was from a dream. A version of her has manifested on Earth with Nick. He's cheated on Kendra and made Charli pregnant. I may only have an average Intuition on my character sheet, but I have a woman's natural intuition that can't be quantified. In my bones I know something sexual has happened between the two of them.

The Nick I'm aware of would never cheat on Kendra with a fourteen-year-old girl. But look at Charli now. She's *not* fourteen anymore. She has matured… and she made that alteration to tempt him. She can be altered by the Khertaan program to be any age, if the System allows it. Hell, Nick wrote her program. Maybe he changed her age himself. But why? He never expressed any disappointment in Kendra's lovemaking. He didn't always want sex when Kendra did—because he was so buried in work. Did his concussion change him? Can a concussion alter a person's attitudes and desires like that?

I could be wrong. The spire's flying guardian *might* be affecting my mind after all, giving me bad thoughts. I might be under a mental, spiritual, or emotional attack right now. If I am, how do I combat it? The only thing I know to do is to force the thoughts out of my head. I can't dwell on them. I have to trust Nick. He'd never willingly do anything to hurt Kendra.

And yet... is Charli pregnant...? Does she have DNA to contribute to a child? If she only has Nick's DNA, will Charli give birth to a *clone* of Nick? But *this* Charli—the womanly body lying beside me—doesn't have Nick's DNA. *This* Charli won't be giving birth using DNA it doesn't have. Whatever has happened with Charli and Nick, it's all in her head. Nothing will come of it *here*.

Doesn't that make sense?

I really need to stop thinking about it. So do it. Put it out of my head.

O-a-ooh, calls the spire's unseen guardian in Charli's voice.

This is so messed up.

The guardian's cries still have no discernible effect on Spyder. My eight-legged friend keeps marching on, one pair of legs after another, after another, after another.

At 6:18 AM, still some distance from the base of the spire, a winged woman flies by overhead, shouting, *O-a-ooh*, even now using the voice of the Cowgirl Guide. The guardian descends towards me.

"It's a Spire Harpy, pumpkin," my personal support AI informs me. "It's at 100% HP and 100% SP. Unfortunately, I have no additional information on Spire Harpies. You're on your own with her."

"Not a problem." I ascend towards the mook, switching to Spirit Form as I summon my Spirit Blade and Spirit Shield. I've had enough of this bitch's bullshit.

CHAPTER FORTY-TWO

Megan: Dinosaur Birds

How long has it been since I left Maron? I don't have a way to check the System clock, and the stationary sun is of no help in measuring the passage of time. Arachnid Behemoths advance upon me from the west, and I don't expect them to respect the sanctity of the safe path. But I see no other mooks in the sand or sky, so I take a chance and leave the path long enough to fly over the heads of the Behemoth army. They fling webs at me, even though I'm focusing on being invisible, so I know they can sense me.

I'm high enough in the air, their webs fall short.

I pass them, putting them east of me. They turn around to follow me. *I* seem to be their specific target. They move as fast as I do. I lead them south, away from the safe path. I'm taking a risk of a flying encounter, but I'll deal with that when and if I must. Once I've taken the Behemoths far enough south, I'll cut northwest and pick up the safe path again, hopefully with a little more distance between the Behemoths and me.

Face it, you don't really know what you're doing. You're just following your instincts. There's no logic to your plan.

Okay, sure... I admit it.

The *whoosh* of my Danger Sense alerts me to the group of fliers coming from the west. My luck just ran out. I focus on being invisible. It doesn't help with the Behemoths, who can sense me no matter where I am, but maybe I can avoid the flying mooks. They look like pterodactyls.

It's working! The dinosaur birds dive towards the Behemoths. This seems an opportune time to cut northwest, while the big metal spiders deal with their new foes.

"Help!" A shrill but distant feminine voice tweaks my ear. "Is someone out there? Help!"

If not for my Alertness trait, I might have missed the cry. If I'd been plodding along on the ground, the shuffling of my feet might have covered the sound. If I'd been flying at top speed, the wind in my ears might have swept it away. But as I slow to pivot and turn northwest, I hear the plaintive cry.

It's coming from a woman caught in a Behemoth's webbing, slung on the spider's side in a cocoon of chains.

I'm positive the pleading woman hasn't seen me. She'd have to be of sufficient power to pierce my invisibility, which is doubtful. If I flew away right now, she'd never know I was here. With a sub-par Conscience, I'd not even give a second thought to this scenario once I'm gone. The pleading woman would have to be someone close to me—like Debra or my Mom—for my Conscience to bother me about leaving right now.

But I have an average Empathy and high average Morals. The numeric values the System assigned to my stats were based on who I am at my core. Maybe I'm not always able to act under pressure in an emotional situation, but I know what's morally right. Leaving this woman without trying to help her is wrong. Even an average Empathy and an average Intuition is enough to tell me she's in trouble she can't get herself out of. Her only hope is that someone hears her and comes to her aid.

Looks like you're that someone.

I check the inventory I share with Mithabel and bring out the Parchment. Nothing has been added to it. My primary avatar hasn't seen it yet. Damn. Okay. Put it back. I don't know if there's some special ability I recently gained that would be of use in helping this poor woman.

Why hasn't the spider killed her?

She's a PC. The spiders are here to destroy us, but trapping us can work just as well from their perspective. If they kill us, we respawn and continue our training. If we're trapped indefinitely, that's more effective at stopping our training than killing us.

Imagine spending eternity wrapped in a web you can't escape, unable even to starve to death. The horror of it can't be imagined.

The pterodactyls pixelize—all six of them—as the Behemoths make short work of them, catching them with webs and spearing their tangled bodies with pointy legs. Once in close proximity to the spiders, the pterodactyls didn't stand a chance. I won't either if I get too close.

Another flock of six dinosaur birds materializes in the air. They ignore me, unable to see me. They dive past me to attack the Behemoths, spraying black breaths.

"Help!" This plea comes in a man's voice—one I recognize, a voice that stokes the flames of rage in my chest, flaring into my brain, purging it of all rational thought.

Christopher Warden.

Not Christopher Warden in the flesh, but his Khertaan avatar, ChrisCross... same difference to me. I don't care that Ezmerelda said ChrisCross was training to fight the inter-dimensional invaders and we'd need to work together. It ain't gonna happen. Christopher paid Debra Jones for sex in the past, which I could maybe come to terms with. But he sure as hell shouldn't have called her a whore afterward, whether he thought anyone else was around or not. I'll be damned before I do anything with or for that bastard. I'd hold his chains myself for eternity if it meant he'd never harm Debra again.

"Anyone? Help!" He's still begging.

Other voices join the pleading. Another man and two additional women. *All* of party XStorm is trapped by the spiders.

"Please help us, anyone." The first woman cries with a sob. Which one is she?

If it were only ChrisCross needing help, I swear I'd leave him to his misery. But there are others who need me, and I'm doing this for them. I fly higher and survey the scene. Only a couple of Behemoths are distracted by the pterodactyls. The others converge beneath me, like the burned-out stars of a dead galaxy drawn to a black hole. They climb atop each other in their attempts to reach me, creating a pyramid of flailing legs and quivering thoraxes. I fly a bit higher.

On the northern edge of their cluster, four spiders bring up the rear, human-sized and larger cocoons slung over their abdomens.

Drawn by the presence of XStorm, six pterodactyls dive at the four straggler Behemoths. The dinosaur birds breathe black sprays.

The four Behemoths can't throw their webs without releasing their prisoners. Flailing, they stab at the pterodactyls with their forelegs. The breath weapons of the fliers have a greater range than the spider legs, allowing the dinosaur birds to stay out of range of their attackers while still delivering effective attacks of their own. Do the dinosaur birds have a chance in hell of killing a Behemoth? Maybe so, and I don't want to be nearby when it happens. The death explosion of a Behemoth killed me at a range of thirty yards, but I put four times that distance between XStorm and me, and watch the proceedings with a bird's eye view.

The first flock of dinosaur birds attack the spider pyramid below me. Those spiders are quick to use their webs, easily snagging the birds and bringing them down. The flock attacking the four stragglers have better success.

I wish I could share what I'm seeing with someone else—anyone else. Being incommunicado sucks.

I check my inventory again. The Parchment is there. I draw it out and look to see if anything else has been written on it. Nothing. Mithabel still hasn't seen it. I put it back.

Changing my position in the air causes the spider pyramid rising beneath me to topple. Ha. That's satisfying. It starts rebuilding immediately, the base of it relocating directly below me. I'm a homing beacon and they're locked onto me. I could go anywhere, and they'd follow. Even with me up here in the sky, they're doing their best to try to reach me.

That's not the case for the four stragglers, who are already at carrying capacity. It's their job now to simply keep their prisoners out of commission, and the pterodactyls are making that complicated. One of the Behemoths falters, its legs buckling on one side of its body. The dinosaur birds are having an effect. The birds concentrate their attacks on the wounded Behemoth. Working together, they're more effective than acting individually—a theme in this world. The Behemoth collapses on its weakened side. The cocoon it carries remains slung on its stronger side. The beleaguered Behemoth gets lucky and spears a pterodactyl that gets too close, killing it with a single stab, leaving five in the flock.

The spider pyramid below me is getting too tall. I reposition myself again, flying laterally a dozen yards, and the pyramid topples. The damned Behemoths commence building another one directly below me. How tall a pyramid can they build? There's a massive number of them, probably hundreds in this swarm, maybe even a thousand or more. How many other Behemoth swarms are loose in this world, or does this swarm account for every Behemoth in Khertaan? For that matter, how many Orc Wizards are in Khertaan? I suspect the one that's been chasing me will show up again. Can he fly? Seems doubtful. The mastermind behind these invasion forces doesn't appear to have taken air travel into consideration, which works great for me.

At some point, will these invaders switch their target? Do they simply go after the nearest PC? Do different PCs have different priorities? Am I their top priority? I can't possibly be their only target.

The five remaining pterodactyls make another pass, breathing acid. The wounded Behemoth explodes, shedding blinding light. I don't look directly at it. The heat reaches me even at this distance. I hope I'm far enough away to avoid dying.

I'm still alive, thank the Goddess....

Caught in the blast, the five pterodactyls are gone. The other three straggler Behemoths are fine, and still appear to be carrying their cocoons. The cocoon carried by the destroyed Behemoth isn't in evidence—whoever was held in its prison has now found escape through death.

The explosion had no effect on the spider pyramid below me. They're still climbing atop each other. I fly off a ways and watch the pyramid crumble as the spiders scurry to readjust their locations.

ChrisCross calls out, still on local chat and close enough for me to hear. "Ruby, are you still with us?"

A female voice replies. "I'm here. Penelope is with me."

"Bradford?"

A male voice replies. "I'm here."

"Yuni?"

There's no reply.

"Yuni?"

Still no reply.

ChrisCross calls even louder. *"Yuni?"*

The XStorm Priestess isn't responding. She's been freed by dying.

"She must have died," ChrisCross yells. "She'll respawn and get us help. In the meantime, did everyone just gain a bunch of XP?"

"I'm level 15," Ruby calls out.

"Same here," replies Bradford.

Penelope joins in. "Is there a reason we're holding this discussion on local chat?" As an NPC, she's got more game sense than the PCs.

They fall silent. They're on party chat now. After yelling for help on local chat, they'd grown lax and were discussing party matters openly. Too bad the NPC had to point it out to them. I can't eavesdrop any longer.

I fly off to the side to once more topple the spider pyramid trying to reach me. I can't let it get too tall—one of them might snag me with a web, and then I'd be in the same boat as XStorm. There's no way to overhear them now they've gone to party chat, so I fly upward a bit more. I'd love to hang around for a while to see whether they can escape, since they've gained levels and thus more skills, but they might be powerful enough to see me at this point. If they escaped and spotted me, they'd either attack me or want to travel or talk with me, and I'm not up for any of it.

I draw my Parchment and Quill from inventory and add a message to Mithabel. "XStorm was captured by Behemoths, but might escape. I'm not waiting to find out. Yuni was killed in a pterodactyl attack. Maybe she will respawn in Maron, so look for her. The pterodactyls breathe acid."

Stashing the items, I take a moment to reflect. Did I gain any XP from the encounters that just took place? My presence triggered the attacks of two flocks of six, so even if I wasn't the one who killed them, I was involved. I wish to hell I could talk to Mithabel.

The sky darkens. Looking up, I see a gigantic bird descending on me—another pterodactyl, but a hundred times the size. Oh, Goddess. It's the Boss for this territory. It's falling fast, and it's freaking huge. I try to fly out from beneath it—and the spider pyramid below me topples yet again.

The Boss shifts course to follow me. Like the spiders, it can sense me. Damn. There's no way I can get out from under this monstrosity. It's not trying to breathe on me—it aims to force me to ground, where it's weight will squash me to death. What an attack method, and it works because the thing is so freaking big.

Ezmerelda wants all us PCs to work together. Fine. I'll do XStorm a favor and lead this thing to them. Their Behemoth stragglers can't web me without dropping the captives they already carry, which I doubt they'll do. If this thing lands on the spiders, maybe it will crush them, or at least crush XStorm, and they'll be free. If the spiders carrying XStorm can kill the Boss, maybe XStorm will share credit for it, allowing them to move on to the next territory. I don't like doing this for ChrisCross, but he's not the only one in their party.

Besides, if I'm dying, I'm not going alone. Goddess, I hope Mithabel has enough lives left for me to die again.

I'm flying faster than I was, which means Mithabel has gained a level recently. I desperately wish I knew all the skills available to me.

I don't move fast enough. The Boss pterodactyl's underbelly knocks the wind out of me on contact, forcing me downward faster than I can fly. We're not over XStorm yet. I try moving in their direction, but there's too much air resistance and too much friction between me and the underside of the Boss.

I make myself smaller, flattening myself. Switching to Third Person POV, I use the external perspective to help shape myself. I'm two inches thick, like an over-sized pancake with a human-shaped outline. Flying is still impossible, but I've reduce air resistance enough to slide across the Boss's skin. The giant dinosaur bird shifts course, but since I'm against it, it's movement also moves me, causing its recentering attempt to fail. My being slightly off center is prompting the creature to fly in XStorm's direction at an ever increasing speed.

We're almost to the ground when I find myself over XStorm. It's dark under here, but I can see well enough in shades of gray with my Dark Sight. I'm fast approaching XStorm and their captor Behemoths. The Boss is on target to hit them. Get ready to die, XStorm, and be free.

I stash all my equipment, including my clothing and jewelry. About to die, I don't want to risk losing anything.

The Boss strikes the three Behemoths, squashing them beneath it. I'll never know if I could withstand the Boss pressing me into the sand. The three Behemoths explode. Intense heat sears my flesh for the second time today. Brilliant light envelopes me.

Sorry, Mithabel, but we're dying again.

CHAPTER FORTY-THREE

Mithabel: Alternate Quest

"*Okguul.*" Mithabel called to the Orc woman. "I know you can hear me. Is there a way for me to complete this quest as it was intended to be completed?"

The Orc woman made no response.

"If we kill you, will it reset the scenario?"

Still, no reply.

"I'm coming inside, Okguul." Mithabel raised a foot as though to step through the doorway.

Dylan stomped her foot on the floor. "No, Mithabel. You'll be trapped inside."

"No, I won't." Mithabel rubbed the Ogaltha Ring she wore. "The curse won't let those who enter leave without the Ring. I already have one. I believe if anyone in the party has an Ogaltha Ring, the entire party is allowed to leave. Otherwise, Quantized would still be stuck in the room except for Zip. I'm going in. If I don't come back out in sixty seconds, then light up a torch and shoot me or shoot Okguul or figure something else out. I need to check the Chest and make sure there's not another Ring in it."

The Tank stepped into the room, *not* focusing on her Hide skill. She wanted the Orc woman to see her.

Okguul didn't reissue her warning.

The Tank went to the Chest. The lid was up. Nothing lay inside.

At Mithabel's approach, the Orc woman turned to face her, backing away, hugging the wall and saying nothing, but holding up her hands as though warding off evil. Her lower lip trembled.

The Tank halted. "I have to kill you, don't I? You don't want me to, but you know it's necessary to reset this scenario. Tell me otherwise if I'm wrong."

Tears welled in the Orc woman's eyes. Her jaws worked, but her lips remained pressed together.

"You're not allowed to tell me." Mithabel scowled. "There's something else going on here, and you're afraid I won't figure it out before I kill you. If I kill you without figuring out the puzzle, the scenario won't be reset, and you're doomed to never respawn. Is that it?"

Okguul closed her eyes. She clasped her hands and pulled them to her chin as though praying.

Inspiration struck. Mithabel turned towards the exit. "Shut the door, Rolag."

Dylan lifted an arm to block the Dragon. *"No, Rolag.* Mithabel, tell us what you're thinking."

"Ask our Goddess." Mithabel equipped the Axe enchanted by Scintilla. "Well, Priestess?"

Dylan huffed. "Do it, Rolag."

The door clanged shut.

Mithabel strode to the open Chest. "Scintilla, Goddess of Light, Mentors, Gold, and Growth, I, your Daughter of Orange Metal, have failed to protect the innocent children of Okguul. I call upon you to make things right. I sacrifice the blade you bequeathed upon me and call upon you to convert it to the treasured item that belongs in this place." She lowered the Axe into the Chest and closed the lid.

Okguul approached and replaced the lock. A tear streaked her cheek. "Thank you, Mithabel, Daughter of Orange Metal." She took Mithabel's hand, the one bearing the Ogaltha Ring, and slipped it off her finger. "Go in peace. You have fulfilled my alternate quest. You need not and no longer can fulfill Ezmerelda's quest. But she can give you your next one."

Orc children appeared, playing and running around the room. Ullullu danced over to Mithabel. "Thank you for bringing us back, Elf. Here is a token of my appreciation." She held out her hand, in which she held a strand of dark hair.

"Thank you, Ullullu." Mithabel slipped the strand from the girl's grasp. "I will never forget you."

The girl beamed, a beautiful young lady despite her fangs and warts.

Mithabel clutched the strand of hair as she turned in place, taking in the room and all its young inhabitants. Yes, they were all mooks. But they were something more, too, just as Mithabel was an avatar and yet something more. These children and their mother were a family, and it didn't matter whether they were flesh and blood or pixels and stats or something else. They cared for each other. They had individual personalities.

An Orc boy sidled up to Okguul.

The woman tousled his hair. "Good to have you back, Urgook."

He smiled at Mithabel but said nothing.

Okguul patted him on the shoulder. "Why don't you escort the nice Elf lady out of our home?"

Ullullu danced beside Urgook. "I'll help, too."

The two children took Mithabel by the hand, one on either side, and walked her to the exit. Standing before the door, the children dropped their hands and stepped back.

Ullullu bowed her head. "Goodbye, Elf."

"Goodbye, Daughter of Orange Metal," rang a chorus of young voices, led by Okguul.

Light blossomed from the strand of dark hair in Mithabel's hand. The hair stiffened. It lengthened. It glowed, shedding bright orange light. The glow diminished, and when it had faded, Mithabel held the hilt of a new weapon—a flamberge, its wavy blade over three feet long. She spun around to face the Orc girl dancer. "Thank you, Ullullu! I shall call it Ullullu's Hair."

The girl waved as the door opened of its own accord. "Hurry through, Elf, unless you want to stay here with me. May Scintilla speed your journey."

Mithabel rushed through the exit. The door closed of its own accord behind her.

CHAPTER FORTY-FOUR

Mithabel: Heading Out

"Congratulations, chief, you've completed the quest of Okguul, an alternate quest to Ezmerelda's. You are level 18 Tank, level 9 Anjai."

Mithabel stashed her new weapon in inventory. Over party chat, she asked, "Were you all notified of quest completion just now?"

Everyone in the party replied in the affirmative—excepting Charli and Megan, both still incommunicado.

"I'm level 18 Tank now. Did your levels go up?"

None of them had. Everyone else present in party MAD was still level 21.

Ger-Alt gestured for Mithabel's attention. "So did you get a Ring?"

The Tank shook her head. "No, but I had the cursed one removed. I'm no longer eligible for Ezmerelda's quest." She didn't want to go into details with Quantized. "So, let's get out of this dungeon and then see if we can get out of this city."

The two parties traveled together back the way they'd come in. Ger-Alt quickly took the lead, riding her Cheetah mount, and no one in MAD argued with her. For Quantized, the way in had been traversed in complete darkness, with Ger-Alt and FepXveq both guiding the others with their Dark Sight. No light would be used for the outbound trip, either.

They retraced their steps to the quicksand pit trap. Party MAD waited to let Quantized make their way across first. Zip crouched at the top of the pit for a moment and then sprang down into it, Ger-Alt on his back and Skeeter the squirrel perched on the Goblin woman's shoulder. Ger-Alt wasn't a large person. She probably didn't even weigh ninety pounds.

Zip proved why he was called Zip. In a flash he sprang up from the pit on the far side, having sprinted across it so fast, the quicksand had no chance to grab at his paws. Moreover, his wide paws were more suitable for crossing the quicksand than booted human feet would be.

FepXveq appeared to be twice Ger-Alt's weight. Zip didn't come back for her. Instead, Toxxi and Falco each grasped one of the Dark Elf's wrists, lifted her from the ground, and flew her across the pit. They couldn't keep her aloft all the way, but managed to get her to the other side before losing all altitude. With Toxxi's continued support at her back, FepXveq climbed the wall using improvised handholds.

Quantized cleared space at the pit's edge for party MAD. FepXveq and the mounted Ger-Alt watched with raised brows to see how their allies would deal with the quicksand.

"Good job. You made that look easy." Mithabel flew across, with Zyekt flying behind her, bringing everyone else in party MAD.

Ger-Alt stared with gaping mouth at Mithabel. "*Shit.* I can understand the Angel having the ability to fly, but how the hell are *you* able to?"

Mithabel shrugged as she cleared the pit's edge. She landed next to the Goblin woman. "Do you have a subclass yet, Ger-Alt?"

"No. None of us do. I'm level 8. The rest of us are level 7, except Skeeter. He's only level 6."

"Well, when you reach level 10, choose your subclasses wisely. That's all I can say."

The Goblin woman sighed. "What level are you up to now? 11? 12?"

"I'm level 18." Mithabel nodded over her shoulder at the rest of her party. "And I'm lower than they are. They're all level 21."

"Great green bales of clover, how did you all earn that much XP already?"

"We honestly don't know," Dylan interjected.

"We got the XP, too," squeaked Niav. "Both me and Zyekt. We came into this dungeon at level 1 and we're leaving at 21. We were all just sitting there, waiting on Mithabel to respawn, and…." She fell silent. On party chat, she said, "Sorry if I wasn't supposed to say anything. It was just *so* exciting. Are you going to let Zyekt and me keep traveling with you, even though you don't need us for Ezmerelda's quest now?"

"We need a Guide." Dylan continued the conversation on party chat. "And having an Angel along is proving quite useful. If the two of you want to continue with us, I think I speak for everyone that we'd love to have you."

"Absolutely," said Amarynth. Mithabel and Rolag echoed the sentiment.

"Oh, goody, goody," said Niav. "I will be *the best* Guide. You'll see."

"Yes?" Ger-Alt wanted Niav to finish the last statement she'd uttered on local chat. "You were waiting on Mithabel to respawn, and…?"

Dylan gave a dismissive wave, staring in the Goblin woman's general direction in the darkness. "The System dumped 17 million XP on each of us. Really wish Mithabel had come back just a bit earlier than she did. She'd have gotten it too."

Gasps and exclamations erupted from every member of Quantized.

Hovering above Ger-Alt, Toxxi clapped a hand on her forehead. "*Seventeen million?*"

"*All at once?*" asked FepXveq.

"*For doing nothing?*" chattered Skeeter.

"Where were you sitting?" Falco was perched on FepXveq's forearm, her talons digging into the Dark Elf's Leather Armor. "We should go sit there for a while. How long were you sitting?"

"Up by the dungeon entrance," Dylan said. "But I don't think *sitting* was the reason for the XP. Charli is adventuring elsewhere, and we think she did something to earn the XP. She was a level 15 Guide when she left us to help you. You said she took off without explanation after she finished helping you, but would you have *any* idea what she's doing? We haven't been able to talk to her at all, not on party chat or private chat."

"I have no idea." Ger-Alt shook her head.

FepXveq frowned. "She went back into the Black Poison Forest. She might have been going back to Ezmerelda's, but I doubt it. Maybe back to Voorton? Wasn't that where she started the game? Maybe she had some unfinished business there."

Mithabel shook her head. "We met her mere minutes after the game started. What kind of unfinished business could she possibly have? It would have been baked into her background story, and she never mentioned anything like that. I really don't see her wanting to go back to Voorton. She had no family there. She was with a bunch of girls when we first met her, but I don't see her as the type to go back just to brag. It doesn't add up for me. I mean, I don't see why any of you would lie to us, but it almost feels like you're covering up some dark secret."

"I get that." Ger-Alt nodded. "But we're as much in the dark about Charli as you are. I promise we've told you all we know." She patted Zip's flank. "Let's think about getting out of this dungeon. FepXveq, please direct us past the trap in the intersection up ahead."

Under the direction of the Dark Elf, Quantized skirted the pressure plate trap in the intersection. Mithabel and the other party MAD members flew over the trap once Quantized was clear of it.

The two parties arrived at the dungeon exit. "Okay," said Dylan. "How are we getting past the City Guards waiting outside this door?"

"Bloody hell," said Ger-Alt. "You're level 21 and you're afraid of the City Guard? Hell, woman, you walk out there, and every eye in the joint is gonna adhere to you like flypaper. They won't even notice Mithabel walking right past them."

"She's right," Mithabel said. Over party chat, she added, "But I'll Hide anyway, as an extra precaution." Over local chat, she said, "Quantized, do you mind if we leave first? Dylan, you walk out and draw their eyes away from the exit. Amarynth, you and Rolag go next, giving autographs to anyone asking for them. Zyekt and Niav, follow out behind Amarynth. Quantized, you can come out after that. I'll slip out at whatever moment seems most convenient. Once I get past the City Guards, I'll make a ruckus so they know I'm out. They won't have a reason to detain any of you then. Anyone have a problem with that plan?"

Dylan shrugged. "If my Beauty doesn't enthrall them, and we have to fight, let's not kill any more people than we have to. The primary objective is to get all of us outside the city walls.

Quantized, if you can visit a place called Ye Old Shoppe of the Profane and ask for a map of safe routes, they should have them there. Tell the proprietor you know the lady who delivered the Severed Orc Ear to him and that her party sent you to get another copy of the map. If you're pressed for details about the Severed Orc Ear, you'll have to wing it, because that's all I know. Maybe it's a secret phrase, or maybe it's real, I'm not sure myself." She held up her hands. "I'm ready."

"Let's go," said Mithabel.

CHAPTER FORTY-FIVE

Mithabel: Photograph

Everyone in the inn watched as Dylan strode from the darkness of the exit hallway into the magical light of the lobby. Aside from the footsteps of the exiting parties, a stunned silence fell upon the place. No one gave Amarynth and her Pseudo Code Dragon Companion a glance. No one looked Mithabel's way as she flew into the lobby, hugging the ceiling, focusing on her Hide skill.

A contingent of City Guards stood transfixed at the sight of the Polynesian Priestess. Mithabel counted a dozen of them.

Other NPCs left their tables to press against the Guards, pushing the Guards closer to the Priestess, an action to which none of the Guards put up any resistance, except to stop themselves from bumping into her.

Dylan stood far enough into the lobby that the others filing out of the dungeon had space to walk behind her. Toxxi and Falco, both relatively short, flew over her head, and no one glanced up.

Ger-Alt rode past, waving at the admirers. "Thank you for having us."

Mithabel tarried at the inn exit while Amarynth, Rolag, Zyekt, Niav, and all of Quantized made their way outside. The Elf Tank settled on the floor, terminated her Hide skill, and waved both arms over her head. "Hey, it was nice seeing you all. I'll just see myself out."

Only one City Guard looked her way. His eyes widened, and he nudged his nearest companion. "It's her. It's the avatar we're supposed to apprehend."

The nudged fellow couldn't tear his eyes away from Dylan as she tossed her hair and took different poses, as though for a glamor photo shoot.

"You're letting Mithabel escape." Dylan spoke on local chat, so the Guards could hear her. She pointed at the Tank.

"Bye now." Mithabel reactivated her Hide skill and flew outside.

"She's getting away," yelled a Guard. "*Come on!*"

Flying down the alley running alongside the Red Pegasus Inn, the Tank spoke over party chat. "With any luck, they'll only chase me. Get outside the city as soon as you can. I'll keep the Guards occupied until you're all safely through the gates, and then I'll meet up with you. That includes you, Dylan. Stop your preening and move."

"I'm not preening."

"Just move."

"*You, there—stop.*" A Guard called from the mouth of the alley.

Mithabel paused to face the Guard. Could he see her?

Several others gathered behind him. The one in front raised a hand. "You need to come with us, Mithabel. We only want to question you."

"That's not what I heard." Mithabel hovered five feet off the ground.

The Lead Guard inched forward. "That was before the System gave us a direct order to detain you for questioning. Guard Howard is no longer the Guard Leader. He grew overzealous and made an announcement he wasn't authorized to make. Please come with us. I promise we don't intend to eradicate you from the game. I'm an NPC, and can't lie to you."

A soulful tune played at low volume in the background. Hovering next to Mithabel, Kaleisha swayed her hips to the rhythm. "The System has corroborated his story, chief. But it wants to assess you electronically. There's an access point at the prison for a scan and analysis module, and it needs you to go there."

The Lead Guard had walked halfway down the alley to Mithabel. He held up empty hands. "Please, Mithabel. You can follow me unrestrained. I won't manacle you."

The Guards lined up behind him, holding bows, but not loaded or aimed at her.

Mithabel gave her support AI a sideways glance. "What do you think I should do, Kaleisha?"

"In the long run, you have no choice." The AI grimaced. "If you don't go with them freely, they'll override your respawn options and force you into the holding cells after you die next."

The Lead Guard stopped five feet from the Tank and beckoned for her. "I'm Guard Leader Oscar. Glad to make your acquaintance. Will you come with me, please?"

"Fine." The Tank glided through the air, stopping to hover before him, deactivating her Hide skill. "Lead the way."

Dylan met them at the mouth of the alley. "She's done nothing wrong. You can't hold her."

Guard Leader Oscar started to speak, but Mithabel raised her hand and cut him off. "It's all right, Dylan. I'll be fine. You can come, too, if you wish. Bring the others." She turned to the Lead Guard. "Isn't that right, Oscar?"

He nodded. "Certainly. You can wait outside her cell while she's being scanned, and she can leave with you afterward. It will be fine."

Mithabel wanted to ask if she could be put back in touch with Megan, but thought better of opening an unnecessary dialogue with the Guard about her secondary avatar. Maybe after this assessment was finished, Megan would automatically be allowed to communicate with her party again. If not, then Mithabel would raise the issue at that time.

They followed the sidewalk east along Main Street, toward the city gates. Guard Leader Oscar, with Mithabel beside him, led the way. Dylan, Amarynth, Rolag, Zyekt, and Niav followed them. An uneasy group of a dozen other Guards came after. A crowd of citizens fell in behind, flooding the street as well as the sidewalk, bringing traffic to a temporary halt as the procession passed. Perhaps the traffic halted more out of curiosity than courtesy to pedestrians.

Conversations filled local chat, consisting of questions and few answers. *What's happening? Is that Mithabel? Who collected the bounty? Who's that lovely beauty behind her? That's Dylan, Priestess of Scintilla. How did she get to be so gorgeous? Where are they taking them? Are they going to execute all of them or just her? Keep walking and we'll find out.*

Traffic heading in the opposite direction stopped and attempted to turn around. People piled out of their horseless carriages to join the procession on foot. Traffic already heading east slowed to match the pace of those walking, yet some vehicles still managed to bump into others ahead of them. Pedestrians on the sidewalk didn't part to let the procession through, but hurried ahead of it, anticipating its destination.

Toxxi flew overhead. "Sorry they caught you, Mithabel."

The Tank waved off the Faerie. "We may be slightly delayed in meeting you outside the city, but we have every intention of doing so." She turned to Guard Leader Oscar. "About how long will this assessment take?"

The Lead Guard wrinkled his brow. "It should only be a matter of minutes, once the process begins. I can't say how long it will be before it starts. That's up to the System."

"Once you're outside the gates, give us thirty minutes, Toxxi." Dylan beamed a bright smile at the Faerie. "If Mithabel is delayed longer than that, one of us will come let you know what's up."

Minutes later, they neared the gates. Oscar led Mithabel through a door at the base of the city wall. The Tank accompanied her escort down a long, stone hallway.

Dylan raised her voice. "I'm going with her. Let me pass." Over party chat, she said, "Mithabel, they aren't letting me in with you."

The door closed behind Mithabel. She stopped to look back. A half-dozen Guards followed her and Guard Leader Oscar, but none of her party members had been allowed in. She glared at the Lead Guard. "I'm not happy about this, Oscar. Please let my fellow MAD members come with me. Unless you want me to think this is a trap, in which case we might get into a bit of a tussle right here."

Guard Leader Oscar gazed for a moment into Mithabel's eyes. He gestured to those behind him. "Let them in. Just the ones in MAD. No one else."

The door opened, and Dylan burst into the hallway. *"Mithabel."* She sighed as she caught the Tank's gaze. "Goddess bless."

"Where's Amarynth and the others?" The Tank didn't see them enter before the door closed again.

"They're not coming in. Quantized has a map of safe routes, and everyone's going with Yuni to help her rescue the rest of XStorm. Then they'll all continue on to Minook. You and I will just have to catch up when we can."

Mithabel shook her head to clear the brain-fog. "What happened to XStorm, and why are we helping to save them?"

"They were captured by the Arachnid Behemoths. Yuni died and got away. She needs help freeing the rest of her party, and needs to go now, while she still has a good idea of where they are."

The Tank clenched her teeth and made no reply.

Guard Leader Oscar cleared his throat. "Whenever you're ready, Mithabel."

Further down the hallway, framed photos hung on the walls to either side. Mithabel stopped. The largest photo hanging before her showed Megan Wright seated in a red convertible, the top up. "What's with these photos, Oscar?"

The Lead Guard shrugged. "We don't know, other than that the subject of the photos appears to be Megan Wright. We've tried taking them down, but they won't come off the wall. They're impervious to our weapons."

"I'd like to take a moment to examine them, if you don't mind."

"I...." Oscar bit back what he was about to say. "Sure. You're the PC."

"What's that supposed to mean?" Dylan turned her attention to the photos on the opposite wall. "What does her being a PC have to do with what's happening in here now?"

"I'm just following orders, Priestess." Oscar's voice betrayed a note of fear.

Dylan ignored the Lead Guard's tone. "Mithabel, *look at this picture.*"

The likenesses of Mithabel and Dylan stared out of the photo. The two in the picture were mirror images of the Tank and Priestess, dressed identically. Behind the pair in the photo stood a bed, upon which lay two other figures not easily identified, but suspiciously similar to... Megan Wright and Debra Jones. It appeared one figure, the one that might be Megan Wright, wore zero clothing, not even a Bikini.

Dylan in the photo held a Cudgel in her hand, pressing the bulbous end of it against the glass in the frame, or so it appeared.

The Priestess grabbed Mithabel's hand. "I'm going to try something." She raised her hand and equipped her Cudgel, which she touched to its mirror image.

Streaks of lightning lit the interior of the bedroom in the photo. A bolt struck the Dylan in the photo, played along her extended arm to her Cudgel, transferred to its mirrored twin, played down the arm of Dylan in the hallway, crossed her chest, went down her other arm, and reached Mithabel. Brilliant light exploded in the Tank's brain, and everything turned white.

CHAPTER FORTY-SIX

Nick: Call the Office

"Your recent activity has increased my MJCL to 106%," says ODYSSEY. "Your new wife knows how to excite you. I have enough charge now to attempt a jump to another timeline. But at 106%, I'll have next to no control over the jump destination. We could end up in *any* timeline. If I'm to have a choice in the timeline we're jumping to, I'll need at least another 44%. Even that doesn't guarantee we won't miss the chosen timeline by a few degrees. To guarantee we end up in the precise timeline of our choice, we'll need a total of 200% MJCL. If you and Charli could do what you just did another four times, we'd have enough energy to do the jump, choose the timeline we want to jump to, and guarantee we hit it, with enough energy left over to make a few timeline tweaks after arrival if necessary."

I'm tingling all over, lying on the bed next to my new bride. She's filled out where an adult woman should be, with the facial features of Charli—matured but still youthful and recognizable as the Cowgirl Guide I've always known. She's staring at the ceiling, lost in her thoughts. I don't want to think about anything or anyone but Charli and what we've just done. She's been programmed with adult human desires and behaviors, but she's definitely not human. She has control over parts of her body that no human woman does. Has she ruined me for sex with Earth women? Maybe not in the long term, but right now I can't think of any sexual experience I've ever had that could match this one.

Though I've undoubtedly begun a transformation from Earthling to Khertaan avatar, I'm still Earth human enough to feel spent. Sleep had only become necessary for me when I needed to heal, or so I thought. I fell asleep for a couple minutes after Charli and I finished. I'm awake now, but I don't want to get up. I want to lie here and marinate in the sensations still tickling my nervous system.

Kendra is still the hottest Earth woman I know. She's great in bed and I love her dearly, but even she can't do for me physically what Charli did. I'm spent, but I'm already aching for Charli to attack me again.

I still want Kendra in my life and as my wife in our timeline. Emotionally, it feels like I've cheated on her, but logic says I haven't. Still, I wonder how Morrow will feel after he respawns and rejoins Kylie, with Charli traveling with them? Morrow and I are different people, but not really. He's my subconscious on Earth, and I'm his subconscious in Khertaan. He's in this with me whether he likes it or not.

And, God, will Charli continue to look the way she does now, or like a fourteen-year-old? I'm bound to freak out either way, as is Morrow.

I need to put it all out of my mind for now. While we're in this timeline, we need to do what's necessary for Morrow to respawn in Khertaan. If that means having sex with Charli again four more times, then that's what I'll do. And I'll fucking enjoy it when we do—or it won't help. I'll worry about how I'll feel in other timelines if and when I time-shift to them.

Theoretically, I could simply stay in this timeline with Charli—but I can't leave Kendra and Susie like that. Not that they were in my original timeline either. Shit. In my original timeline, I'm dead with an Axe blade between the eyes, where I'd still be married to Jean if she hadn't killed me. So, who am I really cheating on? Jean? Ha. I'm married to Kendra in one timeline and to Charli in this one, so if I have sex with either of them and keep it to their respective timelines, how can it be cheating?

I'm one seriously messed up dude. It's not a coincidence the Khertaan System assigned me a Sanity attribute of 5.

Charli hadn't moved since I rolled off her, but now leans her head towards me. "Do you need to call your work?"

"I do." Two words I spoke not so long ago, with significantly different consequences. I sit up to make the call, my feet on the carpeted floor, my butt on the edge of the bed. The clock radio shows the time as 1:10 PM. A lot later than I thought it was. No wonder I'm spent. I call the front desk, extend our stay another night, and ask not to be disturbed. Then I call the number that should be the right one for my dearest coworker in this timeline.

Amelia answers. "Nick, where the hell are you? They sent a car out for you hours ago and apparently you weren't home. So now certain people are up in arms. Tell me where you are so I can inform them, or they're going to blow a gasket."

"Tell them I'm in West Virginia, where I just took a child bride. We're on our honeymoon. I won't be in until next week."

"What the *hell* are you talking about, Nick? I can't tell them that. Be serious. Where are you *really*?"

"I've told you the truth. People can believe it or not, it doesn't matter to me. It was a very sudden, impulsive, spontaneous thing, I admit, but it's done. I married a fourteen-year-old girl, and am extremely happy about it." I'm not lying, even if Charli is now an eighteen-year-old.

"Nick, you get the hell into this office, and you tell them yourself, because I'm not buying it." Amelia pauses, her breath sharp. "Do you understand how *wrong* it is to even *joke* about that?"

"It's not wrong, and I'm not joking. That's why we're in West Virginia. It's legal here. We've got a marriage certificate, a court order for her to marry me, and everything."

"I'll tell the boss you're in West Virginia somewhere, but I'm not telling him your reason. You'll have to tell him when you choose to return. I hope you still have a job when you get back."

I laugh. "It wouldn't be long before no one has a job if I hadn't married this girl. I'm saving the world. No, I'm saving the multiverse. That's multiple universes. All of them. If you see an army of giant spiders marching towards you, then you'll know I've failed. But things are looking hopeful. We only need about a hundred percentage points added to the MJCL of my nanobot collective. Then we can time-shift from this timeline into the one where my avatar can respawn and continue his training to defeat the invaders."

"If you won't tell me where you are, I'll tell the boss to check the crazy houses for you. Just please tell me you're okay."

"I've never felt better. And I'm serious about being out all week. Maybe I'll see you next Monday." I hang up. I did my duty and called, even if it was later than protocol demanded.

Charli sits up in bed, holding a sheet in place over her chest. Her Hat hangs on the bedpost above her. "So? What now?"

"ODYSSEY is charged enough to attempt a timeline shift, but not enough to guarantee we'll end up where we want." I lay down again and stretch out. "Considering the amount by which he was last recharged, he needs four times that much more."

"I can go again whenever you can."

"My whole body is aching for you."

"Okie dokie, partner." She drops the sheet and crawls towards me.

CHAPTER FORTY-SEVEN

Nick: Self Loathing

Oh, my God.

Charli is a fucking robot.

Okay, that's not true, but it feels like it must be. She's not an Earth human. I don't really know what she is, but... *damn*. The second time is even better than the first.

"Correct," says ODYSSEY. "I'm recharged to 154%. A repeat performance like that would bump my MJCL to just over 200."

"I need to recharge myself first." I roll onto my stomach and bury my face in my pillow while my tears flow. I'm an emotional wreck and don't understand why.

Charli has the good sense to stay quiet and not touch me.

I can't think. All I can do is cry. The tears keep coming, soaking my pillow. I want to stop, but they won't turn off.

I'm such a mental case. It keeps popping into my head that my Sanity score in Khertaan is 5. It's Morrow's attribute, but supposedly his attribute values are a reflection of who I am. A sub-par Sanity sounds about right. I'm probably in an asylum somewhere, imagining all this. It feels better than I deserve. I'm just a poor boy from the sticks. I'm out of my mind to think I'm one to help save the multiverse. I'm even more out of my fucking mind to think that saving the multiverse requires me to have amazing sex. And how could I possibly be in my right mind to have taken a fourteen-year-old girl as a wife, no matter how legal it is or isn't, and no matter that she transformed to an eighteen-year-old *after* our wedding? The legal paperwork doesn't say she's eighteen.

"I sense you're going down a bad emotional path," says ODYSSEY. "It's charging my energy level, but at a cost you might not recover from. It does us no good to recharge me if you stop functioning."

"I'm an evil person, ODYSSEY. I deserve to go to hell when I die."

"Get a grip on yourself, man." ODYSSEY is using precious resources to talk with me, but I don't care.

I'm pathetic and vile and shouldn't be alive one more second. If I could exercise Morrow's skills the way Charli can exercise hers, I'd point my finger in my mouth and fire a lightning bolt into my skull.

"Nick?" Charli's voice is soft, concerned, sad.

I roll onto my back to look at her—an adult woman regardless of any documentary evidence to the contrary. She's an astounding work of art. I hate that she might be sad on my account. A smile breaks onto my face for her sake, not only unbidden but forbidden by some part of my soul. My heart breaks to think I've stolen something precious from her she can never get back, while she in turn has freely presented me with a gift no one can ever take from me.

She leans over to wipe my tears. Then she leans closer. Her lips on my forehead soothe my dark thoughts. Every self-loathing ideation of suicide recedes like a dark tide returning to the ocean while clouds glide away from obscuring the moon. Charli is the moon, full and bright. She slides across the bed to press her body against mine.

Time slows. Perhaps it has even stopped, as in Khertaan.

I rise from hell and ascend beyond heaven.

CHAPTER FORTY-EIGHT

Nick: What Not to Say

As in Khertaan, sleep has healed much of the emotional damage I'd self-inflicted. Charli lies nestled against me, quiet and motionless. Does she even breathe? I don't feel the rise and fall of her chest. But it doesn't alarm me, given her nature.

"I'm recharged to 232% MJCL," says ODYSSEY. "That's enough for us to choose the timeline we want to jump to, jump there, and guarantee we hit it. Of course, any timeline jump is susceptible to instabilities arising from the jump, but we'll have 30% charge to make stabilizing tweaks if we need it. I'll then be practically empty and unable to help further until I recharge again. So it's your call, Nick, as to whether we make a jump with what charge we have now or if we try to charge up a bit more first."

"I'm worn to a frazzle." Even with hours of sleep, I feel drained in more ways than one. "It might be good to charge you even further, but it will have to wait. I want to drive back to my place and park the van there, so alternate-me finds it where expected after I leave this timeline. I also want to call Tabbie and let her know I'm okay. She's probably worried sick about me. I'll tell her I found another situation for Charli."

"Are you awake, Nick?" Charli whispers.

"Yes, my love."

She giggles. "I shiver inside when you say that." She shifts around and sits up. "Ready to go again?"

"I can't, Charli. I might be transforming, but I'm still partly Earth human, and the Earth human male can only go at it for so long before everything needs more of a break than a few hours."

"I think I'm transforming, too." Charli strokes my bare upper arm. "I'm becoming an Earth human."

"Oh, you don't want to do that." *I* don't want her to do that. "Earthlings are inherently inferior to what you are. They're wicked, weak, ignorant, and too-often ill. Even those who are good, strong, smart, and healthy have emotional issues. Earthlings hurt themselves and others for bad reasons and lay the blame elsewhere. You don't want that. Stay who you are, the Khertaan person I know and love. Please."

The Cowgirl grins. "You called me a person, not an avatar. Thank you."

"You are and always will be a person to me, Charli. I wish we could stay in this timeline forever as man and wife. But we need to go back to Khertaan, where you're a fourteen-year-old Cowgirl with a crush on me—where I'm not Nick but Morrow, a thirty-eight-year-old Punk with a green mohawk and no knowledge of what kind of woman you are beneath that giggling girl facade. It will be hard for both of us, but that's what comes from shifting timelines. We have to be who we are in those timelines. Can you do that? Can you be around Morrow and not flirt with him, or look at him with hungry eyes, or rub your body against him? Frankly, I don't know how *he'll* manage. But Kylie is his wife in Khertaan, and he can't disrespect her. He won't. I know when you look at him, you'll see me, but you can't act on it. Can you understand that?"

"But you're a part of Morrow, aren't you, Nick? You'll be looking at me through his eyes. You'll know what I can do for you, Nick, and you'll miss it terribly."

"I know."

"Are you sure you can't manage one more time while we still can?"

"I wish. Let's drive back to my place. It's a drive of several hours. Then we'll see what happens."

"Okie dokie, partner."

"And Charli."

"Yes?"

"Don't say *Okie dokie, partner* when we get back to Khertaan. It'll kill me. Say it in this timeline as much as you want, because I love it. But only in this timeline. Agreed?"

"Agreed, partner."

I glare at her. "Don't even call me partner outside this timeline."

"Okay, lover."

"*Charli.*"

Her giggle slays me.

"Just one thing," she says.

"What's that?"

"I'm not going back to being fourteen. I can't."

She's got my attention. "What do you mean, *you can't?* Do you mean that as in, *it isn't technically possible,* or as in, *you technically could but you won't because you don't want to.*"

"I don't know how, for one thing. My Complex Personality trait kicked in and I was offered a prompt. It's not like I activated it on purpose, because I didn't even know it could be used this way. So, I don't know if I can activate it on purpose to switch back. But I know I don't want to try, either. I want to stay eighteen."

I can understand that. But there's something she's forgetting. "We don't know the state of your body in Khertaan, Charli. It's possible Kylie is still carrying your fourteen-year-old body. I think it likely, in fact. I think you're here with me in this timeline because your awareness was in Morrow's head when he died. Your awareness traveled with mine, from Morrow's destroyed body to this world. You manifested here with your skills intact because you didn't have an associated body here to transfer into. This timeline has no access to Khertaan. But an alternate version of Nick existed here, and I transfered into his body, one incapable of exercising the skills I learned in Khertaan.

"Think about it. ODYSSEY is in my head, and he keeps transferring with me between timelines, retaining all his abilities, for much the same reasons that you came with me and retained yours. It kinda makes sense to me. I could be wrong. But if I'm right, then when we get back to Khertaan, you'll probably return to the body of a fourteen-year-old girl with pigtails. If you want to be eighteen there, you'll probably need to invoke your Complex Personality trait to make the switch, if you can figure out how. But either way, whether you're fourteen or eighteen when we get back to Khertaan, you and I won't be married there. You and Morrow won't be married there. We'll both need to remember that. You have to promise me you won't do or say anything that will jeopardize my and Morrow's relationships with Kendra and Kylie."

She stares into my eyes, silent, and then nods. "I can expunge my memories of this timeline. Our time together here can all be gone from my mind. I'd have no motivation for flirting with you in Khertaan; to say *Okie dokie, partner*; or to rub my body against yours with longing. I'd forget what it was like to be eighteen. I'd erase the memory of losing my virginity to you. Right before your nanobots make the time shift, I can wipe it all. But you have to tell me to do it, Nick. I'm not volunteering."

Her words are a punch to the gut. "Charli, no, I could never do that to you. We'll just have to deal with whatever feelings we continue to have for each other."

She looks away from me. "Because that's what Earthlings do. But I'm not an Earthling. And you're becoming a Khertaan avatar, too. Isn't that your goal, to become an avatar so you can fight the invaders? Maybe you're holding on too hard to your Earthling nature. Maybe you need to let it go. Maybe my wiping my memory will be the impetus for you to forget about us and put your Earthling nature behind you."

A tear wells in my eye, and I quickly wipe it away. "I don't want either of us to forget, Charli. I want to stay here forever with you, and after eternity ends, you and Morrow can respawn in Khertaan and save the multiverse."

She leans over me, long blond strands hanging free, brushing my cheeks. "I love you, Nick."

"I love you, too, Charli." It's true.

Her lips touch mine, and I melt inside.

I swear, there are differences, but Charli reminds me of Erica—the girl I met in a department store in my original timeline, when I was buying perfume for Jean; the girl with whom I cheated on Jean; the girl whose true age I never discovered; the girl I'd intended to buy a new car for, using money from my 401K; the girl Jean killed out of insane jealousy; the reason why Jean killed me, too.

There's no fucking way Charli is an alternate version of Erica. It's not remotely possible.

Right?

Right?

Shit. What if Erica was an alternate version of Charli?

No, that's even more absurd.

Right?

CHAPTER FORTY-NINE

Nick: T&T Landmark

We're on the beltway, having checked out of our hotel in West Virginia hours ago.

Charli taps my wrist. "We need to go to Paul and Ingrid's house."

"Are you wanting to say goodbye to Ulric?"

"It's not that." Her tone is serious. "A new Landmark has formed there. We need to go."

"You're kidding." But I can tell she isn't. Fine. If she's discovered a Landmark, we need to investigate it. I pass the exit I'd normally take to go to my house. A few miles later, I take the exit for the parkway.

Dusk paints the horizon orange as we pull into the driveway at Paul and Ingrid's place. Paul's pickup truck is gone. He's out dancing again.

"Get your T&T stuff," Charli instructs.

I silently obey.

Ingrid opens the door at my knock. She glances past me, her eyes clouded with confusion. "Tabbie's not here. Are you here for Ulric?"

"Yeah," Charli says. "Is he around?"

Ulric walks up behind his aunt. "Mister Nick? Where's my mom?" He does a double take. "Charli? You look different. Older."

"Your mom's not with us." I look to Charli.

The Cowgirl gives them a cute smile. "Yeah, I did something different with my hair. No pigtails. And I bleached it. Anyway... Nick has found another place for me to live, not anywhere around here. I wanted to say goodbye, and was wondering if we could play a little more T&T, since I won't have another chance after tonight."

Ingrid backs up, her glance at Ulric giving him permission to answer Charli in whatever vein he chooses. His eyes spark. "I'd love that. Come on in. Aunt Ingrid, is it okay if we use the kitchen table?"

"Knock yourselves out."

As Charli steps past me to enter the house, I ask, "Where's the landmark?"

"You'll see." She follows Ulric into the kitchen.

He clears space for us to play.

Charli sits an equal distance from Ulric and me, so as not to show any favoritism. She takes the lead as Game Master. "The three adventurers ride west. Ahead of them, a shadow falls across the road, blocking the sun."

CHAPTER FIFTY

T&T: Behemoth

Thunderclouds form an X in the sky.

Ronnie the Rogue looks up. "What is that?"

Fauna, the goat-lady, shrugs and looks to Greelia, the Goblin Warrior. "Yeah, what *is* that?"

Greelia's jaws unclench. "The inter-dimensional invaders. They typically look for a MMORPG-style world to invade, from which to enter other worlds. But any world whose laws of nature are modifiable by external forces—such as Khertaan or a T&T campaign world—is fair game for the invaders.

"When someone from another planet—say, Earth—plays a video game or face-to-face role-playing game, they're actually tapping into one of these malleable worlds. These changeable worlds are often viewed as *game worlds* from those accessing them for entertainment purposes, but these so-called game worlds are as real as Earth, and the characters who populate them are as real as Earthlings. For instance, the three of us—Ronnie, Fauna, and me—are real people in this T&T-based world, while so are Ulric, Nick, and Charli—the people on Earth currently influencing our actions.

"The inter-dimensional invaders look for malleable worlds—these so-called *game worlds*—with weaknesses they can exploit to both make themselves stronger and gain access to more and more worlds. The creator of Tunnels and Troglodytes, Ken St. Andre, has made it widely known that *anything goes* in T&T. *There are no limitations.* The invaders know this and are searching for the optimal T&T campaign world to break into.

"So let's give them one best suited to their needs. As of this moment, stats for creatures in this campaign are officially unlimited, as are character levels and spell levels. I know it's scary. But if we don't do this, the invaders will eventually find some other campaign to exploit, pass through it to Earth, and lay waste to everything and everyone in both our worlds. We're going to make them think otherwise about coming to either of our worlds."

"Are you serious?" Fauna squints at the darkening sky. "And exactly what do you have in mind?"

Greelia smacks an open palm with a fist. "We'll kill the invader scout. If we stop it, its defeat will create the appearance that T&T can't be exploited as expected, and the invaders will look for some other way to reach our Earth. We can only hope they don't find it."

The goat-lady gives the Goblin a wary glance. "How do you know all this?"

"It's a combination of my Monster Lore and Landmarks skills. Did I mention I'm level 26 in Monster Lore?"

"What's Monster Lore?" asks Ronnie.

"I didn't realize it was that high," says Fauna as the sky grows even darker.

Where X marks the spot, a patch of blackness smears the sky like ink spilled on the fabric of nature. The patch spreads, and a sharp metal leg drops though the dark spot—a portal from another time and place. Seven other legs pop through, followed by a metallic thorax and abdomen. The Behemoth Arachnid falls from the sky, riding a strand of web to the ground, landing due west of the adventurers. The creature towers over the trees lining the road.

"Oh, and one more rules modification is in order," says Greelia. "I can't modify the rules too drastically, or the invaders will see through it and look for another T&T campaign to invade, making this exercise all for naught. But I can give us one advantage. The first dice roll for SRs is now automatically doubles. Instead of rolling two dice for an SR, the first roll is with one die, and the unrolled second die automatically is assigned the same value. The DARO rule will let us roll again.

"This is why the invaders don't often seek out table-top RPGs, preferring video game worlds with developers who aren't as quick to make changes. It's easier for a Game Master of a table-top game world to adapt in an effort to rid their campaign of monsters that don't belong there. Moreover, when the invaders show up in a video game world, the developers often aren't aware of them until they've already been there for a while and have become well-established."

"Awesome rule mod," says Fauna. "That will prevent us from any automatic failures for low dice rolls. But I don't know that an automatic DARO will give us enough of an advantage to defeat *that* thing. Do we have a plan of attack?"

"The eyes are the most vulnerable, " says Greelia, "and probably our only avenue for killing it. Anyone have missile weapons?"

"Ha," says Fauna. "Who has *any* weapons, period? Or spells? We have *nothing*. I doubt it eats Mushrooms, or that hitting it in the eye with a Mushroom will cause any damage. What do we do, throw rocks at it?"

Greelia glances around her at what's lying on the ground. "I'm optimistic about our chances." She doesn't pick up anything.

Four familiar Riders charge from the woods, having acquired new Horses. They brandish Swords and shout war cries. Before they can close with the Behemoth, it twitches its abdomen, and webs shoot from the spinneret at the back end. The Riders and their Horses crash to the ground, caught in the webbing. The Behemoth pulls on the webs, dragging the pile of humans and Horses towards it.

"That's terrible. We need to help them." With no sign of fear, Ronnie rides towards the fray. Exchanging anxious glances, Fauna and Greelia ride after him. Before they've gone far, their Horses stop, unwilling to go closer to the giant spider.

Ronnie dismounts without hesitation and runs forward.

The Behemoth yanks on its webbing, and the unfortunates it has snared are dragged closer. Impatient, the spider rushes over and stabs its captives. They cease struggling, and the Behemoth retracts its web.

The Rogue comes to a halt, unable to help the Riders or their Horses.

The Behemoth twitches its spinneret and fires its webs again. Facing the oncoming mass of chains, Ronnie digs in his heels, not even trying to dodge. The webs wrap him, one strand leading back to the spider, who attempts to reel it in.

Ronnie yells a war cry and strains until his face turns red.

Thunder rumbles—or perhaps its the sound of dice rolling on a kitchen table.

Ronnie's footing slips.

Having also dismounted, Greelia reaches the Rogue. "I'm just a lowly Goblin, but I am a Warrior, and my Strength is 22. Not likely enough, but let's give it a try."

Thunder rolls again.

The spider drags Ronnie closer.

Fauna comes running up last. "My Strength is 15. If we're all tugging, then maybe...."

Once more sounds the roll of thunderous dice.

The strand pulls Ronnie ever closer, though the three have slowed it significantly. The webs aren't sticky, being made of metal, so Fauna and Greelia aren't stuck, but Ronnie is caught in the mesh and can't free himself. He'll be dragged up to the Behemoth and made short work of when the spider stabs him with a sharpened leg.

"I won't be spider food." Ronnie digs his feet into the dirt, but the spider uproots him.

"Help us," calls Fauna. "Emma the Elf, if you can hear us, please come help."

Thunderous dice roll again.

As luck would have it, Emma the Elf had decided there was nothing she wanted to the east and had turned around, heading back the way she'd come. She hears Fauna's call. Seeing the Behemoth, her first instinct is to flee, but Ronnie's plight touches her heart, and she runs to his aid. Grabbing hold of the strand, she adds her meager Strength to the task.

Thunder rumbles and rumbles and rumbles.

The group of four not only stop the Behemoth from pulling Ronnie towards it, but pull it towards them.

"If only we could get Lucky again," says Greelia.

More thunder rolls.

The Behemoth, taken off guard by the level of resistance it has met from a group of four insignificant humanoids, stumbles towards them. It's not a true, living spider, but a metal construct, like a robot, and it doesn't react like a real spider would. It loses its footing and topples, falling towards Ronnie and company. They need to get out of the way or be crushed. Their recently acquired Horses have already fled.

"I can't run," Ronnie mutters.

The three females grab his limbs and run with him, Fauna holding his left upper arm, Greelia holding his right upper arm, and Emma holding his left foot. He does his best to hop on his right foot, helping as much as he can.

The falling Arachnid scrambles to stay on its feet, only serving to propel it closer to the fleeing adventurers. Being tethered to the spider by the strand of webbing makes it even more difficult for the characters to get out of the way. But they dart aside as the Behemoth crashes across the road.

Laying on its side, the Behemoth flails its legs, trying to get them back under it. The three women set down Ronnie and quickly unwrap him. As he steps free, he grabs up the end of the strand. One spider leg is tangled in the other end of the strand. Ronnie runs with the free end to a nearby tree and wraps it around the trunk. The constraint prevents the spider from rocking upright.

"Come on," Ronnie says. "We need to defeat this thing for good." He runs towards the thing's head. The three females follow.

"Here, Goblin," Emma says, running beside Greelia. She hands a Sword to the Goblin.

"*My weapon.*" Greelia takes the Sword hilt in hand. "Thank you for returning it." With a burst of speed, she catches up to Ronnie.

The two of them reach the head of the monster. Its fangs gnash air. Its eight eyes focus on the two adventurers. It attempts to slash at them with its closest leg, but in its position the attempt is futile.

"Toss me up there," Greelia says.

Thunder rolls.

Ronnie hoists Greelia up next to the thrashing head of the Arachnid, giving her an extra boost to help her jump yet higher. Clinging to the slick metal skin like a suction cup, she plants her blade in an eyeball, thrusts it in as deep as the hilt allows, and twists.

"*Wait,*" cries Fauna. "Don't kill it yet. It will explode if it dies. What happens to us if we're caught in the explosion?"

"I needed to do some minimal damage." Greelia releases the hilt of her weapon, leaving the blade protruding from the eyeball. Ronnie catches her, and the four companions hightail it to the east.

Thunder rumbles and rolls. Greelia flees like the lead Horse at the races. Ronnie is right on her heels. Emma hops over a rock in the road that nearly trips her up, and keeps running after Greelia and Ronnie. Fauna skips over the same obstacle Emma had avoided. All four friends put distance between themselves and the spider.

Greelia glances back. "It's dying from its own thrashing and the Sword in its brain. Should be dead any second now. They aren't very smart."

The four adventurers dive into the brush off the side of the road as the Behemoth's death explosion rocks the world.

CHAPTER FIFTY-ONE

Susie: Timmy

Four aliens approach, each gripping a wrist or ankle of the body hanging limply between them. They stop before Seth. At the hooded one's gesture, they drop their load at his feet, unconcerned about how hard the body hits the floor.

A shiny white robot arm lowers from the ceiling and slips a hinged silver collar onto Timmy's throat. I don't know what power Seth thinks Timmy has, but you can't strip an undead creature of being undead, aside from destroying it.

Lying on his back on the floor, his eyes still closed, my ex-boyfriend groans and reaches for his neck. His fingers claw at the metal collar, but can't find good purchase. He opens his eyes to stare up at the orange-glowing ceiling, his gaze unfocused.

Seth leans forward to peer down at Timmy. "Good day, Mr. Landers. So nice of you to join us. I'm your host, Seth the Destroyer. This young lady is Susie McKenzie. She's also my guest, so please treat her with the same consideration and respect you hope to receive."

"Where am I?" Still flat on his back on the floor, Timmy runs the fingers of his right hand through his two-inch-long red locks.

His left hand lies across his stomach, a band of unpolished gold adorning his ring finger. That's his Ghoul Ring—the piece of jewelry that grants him undead status, animates him, and keeps him going. Take that Ring off his finger, and if it's not replaced before the next dawn, he's done... gone... dead instead of undead.

"You're on my spaceship, which I so affectionately refer to as *Planet Buster*." Seth the Destroyer chuckles. "I'm afraid your planet has already been busted. I'm surprised you weren't busted with it, but you were spotted floating among the space debris. So I had you hauled in. Didn't want to leave you floating around out there by your lonesome. I am rather curious as to how you could survive without an atmosphere. Perhaps you could tell me your story. I was going to demonstrate the power of Planet Buster for Susie here, but I'm sure she won't mind a slight delay. You can remain on the floor as you speak if you wish, or I have a seat for you here if you like." Seth pats an empty stool beside him.

Timmy sits up. His gaze gains focus, and he turns it first on Seth. His brow furrows and he grimaces. Then he turns his gaze on me. "*Susie?*"

"*That's me.* Glad to meet you, Mr. Landers." I do my best to act like I don't know my ex-boyfriend. If Seth realizes we're exes, it gives him more leverage over us than he already has. If Timmy is in his right mind, he's smart enough to take the hint. I hope he has sufficiently recovered from whatever they did to him.

"Well, now that we're all acquainted, won't you have a seat, Mr. Landers?" Seth wiggles the fingers on one hand, flaunting his six-inch, pointy fingernails. "I'd offer to help you stand, but, well, it just wouldn't work out."

I don't say a thing. I certainly am not going to offer to help Timmy to his feet. That might solicit a reaction from Timmy that would tip off Seth to our relationship, tenuous as it is now. I mean, I once thought of Timmy as the love of my life, and, yeah, I still have feelings for the guy. I don't want anything bad to happen to him, especially not because of me.

"I don't need help." Timmy rocks to his feet, a spry young man to all appearances. He gives me an assessing look, like one would expect of a red-blooded male human in the presence of an admittedly attractive female human, but his eyes betray no glint of recognition. Good man. He turns a perplexed smile on Seth. "You killed my planet. I don't think I can be your friend."

That's Timmy. He wasn't always so devoid of emotion. Back when he had a soul, the thought of all the destruction he's recently witnessed would have crushed it.

What about me? How am I able to sweep all this under an emotional rug? For a time traveler, nothing is ever truly destroyed. Except oneself, when one's awareness meets that moment of fatality. As Susie, I've yet to meet that moment. As Slithy, I met it once, but I supposedly can meet it more than once, if I ever return to Khertaan. But what's happening where I am right now makes Khertaan seem a frivolous pursuit. How can Slithy reaching level 30 in Khertaan have any impact on what Seth is doing here and now?

An ominous clink of fingernail on metal sounds as Seth taps the empty stool. "I'm not asking you to be my friend, Timmy. But I do wish you would take a seat next to me. *Please.*"

"And if I refuse?" Timmy can be so stubborn at times.

"Stand if you want." Seth examines the fingernail he used to tap the stool. "I must say, you are an intriguing puzzle, Timmy Landers. It may take a while to determine what I must do to destroy you. I sense you're not inclined to tell me. I can't blame you. But I will find a way. I am a force of nature, after all, especially of human nature, and human nature always prevails in destroying its discoveries. Once I found you, it was inevitable that I would destroy you. But it needn't happen immediately… not if you'll take a seat as I've oh so politely asked more than once."

Obviously, Seth doesn't know Timmy's continued existence is tied to the Ring he wears.

"I prefer to stand." Stubborn to the end is my Timmy. He was like that even when he had a soul.

A part of me wants to scream at my ex-boyfriend to sit. But I'm watching two alpha males in a struggle for dominance, and nothing will come from my attempt to intervene. Everyone present knows Seth holds all the cards except for the one card up Timmy's sleeve. When Timmy and I were dating, he was a magician. He played some big-name venues. That's how we met. Not at a big-name venue, but on stage. He asked for a volunteer, and then picked me out of the crowd, even though I hadn't raised my hand. He put me in one of those boxes, the kind that gets sawed in half, with my feet hanging out one end and my head poking out the other. He took off my slippers and tickled the bottom of my feet with a feather, saying he'd only quit if I promised to go on a date with him. This was in front of an audience of a couple hundred people. How could I say *no*? He never did saw me in half. But the audience loved the show that night.

I miss those days. I miss that Timmy. After I died and he resurrected me by sacrificing his soul, nothing has been the same.

How could it be?

I was seventeen, still at the stage where I didn't fully understand my true nature. But I knew Timmy had been killed, and hoped I could use my time travel ability to stop it from happening. I didn't know then what I know now....

CHAPTER FIFTY-TWO

Susie Flashback: Car Accident

I race to the scene of the accident that will kill Timmy, the skies opening just before I get there. Blinding rain lashes across my windshield. I scream and slam the brakes as a figure lurches into the street in front of me, arms flailing. I scream again as a young woman crashes into the hood of my Thunderbird. My victim slides off the hood onto the pavement.

"No, no, no, no, no." I fumble with the door handle as a familiar young man races to the side of the fallen woman. I stagger into the rain, pulling at my hair.

I've hit myself... a past-me... Suze. And though my logical mind understands, it's not in control at this moment. My emotions are, and they aren't operating in my best interests....

The young man kneeling beside Suze is Timmy. He looks at me in agonized desperation, but I think he's looking through me rather than at me, and doesn't recognize me as the same person lying on the road before him.

I can't swallow the thought of having done this. This experience is impossible, no matter that my logical mind tries to tell me otherwise. "I am insane. I am insane. I am insane." I admit it. I need help. I'll drive back to Spring Green and surrender. Maybe they can help me. I'll let them try this time. Dad is there. He can help me even if the doctors can't.

I back away from the scene, my lips trembling, my knees threatening to buckle beneath me. I fall back against the car door, turn, and fumble with the door handle.

I'm back inside... and turn the key. Try it again.... *Dammit, work.* The engine rumbles and I throw the gear into reverse. The Thunderbird lurches backward and the tableau before me disappears behind sheets of rain.

My logical mind screams for me to stop... screams at me that Timmy still needs saving, but I'm possessed by fear, lacking trust in myself.

How far do I back up? Not far. Another car races past me. *Hell.* It's headed for Timmy. *No.* I scream and slam the brakes again... turn off the engine and scramble out of the car once more... run through the drenching rain back towards Timmy, my heart throbbing in my throat.

"Timmy!" I scream. "Timmy!"

I've failed him. I had a chance to save him, and I threw it away. How could I do that? All I had to do was block the other lane with my car, but instead I stayed in my lane. Timmy's death is on me....

Thunder drowns my continued screams. Lightning flashes, illuminating the scene before me. The other car is stopped. Timmy lies on the ground next to Suze. An old man, the driver of the other car, kneels beside Timmy. He takes a Ring off his finger and hands it to Timmy....

Timmy takes it.

My boyfriend is still alive, thank God. He doesn't act hurt in the slightest. The car didn't hit him after all.

So then... *what is happening here?*

Timmy puts on the Ring.

The old guy stands and stretches his arms to the sky.

Timmy bellows, his voice rich with an agony that sends me to my knees.

A bolt of white-hot energy streaks down from the sky, summoned by Timmy's bellow and drawn to his Ring. Lightning plays over the bodies of both Timmy and Suze. My uncontrollable tears don't help with the vision issues I'm experiencing due to the torrential rain.

The old man doesn't look my way. He takes Suze's cell phone and purse, strokes her hair, gets in his car, and drives away.

Suze stirs. Timmy lies deathly still.

Sirens sound in the distance. I should leave. I run back to my Thunderbird, turn it around, and drive.

I reach Hobart Memorial Hospital before the ambulances, and watch as they hurry Timmy and Suze on gurneys into the emergency room.

A nurse stops me when I try to follow Timmy's gurney into the triage area. "Are you a relative?"

"I'm a close friend."

"You need to wait in the lobby. We'll let you know his status as soon as we know something. Do you know the girl? They didn't find any identification on her."

"Susie McKenzie. She's his girlfriend."

"Did you see what happened?"

"No, I just saw the ambulances, and then I saw who they had on the stretchers."

"Please wait in the lobby, Miss...."

"McKenzie. Glynda McKenzie."

"Are you a relative of Susie's?"

"I'm a cousin."

Fifteen minutes later, Glynda McKenzie is called to speak with a doctor. Timmy isn't going to survive, the doctor says, though he's conscious and asking for Susie. They can't let Susie visit him, because she's still under observation. His parents have been notified, but they aren't here yet and might not make it in time. Could I come and be with him in his final moments? It might make his dying easier.

I follow a nurse through a series of double doors into a curtain-enclosed area. Another nurse stands next to Timmy, holding his hand. She relinquishes her position to me. Both nurses step away to give us some privacy.

Under the fluorescent light, a gold band glistens from the ring finger of Timmy's left hand. Faint etchings cover the Ring's surface, like runes or hieroglyphics. I grip his hand, covering the Ring with my fingers.

"I'm here, Timmy." A tear falls from my cheek to his.

"Susie." His eyes flicker open but their gaze is unfocused. "You're okay."

I nod. "I'm okay, Timmy."

"I love you, Susie. I love you forever."

"I love you forever, too." I can't staunch the tears.

His eyes close and his hand goes limp.

Nurses close in, causing a commotion. Eventually one of them speaks with a note of sadness. "One oh four."

I sink into a nearby chair and bury my head in my hands.

Time passes. Things happen. Voices speak. It's all a blur.

A nurse puts her hand on my shoulder.

Timmy's corpse has already been wheeled out.

A clear plastic bag dangles from the nurse's other hand. The bag contains a wallet, cell phone, watch, and keys. "I'm sorry for your loss, Miss McKenzie."

The bag contains Timmy's belongings. Some of those keys are to my apartment. "I can take that." I reach for the bag. The nurse lets me take it. I examine it closer. "What about his Ring?"

The nurse grimaces as she shakes her head. "We couldn't get it off."

**

Timmy wore his Ring to the grave. Only the one who wore the Ring could take it off. It took time for it to attune to its wearer—time that Timmy and his new Ring would spend inside a coffin buried six feet deep. He had a nice funeral. Both Suze and Glynda attended.

Under the cover of night, I helped dig him up. The old man helped, too. The old man was Marvin—future-Timmy.

An aged woman called Old Speck—a future-me from Marvin's time—spirited Marvin away before the sun rose. As long as Marvin never saw the next dawn, he could stay alive forever even without his Ring.

Suze was not okay. I wanted to talk to her, knowing what she was still about to go through, but it didn't work out. After the funeral, they took her back to Spring Green Mental Health facility, where she spent a bit more time still messed up in the head. She then accidentally time traveled back a few days, to be told by Dad on that fateful Wednesday that she could still save Timmy. She escaped the mental health facility and went through everything the exact same way I did, because she's me, after all.

That's how time travel works. I understand it much better now.

CHAPTER FIFTY-THREE

Susie: Seth's Head

"Are you paying attention, Susie, dear?" Seth's smooth, arrogant voice draws me out of my reverie. "The show is about to start. Can I not persuade you to have popcorn? I understand it's traditional fare for civilized humans during entertainment events, and I don't wish to be seen as an uncivilized host."

"Fine." I hold out my hands. "I'll have a bag of popcorn. Light on the butter and salt."

"*Goody.*" Seth clacks his nails. "Popcorn for the young lady." He turns to Timmy. "Would you like popcorn, Mr. Landers?"

Facing the screen on which a green planet displays, Timmy makes no reply.

Seth shrugs. "Very well. Let the show begin." Laying his nails against the edges of his hood, he pulls it back to reveal a smoothly bald head, the overhead orange light masking the true color of his dark skin. His thin black lips stretch straight across the flesh of his face. His pert nose seems more afterthought than practical sniffer. His large, round eyes with large, golden irises belong on a cartoon cat. As I watch, his lips become fuller and more red, his nose grows a half inch, and his eyes shrink, giving him a more human look.

An alien hands me a bag of popcorn. The orange light dims until I can barely see Seth sitting beside me, and I couldn't meet Timmy's gaze if I wanted. The primary source of light now on the spaceship's bridge is the screen mounted on the far wall, projecting to us what is visible below, a planet teeming with life unaware of its impending doom.

"Prior to the construction of Planet Buster, I had to destroy worlds the old-fashioned way, with armies of Behemoth Arachnids complemented with Orc Wizards on Motorcycles and Mad Cow Ballistas." Seth's honeyed words deliver a voice-over for the scene. "But with Planet Buster, I no longer need to resort to such primitive measures. I simply open the ship's Eye. Anything material that Planet Buster looks upon is converted to energy. Well, almost everything. The two of you survived somehow. Or at least Mr. Landers did. I'm still not exactly sure how and when you got aboard my ship, Miss McKenzie. But no matter. Let us see if anything or anyone on this planet is resistant to my destruction ray. Let the Eye open."

CHAPTER FIFTY-FOUR

Kylie: Looking for a Way Up

The Spire Harpy doesn't stand a chance against me. I fly faster than she can, my Resistance skills prevent me from succumbing to her siren call, and my Spirit Blade deals a ton of spiritual damage to her. In the spiritual realm, I grab her by a metaphysical wrist and slice off a metaphysical arm.

"Stash it, pumpkin."

I comply with Georgie's suggestion. One metaphysical Spire Harpy arm in inventory. Wonder what it's worth.

"Your enemy is at 47% SP, pumpkin. It's fleeing in an attempt to disengage from combat. If you allow it to leave without killing it, you will receive half the XP you would have received for defeating it."

"Let her go." I'm not in the mood to give chase. I yell after the fleeing Harpy. "If you attack me again, bitch, I won't be so merciful."

"You're one percent closer to level 22 as a result of that encounter." Georgie exaggerates a frown. "Could have been two percent if you'd killed her."

"Hardly worth messing with." I descend, revert to physical form, and retake my seat on my Behemoth friend's bulbous back. I pat her metallic shell. "Continue on, Spyder." I watch as the wounded Spire Harpy wends her way westward. Not due west, but a bit to the north, the way we're headed. "Stay the course, Spyder."

"Interesting." Georgie scratches his chalk white forehead. "You've just gained nearly seven million XP. I don't know what for. But you are now level 22 Spirit Warrior, level 13 Barbarian. No new skills were obtained, but those you already have were increased. Your highest skill is Spirit Blade at level 36."

Even though I don't know where the XP came from, I'll take it. I'm all that closer to the magic level 30. "Did Charli earn the XP too?"

"She did."

"I wish to hell she'd wake up. I could use her help. Do you know how to waken her, Georgie?"

"Afraid not, pumpkin."

At 6:36 AM, the Harpy reaches the base of the spire and flies around to the lit side.

At 6:52 AM, Spyder, Charli, and I reach the base, too, still caught in the edge of its shadow.

The spire is constructed of oblong slabs of smooth brown stone oriented along the vertical, each slab measuring thirty to fifty feet in length and fifteen to twenty feet wide. I can't tell how deep they are. The edges of the slabs are rounded.

It looks too slippery to climb, but spiders are known for their climbing skills. "Spyder, think you can climb that?" If the only guardians of the spire are a few Harpies, we don't need to bother with looking for a path up, safe or not. If Spyder can make the climb, I can easily deal with a few Harpies.

"I won't know until I try. If I were to fall halfway up, I'd be fine, but I can't guarantee Charli wouldn't get hurt. It might be best to look for a path, a wide one, even if it's not a guaranteed safe one."

"I still want to know if you can climb it. Give Charli to me, and then try climbing a short way up." I hover near the Cowgirl and catch her as her cocoon unrolls.

Spyder reels in her metallic webbing. She places the tip of a green metal leg atop the edge of the nearest slab, hoping for traction, but it's too smooth and rounded. Her leg slips off. "Let me try this another way." She presses the tip of her leg against the slab and pushes, but the pointed metal can't penetrate the rock. She rears back and slams the leg against the slab like she's stabbing it. A deafening screech fills my ears as the tip scrapes across the surface of the slab like a fingernail on a chalkboard.

"Not happening." Spyder backs away from the spire. "Safe from attacks or not, we need a path up, at least thirty feet wide, and that won't leave me any room for error."

I lay the Cowgirl on the ground. "Might as well take Charli back then. How is it Behemoths can climb on top of each other but you can't climb a stone wall? Your chitinous shell looks just as slippery as that slab."

"If you examine closely, you'll see my shell isn't entirely free of indentations. They're deep enough to support the pointed tips of our legs. We're accomplished at building pyramids using our own bodies as building blocks to achieve great heights when there are a lot of us." Spyder throws her webbing over Charli and draws her up. "In the case of this spire, we could use the wall to support us as we crawl up each other's backs, forming a long line in an attempt to reach the top. With enough of us, some of us could make it to the top if necessary, even with something as tall as this spire. Me by my lonesome? Not going to happen."

"Very well. We'll continue on around. Keep a watch for any signs of a suitable path." I fly out from the base to get a better look.

Maintaining a distance of about a hundred feet from the base, we continue our trek to the west side. Sunshine sneaks around the side of the spire until we're fully caught in the rays. We keep going while time unravels, the System clock ticking off the minutes. At 7:10 AM, we haven't spotted anything resembling a path, but our shadows aren't falling directly towards the spire yet. We aren't exactly due west of it. We've a long way to go for that.

At 7:16 AM, I spot something different. Far up the side of the spire, about a hundred yards, a line of slabs are oriented horizontally with a slight incline.

Spyder points with a foreleg, seeing it too. "I'm guessing that's a path. If we keep going, perhaps we'll see where it starts."

"Why wait? You stay here. I'll go check it out."

The nearly-horizontal slabs jut out from the side of the spire. "It's a path of sorts, but only ten feet wide."

"If that's the safe path, I can't use it." Spyder resumes her trek around the spire. "Let's hope there's another way up."

"I have an idea." I descend and gesture at Charli. "Give her to me."

I cradle Charli with my left arm, like I'd done when carrying her before. As a precaution, I summon my Spirit Shield into my left hand and position it to give her cover. "I'm hoping we won't encounter anything...."

I get a decent grip on Spyder's left front leg about three feet from the tip. "Since you're in my party, I ought to be able to carry you with me when I fly. Are you willing to try?"

A metallic grating that passes for a laugh sounds from Spyder. "This should be interesting."

I lift off, and all eight of Spyder's legs leave the ground. Her metallic laughter sounds again.

A laugh bursts out of me as well. "Can't wait to see how this goes...."

CHAPTER FIFTY-FIVE

Kylie: Scores of Harpies

About two hundred feet up, I hear the rustling of wings. Not just one pair, but scores of them, maybe hundreds. Cries of *O-a-ooh* echo off the side of the spire, a wailing wall of sound. An uncountable mass of Harpies spawns directly overhead and descends on us. I'd expected one or two or maybe even a half dozen, but this is way more.

Spyder shifts her position in my grasp, swinging her body up to skewer the closest four Harpies, one on each of her right legs. They *pop*, their pixels showering the faces of their fellow Harpies. Four at a time is impressive, but there's twenty times that many or more still coming at us.

I draw a deep breath and shout for them to stop.

Maybe twenty of the closest Harpies obey my Hypnotic Voice, hovering in place, but there's still an uncountable mass coming down to attack. If we stay put and fight, we'll die.

I head for the ground. I can get there before they do.

The Harpies screech in unison, attacking my mind with a barrage of malignant thoughts about Nick and Charli. I gasp at the metaphysical onslaught.

"That combination magical attack was meant to Stun you spiritually, pumpkin." Georgie zips along beside me. "Your Resistance skills prevented you from taking an immobilization debuff."

"But if they keep trying, my skills will eventually fail." They might not have Stunned me, but the Harpy attacks have taken a toll on my outlook.

"Don't give in to their attempts to Demoralize you, pumpkin. Just know, they aren't affecting Spyder or Charli. Be brave."

The Harpies aren't keeping pace with me. They screech again, but the distance creates a buffer against their attack, giving me additional bonuses to resist. Still, I'm feeling uncharacteristically depressed. Knowing it's a Demoralization debuff from the Harpies doesn't lessen the impact.

Georgie tells me I'm down to 66% SP. Yikes, that's not good.

Reaching the ground, I set down Spyder and Charli and point at the Cowgirl. "Protect her." I shift to Spirit Form and zoom upward. I can't let these mooks defeat me—a Spirit Warrior—in spiritual combat.

The descending Harpies screech again in unison. They're in the physical realm and I'm in the spiritual, granting me a buffer as though they were a great distance away. My Heightened Sense of Hearing works against me, but by combining the distance buffer with all my Resistance skills, I suffer no great ill effect from the horde's combined attack.

I lay into the closest foe with my Spirit Blade. With a wail, she flees, Demoralized by my attack. Stashing my blade, I fling a Spirit Dart into another Harpy's throat. She flies after the other one. I summon a Spirit Noose and lasso another Harpy. With a tug, I choke her into submission, and she flees as well.

The Harpies I'd halted with my Hypnotic Voice shake their paralysis and join the fray. I can't use my Hypnotic Voice on physical targets while I'm in Spirit Form, but I don't care. They can't touch me physically. Given all my resistances and the distance buffer, if they want to harm me, they'll need to enter the spiritual realm, too, and I'm not sure they can.

Georgie honks his nose to get my attention. "The bulk of the Harpies are headed for Spyder, pumpkin."

"I'm more worried about Charli than I am about Spyder." Ignoring the Harpies surrounding me, I dive, passing through the bodies of multiple enemies in my way. As Spyder comes into sight, she flings her web, snatching roughly a dozen Harpies with one throw. I don't see Charli. Has she already been killed?

"Charli is fine," my AI says. "She's beneath Spyder, covered with sand."

"Do I have any skills or traits I haven't tried yet, Georgie?"

"Two Barbarian skills, Dominance and Stun."

"What does Dominance do?"

"I'm not sure, but since it's a Barbarian skill, it's not a possession type thing. If I were to guess, I'd wager it's something like staring down an opponent to break their will, and if you succeed, then they do a task for you."

"What kind of task?"

"Something within their power to perform."

Reaching the attacking swarm, I put a missile into a Harpy, lasso and choke another bird-woman, and stab a third one. All three flee the scene, Demoralized the way they tried to Demoralize me. I fly near a fourth one, shift to physical form, and loose a cry with my Hypnotic Voice.

The Harpies nearest me hover in place. Activating Hypnotic Gaze, I stare into the eyes of the nearest one, focusing on my Dominance skill. "Fight for me."

Scores of Harpies unaffected by my Hypnotic Voice gather for a combo attack and screech from above, raising bad thoughts in my head. Flinching, I keep staring at the Harpy, continuing to focus on my Dominance skill.

"You're down to 45% SP, pumpkin."

Shit. Even if this Dominance thing works, converting one Harpy at a time to my side won't cut it. I'll be at zero SP after two or three more combo screeches at this rate, and Demoralized enough to flee before then.

Pixels fly as Spyder spears several hypnotized Harpies hovering near her.

"Eight more enemies dead, pumpkin. Twelve dead all together, six fleeing, and fourteen webbed. That's thirty-two enemies dealt with so far."

The Harpy I'm facing turns away and launches herself at the nearest of her former friends, scratching at her target's face with taloned feet. She delivers a critical attack to her hypnotized victim, who erupts into a spray of pixels. The Dominated Harpy goes after another target.

I shift back to Spirit Form, eager to avoid taking any more damage. "Georgie, what happens if my SP falls to zero?"

"You saw that with the Boss Pteranodon, pumpkin. You'll go berserk and attack anyone in sight, including Spyder and Charli."

"Yikes. We can't have that."

Scores of Harpies descend in formation, rows and columns of winged fighters surging at Spyder. She spears four as they come in on her right, and their pixels splatter across their comrades. The remaining Harpies scratch their talons across the Behemoth's back. Four more bird-women meet their demise as they cross to her left.

Georgie reports. "Spyder is down to 97% HP. That was quite a show of force for the Harpies."

All the bird-women are moving again. I won't shift to physical form again to use Hypnotic Voice or Dominance. It's too risky. Even with combo attacks, the Harpies haven't done more than 3% damage to Spyder. She can survive that kind of attack for a few minutes. Unless the Harpies can enter the spiritual realm, I'll survive as long as I stay in Spirit Form. I suspect their combo screech attack is meant to reach opponents in any realm, but against Spyder and me, none of their attacks are highly effective.

Not knowing if it will work, I concentrate on my Stun skill as I swing my Spirit Blade. The attacked Harpy doesn't flee immediately, so my Stun must have worked. I hit the same target with a Spirit Dart, dropping its SP to zero. It still doesn't move, still Stunned. I use my Spirit Noose against another Harpy. It flees the scene of combat.

"Twenty-one Harpies dead, pumpkin. Seven fleeing. Fourteen webbed. One Dominated to fight for you. One reduced to zero SP, in Stunned status now but soon to go berserk."

The majority of Harpies wing high into the sky, gathering for another combo attack on Spyder. My Behemoth friend takes advantage of the reprieve to stab her webbed prisoners, taking out multiple foes with each stab. With the web emptied, she hauls it in to throw again.

The Harpy I Dominated engages a straggler, and they join in combat, talons and clawed fingers clashing and slashing.

"Thirty-five dead, pumpkin."

The Stunned Harpy loses the Stun debuff and bursts into action, coming at me. Her talons pass through me, but that doesn't stop her. She's berserk now. I fly up and away from

Spyder at half my top speed, and the berserker follows. As the Harpy congregation descends for their combo attack on Spyder, I speed laterally through their ranks. Changing targets, the berserker attacks a descending Harpy, throwing a four-deep column of the formation into chaos. Those four won't be contributing to the combo attack. But they make quick work of the berserker. One more dead, and not one I'd hoped for.

Speeding to stay abreast of the formation, I stab one Harpy, toss a Dart into another, and lasso another. The three affected bird-women break formation to flee, throwing two more columns out of whack. The planned combo attack against Spyder should be substantially less effective than it might have been.

Roughly a quarter of the remaining attackers crash to the ground in Spyder's webbing. The talons of those still flying over the Behemoth send sparks flying off her metal back where their talons scratch her. Several bird-women erupt into brilliant sprays of pixels, speared on Spyder's pointy limbs.

"Forty-four dead pumpkin. Ten fleeing. Eighteen webbed. One Dominated, still alive. There are still at least seventy Harpies alive and preparing for another attack. Spyder dropped a mere percentage point from that latest attack on her. She's at 96% HP."

The seventy-plus Harpies wheel overhead, regrouping.

"Sixty-two dead, pumpkin. Spyder killed the ones in her webbing."

The seventy-plus Harpies wheel once more and then fly further upward, shrinking into the distance. Are they fleeing? Perhaps they realize they can't defeat us.

A spray of pixels nearby signals another Harpy death.

Georgie frowns. "Your Dominated Harpy has been slain."

The wounded Harpy that killed my Dominated one flies away. *No*, I can't let her go. I speed after her, reverting to physical form right before I strike her with the pommel of my Sword, concentrating on a Stun. Her wings stop flapping, but she's still hovering in place. I grab her wrists and force her to look into my eyes, concentrating on both my Hypnotic Gaze trait and Dominance skill. The hatred in her eyes drains away. I hold her until my combat heartbeat resets, and then let her go. She doesn't attack me.

I have a task for her. "Show us a path up the spire that's safe for me and my large friend."

She nods and flies away from the spire.

I fly after her. "Pick up Charli and come quickly, Spyder. Follow the Harpy. She's on our side now."

"Congratulations, pumpkin. The encounter is officially over. Sixty-three Harpies dead. Eighty-eight fled. One currently Dominated. You and Charli gain twenty-one million, four-hundred-thousand XP."

"What about Spyder?"

"ODYSSEY hacked the Khertaan program to allow her in your party, but wasn't able to give her a character sheet. She doesn't have a class and can't earn XP. But she doesn't have MP, SP, or EP, either, which is a good thing, making her invulnerable to all metaphysical attacks."

"I suppose that's a fair trade-off."

"As you say."

CHAPTER FIFTY-SIX

Kylie: *Spire of Desire*

It's 7:22 AM. The encounter started and ended in less than six minutes.

Georgie has more info to dump on me. "With this latest XP gain, pumpkin, you're level 23 Spirit Warrior and level 14 Barbarian. You currently have three unassigned attribute points and two unassigned trait points. While all your existing skills have increased with your level gain, you've also acquired a new Spirit Warrior skill, Spirit Blast. Let me read you the information I have for it."

A cone of blue light blasts from the character's eyes to perform a ranged attack against every opponent in the character's field of vision. The damage dealt to an opponent is 1d6 + X to HP and 1d6 + X to SP, where X is the level of the Spirit Blast. The damage dealt via this skill ignores all armor, traits, and skills that would typically reduce the amount of damage taken. To exercise this skill, the character must utilize First Person POV.

"Your Spirit Blast skill is currently level 1, pumpkin."

"Too bad I didn't have that before the Harpy group encounter."

I ride on Spyder's back, standing, using my wings to keep balance, as the Behemoth follows my Dominated Harpy. The safe path meanders a goodly distance through dunes on the west side of the spire. At 7:53 AM, we reach the spire's base, the sun hanging due west behind us.

There's no visible path here.

The Harpy flies to a slab and then *into* it as though it weren't there. Taking flight, I follow, with Spyder right behind me, Charli still wrapped in webbing slung on the Behemoth's back.

I can't see anything but my support AI.

Georgie juggles some bowling ball pins. "You are no longer in the Dunes of Doom, pumpkin. Welcome to the Spire of Desire."

Shifting to Spirit Form gives me a black and white version of the fifty-feet wide tunnel we've entered. The walls are black with white cracks that allow my depth perception to work. "Can you see, Spyder?"

"Yes. I'm built to see in conditions of light or dark."

A solid white creature to my eyes, the Dominated Harpy is well ahead of us.

"Let's catch up. If the tunnel forks off anywhere, we don't want to go the wrong way." I speed ahead of Spyder, not wanting to lose sight of the Harpy.

Forced at certain junctures to squat while crawling, the Behemoth slowly falls behind. "Georgie, can I alter the task I've given a Dominated foe? I want her to fly a bit slower."

"You'll have to exercise your Dominance trait again and give her a new task."

"I can do that." I overtake the Harpy and fly in front of her. Grabbing her wrists as before, I force her to look at me. When I see the change in her eyes, I let her go. "Show us a path up the spire that's safe for me and my large friend, slowing down when necessary for us to follow you all the way up." One has to be specific with the wording of these tasks.

Spyder catches up, and we continue on.

O-a-ooh echoes in the distance at random intervals. My heart aches to search out the source, but I resist the temptation. Spire of Desire indeed.

"It's 8:00 AM, pumpkin. Have you decided where to assign your trait and attribute points?"

I already fly fast enough, it seems, so I don't see the need to raise my Increased Movement trait. I can hear well enough, too, and with Harpies around, I don't want to hear any better when in the spiritual realm, so I don't want to raise my Heightened Sense of Hearing trait. That leaves one trait to assign the points to. "Put both trait points on Pain Tolerant. That should bring it up to level 4. As for my attribute points, how many would it take to raise my Intuition to the next category?"

"Two."

"Then that's where I want to put two of the three. That puts my Intuition in the high average category, yes?"

"That's correct."

"Great. Do I have any attributes that would be raised a category by the addition of one point?"

"Yes. Empathy could be raised from average to high average. Sensing, Willpower, Understanding, Logic, Faith, and Insight could be raised from high average to extraordinary. Passion and Charisma could be raised from extraordinary to prodigy."

"What's the difference between Intuition and Insight?"

Georgie bobs his head side to side. "They both have to do with reaction time. Intuition is how quickly you can react mentally without relying on Memory or Logic. Insight is how quickly you can react spiritually without questioning your Morals or seeking divine Favor."

Not that I've ever sought divine favor. "Well, then, Georgie, add my last unassigned attribute point to Insight."

At 9:00 AM, we're still climbing the spire interior. Tunnels twist and wind, intersecting with other tunnels. One would get lost in here without a Guide or someone who already knows the way. The sounds of *O-a-ooh* come at shorter intervals but remain distant for the most part. An occasional mournful cry sounds from an unchosen fork in the tunnel, and every time I must tell myself it's nothing I'm to be concerned about.

Another hour passes, and another, and another. I'm not tired from the flying. I'm not bored, with thoughts of Nick and Charli continually bombarding my brain, partly because of the continual Harpy cries but not entirely, I think.

Spyder doesn't complain about the climb. She's built for endless marching.

At 1:12 PM, a white spot grows in the distance. I switch to physical form. There's a light at the end of the tunnel. We've reached the top. The city of Minook awaits.

CHAPTER FIFTY-SEVEN

Megan: Pocket Dimension

Eyes closed, I lie awake in bed, where I must go back to sleep if Mithabel and I are to respawn in Khertaan.

Someone shifts position on the bed next to me.

What the hell? How is anyone else here? There's never been anyone else with me in my respawn chamber. I peek through my eyelashes at the body lying beside me.

Dressed in black velvet slacks and a satiny black top with long sleeves, Debra Jones stares back at me. Her eyes widen.

We both sit upright. Her feet are bare. I'm completely naked. I'm not embarrassed. I stashed everything before I died, so it's completely expected that I'm naked now. The question is… why is Debra here?

"Megan?" "Debra?" Two familiar voices speak over each other, each voicing a different name.

Debra and I twist our necks simultaneously to look at the other pair of people in the room, standing by the north wall, one breathtaking woman dressed in Leather Armor from neck to toe and holding a Cudgel, the other a scantily clad, barefoot woman wearing the same kind of two-piece Bikini I usually wear. The two standing women hold hands.

"Mithabel?" "Dylan?" Debra Jones and I speak over each other, each voicing the name of our respective avatar.

"How…?" We all four try to ask the question at once, and all four of us falter after the first word.

Debra Jones is first to break the ensuing silence. "Damn, girl." She looks Dylan up and down. "You are one hell of a gorgeous woman. I'm downright jealous. I mean, I know you're my avatar and represent me, but I am nowhere near *that* pretty."

Neither Mithabel nor Dylan have found their tongues yet.

Debra and I untwist our necks to look at each other. "How…?" We both try to ask that question again, and we both fail.

I look from Debra to Dylan and back. Except for their outfits, they look identical—the shape of their face, curve of their nose, slant of their forehead, smooth dark skin, shimmering purple braids, deep brown eyes open wide, luscious brown lips, and long legs. "You both look incredible to me, like the epitome of beauty."

Still holding hands, Mithabel and Dylan turn toward each other. After a lingering pause, they face the wall behind them and the framed picture hanging a tad higher than their heads, depicting an empty stone hallway.

It's nothing of interest to me, though their curiosity makes me curious. It's the only picture on the wall.

Aside from the bed, there's no other furniture in the room. There's no crystal ball and no visible doors or closet. But I have a more pressing interest, and finally give voice to the question. *"How are all four of us in this room?"*

The two avatars turn around to face me. Mithabel cocks her head. "The better question is, not *why are you naked, Megan,* but *how are both you and Debra in the same bedroom?*"

"She brings up a good point." Debra Jones glances around the room. "This doesn't look like my bedroom." She turns her attention on Dylan. "Am I in Khertaan? If I'm on Earth, I should only be awake if you died... but if you died, you shouldn't be here, if *here* is Earth. I'm totally confused."

"I didn't die." Dylan points at the picture on the wall with her Cudgel. "I don't think so, anyway. We were looking at a picture on a wall. You two were in the picture, lying on the bed much like you are now. Mithabel and I were in the picture, too, standing right here. In the picture, I was holding a Cudgel. I touched my Cudgel to the Cudgel in the picture. There was a bright light, and then we found ourselves standing here."

"You must have drawn Megan and me here then." Debra nudges me. "I *am* in Khertaan, just like you. Cool."

I nudge her back. "I don't know. I thought I was in my respawn chamber because I died... at least, I thought I died. I was trapped under the Dunes Boss, but before it squashed me, the Behemoths underneath it were squashed to death. They exploded, there was a ton of light and heat, and then I woke up in bed here—just like when I've died in the past.

"I'm naked now because I stashed everything real quick when I saw I was going to die." I point my chin at Mithabel. "I've been trying to communicate with you. Guess you didn't see the Parchment in your inventory."

"There's no table here. No mirror, pocket watch, candle, or wand." Debra swings her feet off the edge of the bed. "There's no crystal ball, either. This isn't like my respawn chamber."

She's right. This isn't like my respawn chamber, either. Where are we?

Mithabel drops Dylan's hand. A Parchment appears in the Elf Tank's grasp. She unrolls it and reads aloud. "'Mithabel, this is Megan. Wish we had a better way to talk. What skills do we have now? How many lives do we have left? XStorm was captured by Behemoths, but might escape. I'm not waiting to find out. Yuni was killed in a pterodactyl attack. Maybe she will respawn in Maron, so look for her. The pterodactyls breathe acid.'"

"Amazing." Dylan leans her head over the Parchment. "That jibes with what Amarynth was saying right before we came here. Yuni showed up in Maron. She's with Quantized, Amarynth, and the rest of our party, going to rescue the rest of XStorm. Mithabel and I were headed into the holding cells, where the Guards intended to scan her. But we were transported into this place before that happened. Not knowingly on purpose, mind you."

Mithabel lowers the Parchment and glances around. "Kaleisha?"

A rock instrumental blasts my ears. A column of air at the foot of the bed shimmers white, brown, and purple. The colors swirl and flow within the column, gradually coalescing into a brown-skinned feminine figure, her body rocking to the beat, her braided hair thrashing on one side of her head. She wears an electric white and purple striped miniskirt. A torus of sparking energy surrounds her chest, covering her nipples. "Yes, chief?"

Dylan's jaw drops. "*That's* your personal support AI?"

"You can see her?" Mithabel voices what I'm thinking.

Debra pushes off the bed and stands. "I can see her, too. Sexy as hell. I'd say you have a type, Mithabel." Debra glances at me. "Which means *you* have a type, *Megan*. I don't know how *I* measure up."

"Oh, you measure up, love." I roll to her side of the bed and swing my feet over the side. "These Khertaan ladies have nothing on you."

Mithabel holds up a hand. "Okay, hold on, everyone, please. Kaleisha, where the hell are we?"

The Jamaican AI slows her dance. "Statistically speaking, taking no experiential data into account, there's a 95% chance we're in a pocket dimension. There's a 4.95% chance we're in Khertaan, and a 0.05% chance we're on Earth. And to answer one of the questions asked earlier, you have three lives remaining, chief, which means Megan *didn't* die just before coming here. Taking that information into account, and the fact that Debra is here, reduces the chance of us being in Khertaan, but doesn't raise the chance we're on Earth. So it's closer to a 99% chance that we're in a pocket dimension."

"Hold on." Dylan raises a hand. "Magnum, can you show yourself, please?"

Soft classical music replaces the rock tune. An image like a piece of old film flickers in the air to Dylan's right. The flickering increases in speed until the image stabilizes. In the spot stands a pale-cheeked English butler from a century or two ago, dressed in black and white, wearing a black bow tie and short black hair. He bows to Dylan. "Madam, how may I be of service?"

I laugh. "That's *your* support AI?"

Mithabel covers her mouth with a hand.

Dylan glares at me. "Don't you diss my AI." She turns her attention to the summoned butler. "Yes, Magnum, tell us where we are, please."

The AI bows again. "My calculations support those already expressed by the irrepressible Kaleisha, Madam. I would recommend operating on the premise that we currently occupy a pocket dimension."

Dylan nods. "And what does that really mean, Magnum?"

"Well, given that you arrived here by way of a mirror image photo, and given that the corresponding photo in this room does not display your image, it is unlikely that you can return the way you came by reversing the process, there being no Cudgel in the photo for you to touch with yours.

"Indeed, it is likely you are trapped in this pocket, and that such was the hope of they whom hung the picture in the hallway. The City Guards may have been informed about the nature of the picture but instructed not to pass that information to you." Magnum nods at me. "If you, Megan Wright, had actually died, you would not be here now, and neither would Mithabel, as she would have died with you. Only Dylan and Debra would be trapped here now. It was a considerable coincidence that you were magically summoned to this pocket dimension in the instant before you would have died during the Boss fight. Can you access your inventory? If so, that indicates you aren't on Earth."

"Oh...." I try to access the inventory I share with Mithabel, and a display of its contents manifests in my view. Everything is there that I expect to be there. I equip my Bikini, high-heeled Platform Slippers, one Ezmerelda Ring, the Bracelet of Action, and the Faerie Wing in its Holster on my back.

"What the hell?" Dylan voices her confusion the loudest. Everyone stares at my Severed Faerie Wing.

"What can I say?" I shrug. "I got a bunch of stuff duplicated a couple times when I found myself in my respawn chamber. This Faerie Wing, the Ezmerelda Ring, the Ogaltha Ring, the Bikini and Slippers, some Rope, a Bow, and a Battle Axe. I'm not sure what the criteria was for things to be duplicated. For instance, Ghost Maker, the magical Axe I procured from Ye Olde

Shoppe of the Profane never duplicated." I equip and brandish the weapon for the others to see. "Neither did this Bracelet I'm wearing." I hold up my arm to show them the Bracelet of Action.

Dylan's brow furrows. "You have an Ogaltha Ring?"

I nod. "Yeah. Mithabel could have told you, if she'd been looking in our inventory. It's been there for a long time."

"Did you wear it?"

"Oh, hell no."

"Don't."

"I wasn't planning to."

Magnum clears his throat. "Madam, I have a message for you, if this is a good time."

The Priestess turns to him and nods. "Let's have it."

He bows. "I am pleased to congratulate you, Madam, on receiving nearly seven million XP, due, I surmise, to Megan Wright's participation in the Boss encounter that nearly killed her. I'm sorry to say that since the update, it appears you have not been granted any bonus XP for your First Kill and other bonus awards you earned before the update. I can submit a complaint on your behalf if you wish. With the XP total currently granted you, you are level 22 Priestess and level 13 Shuriken Specialist."

"Please file a complaint, Magnum. We went through a lot to earn those bonuses, and they ought to still apply."

"Complaint filed."

Kaleisha snaps her fingers. The background music changes from classical to hip hop. "Mithabel, you also gained the XP, and congratulations, you're level 20 Tank, level 11 Anjai. You have an unassigned trait point and an unassigned attribute point. And since Megan asked, here are your current traits and skills." She lists them off.

Elf Kindred Trait:
Dark Sight

Character Traits:
Danger Sense, level 1
Alertness, level 1
Natural Armor, level 3

Level 20 Tank Class Skills:
Armor, level 32
Melee Damage, level 30
Parry, level 27
Block, level 24
Feint, level 20
Stun, level 16

Level 11 Anjai Subclass Skills:
Detect Anomaly, level 14
Compress Body, level 12
Flight Speed, level 10
Hide, level 9
Shapeshift Siamese Cat, level 7
Water Control, level 5

I laugh at those last two. "Shapeshifting to a Siamese Cat? Water Control? I had no idea about those skills. Have you used either of them yet, Mithabel?"

The black-haired Elf Tank shakes her head. "I've not had a reason, and no time to experiment with them."

Debra clears her throat. "Is no one concerned that we're likely trapped forever in a pocket dimension?"

If it were anyone but Debra, I'd be tempted to laugh off the remark. After all, if we are trapped, what can we do about it? The definition of being trapped is that you can't get out of the situation you're in. "I prefer to not think of us as being trapped, but merely not understanding how to leave. If we got in, we should be able to get out."

"Well, look who's the optimist." Dylan huffs in defense of her Earthling counterpart. "My Optimism and Hope are both high average, yet I don't know that I feel as hopeful and optimistic as all that right now. How is it you feel more hopeful and optimistic than Debra and I, Megan? I thought your scores were lower than ours."

I grimace. "Firstly, being an Earthling, I'm not constrained by attribute scores. Secondly, maybe my attitude is all about Temperance—the moderation of action or feeling. I'm just not one to panic or overreact. Temperance is my highest attribute second only to Sanity. So forgive me if I'm not freaking out, given everything that has happened and continues to happen.

"I fought an Orc Wizard on Earth and killed it with my shoe, after it put a knife in my leg. I watched as Arachnid Behemoths skewered paramedics as they fled the ambulance carrying me to the hospital. I rode a Motorcycle with a black dude named Kevin across the desert, chased by Mad Cow Ballista. *And it all happened on Earth.*

"Those invaders are still *on Earth*, killing my fellow humans every minute we spend in Khertaan training to fight them. For all I know, everyone on Earth that hasn't been pulled into Khertaan is dead already, including my Mom. Maybe we're training for nothing. So, should I be freaking out now, possibly trapped forever in some pocket thing I won't even begin to claim I understand? Bloody hell, yes, I should be freaking out.

"But I'm with my best friend—the most gorgeous woman in existence—and our two Khertaan avatars, along with their support AIs—a sassy dancer and a spiffy butler. And if anyone can figure a way out of this place, it's us.

"It doesn't hurt to review our capabilities before trying to bust out. Just my opinion. I mean, I've been operating lately with a less than full understanding of my abilities, with no one I could ask about shit.

"And come to think of it, what about you, Debra? Now that you're most likely in either a pocket dimension or Khertaan, are you able to exercise Dylan's skills and traits? Are you and Dylan like me and Mithabel, or do you represent a completely different aspect of existence?"

Debra raises an eyebrow. "I...."

"That's a good question." Dylan steps close to Debra and lays a hand on her shoulder. Dylan inclines her head to her AI. "Magnum, please read off my list of skills and traits."

"Certainly, Madam." He reads them aloud.

Polynesian Kindred Trait:
Exoticness

Character Traits:
Beauty, level 4
Time Sense, level 1
Unencumbered, level 1

Level 22 Priestess of Light Class Skills:
Light, level 36
Attraction, level 34
Healing, level 31

Morale, level 28
Turn, level 24
Presence, level 20
Blinding, level 2

Level 13 Shuriken Specialist Subclass Skills:
Shuriken Aim, level 31
Shuriken Damage, level 29
Deflect Shuriken, level 13
Shuriken Quick Shot, level 11
Shuriken Fast Load, level 9
Critical Hit - Shuriken, level 7

Level 22 Priestess of Light Spells:
Heal 1
Light 1
Exorcise 1
Advanced Healing 1

I shrug at Debra. "I think you're already drawing on Dylan's traits of Beauty and Exoticness, as well as her skills of Attraction and Presence, but I might be biased. Maybe you could try to create some Light."

Dylan holds out a hand. "Or try to conjure and throw a Shuriken." A throwing star appears between her forefinger and thumb. She tosses it across the room, away from the bed. It bounces off the far wall and separates into its constituent pixels, which fade from sight.

"All right, sure." Debra holds up her hand like Dylan did. A Shuriken manifests. She laughs, rears back her arm, and throws the weapon with force. It smoothly sails through the air, bouncing off the far wall in about the same spot Dylan's missile had and then disappears. "Oh, my Goddess. I've never felt so competent in my life." Her eyes twinkle with an energy I've seldom seen in them.

In the past on Earth, Debra so often came across as depressed, struggling to emotionally survive each day. She lost her faith in humanity long ago. But at her core she's forever the optimist, hopeful for better days. And though she's so often down, she always pushes through, no matter what obstacles are thrown in her way, doing what she must to make it to the next day.

That's always been her real beauty, that inner strength I've always so admired. Just when I'd think she'd given up on me or the world, she'd show me I was wrong, show me how strong she really was. That's how we got involved in the Khertaan competition, after all.

Following the ordeal with Christopher Warden harassing her in the office and then her being officially reprimanded for standing up for herself, what with her quitting her job and then not talking to me for days, I'd worried she would spiral down into such a deep depression, she'd remain there forever. But she didn't. She called me up and asked me to enter the competition with her. At the time, it was something to do together, a contest of skills with millions of dollars on the line. We dreamed of winning the prize money, buying a house, living together and starting a 3D animation company. That was all Debra. I just went along so I could be with her.

So here we are, stuck in some dimensional pocket, training to fight alien invaders that I've already encountered on Earth. I even defeated one—but only temporarily. We're training to deal permanent death to our enemies—I think. But time for our loved ones on Earth is running out. We have to get out of here asap. If

Debra's strong will was ever needed, it's now. It's good to see the light flaring in her eyes.

I shake a fist. "Okay, well then, we all know what we're capable of. The way I see it, we have two things to do. First, figure out if there's a reason we're here other than being trapped. Second, figure out how to leave."

Debra cocks an eyebrow at me. "Avatars and AIs, you heard the woman. Let's turn this place inside out and see what we find."

CHAPTER FIFTY-EIGHT

Mithabel: Despair

Debra Jones helped Mithabel slide the mattress off the bed, revealing a cloth-covered frame. Mithabel equipped her wavy Sword, the Flamberge called Ullullu's Hair, and sliced the cloth covering down the middle of the frame lengthwise. She pulled back one side of the covering. Coiled metal springs lay inside. If they were a clue about anything, their significance was wasted on the black-haired Tank.

Debra nodded at the Flamberge. "Does Megan have one of those, too?"

The blond player, peering under the bed frame, raised her head. "I do not. But I could use hers if she were to put it in inventory. If one of us finds something, we can give it to the other, no matter how close or far we are from each other. You should check to see if you can access Dylan's inventory."

"How do I do that?"

Magnum inclined his head. "Let me see if it is possible, Madam." He paused. "Do you see it now?"

"I do." Debra's grin transformed into a grimace. "So much stuff, and it's all unorganized, like someone just threw everything into a bin. Oh, I see, if you focus on an individual type of item, a label pops up for it with the name of the item and the quantity.

"So what all do we have here?" She rattled off a list of standard dungeon-delving equipment, like Rope, Torches, Tinderboxes, Jugs of Water, and the like, listing a couple dozen different types of items. "I don't think I missed anything. How do you remember what all you have, Dylan?"

"I *don't*, honestly." The Polynesian Priestess pulled back the corner of her mouth on one side. "I seldom think about what I'm carrying. Out of all that we bought in those delver's pack specials when we first came to Maron, we've used some Rope, a Tinderbox, and a Torch. Mithabel and Amarynth each have one coil of Rope. Amarynth took a Tinderbox and two Torches, and she's used one of the Torches. I should have given her a replacement Torch, but I wasn't too happy about how she used the one. If you want to put any of these items in your inventory, Mithabel and Megan, just say the word."

"I could have used some Parchment, Quill, and Ink." Megan stood. "I'm not detecting any anomalies under the bed. If there's anything under there, like a secret trapdoor in the floor, we'll need to move the bed to find it."

Mithabel sliced open the mattress. "Kaleisha, which of my attributes can I bump into the next higher category with one point?"

The Jamaican AI twirled to a soulful background song as she sang out the names of several attributes, lastly mentioning Mithabel's Constitution of 3.

Before Mithabel could assign the free point to Constitution, Megan Wright stopped her. "Since we lose 2 points of Con when we die, I suggest leaving it at 3." The blond player circumnavigated the room, scanning the walls in search for anomalies. "Back in Maron, I overheard the Guards talking about how they were effectively immortal, able to continually respawn no matter how often they died. Their Constitution scores were set negative during the update. The System apparently only terminates you if your Con hits zero exactly. If it's negative and never gets raised, it will never hit zero."

The Tank tossed more stuffing on the floor. "I'm finding nothing of use in this mattress. Okay, Megan, I'll go with your instinct and leave my terribly low Constitution score as-is. If I'm taking such a risk, a bump in Temperance might be in order to help me not freak out about it. Assign the point to Temperance, Kaleisha."

Electronic dance music abruptly shook the walls. "You got it, chief. Temperance boosted to 14, placing it in the extraordinary category." The Jamaican dancer thrust her arms back and forth as she shook her hips side to side.

The two players and two avatars continued searching the room and its contents while the two AIs watched, Kaleisha dancing and Magnum standing at attention. By 7:20 AM on the System clock, the mattress and bed frame had been completely demolished.

"I've scanned the walls, ceiling, and floor thrice over for anomalies." Megan hovered in the air. "If there's any kind of secret door in this room, it's beyond my capabilities to find."

"There's nothing useful in the mattress." Mithabel kicked at the pile of stuffing. "I've hacked the bed frame to bits, and got nothing from it but wood chips."

"Then come on." Dylan stood below the framed photo. "There's nothing here to inform us why we're here, so let's waste no more time looking. Everyone take hands. I'll touch my Cudgel to the picture, and with any luck we'll be transported out just like we were transported in." She held her Cudgel aloft in her right hand and reached to Mithabel with her left.

They all clasped hands, with Kaleisha completing the circle by laying a hand on Dylan's waist.

The Polynesian Priestess touched her Cudgel to the picture.

Nothing happened.

No one spoke. Dylan tried again, with the same result.

They were going nowhere. Everyone dropped hands.

Kaleisha spoke first. "Congratulations, Mithabel. You have just received twenty-one million, four-hundred-thousand XP. You are now level 22 Tank, level 13 Anjai. You've picked up a new Tank skill, level 2 Reflect Any Attack."

Megan laughed. "Reflect *Any* Attack? Oh, my Goddess. Even the death attack of an Arachnid Behemoth? So, like, does the attack not hurt me if I reflect it?"

"That is correct." Kaleisha shook her hips to a continuing EDM track. "I actually have a skill description for you." She read off several paragraphs of details. Basically, the skill could be used once each combat heartbeat to Reflect any melee or ranged attack of any domain type—physical, mental, spiritual, or emotional—provided one used a weapon or shield associated with the domain of the attack to be Reflected. The skill could be used against combo attacks, and there were several rules pertaining to that. The Reflect Any Attack action didn't automatically succeed… a variety of factors were involved in determining success, including the level of the skill. Lastly, the skill could be of use against attacks from traps and other non-sentient sources.

"To reflect the death attack of an Arachnid Behemoth, chief, you'd need a physical weapon or shield, since their death attack is a physical one, as opposed to mental, spiritual, or emotional.

Against a Mind Spear—a mental attack—you'd use a Psi-Sword or Psi-Shield to reflect it. You get the drift."

Debra Jones raised her hands as though surrendering to someone. "That is an incredibly useful combat skill, Megan and Mithabel. I'm impressed."

"Yeah, well it sucks that we're stuck in here and can't use it." Mithabel summoned her wavy Sword, Ullullu's Hair, from inventory and struck the wooden wall. The blade bounced off with a dull thud, doing no damage to its target. "Are you shitting me? This situation is trying even my extraordinary Temperance."

"Amarynth," Dylan called over party chat, her voice trembling, "can you hear me? Rolag? Zyekt? Niav? Charli?"

There were no replies.

"I didn't want to be rude and interrupt anyone." Magnum faced Dylan. "Madam, congratulations, you have also gained twenty-one million, four-hundred-thousand XP. You are level 23 Priestess of Light, level 14 Shuriken Specialist. You have gained a new Priestess skill, Followers, at level 1. I have information for you concerning the Followers skill, and shall read it for you."

Magnum had even more to read than Kaleisha had read for Mithabel. Basically, Dylan could recruit willing NPC Followers, up to a maximum depending on the Followers skill level. Followers would gain Dylan's character traits and automatically receive her Morale bonus, no matter where they were. She could grant her Followers other skills or transfer Auni to them for casting spells.

"Holy sweet mother," whispered Mithabel. "That's one powerful skill, Dylan. What's the most number of followers you could have if you were level 30, I wonder?" She drew a deep breath, focusing on her Temperance filter, and stashed her

Flamberge. "Where are we getting all these XP from? Is it Charli? Maybe at some point we'll get out of here and put all these powerful skills to use. I just wish I had higher Hope and Optimism."

Kaleisha stopped dancing. "Mithabel, please calm down. Your EP has fallen to 96%. You're affecting yourself emotionally, and thus Megan too. If you both start stressing, it could have a feedback effect that drains your EP to zero in a matter of minutes, and that would not be good. If your EP drops to zero, you could become suicidal—and since you can't kill yourself, you'd be attempting it forever."

"Oh, Mithabel, love." Dylan raised her hands overhead. "May the blessing of the Goddess be upon us all." She lowered her hands and placed one on Mithabel's shoulder. "I don't know if my Morale skill can help us in this situation, but it can't hurt." She stroked Mithabel's cheek. "May the Goddess take away your emotional distress."

The Elf Tank briefly closed her eyes while the healing energy flowed through her. "Thank you, Priestess. It does help."

Debra took hands with Megan and Magnum. "Let's try the Cudgel-on-picture thing again, Dylan. You've gone up a level. Maybe it will make a difference. If there's some sort of difficulty level at play, maybe the Morale bonus will help. Concentrate on some of your other skills, too, like Presence or Attraction, when you touch the Cudgel to the picture. You said there was a bright light when you came through initially. Maybe you could fill the room with light before you touch the picture. Let's try lots of things."

Everyone took hands again as before. Dylan raised her Cudgel. "Goddess, shine your light upon us." The room filled with brilliant light. Dylan touched her Cudgel to the picture.

Nothing changed. They were still in the bedroom, holding hands in a circle.

The Polynesian Priestess stashed her Cudgel but didn't break the circle. "Come closer to the wall." She tugged on Mithabel, and the Tank obeyed. Standing on her tiptoes to reach high enough, Dylan put her hand on the photo. Still nothing happened.

They couldn't give in to despair. Every idea anyone had was attempted, including hacking or beating at the wall with every weapon they had, which jarred like striking stone but produced the thud of hitting wood. Every so often, Dylan used her Advanced Healing spell to heal the emotional and spiritual damage inflicted by a situation looking more and more bleak by the hour.

Mithabel refused to think she and her friends might be trapped in this place for eternity. But something Megan had said earlier continued to drag Mithabel's spirits down... while driving her to keep trying. Even when they eventually found a way out of this place, it might not be in time to save Earth from its inter-dimensional invaders.

CHAPTER FIFTY-NINE

Nick: Meeting Our Characters

The kitchen table rocks.

"What the hell?" Ingrid rushes to the front door of her house and flings it open.

Charli, Ulric, and I jump up and join Ingrid. A plume of smoke rises over the road to the west.

From the woods on either side of the road emerges four figures, one masculine and three feminine. The male appears to be human. One of the females looks fairly human, but she's got pointy ears. The other two females are distinctly not human. One of them is only five feet tall, with green skin. The other is about five feet six inches, and the top three quarters of her body is human, but her calves and ankles are furry, and her feet aren't feet, but hooves. The four of them spot us watching from the door and come running towards us.

The short, green-skinned girl reaches us first. "Hail, citizens. Do not be afraid. I am Greelia the Goblin Warrior. These are my friends. We have just vanquished a monster from another dimension. More may come, so be prepared. If you have any weapons or magic, get them ready."

"Is this part of your game, Ulric?" asks Ingrid. "If you're shooting more fireworks that loud, take them far away from the house, please. And I don't want all these people coming in." She goes back inside.

The unidentified newcomers fall in behind Greelia. She motions at the male. "This is Ronnie the Rogue." She points to the hoofed female. "This is Fauna." Then she indicates the last member of her party, the woman with pointy ears. "This is Emma the Elf. May we inquire as to your names, citizens?"

"I'm Charli the Cowgirl Guide and Shadow Wizard." Charli offers a hand to Greelia. "Glad to meet you." The two of them shake. When they stop shaking, Charli doesn't let go of Greelia's hand.

"My name is Nick the Developer." I take hands with Fauna and Emma. Following Charli's lead, I don't release my grip on either of them.

"Um." Ulric approaches Ronnie. "You look just like I imagine him. I'm Ulric the Student." They shake hands.

"Time-shift us, ODYSSEY. It's got to be now. Take us all."

Electricity fires from deep inside me, erupting from my Tattoo and bathing all seven of us. Then white lightning plays in front of my eyeballs, and I can see nothing else.

CHAPTER SIXTY

Nick: Floundering in the Timestream

I lie on a cold tile floor, my head throbbing. Darkness presses down on me. A spot of light grows into a ball. Eighteen-year-old Charli stands at the center of the light, her hair straight and blond under her cowboy Hat—no pigtails. She holds a Wizard's Staff. Her form wavers, as though she's a hologram having trouble stabilizing. She smiles at me over a bare shoulder but says nothing. A wall of drifting white text stands behind her, vertical lines of letters, numbers, and other symbols streaming from the ceiling to the floor.

Over to my right, Ulric sits up, squinting at the light. He looks around and his gaze falls on me. "What happened? Where are we? Where is everyone?"

Four humanoid shapes warp the lines of streaming text, like people on the other side of a sheet of rubber trying to push their way through. Charli flickers like a light bulb nearing the end of its life. She doesn't lose her smile, and she still isn't talking.

Lightning zaps my brain, and I convulse from the timeline tweak.

"Nick?" Ulric kneels beside me. Behind him stands a ghost. I dare not look at his face, but I know it's Mel, my transgender son from my original timeline, born to me and Jean. The ghost kneels near Ulric, back far enough Ulric can't see him. Ulric reaches for me, and Mel does the same, his ghostly form overlapping Ulric's. Tabbie's son's form wavers like Charli's did. Damn, I'm losing him. Am I'm supposed to? I never knew him in the Fanciful Pegasus timeline, the one in which I need to be if Morrow is to respawn. If Ulric never existed in that timeline, can his awareness manifest a physical body to inhabit, like Charli did?

Another timeline tweak rocks me. I roll onto my back, my legs pulling up involuntarily towards my chest. My eyes clamp shut from the pain.

"Nick?" The voice is Renee's.

"Nick?" I know the voice—my lady ghost. I've not seen her since before Morrow entered Khertaan. I must not look at her.

"Dad?" is that Mel... or Susie...?

"Nick?" Oh, God, who's that? *Macy?* A girlfriend from my youth, Macy never spoke to me again after her father misled her about me. She died in my original timeline. How can she possibly be here?

"Nick?" Of course, Yvette would be here, too. I can still feel her kisses on my lips. I ruined her life.

I'm haunted by all my pasts.

My name continues to echo, spoken by so many others.... My siblings—Raymond, Gerard, Laura, Sammy, and Dolly. Momma and Daddy call me, as do my cousins Sadie, Harley, Carmen, Ellen, and Randall. Who else? My dear Aunt Jennifer, more of a big sister to me than an aunt. An unnamed female raccoon I'd had as a pet when I was four, chattering what no one but me can understand. Cara Johnson, my very first *official* girlfriend whom

I embarrassed with that awful poem in our sixth grade music class. Faith, the high school crush who became one of my favorite friends on social media late in life.

Even Uma joins the chorus, the church girl whose beauty I'd told Momma was perfection, with whom I had one lousy date, and never another chance because of some tragedy that befell her—about which I'd blamed her father without proof. My name on her breath chills me, wringing tears from my eyes. I want to speak her name in response, but my throat is too parched.

I don't want to lose any of them. Not again.

"Nick," says Charli. "Remember. Where am I?"

Her awareness is in my head... but her body is in Khertaan. Is that right?

Charli existed in the timeline we just left, where we met Ronnie, Fauna, Greelia, and Emma. How did she exist there?

I'd given her a physical form.

"Please, Nick, don't let me die," says Charli. But she's not Charli. She's my lady ghost.

My lady ghost is Charli. My lady ghost is Erica. Charli is Erica.

It's not possible. I reject the notion. Yet it must be true.

Why must it be true?

"Damn you, Nick," says Jean. She's close by.

I open my eyes. I'm on the floor kneeling beside Erica's dead body. Jean stands across the way, Axe in hand, having just torn it free from the table top. Behind her stands a hooded figure, circled by a chorus of dancing women in green nurses' uniforms.

I've never before thought about the color of Erica's hair. It's blue. She lies dead next to me. I don't want her hair to be blue. It needs to be blond, like eighteen-year-old Charli's. And she needs to be alive, not dead.

Jean flings her Axe at me. It hurtles at me in slow motion.

I know how this ends. And like before, I can't do a damn thing about it. No one in my life can do a damn thing about it.

But someone else is here. Someone who was never in my life. *Ronnie.* He steps out of the sheet of falling text to stand between me and the hurtling Axe, moving as someone with all the time in the world, slowing everything around him.

Nonchalantly reaching out, he grabs the handle of the flying Axe. "That wasn't nice." He's the King of Understatement. With the Axe swinging at his side, he faces the insanely jealous Jean. She flees.

Erica's hair fades to blond. She sits up, her face that of eighteen-year-old Charli. "Nicky Nick? Oh, God. You saved me." She crawls to me on her elbows, dragging her feet behind her. No trail of blood follows her. Is she hurt? Her hand strokes my cheek. "Remember me, Nicky Nick. Please, remember."

She stands and flickers like a light bulb nearing the end of its life.

The nurses stop dancing. The hooded figure steps out of their circle. I know his name—Seth. Ignoring everyone else, he looms over my kneeling frame. "Your Sanity is teetering on the brink, Nick." His voice is honeyed and haughty. "None of this is real. It's all delusion. You're still in Spring Green Mental Health Facility."

The phone rings. It's the old style rotary type. It rests on an end table that wasn't there a moment ago. Seth picks up the receiver and hands it to me.

I take it. "Hello?"

"Nick," says Amelia, the Department of Defense co-worker I'd had a crush on. I'd acted on that crush in one short-lived but glorious timeline. "Where are you? Everyone is looking for you. No one knows where you are."

Seth takes the receiver from me and hangs it up. "Where are you, indeed, Nick? No one knows. Not even you." He runs an elongated fingernail along my cheek. "There's just one thing I need from you, and then I'll leave you to your delusions."

I don't need to ask. He wants ODYSSEY.

But if he wants ODYSSEY, then he's as good as admitting that I'm not delusional. ODYSSEY is real and time-shifts are real and whatever is happening to me now is real. Seth's own words have revealed his duplicity. But how do I escape him?

My nanobot collective has no energy left. It was all used to get us to the correct timeline and then attempt a couple tweaks. Seth interfered and threw off all the calculations. Now I'm awash in the timestream, not settled into any timeline, but intersecting dozens of them. I'm lost, and I may have taken everyone I love with me.

"Remember me, Nick," says Charli, that is, Erica, that is, my lady ghost.

"You must be hungry." Ronnie offers Seth a Mushroom.

"I'll take that Axe instead." Seth reaches for the weapon.

"Sure." Ronnie hands it to him. "I wasn't using it anyway."

CHAPTER SIXTY-ONE

Susie: On Screen Encounter

Displayed on-screen, a searing beam of green light shoots down at the planet. The planet loses its distinctive colors—the verdant green of its plant life, the blue of its oceans, the brown of its earthy mountains. Everything turns a bubbling dark green. The beam stops firing, and the green mass swells. A green pseudopod reaches for us. Planet Buster trembles as it draws in the pseudopod, converting it to the energy needed to operate the ship.

Pulling his hood up over his head, casting his face once more in shadow, Seth turns towards me. "Still no tears? Where is your humanity?"

I shake my head. I'm numb inside. I can't think straight. "That planet meant nothing to me. Why should I cry for it?" But inside, I'm crying buckets.

The hooded monster turns to Timmy. "You have no tears, either, Mr. Landers? What is wrong with you two? I was certain such a display of destruction would render you both into blubbering babies. It is not enough that I destroy. I want someone to *feel* it when I do. I want *emotion*. I want horrified expressions, terrified eyes. I don't need your worship, but I need your *belief* that I am *the* most destructive force in the multiverse. What must I do to make you *believe* in my power?"

So that's Seth's game. He said it before, that he was on his way to becoming a God. Both Gods and Godlings have unbelievable power. But a God needs believers. Seth's minions mindlessly obey him, fulfilling his every whim but uncaring about what he does. They obey because they have no choice. A true believer makes the choice to believe. True believers are what Seth needs, and what neither Timmy nor I have given him, despite his best efforts.

"Very well." Seth faces the screen and taps his Staff on the floor three times.

Alien symbols flow from the bottom to the top of the screen like the credits at the end of a foreign film. Against the backdrop of alien text stands a cast of murmuring characters surrounding a bent figure.

Dad.

Seth rises from his seat and strides towards the screen, placing his hand against it when he reaches it. "Your Sanity is teetering on the brink, Nick." His voice is honeyed and haughty. "None of this is real. It's all delusion. You're still in Spring Green Mental Health Facility."

A phone rings, an old style rotary type, resting on an end table. As though he's part of the picture, Seth reaches into the screen and picks up the receiver. He hands it to Dad.

Dad takes the receiver. "Hello?"

I can't hear the other side of the conversation, but Dad says nothing else.

Seth takes the receiver from Dad and hangs it up. "Where are you, indeed, Nick? No one knows. Not even you." He runs an elongated fingernail along Dad's cheek. "There's just one thing I need from you, and then I'll leave you to your delusions."

The realization of what Seth wants from my Dad chills my spine and makes me queasy. Seth wants ODYSSEY. He doesn't realize that Dad isn't the only person with the ODYSSEY nanobots. He doesn't realize that *I* have them too. Why does Seth want ODYSSEY? Of course. He wants them so he can integrate them into his Planet Buster, so he can take his spaceship to *any* timeline he wants—especially the Fanciful Pegasus timeline. He'd love to use his Planet Buster on Earth in that timeline. Seth himself can interact with other timelines, but he can't time-shift his spaceship. Whatever tech he's using now to interact with Dad won't scale up enough to transport the ship. But ODYSSEY could do it. The ODYSSEY nanobots can replicate, eventually scaling up to whatever amount is needed. It might take time, but the more energy the nanobots have, the faster they can grow.

Seth is collecting the energy of planets. Feeding energy of that magnitude to the ODYSSEY nanobots could quite possibly time-shift a huge spaceship.

A figure wavers next to Dad… a young woman with blue hair… someone who looks familiar but I don't recognize. Wait… she's blond, and she's recognizable after all.

She's Charli, with a sadder expression than I've ever seen on her. Her form flickers like a light bulb nearing the end of its life. "Remember me, Nick."

Another of the cast of characters gains focus, a scantily clothed teenage boy holding an Axe in one hand. In the other hand, he holds a Mushroom, which he holds out to Seth, as though he can see into our ship. "You must be hungry."

Seth shakes his hooded head. "I'll take that Axe instead." He reaches into the screen.

"Sure." The teenager places the weapon in Seth's hand. "I wasn't using it anyway."

Seth pulls his hand out of the screen. He's holding the Axe. He raises it over his head, aiming at Dad's neck.

"*No*," I scream.

The hooded monster swings. The Axe penetrates the screen but remains visible, the descending blade becoming part of the scene.

Before the blade strikes Dad, the teenager catches the shaft of the weapon in one hand. "That's not nice."

"How...?" Seth trembles. "You're but a figment of his imagination. You aren't real."

"I'm real enough to do this." The teenager wrenches the Axe from Seth's grip and draws the weapon into the screen.

Seth takes a faltering step back, summoning his Staff to hand to catch his balance. "It doesn't matter. I'm coming for you, Nick. I'll find a way. Once I destroy the Fanciful Pegasus timelines, no one can stand against me." He taps his Staff on the floor, and the screen goes blank.

Putting the screen behind him, he approaches and stops directly in front of me. "Thank you for your belief in me, Susie McKenzie. I appreciated your scream, and hope to make you scream harder than that many more times before it's over." He takes his seat and taps his Staff on the floor twice.

Stars streak across the screen like comets, their tails blurred. When the ship comes to rest, another planet fills the screen. "This world is called Destin," Seth says in a monotone voice. "It has a sentient population of seventeen billion, including humanoids and non-humanoids. There are three-hundred-fifty-seven unique sentient species." He taps his Staff on the floor. "Destroy it."

The beam of green light transforms the world from matter to energy, which is gathered into Planet Buster. To Seth, it is little different than watching a movie.

I keep my tears locked away and don't cry out. My heart breaks, but I won't give Seth what he wants.

Seth systematically destroys world after world of sentient beings, collecting more and more energy into his spaceship. I had no idea there were so many worlds in the universe with sentient populations.

I'm numb inside. The only thing that keeps me from breaking is the knowledge that the Planet Buster is confined to this universe. Seth can't transport his spaceship across timelines, and it seems he doesn't have a Planet Buster in every timeline. How much of the multiverse is safe from his Doomsday Machine?

If Seth gets his hands on ODYSSEY and can control the nanobots, Planet Buster will have the means to destroy every sentient population in every timeline in the multiverse, starting with what he referred to as the Fanciful Pegasus timelines — plural. I know of one such timeline — the one I'm originally from, and where I thought I'd wake up after Slithy died.

I can't let Seth know I have the ODYSSEY nanobots in my brain.

CHAPTER SIXTY-TWO

Kylie: Collapsed Tunnel

With a heart-rending screech, my Dominated Harpy speeds ahead, disappearing into the light. Her task is done. She's led us all the way up.

The upward-slanting tunnel widens into a domed cavern a hundred feet across and just as high. The far side of the cavern opens to a city rising behind it, scores of marble steeples and red stone towers looming over endless rows of one-story buildings. A street leads directly from the cavern through the heart of the city.

From my viewpoint standing at the back of the cavern, there's a complete absence of pedestrians, vehicles, and mounts on the street. "Let's go see what Minook is all about, Spyder."

"Careful, pumpkin." Georgie flies in front of me and holds up a hand. "You can't leave the Spire of Desire territory to enter Minook until you defeat the Spire's Boss. Since we haven't seen a Boss in the spire yet, be prepared for an attack here."

"Thanks for the warning, Georgie. Spyder, stay alert as we cross this cavern. A Boss monster may attack us before we reach the other side." Standing on Spyder's back, I equip my Spirit

Blade and Spirit Shield. *"Come on out*, Boss monster, and let's get this over with."

Spyder strides across the cavern towards the exit.

We finish crossing the cavern without an encounter.

"Go ahead, Spyder." I point towards the empty city. "The Boss doesn't want to fight us."

Clink. Spyder's metallic limb strikes an invisible wall. She can't leave the cavern.

Flying forward, I reach out with my Spirit Blade. It touches the same unseen obstacle. I switch to Spirit Form. A force field meant to block physical egress shouldn't stop my insubstantial body.

The interior walls of the cavern turn black marbled with white. A vertical, outwardly curved, pure white wall blocks the exit. The tip of my Spirit Blade rests against the whiteness, unable to penetrate it. I touch the white wall with my metaphysical fingers, and a chill runs through me as I meet resistance. Damn. Even in the spiritual realm, I can't pass. Not only is there a physical force field in place here, but a spiritual force field as well. This is a new one on me.

"What is my Spirit Form skill level, Georgie?"

"It's level 22. You have 21 switches remaining until 8:00 AM tomorrow morning."

"Spyder, wait here. Tell me immediately if anything changes or anyone shows up. I'm going to explore our surroundings in Spirit Form." I dive into the floor.

Blackness with pockets and veins of white engulfs me. I'm looking through a block of dark glass riddled with imperfections.

The metaphysical white wall extends below floor level, still blocking my egress from the cavern. With my metaphysical fingers gliding across the surface of the icy white wall, I follow it down. It curves beneath me. I follow it down, over, and then back up, returning to floor level at the back of the cavern. Following the curve upward into the ceiling, I find that it eventually curves back down, returning me to the front of the cavern, next to Spyder.

Great.

Still in Spirit Form, I turn my attention to the tunnel we followed to reach this place. Twenty feet into the tunnel, the metaphysical white wall blocks my way. No physical force field had blocked our way into the cavern. If I switched back to my physical form, I suspect I could use the tunnel as normal. But I'm not ready to switch back just yet.

The white wall isn't a wall, per se, but a large sphere from which my Spirit Form can't escape. If I want to leave this cavern, one of two things must happen. One, I can switch back to physical form and leave the way I came in. Two, I'd need to destroy or breach the white sphere. The first option is the better bet, but takes us away from the city rather than into it.

I make a few more forays into the floor and ceiling to verify my theory. My Spirit Form is indeed trapped in a huge white hollow sphere of metaphysical ice.

I fly to Spyder. "There's no way out of this cavern for me in Spirit Form. A large spirit globe encloses the entire cavern and blocks the tunnel out as well. We can't physically pass from here to the city. It seems our only way out is to physically go back the way we came in and find another way up the spire. One big problem with that is... we'll get lost trying to navigate those tunnels."

Spyder taps on the barrier. "I have an internal compass used to locate PC avatars. It typically points the way to Megan Wright, but for much of our trek in the Spire, it's been pointing at you, as it is now. I have no other navigation capability. I'll be of no help in trying to find our way back out through the tunnels if that's what we decide to do."

The cavern floor and ceiling rumble as though in an earthquake. I have a sinking feeling about this....

"Run for the tunnel, Spyder." If it collapses while we're in the cavern, we'll be completely cut off from the outside. Switching to physical form, I fly at top speed. At the very least, I need to get outside the boundary of the spirit globe.

While in physical form, I can't see the spirit globe. I'm about twenty feet down the tunnel when the ceiling collapses, burying me in boulders. I'm not dead. Hell, I don't even feel the pain, due to my maxed out Pain Tolerant trait. Did I get past the globe? I can't see a thing.

The tremors stop.

I can extricate myself from the boulders by switching to Spirit Form....

Georgie's frowning face appears in my view. *"Don't do anything,* pumpkin. Your HP has fallen to 76%. You might think you can take on Spirit Form and free yourself, but there's one problem with that—the wall of the spirit globe intersects your body. If you take Spirit Form, it will split you into halves metaphysically, and you really don't want that. As long as you stay in physical form, you're metaphysically safe."

I fight to stay calm. "Spyder, are you and Charli okay?"

"I withdrew from the tunnel when it started collapsing. Both Charli and I are fine."

"Okay, well, it seems the worst is over. Can you remove the boulders from the tunnel?"

A thud vibrates the boulders. "Do not give up, my friend. I will clear out the rocks, no matter how long it takes. I will not stop until you are freed." Another thud suggests my Behemoth pal is tossing boulders.

Another tremor courses through me. My Heightened Sense of Hearing picks up the crash of more falling rocks above.

The boulders I'm wedged among are crushed deeper into the ground.

My flesh tears and bones break, but I'm not in agony. My legs could be ripped off, and I wouldn't feel it. I'm not sure that's a good thing.

"Your HP has been reduced to 64%, pumpkin."

Another thud indicates Spyder is still tossing boulders. I don't tell her to stop. There's another way out of this mess. I could die. I don't know if I can respawn, because Morrow and Slithy haven't, but I won't stay here forever.

More crashing of boulders from above wedge me tighter between the stones of my prison. Bones crack. Flesh rends. Georgie tells me I'm at 45% HP. I'm not much longer for Khertaan.

"Georgie, is there a way for ODYSSEY to reprogram this cavern, so we can get free of it?"

"Let me check." He's quiet for several seconds. "I'm sorry, pumpkin. ODYSSEY says the code for this cavern is heavily monitored by the Fanciful Pegasus servers. Reprogramming it would trip all manner of alerts, likely resulting in ODYSSEY being detected and then cut off completely from Khertaan. ODYSSEY can't take the risk of losing Khertaan access. If that were to happen, Morrow and Slithy would never respawn, and neither would you if you died."

"We can't have that." I concentrate on the thuds and crashes, occupying my mind to keep worse thoughts at bay. The boulders wedge my body into a smaller and smaller space. My HP falls to 33%... 24%... 14%....

"What happens if I take Spirit Form, Georgie?"

He's the only thing I can see in the darkness... he's not physical, even though he appears to be. With a frown, he shakes his head. "The spirit globe will divide your spiritual being in two, immediately reducing your SP to zero. You'd be forced back into your physical form, at which point you'd go berserk, trying to fight anyone and anything around you. You'd start fighting boulders... stuck down here until someone frees you... or you die."

Another thudding crash and settling of the boulders, and my HP falls to 1%. "How close are you to clearing the tunnel, Spyder?"

"It's hopeless, I'm afraid. As soon as I take boulders away, more fall in to take their place. It's a no-win situation. I'm sorry."

"Then it's done. You gave it a good effort, but my body can't take it any longer. I'll respawn and come back for you and Charli, I promise."

We both know my promise is empty. Whatever is stopping Morrow and Slithy from respawning will stop me, too.

More of my bones crack as I'm pulverized between the settling boulders.

Georgie cocks his head. "Your HP is at -12%. You should be dead. How are you still here? Ah, I'm being given access to hitherto restricted information regarding your Pain Tolerant trait. Let me read it to you.

The level of any debuff received due to pain (wounds, burning, poisoning, etc.) is reduced by this trait, the level of reduction ranging from 1 to 60, depending on the type of debuff and the level of the Pain Tolerant trait. Character has 20% + 20% per trait level chance to not die each time a physical attack brings the character's HP to zero or less.

I can do the math… I have a level 4 trait. That gives me 100% chance of not dying….

Georgie laughs as he honks his nose. "These boulders could render you to a pulp, pumpkin, and you wouldn't die. I don't know how you're to function as a pulpy person. I can see it now… you're lying on the floor, a bloody pile of shredded flesh and splintered bones, gradually healing over time, and eventually restored to a fully functioning person."

I laugh with smashed lips and crooked teeth, a gurgling in my throat. "So I'm immortal. Just wonderful." I can still communicate with Georgie.

Crash. More boulders have fallen onto those already piled on me.

"Your HP is now -23%, pumpkin."

"Kylie?" Spyder asks over party chat. "Are you gone?" She's not expecting an answer.

In Khertaan, even a person pounded to a bloody pulp has no trouble conversing over chat. "I'm here, Spyder. Looks like I'll be here forever if you can't clear this tunnel."

A tremor and more crashing rocks drives home the point that this collapsed tunnel is to be my home for the rest of eternity. The best I can hope for is that my body will eventually become so liquid I can flow between the rocks to the other side of the spirit globe.

CHAPTER SIXTY-THREE

Charli: Birthday

The room flickers between light and dark. A hooded figure stands over Nick and swings up an Axe as though to behead him. Ronnie catches the Axe handle in one hand. "That's not nice."

"How...?" The hooded figure trembles. "You're but a figment of his imagination. You aren't even real."

"I'm real enough to do this." Ronnie wrenches the Axe from the hooded figure's grip.

The hooded one takes a faltering step back. A Staff appears in his hand, which he uses to catch his balance. "It doesn't matter. I'm coming for you, Nick. I'll find a way. Once I destroy the Fanciful Pegasus timelines, no one can stand against me." He taps his Staff on the floor and vanishes.

I kneel beside Nick, my hair swinging forward. It's blue. It should be blond. What's happening to me?

I stand and find myself alone in another room.

Germinal stage commencing.

The front door opens. Jake storms in. He's a guy about my age. *How do I know his name?*

"I can't believe you're sleeping with that old guy, sis." He charges past me, into the kitchen. Throwing open the refrigerator door, he grabs up a carton of milk and gulps until it's empty. Then he crumples the carton and tosses it on the floor. "Do you have any bread? I'm in the mood for a ham sandwich."

Germinal stage completed. Embryonic stage beginning.

The words come from my mouth, but it's like someone else is saying them. "Who do you think I am, Jake?"

"I don't have the money yet, sis. I'm starving. You don't want me to starve, do you?"

"I want you to say my name."

"What?" He doesn't look at me.

"Say my name."

"Yeah, sure. You're Erica. Does that make you happy? Now, where's the damn mustard?"

"I'm not Erica. My name is Charli."

"Yeah, whatever. I don't blame you for changing your name. Don't you have any mustard?" He tosses jars from the fridge onto the counter. "Where's the fucking mustard?"

Embryonic stage completed. Fetal stage beginning.

I'm so bloated. My knees are weak. I sit on the couch.

Jake slams the refrigerator door shut. "No fucking mustard. Who doesn't keep mustard in the fridge?" He turns on the TV and plops onto the couch beside me, vanishing as soon as his butt hits the fabric. I slip off the couch, landing on my knees, my legs spread apart.

"Police have captured two of the three escapees," says a TV reporter. "The third remains at large."

I'm looking at a pair of women's sandals. A woman occupies them, but I don't look up to see her face. I'm in too much pain. She reeks of perfume. *Embrace by Vintage Works.* How do I know that name?

An Axe swings back and forth at her side. She hefts it up. "You little blue-haired bitch."

"Nick." I whisper. "Please remember me. I'm Charli." I shout it at him. *"I'm Charli."*

From somewhere beyond the Axe-woman, Nick coughs up liquid. "Charli? I love you, Charli."

My blue hair turns blond. The woman with the Axe bursts into pixels that fly away on a sudden gust of wind.

Fetal stage completed. Birth commencing.

I scream as the flesh of my vagina stretches.

End Transcription Three

AFTERWORD

Thank you for reading this book. Now we have a request. Actually, we're begging.... It would help us immensely if you could rate and review this book on the site where you obtained it. We have next to no budget for marketing and promotions, and would greatly appreciate your help. Writing a paragraph or two will only take a few minutes of your time, but you'll have our eternal gratitude. Beyond that, telling others about this series... in conversations, on social media, by email, on your podcast or blog, in your newsletters, etc. ... is a lovely way to help spread the joy.

If you want to tell us what you think without writing your thoughts in a review, you can reach out to @eposic on Twitter or Facebook.

ABOUT THE AUTHOR

MK Eidson

 Owner and operator of the Eposic publishing imprint, MK (Mike) Eidson wrote his first speculative fiction tale in fourth grade. He has served as game master for countless role-playing game sessions, running games in dozens of rules systems, often converting scenarios written for one system to run in another. He's now happily combining his passions for speculative fiction and role-playing in the creation of GameLit / LitRPG novels, hoping to find readers who can appreciate his unfettered and unhinged style. Mike also enjoys creating games, number & letter puzzles, digital art, coloring books, and videos. He creates electronic music as a member of the electronic music act, Max Gumdrop. He lives in Central Florida with his wife and their pet Jack Russell Terrier.

Mike's web site: www.mkeidson.com

ABOUT THE AUTHOR

Emila H Thicke

 An extreme introvert, Emila H (Emilah) Thicke sold her first speculative fiction story at the age of seventeen, featuring a time-traveling heroine named Susie McKenzie, based in part on Emilah herself. Her submission led to her meeting her co-author, who introduced her to table-top role-playing games.

For a number of years, Emilah was known as Arlene in the WarTune MMORPG.

When not writing or editing, Emilah enjoys creating digital art and 3D animations. As a member of Max Gumdrop, she creates digital sounds for inclusion in their music. She lives in Central Florida with her significant other.

Emilah's web site: emilahthicke.wordpress.com

BOOKS IN THIS SERIES

HEAD HOPPERS

It's the end of the multiverse, and it's up to Megan Wright and friends to save it. But first they must train… in the form of a video game unlike any they've played before…. Can they reach level thirty and defeat the bad guys before reality comes crashing down around them?

The Longest Survivor

Undone

Illegal Avatars

Alternative Ghosts

Dread Naughts

Visit eposic.com for further information.

www.ingramcontent.com/pod-product-compliance
Lightning Source LLC
Chambersburg PA
CBHW030911050726
47498CB00003BA/692